The arts of Angela Carter

Manchester University Press

The Arts of Angela Carter

A cabinet of curiosities

Edited by Marie Mulvey-Roberts

Manchester University Press

Copyright © Manchester University Press 2019

While copyright in the volume as a whole is vested in Manchester University Press, copyright in individual chapters belongs to their respective authors, and no chapter may be reproduced wholly or in part without the express permission in writing of both author and publisher.

Published by Manchester University Press
Oxford Road, Manchester M13 9PL
www.manchesteruniversitypress.co.uk

British Library Cataloguing-in-Publication Data
A catalogue record for this book is available from the British Library

ISBN 978 1 5261 3677 0 hardback
ISBN 978 1 5261 6360 8 paperback

First published 2019
Paperback published 2022

The publisher has no responsibility for the persistence or accuracy of URLs for any external or third-party internet websites referred to in this book, and does not guarantee that any content on such websites is, or will remain, accurate or appropriate.

Typeset by
Servis Filmsetting Ltd, Stockport, Cheshire

For Nigel, as always,
Sandi and Jools, and
in memory of my cousin Susan

Contents

List of figures	page ix
Notes on contributors	x
Acknowledgements	xv

	Introduction: Angela Carter's curious rooms – Marie Mulvey-Roberts	1
1	Intermedial synergy in Angela Carter's short fiction – Michelle Ryan-Sautour	17
2	Psychogeography in the curiosity cabinet: Angela Carter's poetics of space – Anna Kérchy	39
3	Bloody chamber melodies: painting and music in *The Bloody Chamber* – Julie Sauvage	58
4	Angela Carter's poetry – Sarah Gamble	80
5	Angela Carter's *objets trouvés* in translation: from Baudelaire to *Black Venus* – Martine Hennard Dutheil de la Rochère	98
6	Myths, meat and American Indians: Angela Carter and Claude Lévi-Strauss – Heidi Yeandle	127
7	Angela Carter's 'rigorous system of disbelief': religion, misogyny, myth and the cult – Marie Mulvey-Roberts	145
8	'Clothes are our weapons': dandyism, fashion and subcultural style in Angela Carter's fiction of the 1960s – Catherine Spooner	166
9	Desire, disgust and dead women: Angela Carter's re-writing women's fatal scripts from Poe and Lovecraft – Gina Wisker	183
10	The 'art of faking': performance and puppet theatre in Angela Carter's Japan – Helen Snaith	204

11 'I resented it, it fascinated me': Carter's ambivalent cinematic fiction and the problem of proximity – Caleb Sivyer   223
12 The rough and the holy: Angela Carter's marionette theatre – Maggie Tonkin   246

Index   263

Figures

1 Original cover of *The Sadeian Woman* published by Virago in 1979. Photo by Martine Hennard Dutheil de la Rochère   109
2 Cover of *Black Venus's Tale* published by Next Editions in 1980. Photo by Martine Hennard Dutheil de la Rochère   113
3 Penitent Magdalen sculpture (1455) by Donatello, Museo dell'Opera del Duomo, Florence. Photo by Sailko, via Wikimedia Commons   150
4 Original cover of *American Ghosts & Old World Wonders* published by Chatto & Windus in 1993.   151

Notes on contributors

Sarah Gamble is Reader in English with Gender at Swansea University, where she teaches modules on contemporary women's writing, the Gothic and gender theory. She has published extensively on the life and work of Angela Carter, including *Angela Carter: Writing from the Front Line* (1997) and *Angela Carter: A Literary Life* (2006). Sarah is currently writing on the significance of the somersault in Carter's fiction, and planning a third monograph that will explore the influence of figurative art upon her work.

Martine Hennard Dutheil de la Rochère is Professor of English and Comparative Literature at the University of Lausanne, Switzerland, and former Associate Dean of the Humanities. She is International Corresponding Member for the British Comparative Literature Association (https://bcla.org/about/international-corresponding-members). She has published on various aspects of modern and contemporary literature (including Dickens, Conrad, Nabokov, Carter, Rushdie, Donoghue, Yolen), the international fairy tale tradition from antiquity to the present, and literary translation (theory, practice, reception). She is the author of *Origin and Originality in Salman Rushdie's Fiction* (1999), which focuses on the poetics and politics of cultural translation, and *Reading, Translating, Rewriting: Angela Carter's Translational Poetics* (2013), which traces the interplay of translation and rewriting in Carter's fiction. She guest-edited *Angela Carter traductrice – Angela Carter en traduction* (2014), and co-edited *Des Fata aux fées: regards croisés de l'Antiquité à nos jours* (2011), *Cinderella Across Cultures: New Directions and Interdisciplinary Perspectives* (2016), and *Translation and Creativity – la traduction comme création* (2016).

(For a full list of publications, affiliations, and projects, see https://martinehennarddutheil.wordpress.com.)

Anna Kérchy is Associate Professor and a member of the Gender Studies Research Group at the English Department of the University of Szeged, Hungary. She holds a PhD in Literature from the University of Szeged, a DEA in Semiology from Université Paris VII Denis Diderot, and a habilitation degree in Literature and Culture from the University of Debrecen. Her research interests include gender and body studies, the post-semiotics of the embodied subject, intermedial cultural representations, interfacings of Victorian and postmodern fantastic imagination, women's art and children's literature. She is the author of *Body-Texts in the Novels of Angela Carter: Writing from a Corporeagraphic Point of View* (2008) and *Alice in Transmedia Wonderland* (2016), editor of *Postmodern Reinterpretations of Fairy Tales* (2011) and *Posthumanism in Fantastic Fiction* (2018), co-editor of *What Constitutes the Fantastic?* (2010), *The Iconology of Law and Order* (2012), *Exploring the Cultural History of Continental European Freak Shows* (2012) and special journal issues: of *EJES* on *Feminist Interventions into Intermedial Studies* (2017) and of *Bookbird* on *Translating and Transmediating Children's Literature* (2018).

Marie Mulvey-Roberts is Professor of English Literature at the University of the West of England, Bristol and is the Editor-in-Chief and co-founder of the journal *Women's Writing*. She publishes in the areas of Gothic, gender and human rights and has authored, edited and co-edited over thirty books including *Strange Worlds: The Vision of Angela Carter* (2016). Her most recent monograph is *Dangerous Bodies: Historicising the Gothic Corporeal* (2016), winner of the Allan Lloyd Smith Memorial Prize. Her next book is *Pyrotechnics: The Incendiary Imagination of Angela Carter*, co-edited with Charlotte Crofts, with whom she runs the website, getangelacarter.com. She co-curated the first art exhibition relating to the work of Angela Carter, hosted at the Royal West of England Academy in Bristol to commemorate the twenty-fifth anniversary of her death and produced two musical adaptations of Carter's *The Bloody Chamber*, about which she made a film for Massolit for use in schools. With Charlotte Crofts and Caleb Sivyer, she is a co-founder of the Angela Carter Society.

Michelle Ryan-Sautour is *Maître de Conférences* (Senior Lecturer) at the Université d'Angers, France, where she is co-director of the Short Story and Short Forms section of the CIRPaLL research group and Editor of *Journal of the Short Story in English*. She is one of the founding members, and currently Director, of the newly formed European Network for Short Fiction Research (ENSFR). Her research focus is the speculative fiction and short stories of Angela Carter, Rikki Ducornet, Ali Smith and Sarah Hall with a special emphasis on authorship, reading pragmatics, game theory and gender. Ryan-Sautour's work has been published in *Marvels and Tales, Journal of the Short Story in English, Etudes Britanniques Contemporaines, Short Fiction in Theory and Practice*, and in several collections.

Julie Sauvage is Assistant Professor at Université Paul-Valéry Montpellier 3 and a translator. She holds a PhD on 'Theatricality in Angela Carter's novels' (University of Bordeaux). She has published several articles on novels and short stories by Angela Carter and Kate Atkinson. She specializes in the study of narrative voice and image/text relationships, as well as myth and fairy tale rewriting in contemporary British fiction, and has recently been reorienting her research towards periodical studies. She is a member of EMMA (Etudes Montpelliéraines du Monde Anglophone). Univ Paul Valéry Montpellier 3, EMMA EA741, F34000, Montpellier, France.

Caleb Sivyer is Senior Lecturer at the University of the West of England, Bristol, where he teaches undergraduate and foundation year modules on a wide range of subjects including myths and fairy tales in literature and film, political and cultural theory, and contemporary literature. He holds a PhD in English Literature from Cardiff University, with a thesis that analysed the politics of gender and the visual in selected works by Virginia Woolf and Angela Carter. He also has a background in philosophy, holding a BA in philosophy from the University of Kent. His research interests include contemporary literature, women's writing, gender and sexuality, film studies, literary and cultural theory, myth and fairy tale and philosophy. He has published a number of articles and book chapters on Angela Carter, as well as articles on other writers, including J.G. Ballard and Alison Bechdel. He is the co-founder (along with Marie Mulvey-Roberts and Charlotte Crofts) of the Angela Carter Society and he runs a website devoted to the life and works of Angela Carter (www.angelacarteronline.com), which has a thriving online community.

Helen Snaith has recently completed her PhD at Swansea University and is now working as an independent scholar. Her research focuses on Angela Carter's time in Japan, drawing specifically on the representation of Japanese cultural, literary and theatrical influences in Carter's work. In 2017, she published an article on Margaret Atwood's dystopian fiction for a special issue of the *Feminist Review*. Her research interests include gender and sexuality, contemporary women's writing, and Japanese literature. Helen currently works as a senior policy advisor, investigating the role of open access academic books in the scholarly communications landscape.

Catherine Spooner is Professor of Literature and Culture at Lancaster University. She has published widely on Gothic in literature, film and popular culture, with a particular emphasis on fashion. Her six books to date include *Fashioning Gothic Bodies* (2004), *Contemporary Gothic* (2006) and *Post-Millennial Gothic: Comedy, Romance and the Rise of Happy Gothic* (2017). She has made multiple media appearances ranging from *BBC Breakfast* to *The Steve Lamacq Show* on Radio 6 Music, and her work has appeared in volumes accompanying major exhibitions at the British Film Institute, British Library and Victoria and Albert Museum. She was co-president of the International Gothic Association 2013–17.

Maggie Tonkin is Senior Lecturer in English at the University of Adelaide. She has written substantially on Angela Carter, being the author of *Angela Carter and Decadence: Critical Fictions / Fictional Critiques* (2102), as well as a number of journal articles and book chapters on Carter and on other contemporary women writers. She was the joint editor of *Changing the Victorian Subject* (2014), a collection of essays on Victorian literature, and is currently working on a project examining cultural representations of existential psychiatrist R.D. Laing. Her other research interest is in dance and performance studies: she writes for the Australian dance press, is the author of *FIFTY: Half a Century of Australian Dance Theatre* (2016), and is a partner on a research project on the work of seminal Australian choreographer, Meryl Tankard.

Gina Wisker is Professor of Contemporary Literature & Higher Education with principal research interests in contemporary women's Gothic and postcolonial writing. She has published: *Contemporary Women's Gothic Fiction (2016); Margaret Atwood, an Introduction to Critical Views of Her Fiction* (2012): *Key Concepts in Postcolonial Writing* (2007), *Horror* (2005). Other interests are postgraduate study and supervision: *The Postgraduate Research Handbook* (2001, 2008), *The Good Supervisor* (2005, 2012), *Getting Published* (2015). Gina edits online dark fantasy journal *Dissections*, poetry magazine *Spokes*, and is a member of the World Horror Association, board member of Femspec and the Katherine Mansfield Association and past chair of the Contemporary Women's Writing Association.

Heidi Yeandle is based at Swansea University where she was awarded a PhD on Angela Carter in 2015. Her first monograph, *Angela Carter and Western Philosophy* (2017), has been published by Palgrave, and stems from her doctoral research. Her current research on Carter is related to Chinese philosophy. Her broader research interests include dystopian and post-apocalyptic fiction, twenty-first-century women's writing, and depictions of female writers in contemporary women's writing.

Acknowledgements

SELF-EVIDENTLY, THIS IS A collective endeavour inspired by a growing community of Angela Carter scholars, and one which has recently been consolidated by the founding of the Angela Carter Society. I am very grateful to all the contributors and to my colleagues at the University of the West of England, Bristol, most notably Charlotte Crofts and Caleb Sivyer for their support and encouragement. My gratitude goes to my university for granting me some teaching relief and I would like to give special thanks to my colleagues there: Gill Ballinger, Zoe Brennan, Hazel Edwards, Rehan Hyder, James Lee, Steve Poole and Sarah Robertson. I have benefited greatly from conversations about Carter with Scott Dimovitz, John Ellis, Christopher Frayling, Edward Horesh, Lorna MacDougall, Christine Molan, Mark and Alex Pearce, Martine Hennard Dutheil de la Rochère, Victor Sage, Sharon Tolaini-Sage and Anna Watz. The support and help of Marion Glastonbury and Nigel Biggs has been hugely appreciated. I am grateful to the British Library staff for helping me access the Carter archives. The catalyst for this book was the exhibition I co-curated at the Royal West of England Academy in Bristol and I will always be grateful to them for giving me this opportunity. Janette Kerr, Peter Ford and Christine Higgott provided invaluable support. I would like to thank my ex-student Sandi Fish for her help and continued enthusiasm for Carter and my Gothic literature students over the years for their Carter-related projects. I am very grateful to Manchester University Press for taking on this book and especially Matthew Frost – there is no-one better to work with. My thanks go to the entire team. Finally, I wish to express my gratitude to Andrew Kelly, the Director of the Festival of Ideas, and Susannah Clapp for supporting so many of the Angela Carter activities in Bristol relating to Carter's twenty-fifth anniversary for which this volume intends to serve as a lasting reminder.

Introduction: Angela Carter's curious rooms

Marie Mulvey-Roberts

There's a theory, one I find persuasive, that the quest for knowledge is, at bottom, the search for the answer to the question: 'Where was I before I was born?'
In the beginning was ... what?
Perhaps, in the beginning, there was a curious room, a room like this one, crammed with wonders; and now the room and all it contains are forbidden you, although it was made just for you, had been prepared for you since time began, and you will spend all your life trying to remember it. (Angela Carter, 'Alice in Prague, *or* The Curious Room', 1996: 401)

THE FANTASTICAL AND MULTI-DIMENSIONAL work of Angela Carter is like a series of curious rooms or textual cabinet of curiosities.[1] Maestro of bricolage and doyenne of the fabulous, strange and surreal, Carter was fascinated by the collections of wonders and curios compiled by the eccentric Austro-Hungarian Archduke Rudolph II (1552–1612). She described his 'extraordinary room' as 'a kind of ur-museum, a manifestation of an omnivorous curiosity, a gluttony for the world, but also a potent image of the unconscious' (1990: 217). Indeed, these are observations applicable to her own literary inventiveness, which includes: novels, collections of short stories, radio plays, translations, children's books, poetry, non-fictional works, journalism and even a libretto for an opera. Carter's proclivity for the transgressive, subversive and iconoclastic forged the key she left in the lock of many a forbidden room for her curious readers. Gaston Bachelard's comment in *The Poetics of Space* (1958) about the psychology behind the locks and keys of 'the houses of things: drawers, chests and wardrobes', bearing 'within themselves a kind of esthetics of hidden things' (2014: 21), can be applied to such secret rooms.

My idea for an Angela Carter exhibition, Strange Worlds: The Vision of Angela Carter, eventually manifested in 2017 as a series of interconnecting rooms whose contents were like a cabinet of curiosities. These included a large globe containing a moon-lit mysterious castle, which went in and out of visibility, a hologram of a drowning Ophelia, and a life-size baby in a box on the wall. This collection of essays arose from the same inspiration of seeing Carter in terms of place and space, as well as through her multi-disciplinary reach.

Ever since her untimely death in 1992, critics have been hunting for conceptual, biographical and historical keys to unlock hidden meanings within the work of this complex, erudite and at times esoteric writer, and explore her wide-ranging output. Notoriously difficult to pigeon-hole, Carter admits in her essay, 'Notes from the Front Line' (1983) to 'various intellectual adventures in anarcho-surrealism' (1997a: 37) and in the BBC's *Angela Carter's Curious Room*, referred to her own writing as 'overblown, purple, self-indulgent prose'.[2] Recent scholarship has shown how her writing was influenced by her love of art, cinema, experiences as a translator, folk-singer and practitioner of inter-textuality.[3] As well as often being allusive, Carter's writing has an elusive quality and, as the grandmother in her 'The Company of Wolves' from her most celebrated collection of short stories, *The Bloody Chamber* (1979), reminds us, things are never quite as they seem. Her love of the fantastic and folk tradition has travelled hand-in-hand with a commitment to international socialism and feminism, through which she saw everything emerging out of history and flowing back to the world. Her descriptive and intensively visual language merges with the philosophic and the abstract through a post-modernist play of ideas, for she regarded narrative as 'an argument stated in fictional terms' (Haffenden, 1985: 79). As she indicated in the preface to her book of radio plays, *Come Unto These Yellow Sands* (1978), she was able 'to create complex, many-layered narratives that play tricks with time' (7). Her work has also been seen spatially, for her word labyrinths are like Piranesi's drawings in prose or, as Scott Dimovitz describes it, 'architectonic allegories' (2016: 1).

Carter was keenly aware of the relationship between writing and space. In the Afterword to *Fireworks: Nine Profane Pieces* (1974), she says that the reason why she started writing short pieces was because the room she was writing in was too small in which to write a novel. This might be a reference to the size of the rooms in Japan where she was living at the time, for as she explained, 'So the size of my room modified what I did inside it and it was the same with the pieces themselves' (1996, 459). When it came to objects and words, she was certainly no minimalist; her study was as gloriously cluttered and colourfully over-blown as her prose. For Carter, writing and space range from the claustrophobic Poe-esque sweating walls of the bloody chamber contained in the Bluebeard title story of her most celebrated collection of tales, through to the Georgia O'Keefe-like expansive openness of the Californian desert in *The Passion of New Eve* (1977). Within each kind of space constructed through writing, however immense or constricted, the repercussions of Carter's work proliferate effortlessly and endlessly.

Place, as well as space, characterizes much of Carter's work. Since she is regarded generally as a London writer, it may come as a surprise, even to ardent fans, that she actually wrote more than half her novels while living in the city of Bristol, where she spent most of the 1960s. These include the so-called Bristol Trilogy, three novels set in the city: *Shadow Dance* (1966), *Several Perceptions* (1968) and *Love* (1971),[4] as well as *The Magic Toyshop* (1967), for which she wrote a film adaptation directed by David Wheatley, and *Heroes and Villains* (1969), a post-apocalyptic novel depicting a society split between professors and barbarians. Here, the heroine Marianne traverses these two worlds and it is tempting to see them as a fictionalization of how Carter's own life was divided between the dons at Bristol University, where she was studying for a degree in English, and her life in bohemian Clifton, which was then a downtrodden area, full of the junk shops that provided a setting for her first novel *Shadow Dance*. It was while she was in Bristol that Carter started getting her poetry published and gaining her first experience as an editor, which was for a student literary magazine. Between 1972 and 1977, she lived in the Georgian city of Bath, where she wrote her most important non-fictional work, *The Sadeian Woman: An Exercise in Cultural History* (1978), the dystopia *The Passion of New Eve*, began her collection of fairy tales *The Bloody Chamber*, now widely studied in schools, colleges and universities, and made notes in preparation for *Nights at the Circus* (1984). Clearly, the time Carter spent in the West Country was pivotal to her writing career and indeed she proved to be more productive in Bristol in terms of fictional output than anywhere else. Without doubt, this was the place where her writing career began and where it most decidedly flourished, resulting in not one but two literary awards.[5]

For the commemoration of the twenty-fifth anniversary of her death, it seemed appropriate to draw attention to Carter's neglected links with Bristol through local events celebrating her multi-disciplinary interests.[6] While living in the city, Carter pursued her interests in art and music and, as chapters in this book reveal, these influenced her fiction. Carter was fascinated by the surrealists, in spite of reservations over certain male attitudes to women, and was especially drawn to the work of Frida Kahlo, bringing out a box set of postcards of her artwork with an accompanying booklet. Towards the end of her life, she made a surrealist film on the history of religious painting called *The Holy Family Album* (1991). The first critic to have written about this film is Charlotte Crofts, whose book, '*Anagrams of Desire*' (2003), was a source of inspiration for the art exhibition on Carter for the 2017 anniversary.[7] The originals of three paintings shown in the film were exhibited in a gallery, making it resemble a Gothic chapel. These were William Holman Hunt's *The Shadow of Death* (1970–73), Stanley Spencer's *Wedding at Cana Bride and Bridegroom* (1953) and Arnulf Rainer's *The Wine Crucifix* (1957–78). Together, they formed a trinity of paintings on the subjects of transformation (water into wine) and transubstantiation (wine into blood), prefigured by the life-affirming sight of a joyful half-naked Jesus surrounded by his carpenter's tools, represented as sinister symbols of the tortures lying ahead.

The venue was the majestic Royal West of England Academy (RWA) in Clifton, not far from where Carter used to live in Royal York Crescent. Shortly before the opening, it dawned on me that this was the very same building in which Carter herself had taken art-classes.[8] She enrolled part-time in the summer of 1967, but when she was turned down for a full-time place on the grounds that her vocation seemed more in the direction of a writer than artist, she took the rejection badly. However, it did not prevent her from continuing to paint and draw throughout her life and fictionalizing the artists she came into contact with in Clifton through her Bristol trilogy. Not only had she produced paintings at the RWA, but she would have walked the galleries, never dreaming that one day they would contain an exhibition inspired by her life and work. The show, Strange Worlds: The Vision of Angela Carter, attracted over 11,000 visitors during a period of three months and opened up her work to new audiences. On display was the work of artists who had inspired or influenced her, including Marc Chagall, William Holman Hunt and Leonora Carrington, and contemporary artists such as Eileen Cooper and Heather Nevay, whose artwork has parallels with her writing (see Mulvey-Roberts and Robinson, 2016).

One theme which emerged was around the very large and the very small, contrasting dimensions that keyed into Carter's fascination with Lewis Carroll's *Alice's Adventures in Wonderland* (1865) and which are mirrored in such stories as 'Alice in Prague, *or* The Curious Room'. Accordingly, installations ranged from the virtually microscopic to the truly gargantuan. For instance, Tessa Falmer's 'The Forest Assassins', a title taken from Carter's description of the wolves in 'The Company of Wolves', depicted a diminutive and sinister fairy-land in which countless minute hostile skeletal fairies, equipped with actual honey-bee wings and armed with spears, flew in aerial skull ships, while others rode on the back of taxidermied creatures and insects. Suspended from the thirty-foot-high ceiling into the wide-open and brightly lit space of the main gallery, it recreated a forest in miniature, constructed out of natural materials, best viewed with a magnifying glass. In stark contrast, five gargantuan carved male figures, whose enlarged heads and real prosthetic human teeth bore an uncanny family resemblance, dominated a much smaller and dimly lit gallery. Four of these carvings were besuited and caught in the act of gobbling up with their eyes a naked man outstretched before them across a table. Called *The Banquet*, these disturbing sculptures by Ana Maria Pacheco can be interpreted as a scene of impending cannibalism and, in this context, are an apt reminder of Carter's identification of the great themes of the Gothic as 'incest' and 'cannibalism' (1996: 459). Concealed behind a black curtain, for the unsuspecting visitor, this curious room, with its connotations of impending slaughter or sacrifice, provided a walk-in version of the forbidden room in 'The Bloody Chamber'.

The exhibition served as a catalyst for numerous activities corresponding to Carter's multi-disciplinary interests. These included a poetry competition in response to artworks, as well as artists' workshops including one on shadow puppets, inspired by the title of *Shadow Dance* and the puppetry in her second novel *The Magic Toyshop*.[9] An original specially commissioned musical adaptation of Carter's short story 'Puss in Boots', entitled *Pussy*, was performed at the Alma Tavern Theatre in Clifton.[10] Contemporary musicians composed music around individual artworks on display, which were then performed in a concert held in the main gallery.[11] A section of the exhibition was devoted to Carter's keen interest in folk-singing, cultivated while she lived in Bristol. It showcased archival material left by her late first husband, Paul Carter, who had been a producer for Topic Records, and was curated with the assistance of Christine Molan, a friend to the Carters and model for the character Ghislaine in *Shadow Dance* (see Mulvey-Roberts and Robinson, 2016: 29–32 and getangelacarter.com). Molan also co-organized with me a folk concert in the gallery, with singers and musicians who used to play with Carter in the 1960s. In 1969, Carter went to Japan, leaving Bristol, her marriage and the folk-music scene far behind, yet her love of the folk tradition continued. She went on to collect folk tales from around the world, editing them for Virago in two collections, whose frontispieces of a man and woman by Corinna Sargood were exhibited in the exhibition, though the apogee of her transposition of folk-music to fairy and folk tale is undoubtedly *The Bloody Chamber*. The typed manuscript of one of the stories from that collection, 'The Lady of the House of Love' (1979), was also put on display. Its origin as a radio play is another indication of Carter's commitment to the oral tradition, quintessential to the folk-music scene (she had a vast repertoire of folk songs in her head). In his book, *Inside the Bloody Chamber* (2015), Christopher Frayling makes a direct link between this tale of a reluctant vampire and the West Country by explaining how his friendship with Carter, which flourished while they were both living in Bath, had been a source of inspiration (20–9). The year after his book was published saw the appearance of the first official biography of Carter by Edmund Gordon.[12]

His biography opened up a hitherto hidden place in Carter's life story, namely the time she spent in Japan, after leaving Bristol in 1969 and returning to England in 1972. The move proved to be transformational on every level and close friends noticed the change on her return. After Carter died in 1992, her friend and biographer Lorna Sage decided to go to Japan and interview Carter's Japanese lover, Sozo Araki, but the plan was cut short by her own untimely death.[13] That episode in Carter's life remained inscrutable until Gordon made the trip himself and when Natsumi Ikoma translated the Japanese memoir written by Sozo. One trusts that the author of

The Sadeian Woman would have been tolerant of voyeurs reading about her experience of love hotels in Tokyo. The city is reimagined in her surrealist novel, *The Infernal Desire Machines of Doctor Hoffman* (1972), though its initial description indicates that she had merged it with Bristol, a blurring which marked her own process of transitioning between cities (Mulvey-Roberts, 2015: 29–30). Another city, New York, forms the backdrop to the first few chapters of *The Passion of New Eve*, which she visited with her husband Paul in the dying days of their marriage. Carter's global reach extends outside the pages of her novels to her readership and in view of the continuing popular and academic interest in Carter, in 2018 the time was ripe for the founding of an international Angela Carter Society.[14] Founder members appear amongst the contributors to this book, who are from various counties, including Australia, France, Hungary, Switzerland, the United States and the United Kingdom, and include leading Carter scholars, as well as lesser-known authors.

In the opening chapter, Michelle Ryan-Sautour explains that the breadth and variety of Carter's short fiction demonstrates the far-reaching intertextual and intermedial diversity of her writing, which includes philosophy, the visual arts, psychoanalysis, cultural and religious iconography, radio, film, and language theory. As a result, the edges of multiple disciplines are played with in the shape-shifting production of short fiction throughout her career and, as Ryan-Sautour argues, provide powerful, multimedial spaces of fictional reflection for her reader. She notes that the words 'short story' appear repeatedly in Angela Carter's journals in the archives at the British Library and are accompanied by fragments of poetry, reflective thoughts and quotations. From this, she concludes that short narrative appears to have been intertwined with her creative process, and seems to have served as an experimental space for playing with ideas. Carter points to short fiction's potential for engaging with certain forms of signification in the Afterword to another collection of short stories, *Fireworks*, where she says: 'The limited trajectory of the short narrative concentrates its meaning. Sign and sense can fuse to an extent impossible to achieve among the multiplying ambiguities of an extended narrative' (1996, 459).

Anna Kérchy is drawn to Carter's short stories with place-based titles such as 'The Bloody Chamber' (1979) and 'The Scarlet House' (1995) and argues that Carter's mapping of the affective, sensorial and psychological components of both spatial and narrative experience springs from the writer's ultimate question: 'Where do stories come from?' In her chapter, 'Psychogeography in the curiosity cabinet', Kérchy explores Carter's poetics of space. She recognizes that Carter's fiction has been distinguished by a topography of the carnivalesque with such liminal settings as Bluebeard's Gothic castle, Uncle Philip's rundown magic toyshop and Colonel Kearney's travelling circus. Here, for the first time, attention is devoted to the metanarrative implications of Carterian spaces from the vantage point of a 'feminist psychogeographer' (Bucher and Finka, 2008: 37) flaneuse, who explores a new way of walking to transform the experience of the city into a playable space which can be applied to approaching literary texts.

The following chapter by Julie Sauvage revisits Carter's short stories by focusing on painting and music in *The Bloody Chamber*. It looks at how Carter plays on the Blakean notion of 'Time is a man, Space is a woman' (Carter, 1977: 57) in *The Passion of New Eve*. Pointing out that the 'arts of time' and 'arts of space' are similarly gendered (Mitchell, 1995: 152–75), Sauvage demonstrates how Carter's use of painting and music allows her to blur the boundaries between gender and genre. The first short story in the collection, 'The Bloody Chamber', with its complex interplay of painting and music is viewed both as tempo and key-note to the remainder of the book, which can be read like a musical score. Similarly, as Sauvage points out, painting seems literally to 'still' life and turn men and women into bi-dimensional archetypes, at the same time as endowing these images with a temporal dimension through repetition and difference. She illustrates this through the image of the tarot pack from 'The Lady of the House of Love' to show how the cards can be shuffled and re-shuffled, while their different combinations give rise to various 'readings', causing readers to lose themselves in a forest of pictures, though this enables them to find their own voices.

A forgotten voice in the case of Carter has been her poetry and, as Sarah Gamble reminds us, this is a neglected aspect of her work, predating her fiction. Part of the reason for this omission has been Carter's own complicity in excising her aspirations as a poet from her autobiographical narrative. Furthermore, the anthologies published after her death by Chatto & Windus did not include any of her poetry. Even after Rosemary Hill brought out a collection of her poems entitled *Unicorn* (2015), Gamble points out that we still tend to follow the script laid out by the poet herself and talk of Carter the novelist, the short story writer and the cultural commentator, etc. In this chapter, Carter's verse is investigated by situating her work in the context of the production of poetry in Britain in the mid-1960s. For her, it was also part of the Bristol scene and it is interesting to consider that when she left the city, the folk scene and her first marriage far behind, she also stopped writing poetry. Gamble considers whether any links can be made between her poetry and her far more successful prose writing and concludes by seeing it as a useful and neglected context for the development of her subsequent writing career.

Another often-overlooked aspect of Carter's work, which gives us a fuller understanding of her oeuvre, are the translations she made from the French. As Martine Hennard Dutheil de la Rochère reveals, translation was an important stimulus for Carter's imagination and creativity. While at Bristol University, she translated Old and Middle English poets and around that time translated French poetry. This laid the groundwork for translating and rewriting Charles Perrault's fairy tales which helped to seed her adaptations of his *contes* in *The Bloody Chamber and Other Stories*. Carter was drawn to French literature and especially to the poetry of Charles Baudelaire, as discussed in this chapter. Her 1980 tale of 'Black Venus' revisits the poet's Jeanne Duval cycle of poems from a female perspective and assesses his legacy in an ambivalent gesture of appropriation, homage, emulation and derision. Baudelaire was taken up by the surrealist poets. While living in Japan, Carter translated a feminist book on the surrealist movement by Xavière Gauthier, which Hennard Dutheil de la Rochère ties into Carter's experiences of being in that particular foreign culture to her interest in surrealism. Ironically, Carter's reluctance to learn Japanese gave her new insights into language and a greater understanding of how, in the words of Henri Meschonnic, 'translation is a laboratory for writing' (1999, 459).[15] As this chapter demonstrates, Carter's method of reading across languages, genres and art highlights the translational poetics that characterized her fiction during this period.

One of Carter's lesser-known interests is anthropology. In the next chapter, Heidi Yeandle investigates her engagement with the eminent anthropologist Claude Lévi-Strauss. After perusing Carter's journals at the British Library, Yeandle discovered that Carter's research on Lévi-Strauss proved to be a defining feature of notes she took from the mid-1960s to the early 1990s, thus spanning most of her career.

During that period, Carter researched a range of Lévi-Strauss's works, as well as reading Edmund Leach's *Claude Lévi-Strauss* (1970). The importance of this research for her fiction is evident from its centrality to her portrayal of supposedly primitive communities and their similarity to the so-called civilized nations in both *Heroes and Villains* and *The Infernal Desire Machines of Doctor Hoffman*. Yeandle argues that Carter's satirical depiction of the 'learned' professors and card-playing soldiers in *Heroes and Villains* stems from her reading of Lévi-Strauss's *Tristes Tropiques* and *The Savage Mind*, and that her knowledge of his *The Raw and the Cooked* influenced *The Infernal Desire Machines of Doctor Hoffman*, which reveals that the eponymous character's methodology for redefining reality actually derives from this work.

The extent of Carter's interest in religion has often been underestimated, which is perhaps not so surprising for a self-proclaimed atheist. As discussed by Mulvey-Roberts in the next chapter, Carter's critiques of Judeo-Christianity and its strangle-hold on Western cultural myths, which hold oppressive gender roles in place, are an attack on patriarchy itself. Carter's most obvious demythologizing of religion was through *The Holy Family Album*, the irreverent film she made on the life of Christ, her short story 'Impressions: The Wrightsman Magdalene' (1993), two wolf stories from *The Bloody Chamber* and the brutal satire of medieval Catholicism and its misogynist theology in *The Infernal Desire Machines of Doctor Hoffman*. In addition to discussing these, this chapter makes the first extensive interpretation of an episode from *The Passion of New Eve* (the title of which evokes both New and Old Testaments) in relation to Zero and his exploited female followers, based on the real-life guru, Charles Manson who, through his infamous sex cult, was responsible for a series of brutal murders, most notably that of film actress Sharon Tate. Carter was present in the United States at the time of the killings. Through this fictionalization, Mulvey-Roberts argues that Carter not only reveals the potential harmfulness of the quasi-religious messianic ideology fuelling certain cults but also exposes the burgeoning disillusionment with the Summer of Love (1968).

Catherine Spooner also invokes the counter-culture of the 1960s through her use of Carter's short essay, 'Notes for a Theory of Sixties Style' (1967), which argues for the mutability of fashion as a liberating force, through which 'girls have been emancipated from the stiff forms of iconic sexuality' (1997b: 109). The essay presents a condensed account of some of the major sartorial concerns of Carter's fiction of the 1960s and throughout her career. These include style as rebellion, performance, dandyism, fetishism, disguise and fancy dress. Spooner shows how the white wedding dress, 'the supreme symbol of woman as a sexual thing and nothing else whatever' (1997: 108), contrasts with the fecund invention of subcultural style, from hippy bricolage to the Hell's Angels' beastly dandyism. Reading Carter's fiction alongside 1960s fashion images, this chapter explores the ways in which subcultural style became a major influence on Carter's aesthetic sensibility. In doing so, it will argue that the 'holiday from the persistent self' (1997: 106) offered by fashion is ambivalent for Carter, either as the intoxicating prospect of liberation or a more hazardous route for escapism.

In the following chapter, Gina Wisker looks at how Carter rewrites the constraining myths for women, maintaining that her writing was crucial for the late twentieth-century rebirth of Gothic horror by providing readers with an impetus to read or re-read Poe and Lovecraft. Carter's work draws us into the rich confusions of the language, the psychology, and physical entrapments, which Poe and Lovecraft play out through their representations of women, and is re-enacted by Carter to expose, explode and re-write. Starting with Carter's tale of the physically, religiously and sexually restricted axe murderer Lizzie Borden, this chapter traces the ways in which Carter unpicks the fascination which Poe and Lovecraft had with the mythologizing of women as monstrous, vulnerable and enthralling. As a late twentieth-century feminist, Carter exposes the underlying sexual terrors, the desire and disgust fuelling representations of women as variously dead or deadly in the work of the two great masters of Gothic horror. She conveys the importance of telling other stories in order to revise and rewrite these constraining myths, so that women are seen to reject the roles of puppets and pawns, as in *The Magic Toyshop*, *Nights at the Circus* and 'The Loves of Lady Purple' (1974), and instead seize their sexuality and agency, thus having the last laugh.

Helen Snaith explores the power dynamics relating to gender and performance within the puppetry and performance of Japanese culture which had fascinated Carter. This is most apparent from the literature she produced during her time in Japan, where artificiality is 'appreciated for its own sake' and in which 'most Japanese spend most of their time acting' (Buruma, 2001: 69). The art of *bunraku*, a form of traditional Japanese puppet theatre, which uses four-foot high marionettes, each controlled by three puppet masters, who appear on stage with the dolls, resonates strongly throughout her short story collection *Fireworks*. Dressed in long black cloaks, the skill of the manipulators is as much revered as it is for the story being told: it is the 'art of faking' that is appreciated by the audience. Alongside a reading of 'The Executioner's Beautiful Daughter' (1974) and 'The Loves of Lady Purple' (1974), this chapter argues that Carter deliberately uses images employed within *bunraku* theatre in order to challenge the dichotomous relationship between the puppet and the puppet master. Using theatrical tropes within both tales, Carter seeks to redefine the power dynamics between actors – real or otherwise – engaged throughout a performance. Challenging authority within an overtly phallocentric society, Carter's marionettes must still ultimately adhere to a performance that is imitative of gendered and socio-political expectations in Japan.

Caleb Sivyer reconsiders Angela Carter's relationship to cinema, arguing that it is important to acknowledge that she was much more ambivalent about this medium than is often noted by scholars. While Carter's love of the cinema is apparent from her journalistic writings as well as the BBC documentary made just before her death, in other essays she is highly critical of Hollywood's colonization of the world's imagination and in particular its portrayal of femininity. This chapter plays on this ambivalence and argues that *The Passion of New Eve* and *The Infernal Desire Machines of Doctor Hoffman* dramatize a simultaneous fascination with and horror at the cinematic image. By observing the ways in which the protagonists from these texts are brought uncomfortably close to the objects of their voyeuristic desires, it can be seen that these two novels employ cinematic-inspired techniques from classic Hollywood film in order to increase the sense of proximity between spectator and spectacle. This is then read as a more productive way to confront not just the illusory images of mainstream cinema but also the desires of the spectators.

Maggie Tonkin, in the final chapter, considers how Angela Carter's writing has often been read through the prism of theatricality. Such discussions invariably focus on the performativity of gender in Carter's fiction, and on her writing as a form of performance, even of spectacle. In contradistinction to this habit of reading performance and performativity metaphorically, this chapter focuses instead on the representations of literal performance in Carter's work. It will investigate the depictions of stage performance in both her fiction and non-fiction, including *The Magic Toyshop, Nights at the Circus, Wise Children* (1991), the short stories, her play script *Lulu* (1996) and her journalism. Here Carter's delineation of the stage will be read as a privileged space in the light of contemporaneous debates about the status of the British theatre from the 1960s until the 1990s, which signalled great changes in theatrical practice with the rise of a new generation of politically radical playwrights. The ideological function of these various modes of theatrical performance across Carter's oeuvre is examined and the extent to which they are informed by political debates about the theatre, during the latter part of the twentieth century, is considered.

Each contributor invites the reader of this collection into a Carteresque curious room or critical cabinet of curiosities. The doors are flung open to throw light on lesser-known aspects of her work such as music and poetry, and also to provide new insights into more familiar areas, as in gender, film and performance. As this book demonstrates, place and space were important to Carter's work, which lends itself to new interpretations, and her extraordinary vitality and multi-disciplinary reach continue to be relevant for us today. In view of the difficulty of representing the extent of her varied interests within the confines of a single volume, this book is best seen as another building block within the edifice of the newly emerging discipline of Carter Studies. The approach taken here foregrounds her multi-disciplinary interests and influences, which allows each chapter to function as part of a cabinet of curiosities even if it might look as though her work has been shoehorned into discrete subject areas, such as music, poetry, psychogeography, theatre, film, translation, anthropology, religion, etc ..., for, like the feet placed in Cinderella's slipper, not all can be a perfect fit. Moreover, Carter relished breaking out of boundaries: as she famously admitted, 'I am all for putting new wine in old bottles, especially if the pressure of the new wine makes the old bottles explode' (1997a: 37). Her crossing of disciplinary lines has been explored in the very first collection of essays on her work, *Flesh and the Mirror: The Art of Angela Carter* (1994), edited by Lorna Sage. The main title here, *The Arts of Angela Carter*, pays homage to Sage's book by building on some of the chapters and continuing to celebrate Carter as an artful Renaissance woman. Other essay collections have focused on more specific areas, such as fetishism and the transsexual subject, as in Joseph Bristow and Trev Lynn Broughton's *The Infernal Desires of Angela Carter: Fiction, Femininity, Feminism* (1997). This was followed by a collection of already published essays on various critical and theoretical approaches edited by Alison Easton for New Casebooks in *Angela Carter: Contemporary Critical Essays* (2000), thereby providing further affirmation of Carter as an established literary figure. The next collection, *Re-visiting Angela Carter: Texts, Contexts, Intertexts* (2006), edited by Rebecca Munford, considered Carter's literary and cultural influences from Jonathan Swift, through to William Shakespeare and up to Jean-Luc Godard, for as she herself pointed out: 'most intellectual development depends upon new readings of old texts' (1997: 37). A more recent collection, *Angela Carter: New Critical Readings* (2012), edited by Sonya Andermahr and Lawrence Phillips, set out to present Carter within new, theoretical and disciplinary perspectives, arguing that besides being a demythologizer, she also re-mythologized cultural narratives. This neatly leads into the present book, which aims for an even wider purview of Carter's multi-disciplinarity in a re-assessment of her oeuvre twenty-five years after her death. The work of Angela Carter continues to be revisited in myriad different ways and for those of us still trying to come to terms with her dazzling achievements, it can feel like trying to catch the tail of a comet.

Notes

1 Besides furnishing the title of a short story and a film, this metaphor is also used as the main title for the book, *Angela Carter, The Curious Room: Plays, Film Scripts, and an Opera* (London: Chatto & Windus, 1996).
2 http://collections-search.bfi.org.uk/web/Details/ChoiceFilmWorks/150391767, accessed 26 November 2018. Directed by Kim Evans, the documentary won the Huw Weldon Best Arts Programme, BAFTA 1993.
3 See Charlotte Crofts and Marie Mulvey-Roberts (eds), *Angela Carter's Pyrotechnics: A Union of Contraries* (London: Bloomsbury, 2022)
4 *Love* was started in Bristol but finished elsewhere.
5 For *The Magic Toyshop*, Carter was awarded the John Llewellyn Rys Prize and, for *Several Perceptions*, she won a Somerset Maughan Award.
6 See the website getangelacarter.com.
7 The exhibition (10 December–19 March 2017) was co-curated by Marie Mulvey-Roberts and Fiona Robinson.
8 This revelation followed leads provided by Carter's friend, the artist

Christine Molan, who has taught there and Edmund Gordon who noted that she had enrolled at the West of England College of Art, but gave no address. He recorded Carter's verdict that it was 'the worst art school in the country' (2016: 116).
9 Other works include *Nights at the Circus*. The workshop was provided by Layla Holzer who exhibited her Carter-inspired work in a show, The Snow, the Crow and the Blood at the Coexist Gallery, Hamilton House, in Bristol, 2–14 February 2017.
10 The composer is Christopher Northam and the librettist is A.C.H. Smith. While working on the *Western Daily Press* as a journalist, the latter met Carter while she was also doing some work for the newspaper and he recalled that she was a hippy looking girl who had expressed her desire to be a writer.
11 This was run by New Music in the South West. More details are on the getangelacarter.com website.
12 It should be noted that Sarah Gamble had already published *Angela Carter: A Literary Life* (London: Palgrave Macmillan, 2006) and Susannah Clapp wrote a memoir, *A Card from Angela Carter* (London: Bloomsbury, 2012).
13 This information was given to me by her daughter Sharon Sage.
14 The Angela Carter Society is run from the University of the West of England, Bristol by Charlotte Crofts, Marie Mulvey-Roberts and Caleb Sivyer. See http://angelacartersociety.com, accessed 26 November 2018.
15 This is a translation from the original French '*un laboratoire d'écrire*'.

References

Andermahr, Sonya and Lawrence Phillips (eds) (2012), *Angela Carter: New Critical Readings* (London: Continuum).
Araki, Sozi (2017), *Seduced by Japan: A Memoir of the Days Spent with Angela Carter*, trans. Natsumi Ikoma, who wrote the accompanying 'Her Side of the Story' (Tokyo: Eihosha).
Bachelard, Gaston ([1958] 2014), *The Poetics of Space*, trans. Maria Jolas (New York: Penguin).
Bristow, Joseph and Trev Lynn Broughton (1997), *The Infernal Desires of Angela Carter: Fiction, Femininity, Feminism* (London and New York: Longman).
Bucher, Ulrike and Finka Maro (2008), *The Electronic City* (Berlin: Verlag).
Buruma, Ian (2001), *A Japanese Mirror: Heroes and Villains in Japanese Culture* (London: Phoenix).
Carter, Angela (1977), *The Passion of New Eve* (New York: Harcourt Brace Jovanovich).

―― (1978), *Come Unto these Yellow Sands: Four Radio Plays* (Newcastle upon Tyne: Bloodaxe Books).

―― (1990), 'Introduction to "The Curious Room"', in *On Strangeness: Swiss Papers in English Language and Literature*, vol 5, ed. Margaret Bridges (Tübingen: Gunter Narr Verlag), 2015–17.

―― (1996), *Burning your Boats: Collected Short Stories* (London: Vintage).

―― (1997a), *Shaking a Leg: Collected Journalism and Writings*, ed. Jenny Uglow (London: Chatto & Windus).

―― ([1967] 1997b), 'Notes for a Theory of Sixties Style', in Angela Carter, *Shaking a Leg: Journalism and Writings*, ed. Jenny Uglow (London: Chatto and Windus).

Clapp, Susannah (2012), *A Card from Angela Carter* (London: Bloomsbury).

Crofts, Charlotte (2003), *'Anagrams of Desire': Angela Carter's Writing for Radio, Film and Television* (Manchester: Manchester University Press).

Dimovitz, Scott (2016), *Angela Carter: Surrealist, Psychologist, Moral Philosopher* (London and New York, Routledge.

Easton, Alison (2000), *Angela Carter: Contemporary Critical Essays* (Houndmills: Macmillan).

Frayling, Christopher (2015), *Inside the Bloody Chamber: On Angela Carter, the Gothic and other Weird Tales* (London: Oberon).

Gamble, Sarah (2006), *Angela Carter: A Literary Life* (Houndmills and New York: Palgrave Macmillan).

Gordon, Edmund (2016), *The Invention of Angela Carter: A Biography* (London: Chatto & Windus).

Haffenden, John (1985), *Novelists in Interview* (London: Methuen).

Kérchy, Anna (2008), *Body-Texts in the Novels of Angela Carter. Writing from a Corporeagraphic Point of View* (Lewiston, NY and Lampeter: The Edwin Mellen Press).

Meschonnic, Henri (1999), *Poétique du traduire* (Paris: Verdier).

Mitchell, W.J.T. (1995), *Picture Theory* (Chicago: University of Chicago Press).

Munford, Rebecca (2006), ed. *Re-visiting Angela Carter: Texts, Contexts, Intertexts* (Houndmills and New York: Palgrave Macmillan).

Mulvey-Roberts, Marie (2015), *Literary Bristol: Writers and the City* (Bristol: Redcliffe Press).

―― and Fiona Robinson (2016), eds *Strange Worlds; The Vision of Angela Carter* (Bristol: Redcliffe Press).

Sage, Lorna (1994), ed. *Flesh and the Mirror: Essays on the Art of Angela Carter* (London: Virago Press).

1

Intermedial synergy in Angela Carter's short fiction

Michelle Ryan-Sautour

We travel along the thread of narrative like high-wire artistes. That is our life. (Carter, 1992: 2)

IN THE INTRODUCTION TO Angela Carter's *The Curious Room: Collected Dramatic Works*, Susannah Clapp speaks of a startling array of images discovered in Carter's study following her death: 'Drawings and paintings spilled out of these drawers' (Clapp, 1997: ix). For Clapp these elements are more than anecdotal; they open up new perspectives on Carter's artistic production, as Carter's interests extend well beyond the realm of prose fiction: 'There was also an unexpectedly large number of plays for theatre, film and radio. [...] By their form and extent, they enlarge the scope and alter the contours of a rich body of work' (Clapp, 1997: ix). Carter's creative imagination was highly literary, yet she was also deeply influenced by other art forms. Clapp's memoir, *A Card from Angela Carter*, which contains reproductions of postcards, points to this sensibility, in that it dwells upon Carter's close connection to image, interweaving fragments of Carter's life story and ideas with a series of postcards 'casually despatched' to reveal a 'zigzag path through the eighties' (Clapp, 2012: 10). Clapp comments on how these cards reflect Carter's preoccupations of the time, and she highlights a statement of intent written early in Carter's career: 'I want to make images that are personal, sensuous, tender and funny – like the sculpture of Arp, for example, or the paintings of Chagall. I may not be very good yet but I'm young and I work hard – or fairly hard' (Carter qtd. in Clapp, 2012: 9). Sculpture and painting appear as lenses through which to visualize her future as a writer.

As Clapp observes, Carter was also 'a child of the radio age' who 'grew up hearing both the sweetness of John Masefield's *Box of Delights* and the sepulchral tones of the Man in Black' (Clapp, 1997: ix); it is well known that Carter's turn to writing for the radio was triggered by a sensitivity to sound: 'I ran the pencil idly along the top of the radiator. It made a metallic, almost musical rattle. It was just the noise that a long, pointed fingernail might make if it were run along the bars of a birdcage' (Carter, 1997a: 499). Such sounds allow Carter to explore a different sort of image, that of the internal visual imagination, where the reader is invited to contribute 'his or her own way of "seeing" the voices and the sounds, the invisible beings and events, that gives radio story-telling its real third dimension'. This space 'interests and enchants' Carter (Carter, 1997a: 497), as it allows her to 'paint some pictures in radio' (Carter, 1997a: 501).

It is such *pathways* between media that seized Carter's attention. Her affection for the cinema, and particularly the culture of Hollywood,[1] also spans much of her career, and her writing for radio, screen and stage has been addressed in depth in Charlotte Crofts' *'Anagrams of Desire': Angela Carter's Writing for Radio, Film and Television*, a work that filled a gap in the critical landscape surrounding Carter's writings. Crofts was one of the first critics to underline the centrality of media in Carter's writing, referring specifically to periods characterized by some critics as being unproductive in fiction writing, but highly productive in projects for other media (Crofts, 2003: 197). I will take up the idea that Carter's writing for media 'is central to an understanding of her work as a whole' (Crofts, 2003: 197), as Carter's awareness of 'the complex processes involved in transforming a text from one medium to another' (Crofts, 2003: 197) is key to understanding Carter's late short fiction.[2] Rather than focus on Carter's turn to other media, I will reverse the question by examining how other media and forms of intermediality act as an underlying force to Carter's writing, which intensifies towards the end of her career. Intermediality appears to give rise to new forms of iconoclasm in Carter's speculative spaces, and proposes surprising vistas for understanding the political and cultural dimension of her short fiction.

Short fiction and intermedial citationality

Joan Smith raises the question of calling Carter a 'Renaissance woman',[3] as Carter was an author whose activities were wide and varied. This

'Renaissance' character carries over into the intertextual dimension of her writing, which is studied in depth in Rebecca Munford's *Re-visiting Angela Carter: Texts, Contexts, Intertexts* (2006), and *Decadent Daughters and Monstrous Mothers: Angela Carter and European Gothic* (2013). But Carter's work is also strikingly intermedial. When one looks closely, her preoccupation with other media appears to be informed by an underlying consciousness of how media shape stories and meaning in different ways. Marie-Laure Ryan has written of the difficulty in defining the term 'medium', explaining how a sociologist or cultural critic might see television, radio and the internet as examples of media; an art critic would speak of music, painting, sculpture, literature, drama, etc.; a phenomenologist might discuss the visual and auditory as factors for defining media; and an artist might speak in terms of clay, bronze, oil and watercolour (Ryan, 2004: 16). It is indeed exceedingly complex to define the nature of media, particularly as Carter's references and work from media stretch across these different areas, reaching into the technologies of film, television and radio, while also pointing to the possibilities of painting, sculpture, oral performance and theatre. Ryan ultimately resists the creation of a definitive definition in favour of the concept of media relativity; media are studied in relation to each other according to their power to shape narrative:

> Hence, what counts for us as a medium is a category that truly makes a difference about what stories can be evoked or told, how they are presented, why they are communicated, and how they are experienced. This approach implies a standard of comparison: to say, for instance that 'radio is a distinct narrative medium' means that radio as a medium offers different narrative possibilities than television, film, or oral conversation. 'Mediality' (or mediumhood) is thus a relational rather than an absolute property. (Ryan, 2004: 18)

Media thus take on multiple forms, and it is the constraints and affordances offered in the telling of a story that reveal their characteristics. This flexible concept in relation to storytelling appears as the guiding principle of Carter's own engagement with media.

In her introduction to *Expletives Deleted*, Carter indeed emphasizes the centrality of narrative, explaining that books act as containers, 'bottles' for stories, and that the story itself is essential: 'because the *really* important thing is narrative' (Carter, 2006: 2, emphasis in original). The story is primordial in its migration across media, an idea that is reinforced in Marie-Laure Ryan and Jan-Noël Thon's introduction to *Storyworlds Across Media: Toward a Media-Conscious Narratology* (2014), in which they present the concept of intermediality as follows:

> Through intermediality, texts of a given medium send tendrils toward other media (see Rajewsky). These tendrils can include cross-medial adaptation (film to video game), references within the text to other media objects (a painting playing an important role in a novel), imitation by a medium of the resources of another medium (hypertext structure in print) and ekphrasis, or other forms of description of a type of sign through another type (music or visual artifacts described in language). (Ryan and Thon: 2014: 335)

Carter's fiction appears to deploy many such 'tendrils' towards various media productions. In *Wise Children*, for example, we are faced with the intersection of cinema, stage and television, an intermedial reflection with carnavalesque overtones that re-examines the relationship between Shakespeare and Hollywood, as Carter explains in a 1988 review of *The Classical Hollywood Cinema*: 'Hollywood was, still is, always will be, synonymous with the movies. It was the place where the United States perpetrated itself as a universal dream and put the dream into mass production' (Carter, 1997b: 385). Hollywood was a place where 'scandal and glamour' were 'an essential part of the product' (Carter, 1997b: 385). *The Passion of New Eve* (1977) is also openly based on an intermedial engagement with not only the form of the cinema, but also its culture, with the character of Tristessa figured as a film star. References to other media are widespread in Carter's writing. In 'The Bloody Chamber', Debussy's *La Terrasse des audiences au clair de lune*, as if played upon 'a piano with keys of ether' is associated with the protagonist's loss of virginity (Carter 1997c: 122), along with the Marquis's collection of paintings, including Gustave Moreau's *Sacrifical Victim* and Paul Gauguin's *Out of the Night We Come* [...] (Carter 1997c: 123). Carter's reflections on George de la Tour's *The Magdalene and Two Flames* also reflects what Karima Thomas describes as an 'urge for intermediality' in 'Impressions: The Wrightsman Magdalene' (Carter, 1997c). According to Thomas, this piece reflects upon the media transference of cultural artifacts: 'Its objective is to perform the permanent construction, deconstruction and reconstruction of meanings out of existing cultural artifacts' (Thomas, 2011: 76).

As Carter developed her writing for other media, this intermedial 'urge' was enhanced. Her fiction underwent shifts, often experimenting with the idea of 'story across media' while creating forms of symbiosis between fiction and radio or screen plays. The short story 'The Lady of the House of Love' (1975) is an emanation of Carter's radio play *Vampirella*,[4] which, as mentioned above, emerged from a sensitivity to sound. *The Company of Wolves*, both the radio play and screenplay, propose three versions of fairy tales, carrying traces of an oral tradition. These fairy tale narratives were initially rewritten in *The Bloody Chamber* (1979),[5] and then transformed through radio and film. Much of Carter's fiction connects with such intermedial trajectories. However, there appears to be an increasing awareness of how media shape meaning later in her career. The intermedial character of the texts in *American Ghosts & Old World Wonders* (1993) reflects a growing consciousness of how media can interrelate with the forms of condensation and concentrated meaning that are characteristic of short fiction.

The short story was an important space of speculation for Carter. A perusal of Angela Carter's journals in the archives at the British Library, reveals a repetition of the words 'short story', accompanied by fragments of poetry, fictional blurbs, reflections and quotations. Short narrative seems to have functioned as a sort of laboratory in which she could play with ideas, and spin out critical fictions that challenge the reader's perception of generic identity. The intermedial thrust of her writings acts in synergy with the generic experimentation present in much of Carter's short fiction. Carter's short pieces indeed fluctuate between the seemingly autobiographical musings of 'Flesh and the Mirror' to the fairy tale and fantasy modes of 'Penetrating to the Heart of the Forest' and *The Bloody Chamber*. Stories also appear as biographical sketches in 'The Cabinet of Edgar Allan Poe' and 'Black Venus', and as fictionalized historical myths such as 'The Fall River Axe Murders'. This heterogeneity is heightened in Carter's last collection, as *American Ghosts & Old World Wonders* proposes pieces collected and published posthumously, and juxtaposes theatrical journalistic fragments such as 'In Pantoland', with screenplay sketches such as 'Gun for the Devil', and speculative enigmas such as 'Alice in Prague or The Curious Room'.

In addition to having produced a heterogeneous collection of short fiction, Carter also wrote pieces that are hybrid in nature, often questioning the limits of fiction, and displaying a baroque quality that leads Salman Rushdie to see Carter as being at her best in her stories: 'Sometimes, at novel length, the distinctive Carter voice, those smoky, opium-eater's cadences interrupted by harsh or comic discords, that moonstone-and-rhinestone mix of opulence and flim-flam, can be exhausting. In her stories, she can dazzle and swoop, and quit while she's ahead' (Rushdie, 1997: x). Carter's short texts often waver between fiction and non-fiction, between sketch and story, glossary and fairy tale, and thus can be destabilizing for the reader. Paul March-Russell comments on this potential of short fiction:

> Like the literary fragment, the short story is prone to snap and confound reader's expectations, to delight in its own incompleteness, and to resist definition. These qualities not only mean that the short story has been of service to experimental writers but that they also relate the short story – and, in turn, modern and contemporary literature – to the mutability of the oral tradition. (March-Russell, 2009: viii)

Ali Smith, in a literary fable that appears in the guise of a foreword to *British Women Short Story Writers: The New Woman to Now*, highlights destabilization as an effect of short fiction; she represents lengthy novels in conversation with a short story who 'walked into a bar' (Smith, 2015: viii). The short story is caught in the fire of adjectives: 'You're far too short. You're far too disturbing. Difficult. Insubstantial. Quite unsettling. Deeply troubling' (Smith, 2015: ix). These adjectives could also be applied to Carter's short stories. The troubling hybridity and heterogeneity of her short fiction is further accentuated by references to diverse media that foster an intermedial imagination, thus multiplying the ways her fiction solicits the reader's creativity, an effect Carter confessed was central to her writing: 'Reading is as creative an activity as writing' (Carter, 1983: 69). Much as Carter saw radio as opening a 'third space' to imagine images, so do intermedial threads open up new spaces for speculation, about specific media productions and their cultural context, as well as the characteristics of the media themselves. This fosters forms of reflection that, like much of her fiction, propose a mix of self-conscious metafictional reflection and cultural commentary.

Meta-medial reflection and intermedial synergy

Carter's short fiction also reaches towards other media in order to incorporate meta-medial reflection into an already self-conscious narrative. This is the case in 'The Merchant of Shadows', where the narrator's reflections about the ontology of the movie star wife of a famous director lead to an investigation of the cultural field of Hollywood as mediated through the written word:

> Decade after ageless decade, movie after movie, 'the greatest star in heaven'. That was the promo. She'd no especial magic, either. She was no Gish, or Brooks, nor Dietrich, nor Garbo, who all share the same gift, the ability to reveal otherness. She *did* have a certain touch-me-not thing, that made her a natural for *film noir* in the Forties. Otherwise, she possessed only the extraordinary durability of her presence, as if continually incarnated afresh with the passage of time due to some occult operation of the Great Art of Light and Shade. (Carter, 1997c: 365; emphasis in original).

The 'Great Art of Light and Shade' functions as an intermedial gesture that is, in turn, transformed into metaphor to reflect upon identity and illusion, as this 'star' turns out in the end to be the famous director in drag. A meditation on illusion and performance is maintained through much of the story through the use of the intermedial thread of the cinematographic image. Sometimes such intermedial tendrils are crossed within the same narrative as in 'The Lady of the House of Love', where the figure of the reluctant vampire is mediated through references to *Nosferatu*, the 1922 film of F.W. Murnau, 'horrorzine'[6] images of the figure of Vampirella, and theatricality; the Lady's catafalque was 'not ebony at all but black-painted paper stretched on struts of wood, as in the theatre' (Carter, 1997c: 208). In Carter's story 'The Kiss' (1977), the visual dimension of architecture and cityscapes meet with the tactile dimension of drawing to engage the reader in a visual, self-conscious construction of a tale of love and transgression: 'Imagine a city drawn in straightforward, geometric shapes with crayons from a child's colouring box, in ochre, in white, in pale terracotta. Low, blonde terraces of houses seem to rise out of the whitish, pinkish earth as if born from it, not built out of it. There is a faint, gritty dust over everything, like the dust those pastel crayons leave on your fingers' (Carter, 1997c: 245).

Such intermedial overtones are intensified when a strong connection exists between two productions. This is the case with 'Overture and Incidental Music for *A Midsummer Night's Dream*' and Carter's radio play 'Come Unto These Yellow Sands'. The radio play is itself intermedial, as the paintings of Richard Dadd are remediated via radio, particularly his 1842 painting of the same title that depicts the dance of the fairies. This title takes up a line from Ariel's song in Act I, scene ii of Shakespeare's *The Tempest*, and is linked to other paintings which figure Oberon and Titania from *A Midsummer Night's Dream*. The radio play explores the nature of dreams and madness, while also proposing a reflection about the Victorian imagination and its perception of Shakespearian sexuality:

> This realm of fictive faery served as a kitschified repository for fancies too savage, too dark, too voluptous, fancies that were forbidden the light of common Victorian day *as such*. If the reality of the artist could not accommodate itself to that of the world of iron, of steam, of labour, of strife, he retreated to the consolation of the Midsummer fairies without the least idea of the true nature of such creatures in any symbolic schema worth its salt. The enchanting light that bathes these whimsical canvases falsifies not only experience but imagination itself. (Carter, 1997a: 38–9; emphasis in original)

This reflection about the Victorian imagination, as mediated through Dadd's paintings, takes on an intermedial quality of increasing complexity, as it is echoed in 'Overture and Incidental Music for *A Midsummer Night's Dream*', published four years later:

> The wood we have just described is that of nineteenth-century nostalgia, which disinfected the wood, cleansing it of the grave, hideous and elemental beings with which the superstition of an earlier age had filled it. Or, rather denaturing, castrating these beings until they came to look just as they do in those photographs of fairy folk that so enraptured Conan Doyle. It is Mendelssohn's wood. (Carter, 1997c: 277).

This last reference, along with the title, of course refers to Mendelssohn's Op. 21 (Overture) and Op. 61 (Incidental Music), an intermedial gesture that underlines the status of the story as being intertwined with Mendelssohn's sentimental portrayal of the fairies, similar to that of Dadd. To this can be added the photographs of the Cottingley fairies, photographs taken by Elsie Wright and Frances Griffiths, beginning in 1917, which incorporate the images of fairies, about which Sir Arthur Conan Doyle wrote. This mesh of intermedial references takes on a transfictional, and even transmedial dimension in this context, as in addition to proposing references to other media, Shakespeare's story migrates across different media and texts, first through the productions of two different artists working in painting and music, and through photographs, and then through two texts, one fictional and one written for radio, which are in turn interconnected.

Both works re-envision the aesthetics of nineteenth-century art, and propose playful commentary about Dadd's life along with his paintings, while the sentimental music of Mendelssohn is placed in relation with an 'Indian boy' figured as a hermaphrodite, Puck as a sexual pervert, and Titania as a large-breasted Titan. The fairies are indeed not shown to be delicate, but rather appear as overtly sexualized beings, particularly Puck: 'The Puck, pressed tight against Titania's magic, sighed heavily, stepped back a few paces and began energetically to play with himself. Have *you* seen fairy sperm? We mortals call it, cuckoo spit' (Carter 1997c: 278; emphasis in original). While the short story 'Overture and Incidental Music' leans towards theatre and music, the radio play negotiates the contours of biography and painting. Both, in turn, are intertwined to propose an overall re-thinking of the cultural value and historical contextualization and appropriation of Shakespeare's play and characters. The result is a dense web of mediations of the same figures, from the same story, fed by the creations of multiple artists. Carter's writing appears at the intersection of these productions, and is crossed by not only the story, but also by the cultural fabric with which it is intertwined. Intermediality, therefore, serves the purpose of bringing these different strands to light and introduces new dimensions into the speculative space carved out by both works.

Such a mesh of intermedial threads reaches a high degree of intricacy in Carter's enigmatic short story, 'Alice in Prague *or* The Curious Room'. The reference to Alice introduces an overt intermedial link between the text/image dynamics of Lewis Carroll's *Alice's Adventures in Wonderland* and *Through the Looking Glass and What Alice Found There*, as illustrated by Sir John Tenniel, and the Czech filmmaker Jan Švankmajer's 1988 film adaptation. The 'Alice in Prague' in the title is an explicit nod to Švankmajer, who is known for working across media. His movie version of the Alice story is informed by a surrealist impulse, and combines live images with stop-motion animation. Inspired by Carroll, Švankmajer emphasizes the importance of dream. *Alice* introduces a curious twist to the text if one considers what Michael Richardson sees in the film as a deep suspicion of words and a favouring of communication through images: 'There is thus in Švankmajer a profound distrust of the word, and understanding emerges, when it does, from touch and recognition of what is contained within the power of images. The superiority of images over words for Švankmajer appears to lie in their mutability: it is precisely because images can lie that they can also tell the truth' (Richardson, 2006: 125).

A meta-medial reflection about image versus language is indeed introduced by the intermedial citation in the epigraph to an earlier version of the story published in 1990: 'Alice said: Now you are reading a story' (Carter, 1990: 218). Švankmajer's film begins with a similar statement: '*Alice* thought to herself '*Now you will see a film* [...] made for children [...] perhaps'. Here Carter plays with the threshold of the wonderland world, but a threshold that superimposes the posture of the reader onto that of viewer, thus inviting the reader to read and 'see' with an inner eye, to link a filmic, and therefore visual, citationality to the experience of reading. This intermedial superposition fosters an intermedial imagination, a reading dynamics that gives a privileged position to a layering of images. The later version of the story, published in *American Ghosts & Old World Wonders*, replaces this initial paratext with an explicit reference to Švankmajer: 'This piece was written in praise of Jan Svankmayer, the animator of Prague, and his film of *Alice*' (Carter, 1997c: 397),[7] yet the meta-medial reflection remains dominant.

Švankmajer's association with surrealism also lends an interesting twist to a reflection on alchemy, which is in turn intertwined with the *Kunstkamer*, or *Wunderkammer*, also known as cabinets of curiosities, where the organizing theme is that of memory, in that objects, relics, various works of art and natural oddities are placed in collections where arbitrary juxtapositions create an aesthetics of defamiliarization and strangeness. Carter's story features the cabinets of Archduke Rudolph II, whose sixteenth-century collections are famous. Such collections function in a mode of patchwork, a recurrent metaphor in Carter's writing that also appears in her story 'The Quiltmaker' (1981). This sense of juxtaposition and heterogeneity is heightened by references to Giuseppe Arcimboldo, whose paintings propose human figures composed of fruits and vegetables, which also function in a mode of *assemblage*. Film, portrait, animation, cabinets of curiosities are intertwined with images of Carrol's Alice, as drawn by John Tenniel. In a review of Pontus Hulten's *The Arcimboldo Effect* (1987), the catalogue of a one-man show at the Palazzo Grassi, in Venice, Carter emphasizes how Arcimboldo's paintings, as typical of mannerism, are 'more interesting to talk about than [...] to look at', thus highlighting the potential of his art to make one think, an aspect that is emphasized in her linking of his work to the surrealists (Carter, 1997b: 431). An aspect of this speculative quality is harnessed here, as Arcimboldo's static paintings, along with the mechanical automata that feature in *Kunstkamer*, are brought into synergy with the medial dynamics of Švankmajer's stop motion play with objects, as Carter's Arcimboldo is the creator of an automaton composed of fruit: 'This thing before us, although it is not, was not and never will be alive, has been inanimate and will be animate again, but, at the moment, not, for now, after one final shove, it stuck stock-still, wheels halted, wound down, uttering one last, gross, mechanical sigh' (Carter, 1997c: 407). The reader is invited to superimpose a reflection about the ontology of the automaton onto the life-like aesthetics of stop-motion:

> Are they animate or not, these beings that jerk and shudder into such a semblance of life? Do these creatures believe themselves to be human? And if they do, at what point might they, by virtue of the sheer intensity of their belief, become so?
> (In Prague, the city of the Golem, an image can come to life). (Carter, 1997c: 406)

Similarly, Tenniel's images are brought to life in the story, in an overt superposition of chronotopes, where literary illustration merges with historical context. Here Alice emerges from the crystal ball of the historical mathematician and alchemist, Dr John Dee:

> How did she get there?
>   She was kneeling on the mantelpiece of the sitting room of the place she lived, looking at herself in the mirror. Bored, she breathed on the glass until it clouded over and then, with her finger, she drew a door. The door opened. She sprang through and, after a brief moment's confusing fish-eye view of a vast, gloomy chamber, scarcely illuminated by five candles in one branched stick and filled with all the clutter in the world, her view was obliterated by the clawed paw of a vast cat extended ready to strike, hideously increasing in size as it approached her, and then, splat! She burst out of 'time will be' into 'time was', for the transparent substance which surrounded her burst like a bubble and there she was, in her pink frock, lying on some rushes under the gaze of a tender ancient with a long, white beard and a man with a coal-scuttle on his head. (Carter, 1997c: 404)

'Time will be' refers to the chronotope of the marvelous wonderland, whereas 'time was' is that of history, that is the period of John Dee and Rudolph II. The figure of Alice travels from Carroll to Švankmajer to Carter, from illustrated story, to film/stop motion animation, to short story, and is in turn placed in synergy with layers of intermedial references. This short story, with its disjunctive narrative and multi-layered images, functions itself like a curious room, an art form that has often been used as a metaphor to refer to Carter's overall style of *bricolage* and citational juxtapositions.[8]

In the introduction of the special *SPELL* (*Swiss Papers in English Language and Literature*) issue, the editors discuss Carter's oral presentation of the story before her reading:

> But few can have expected the moving and playful 'Introductory Speculation' that preceded her reading of 'The Curious Room.' And speculative, in the sense of self-reflecting, it is, with its quotations about mannerism as a strategy of quotation and with the author's self-representation in terms of post-modernism and surrealism. No wonder that Carter pronounces her Alice to be not just Tenniel's, or Carroll's, but also Svankmajer's, and that the Prague of Rudolf II and of Arcimboldo is refracted through André Breton, Wittgenstein (to whom one might also add Chatwin's Utz). Arcimboldo's artifacts, Carmen Miranda's hat, the crystal bubble/tear/ball/looking-glass; all of these are fitting emblems of a colourful, protean work that seduces as it gently incites its academic audience to self mockery. (Bridges, 1990: 10)

Carter speaks of the aesthetics of the curious room: 'The extraordinary room was a kind of ur-museum, manifestation of an omnivorous curiosity, a gluttony for the world, but also a potent image of the unconscious, which is the world, or underworld, in which language develops a life of its own' (Carter, 1990: 217). In Carter's text, this realm of language is fed by the intermedial resonances that emerge between the works integrated into the story. The result is a sense of overlapping, sometimes jarring, artistic chronotopes generated around the idea of Alice and different forms of wonder and dream, as juxtaposed with historical figures and discourse. Carter indeed places different semiotic systems, along with their cultural contexts, into relation so as to foster new literary chronotopes. These heterogenous space-time constructions are self-consciously presented so the reader is led to perceive and experience the intermedial tendrils, while also being led to reflect upon the nature of these different media, as illustrated in the discussion of the ontology of the cinematic star and the sixteenth-century automaton above. The question remains whether the relationship between these different medial manifestations in the text exist in convergence or divergence within the frame of the short story. In an earlier article about this story, I have explored the way in which the intertextual complexity of the piece fosters 'syncretic thinking' through its invitation to link seemingly disparate concepts, arts, references, objects. I would take this a step further in linking this idea to the syncretic, intermedial imagination. Regina Schober speaks of the 'intermedial imagination' and explains the inherent self-consciousness of media:

> The medium itself intrinsically incorporates and conveys its 'image', its version of mediality, either by self-referentially and self-reflexively pointing to its own medial status, by referring to other media and thus determining its own medial boundaries, or simply by displaying performative features of its own mediality in dissociation from other media. In the case of intermedial 'imagination', a medium defines itself by its own potentials, but also with regard to its limitations. Especially when turning to another medium, it automatically embarks on a dialogical contemplation about possible borrowings, impulses and insights which could contribute to enhancing its own (limited) expressive power. (Schober, 2010: 163)

This intermedial imagination is highlighted within a context of 'remediation', a process described by Jay Bolter and Richard Grusin as 'the formal logic by which new media refashion prior media forms' (Bolter and Grusin, 1999: 273). Like Marie-Laure Ryan, Bolter and Grusin emphasize how media are caught in a web of relations: 'Media are continually commenting on, reproducing, and replacing each other, and this process is integral to media. Media need each other to function as media at all' (Bolter and Grusin, 1999: 55). Marie-Laure Ryan emphasizes the versatility and power of this concept, as it also points to how processes of remediation allow for forms of what Bolter and Grusin refer to as *hypermediacy*, that is, media presented in a way so as to highlight their own characteristics (Ryan 2004: 31–2). According to Bolter and Grusin a medium is inherently caught up in processes of remediation, as a medium is defined as 'that which remediates. It is that which appropriates the techniques, forms and social significance of other media and attempts to rival or refashion them in the name of the real. A medium in our culture can never operate in isolation, because it must enter into relationships of respect and rivalry with other media' (Bolter and Grusin 1999: 65). Carter's intermedial layering demonstrates a self-consciousness of such media relations and their 'social significance'. In conjuring up new spaces for the intermedial imagination, Carter highlights not only the characteristics of artistic productions in specific media, but also their potential to *combine in synergy* with a similar goal of 'enhancing' the 'expressive power' (Schober 2010: 163) of juxtapositions. Martine Hennard Dutheil de la Rochère observes such effects in 'From "The Bloody Chamber" to the *Cabinet de curiosités*':

> [In] Angela Carter's 'Alice in Prague *or* The Curious Room' Carter's engagement with the idea of the 'curious room' leads to powerful combinations: The term 'curious room', which has been used by Carter in relation to fiction but also TV ('The Box Does Furnish a Room' in 1979), can thus be traced back to Perrault's *cabinet* and a constellation of other texts and films that demonstrate the creative power of crossing linguistic, cultural, generic and media boundaries, let alone transgressive conjoinings, like the Archduke having 'intercourse with a fruit salad' (Hennard Dutheil de la Rochère, 2016: 129).

This term of 'transgressive conjoinings' is key to understanding the potential impact of Carter's use of intermedial crossovers and layers in her writing.

The intermedial imagination and the screenplay as a field of possibilities

Whereas the intermedial citation in many of Carter's stories functions in a mode of layering and juxtaposition, another dynamic is that of the crossover. Carter spoke openly of the manner in which radio shaped the story of *Vampirella* differently to how short fiction shaped 'The Lady of the House of Love': 'So *The Lady of the House of Love* is a Gothic tale about a reluctant vampire; the radio play, *Vampirella*, is about vampirism as metaphor' (Carter, 1997a: 499–500). But it is interesting to consider not only how media shape a story differently, but also how writing texts for other media influences the creation of new stories. In cultivating the intermedial imagination in the reader, Carter's fiction also engages with the spaces for imagining proposed by the screenplay or radio play, as texts. These are texts of an in-between status, in that they are often performed, but are not always approached as autonomous works. Interestingly, a screenplay or radio play is rarely read for its aesthetic value, but is rather used as a tool through which to structure a potential production or performance. Crofts concentrates essentially on Carter's mediated texts, suggesting how the link between realization and text are an essential aspect of Carter's writing: 'Furthermore, as indicated in the Introduction, Carter wrote a number of other texts for stage and screen which are not discussed in this book, primarily because they were never realized and consequently do not constitute "mediated" texts. These include two original film scripts which demonstrate her ongoing commitment to the cinema' (Crofts, 2003: 195). However, as I have suggested in an earlier study of intermediality in Carter's 'John Ford's 'Tis Pity She's a Whore' (Ryan-Sautour 2011), Carter's writing also raises the issue of the screenplay as a centre of potentialities. Indeed, one does not read a screenplay as one reads a work of fiction, or even a dramatic play. It is read in anticipation of its transfer to the medium of film. The mental space of reading is, therefore, one of projection, as readers are led to imagine a possible future for the text in relation to their previous film experiences and familiarity with the medium.

Carter appears to have found in writing for screen and radio a different form of reading contract, with metafictional/metamedial potential. Ted Nannicelli, in *A Philosophy of the Screenplay* (2013) speaks of the uncertain identity of the screenplay and questions its status as a cultural 'artifact'. Nannicelli insists on the almost insurmountable task of defining the screenplay as an art form. However, in his discussion, he does underline essential aspects of this form of writing as a 'verbal object', with the 'intended function' of '*suggesting the plot, characters, dialogue, shots, edits, sound effects, and/or other constitutive elements of film*' (Nannicelli, 2013: 5; emphasis added). As opposed to a novel or short story, which might appear in adapted forms, a screenplay is 'intended' for production as film (Nannicelli, 2013: 5). However, Nannicelli recognizes how the screenplay might also be written for the express reason of playing with the form, as in Cormac McCarthy's *Cities of the Plain* (1998) and *No Country for Old Men* (2005), which began as screenplays with the intention of developing them into novels (Nannicelli, 2013: 6). Similarly Nannicelli speaks of the fanfiction versions of 'virtual series' that air in the form of screenplays. The form indeed seems to appear not only as a text intended for film production, but can serve as a space for literary experimentation.

Although Nannicelli ultimately resists the formulation of any essentialist definition of the screenplay, in his discussion of possible definitions he cites Ian W. Macdonald's concept of the 'screen idea': 'For Macdonald, a "screen idea" is "any notion of a potential screenwork held by one or more people, whether or not it is possible to describe it on paper or by other means." In short, the screen idea is "a concept … intended to become a screenwork," and the "screenwork" is "the completed film, TV drama, etc"' (Macdonald qtd. in Nannicelli, 2013: 8). The set of moving concepts Nannicelli deploys for his discussion resonate in relation to Carter's practices, where traditional screenplays are brought to converse with texts that play with the 'screen idea'. 'John Ford's *'Tis Pity She's a Whore*' appears as an intentional experimentation with the 'screen idea' in relation with what could be called the 'stage idea' in theatrical performance. In this story, Carter superimposes the storyline that informs Jacobean dramatist, John Ford's *'Tis Pity She's a Whore* onto the Western landscapes of American filmmaker, John Ford. The incestuous couple in the original play, Annabella and Giovanni, are contrasted with their American counterparts, Johnnie and Annie-Belle. The story functions in an in-between space, between two creators, two landscapes, two centuries and two media, in a manner that leads to a self-consciousness of how film has conditioned our imaginations.[9]

This quality of 'suggesting' a film production in the mode of the 'screen idea' is also present in Carter's short piece 'Gun for the Devil', which was originally written to flesh out details for a film production. Mark Bell comments on this in his production notes for the screenplay: '"Gun for the Devil" was originally written as a prose film treatment in the early 1980s […] The screenplay was commissioned by Brenda Reid at the BBC in collaboration with David Wheatley. The script was delivered in September 1987 but did not go into production and was written off in 1989' (Carter, 1997a: 508–9). As a 'prose film treatment'/story, this text functions in a manner similar to that of a screenplay, and thus exists less as a story to be adapted for the screen, and more as a space for imagining a potential screen production.

Unlike 'John Ford's *'Tis Pity She's a Whore*', however, this piece appears to be a posthumously published text of ambiguous status. As a work of prose, it cannot truly figure in Carter's collected writings for other media; it therefore finds its place in *American Ghosts & Old World Wonders*. However, because of the predominance of the 'screen idea' as the guiding aesthetic principle of the work, it occupies an in-between generic space that also invites a different form of reading. The story is strikingly visual and echoes some of the language of screenplays, with its short descriptive, phrases: 'A hot, dusty, flyblown Mexican border town – a town without hope, without grace, the end of the road for all those who've the misfortune to find themselves washing up here' (Carter, 1997c: 349). The screenplay, written after the prose sketch, echoes the structure:

> A town like the town in every Western you ever saw, a little bit of everything.
> Adobe, Clapboard. A single store. Dusty and sleepy under the sun; and very, run down. (Carter, 1997a: 299)

The absence of verbs, along with a description based on Western stereotypes, indicates a mobilization of the reader's previous viewing experiences in order to create an internal landscape. In this in-between space, saturated with the reader's experience of film images, Carter develops a Faustian plot that Crofts describes, in reference to the screenplay, as a sort of homage to Jan Švankmajer: 'Sergio Leone meets Jan Svankmayer – the screenplay combines the *mise-en-scène* of the spaghetti western (recreating the traditional flyblown border town) with supernatural elements reminiscent of Svankmayer's *Faust* (with its animated devils and disturbing transformations)' (Crofts 2003, 195). Here Carter's writing of fiction appears in synergy with her writing for the screen, as it is difficult to read the fictional sketch without in some way referring to or reading the screenplay. The two works appear in tandem, although published in two different volumes, and both function in a mode of projective imagining. Contrary to the intermedial citationality present in the above examples, 'Gun for the Devil' points to a *possible* image. It points to a potential story, while depending on the resources of the reader to do so. It thus deploys the reader's previous viewing experiences, and puts this experience to the service of a text whose intention is to point to possible productions. In *Le Tiers pictural: pour une critique intermédiale*, Liliane Louvel devotes a chapter to the manner in which the pictorial allusion mobilizes the reader's resources in creating an in-between space between two modes of expression, as it appears to vibrate between text and image, and between two separate time frames (Louvel, 2010: 231). In 'Gun for the Devil' this citationality extends more to genre, in that the Western becomes a cultural frame within which to engage the reader's previous viewing experiences as a resource for the imagination to carve out a speculative, fictional space.

Carter's intermedial citationality is far-reaching, as it is intended to stretch the reader's imagination, to engage with the cultural through an exploitation of the reader's 'internal screen'. Louvel uses the term *tiers pictural* (pictorial third) to refer to this in-between space, a dynamic space that emerges between text and image, as a creation by the reader:

> The 'pictorial third' between text and image, makes something else happen, that plays out between the two. This pictorial third would be a floating image [...] suggested by the text, but which remains an image that is created through words, an image that can refer to an extratextual painting, but also to an imaginary painting (or one of its substitutes) to be reconstructed by the reader, an image that would thus be his/her own property, his/her own 'invention'. (Louvel, 2010: 260)[10]

Although Louvel is primarily preoccupied with how the literary text represents and engages with the static visual image, one can see how Carter's superposition of intermedial threads from different visual forms (stop-motion animation, cinema, painting, animation, music, comics) appears to also cultivate a space that Louvel qualifies as one of 'transaction' between author and reader. A dynamic reading posture is cultivated (Louvel, 2010: 259), allowing for a space to emerge beyond the text and beyond the image, as a creation of the reader.

Crofts was therefore correct in underlining the centrality of Carter's writing for other media in her collected works,[11] but we have perhaps overlooked the manner in which other media enhance how her fiction solicits the reader, thus contributing another political dimension to her writing. Intermediality plays out in her short fiction in a dynamic of citationality, synergy, crossover, and even forms of remediation. Given Carter's interest in media, it is highly probable that she would develop an interest in the potential of electronic media if she were still writing today. Indeed, we know she was aware of the changing landscape of literature, as she anticipates a 'science-fiction future world that every day approaches more closely, in which information and narrative pleasure are transmitted electronically and books are a quaint, antiquarian, minority taste. Not in *my* time anyway, I say to myself' (Carter, 2006: 2; emphasis in original). Indeed, not in her time, although she was probably aware of her friend Robert Coover's interest in new technological media, as he became one of the founders of the Electronic Literature Association. Carter's keen interest in intermediality and media crossovers, towards the end of her career, points to a horizon of creation that was never explored. However, much as her work demonstrates prescience as to the development of performance theory in relation to gender, so does it point to a strong awareness of how media shape stories, and how this shaping is interconnected with cultural context. In drawing these reflections into the structure of her stories, she ultimately indicates how different forms of mediation imply different forms of 'seeing'. It is indeed the power of this inner eye that is ultimately solicited by her intermedial spaces for creative reading.

Notes

1 'But it was the movies that administered America to me intravenously, as they did to the entire generation that remembers 1968 with such love. It seemed to me, when I first started going to the cinema intensively in the late Fifties, that Hollywood had colonised the imagination of the entire world and was turning us all into Americans. I resented it, it fascinated me' (Carter, 2006: 5).
2 All short stories quoted in this article are taken from Carter's collected short stories: *Burning Your Boats* (1997).
3 'What she was, in Carter's case, is difficult to define. Novels, short stories, radio plays, fairy-tales, polemic, journalism: the scope of her writing, in an era when authors tend to be pigeon-holed as soon as their work begins to be published, is breathtaking. It is tempting, given this range, to characterise her as a Renaissance woman, were it not for that fact that it is writers like Carter herself who have taught us to be suspicious of such terms' (Smith, 1997: xiii).
4 'Later on, I took the script of *Vampirella* as the raw material for a short story, *The Lady of the House of Love*' (Carter, 1997a: 497).
5 See for example my earlier article, 'The Intermedial Trajectories of Angela Carter's Wolf Tales' and Martine Hennard Dutheil de la Rochère's article, '"La magie des voix dans la nuit": transcréation des contes de Perrault chez Angela Carter'.
6 See Carter's article, 'The Art of Horrorzines', in *Shaking a Leg: Collected Journalism and Writings*, ed. Jenny Uglow (London: Chatto & Windus), pp. 447–51.
7 The earlier version of the story also proposes a different set of

conundrums at the end. There are slight differences between the two pieces that trouble its textual identity. Once the reader becomes aware of the first version, there is a tendency to read both versions in relation to each other.

8 See, for example, Kim Evan's documentary about Carter's life, as well as Angela Carter, *The Curious Room: Collected Dramatic Works*, ed. Mark Bell (London: Chatto & Windus, 1996).

9 See my article, "Intermediality and the Cinematographic Image in Angela Carter's 'John Ford's '*Tis Pity She's a Whore*'.

10 My translation of: 'Le "tiers pictural" entre le text et l'image, fait advenir autre chose, ce qui joue entre les deux. Ce tiers pictural serait l'image flottante […] suggérée par le texte mais qui reste une image suscitée par des mots, une image qui peut renvoyer à un tableau dans l'extra-texte mais aussi à un tableau (ou l'un de ses substituts) imaginaire à reconstruire par le lecteur, image qui sera alors sa propriété, son "invention"' (Louvel, 2010: 260).

11 'Carter's work in media has been sidelined by the academy because it does not fit neatly into generic or canonic categories. But in editing out her mediated texts, contemporary critical responses offer an incomplete picture of her work. As the texts discussed here reveal, Carter's writing for radio, film and television is not a aberration from her real vocation as a writer of fiction, but "an extension and an amplification of writing for the 'painted page'" (Carter, 1985: 12–13)' (Crofts, 2003: 194).

References

Alice (1989), directed by Jan Švankmajer [DVD] (Czechoslovakia: Channel Four Films, First Run Films).

Bolter, Jay and Richard Grusin (1999), *Remediation: Understanding New Media* (Cambridge, MA: The MIT Press).

Bridges, Margaret (1990), 'Introduction', in Margaret Bridges (ed.), *On Strangeness: SPELL (Swiss Papers in English Language and Literature)*, vol. 5 (Tübingen: Gunter Narr Verlag), 9–12.

Carter, Angela (1983), 'Notes from the Front Line', in Michelene Wandor (ed.), *On Gender and Writing* (London: Pandora Press), pp. 69–77.

—— (1990), 'Introduction to "The Curious Room"', in Margaret Bridges (ed.), *On Strangeness: SPELL (Swiss Papers in English Language and Literature)*, vol. 5 (Tübingen: Gunter Narr Verlag), 215–17.

—— (1990), 'The Curious Room', in Margaret Bridges (ed.), *On Strangeness: SPELL (Swiss Papers in English Language and Literature)*, vol. 5 (Tübingen: Gunter Narr Verlag), pp. 218–32.

—— (1992), Interview, *Angela Carter's Curious Room*, Dir. Kim Evans, BBC 2, 15 September 1992. Film Documentary (London: BFI Film Archives).

—— ([1996] 1997a), 'Preface' to *Come Unto These Yellow Sands* [1978], in Angela Carter, *The Curious Room: Collected Dramatic Works*, ed. Mark Bell (London: Vintage), pp. 497–502.

—— ([1978] 1997a), *Come Unto These Yellow Sands*, in Angela Carter, *The Curious Room: Collected Dramatic Works*, ed. Mark Bell (London: Vintage), pp. 33–59.

—— (1997a), *Gun for the Devil*, in Angela Carter, *The Curious Room: Collected Dramatic Works*, ed. Mark Bell (London: Vintage), pp. 299–338.

—— ([1988] 1997b) 'Hollywood', in Angela Carter, *Shaking a Leg: Journalism and Writings*, ed. Jenny Uglow (London: Chatto & Windus), pp. 384–6.

—— ([1987] 1997d), 'Pontus Hulten: The Arcimboldo Effect', in Angela Carter, *Shaking a Leg: Journalism and Writings*, ed. Jenny Uglow (London: Chatto & Windus), pp. 430–1.

—— ([1995] 1997c), *Burning Your Boats: The Collected Short Stories* (New York: Penguin).

—— ([1992] 2006), 'Introduction', in *Expletives Deleted: Selected Writings* (London: Vintage), pp. 1–6.

Clapp, Susannah ([1996] 1997), 'Introduction', in Angela Carter, *The Curious Room: Collected Dramatic Works*, ed. Mark Bell (London: Vintage), vii–x.

—— (2012), *A Card from Angela Carter* (London: Bloomsbury).

Crofts, Charlotte (2003), *'Anagrams of Desire': Angela Carter's Writing for Radio, Film and Television* (Manchester: Manchester University Press).

Hennard Dutheil de la Rochère, Martine (2011), 'The Interplay of Text and Image from Angela Carter's *The Fairy Tales of Charles Perrault* (1977) to *The Bloody Chamber* (1979)', *JSSE*, 56, 93–108.

—— (2016), '"La magie des voix dans la nuit": transcréation des contes de Perrault chez Angela Carter', in Camille Vorger (ed.), *Etudes de Lettres* (Lausanne: Université de Lausanne), 3, pp. 87–108.

—— (2016), 'From the Bloody Chamber to the *Cabinet de Curiosités*: Angela Carter's Curious Alices through the Looking-Glass of Languages', *Marvels & Tales: Journal of Fairy-Tale Studies*, 30:2, 284–308.

Louvel, Liliane (2010), *Le Tiers pictural: pour une critique intermédiale* (Rennes: Presses Universitaires de Rennes).

March-Russell, Paul (2009), *The Short Story* (Edinburgh: Edinburgh University Press).

Munford, Rebecca (ed.) (2006), *Re-visiting Angela Carter* (New York: Palgrave Macmillan).

—— (2013), *Decadent Daughters and Monstrous Mothers: Angela Carter and European Gothic* (Manchester: Manchester University Press).

Nannicelli, Ted (2013), *A Philosophy of the Screenplay* (London: Routledge). Kindle Edition.

Richardson, Michael (2006), *Surrealism and Cinema* (Oxford: Berg).

Rushdie, Salman (1997), 'Introduction', in Angela Carter [1995], *Burning Your Boats* (New York: Penguin), ix–xiv.

Ryan, Marie-Laure (2004), 'Introduction', in Marie-Laure Ryan (ed.), *Narrative Across Media: The Languages of Storytelling* (Lincoln: University of Nebraska Press). Kindle Edition.

Ryan, Marie-Laure and Jan-Noël Thon (2014), 'Introduction', in Marie-Laure Ryan and Jan-Noël Thon (eds), *Storyworlds Across Media: Toward a Media-Conscious Narratology* (Lincoln: University of Nebraska Press). Kindle Edition.

Ryan-Sautour, Michelle (2011), 'Intermediality and the Cinematographic Image in Angela Carter's "John Ford's *'Tis Pity She's a Whore*"', *JSSE*, 56, 59–74.

—— (2012), 'The Alchemy of Reading in Angela Carter's "Alice in Prague or The Curious Room"', in Sonya Andermahr and Lawrence Phillips (eds), *Angela Carter: New Critical Readings* (London: Continuum), pp. 67–80.

—— (2012), 'The Intermedial Trajectories of Angela Carter's Wolf Tales', *Journal of the Short Story in English*, 59, 75–91.

Schober, Regina (2010), 'Translating Sounds: Intermedial Exchanges in Amy Lowell's "Stravinsky's Three Pieces 'Grotesques', for String Quartet"', in Lars Elleström (ed.), *Media Borders: Multimodality and Intermediality* (Houndmills, Basingstoke: Palgrave Macmillan), pp. 163–74.

Smith, Ali (2015), 'Foreword', in Emma Young and James Bailey (eds), *British Women Short Story Writers: The New Women to Now* (Edinburgh: Edinburgh University Press), 2015.

Smith, Joan (1997), 'Introduction', in Angela Carter, *Shaking a Leg: Journalism and Writings*, ed. Jenny Uglow (London: Chatto & Windus), xii–xiv.

Thomas, Karima (2011), 'The Urge for Intermediality and Creative Reading in Angela Carter's "Impressions: The Wrightsman Magdalene"', *Journal of the Short Story in English*, 56, 75–92.

2

Psychogeography in the curiosity cabinet: Angela Carter's poetics of space

Anna Kérchy

Topophilia as a narrative engine

ANGELA CARTER'S FICTION IS distinguished by a carnivalesque topography's liminal settings. Uncle Philip's run-down Magic Toyshop serves as a backdrop to young Melanie's psychosexual maturation; peep show worlds and illusory realities generated by Doctor Hoffman's desire machines are visited throughout Desiderio's picaresque journeys; Colonel Kearney's travelling circus takes on a Trans-Siberian Express tour its birdwoman aerialist falling for a journalist-turned-clown; the vaudeville theatre stages the burlesque performances of the Chance twin sisters; and in the labyrinthine enchanted woods the wolfish Red Riding Hood can meet the tender wolf. These loci all match the borderline conditions and the ahistorical temporal dislocations of Carter's grotesque, metamorphic characters, as well as her (mock) 'magical mannerist' (Haffenden, 1985: 79) style resisting generic categorizations. As Salman Rushdie noted, besides a fable-world turned topsy-turvy in her own iconoclast fashion, Carter's 'other country is the fairground, the world of the gimcrack showman, the hypnotist, the trickster, the puppeteer' (Rushdie, 1995: xi), spaces artistically reimagined on the margins of neatly ordered sites of bourgeois living.

Carter aimed at a daring disruption of demarcating lines: a multilayered transgression of physical corporeal frames, of existential, phenomenological and psychic states, of culturally prescribed social positionalities, as well as of ready-made identity scripts' and the discursive conventions of canonized literary modes. This agenda is encapsulated in her witty *ars poetica*, particularly the spatial subversion implied in her demythologizing project's intent of putting 'new wine in old bottles, especially if the pressure of the new wine makes the old bottles explode' (Carter, 1983: 71).

This *bon mot* highlights how Carterian spaces metanarratively reflect upon creative authorship and textual productivity along the lines of a feminist psychogeographical poetics of spatiality. This chapter scrutinizes the individual affective charge fictive locations hold for the woman writer who composes herself into being within sites of her own mak(e-believ)ing. It starts out from a brief overview of geographical interpretations of Carter's fictional places which associate her trademark challenging of generic conventions and gender roles with spatial explorations which surface both on a thematic and stylistic level of her work. It proceeds with arguing that Carter's decentralization project resonates with the poststructuralist notion of an 'open text' that allows readers to meander in a labyrinthine narrative while tackling the ultimate metafictional dilemma: 'Where do stories come from?' After a brief analysis of the affective investment of spatial imagery on Carter's short fiction, a close reading of 'The Scarlet House' shows how the narrator protagonist's mental mapping of her traumatic past becomes a survival strategy when the stake of maintaining her sense of space is the preservation of her sense of self.

Critical approaches to Carter's demythologization of conventional cartography

Carter's dissatisfaction with conventional cartographical representations takes various forms. She renegotiates boundaries of otherness in search of 'elsewheres' which could fall beyond 'forced mappings' by prevailing ideological technologies, disciplinary regimes or established modes of knowledge formation; and she reconsiders spatiality in terms of the inhabitants' psychic, and imaginative interactions with their own locatedness. In Carter's writing, locatedness seems transitional and kaleidoscopic, no matter how permanent, because of the dynamics of the interpretive agency oscillating between uncertainty and epiphany while calling that specific location into consciousness, and hence into existence. Spaces' reality status is rendered dubious by a strategic destabilization of socio-culturally set signifying systems meant to make sense of the world surrounding us. A select catalogue of some paradigmatic geographical readings of Carter's fictional spaces can illustrate the multidimensionality of the issue.

Susannah Clapp's unconventional biography *A Card from Angela Carter* (2012) reinforced the portrait of the artist as an empathic wanderer and gifted travel writer with a unique feel of capturing the atmosphere of a place; by suggesting that the picture postcards Carter sent to her literary executor Clapp formed 'a paper trail' through her life (Clapp, 2012: 10). The words and images of the cities she visited – inventive, improvised sketches of local colour instead of panoramic tableaux or touristic clichés – mapped their friendship, illustrated her intent to share sightseeing impressions as bases of affective bonds, and documented the 'great swoops'[1] of her artistic imagination.

Carter's trademark generic subversion can easily be interpreted along the lines of rebellious bordercrossing and geographical exploration. From a feminist standpoint, Gina Wisker's essay tellingly entitled 'Behind Locked Doors' examines Carter's horror writing, to unveil how her language, imagery and topography revive E.A. Poe's major leitmotifs. Wondrously nightmarish Gothic settings, spatial symbols of the Unconscious (cracking mirrors, collapsing mansions, haunted forests), terrible consequences of domestic incarceration by male tyrants, and claustrophobic entrapment within cultural clichés of femininity result in the heroine's aggressive or farcical attempts to flee from the confinement of 'his' romantic fantasies and perverse wet dreams illegitimately suppressing her sexuality and power. Relying on Julia Kristeva's theory of abjection, Wisker explains the political stakes of the literary gambit concerned with exposing the boundaries, rejections and repressions of Western patriarchal-based horror. Refusing borderlines (clear-cut distinctions between inside and outside) entails recognizing the abject Other as part of ourselves and fulfilling an egalitarian mission by overcoming 'the need to find victims, scapegoats, and enemies' (2006: 193).

Sarah Gamble celebrates 'domestic deconstruction' as a major feminist leitmotif of Carter's oeuvre. In her view, 'a series of rewritings of narratives of homeliness and domesticity' simultaneously voice and disavow a nostalgia for a home traditionally conceived as a feminized cultural sphere. Carterian homes are no longer solitary, confined, private spaces. They are refashioned into 'open-ended, multitudinous, and polyphonous' territories, matching the 'inner landscapes' of increasingly empowered, self-reflective female inhabitants and their reinvented families – as in Ma Nelson's brothel and the solidarious sisterly community poking fun at the debilitating myth of the Angel in the House. (Gamble, 2006: 279) In Gamble's complex reading, 'home' for Carter is both a place of an intimate encounter with an idealized maternal past, and also a point of origin from where daughters rebelliously break away to find paths of their own making. It is an object of fruitless, absurd nostalgia and from a pragmatic perspective, a 'mundane necessity' (295) of our enworlded embodiment, too.

Carter's woman-centred literary agenda was keen on exploring the voices of women inhabiting heterotopias – utterly neglected by Michel Foucault's original definition of ambiguous, non-totalizable, 'disordered' sites enigmatically falling beyond normative socio-political spheres and incongruous with conventional topographical assumptions (Foucault, 1984: 46). As Eliza Claudia Filimon demonstrates, the lived spatial experience of Carterian heroines transforms 'othered' places into empowering loci by evading patriarchal marginalization of feminized modes of being. Sites of resistance build on counter-discourses of feminist identities mapped in terms of 'empowering reciprocity, politics of boundaries, situatedness, and multivocality' (Filimon, 2014: 24). Heterotopian zones – 'inner depths of outer places' (38), scenes of dynamic performance, storytelling and places to reach towards alterity – can be tracked in Carter's catacombs, castles, prisons, deserts, forests and mazes in a rich fictional corpus organized by the leitmotif of 'worlds in collision', in Filimon's wording (10).

A corporeal narratological analysis provides adequate methodological tools for a literary land-survey that can map the body in/of the text to discover metamorphic corporealities as a major structuring device of Carter's self-decomposing narratives toying with readerly destabilization. As I have argued elsewhere (Kérchy, 2008), in *The Passion of New Eve* the fetishised fragments of surgically sex-changed, transgender Eve/lyn's dismembered body parts (the devouring *vagina dentata*, the sterile womb, the wounded breast, the crying eyes, and the regurgitating mouth) can be interpreted as emblematic stations of the hero/ine's picaresque journey during his/her passion of 'becoming (monstrous) woman' (22). This topography of pain not only maps out a ruthless parody of patriarchal myths of femininity, but also stages the forcibly feminized subject's cultural dis-ease. The pathological indices of the anxieties related to engendering, the psychosomatic symptoms of female body dysmorphia – a misconceived image of the self, resulting in body modifications – infect the novel's language via mutually abortive-castrating, antagonistically engendered, contradictory narrative voices of a male impersonator, an ironic feminist, a post-operative transsexual and a bulimic patient. Using a kinetic, spatial metaphor for the act of writing, New Eve pushes herself forward in a rock cavity 'pressed as between pages of a gigantic book [...] composed of silence: [...] emphatically closed' (Carter, 1977: 180). This scene enacts metafictionally Carter's moving away from a 'ventriloquist' re-enactment of masculine discourse towards a free-flowing, 'cohesively fragmentary' self-reflective feminist voice of her own making (Peach, 1998: 111).

Besides her curious domestic settings, urban territories also hold exciting pychogeographical implications for Carter. Simon Goulding tracks her description of City as a site of dislocation and reorientation. He argues that Carter recycles the classic trope of the displaced orphan with subtexts of cultural, social and sexual misplacement, so as to challenge canonized cartographies and cultural hegemony from the paradoxical position of a social realist fantasist. Her fictionalizations of the 1960s metropolitan landscapes already appeared in *Shadow Dance* and crystallized in *The Magic Toyshop*, which guides to less fashionable districts, 'the streets that did not appear on the maps of smart London' and constituted a counterpart to the stylish 'swinging' image by housing those who were 'not party to the "party"'. Hence urban space is circumscribed as an unmappable collection of marginalized, apparently insignificant smaller sites where the 'characters interact, develop, and simply live out their lives' while bringing into being the city at the intersection of individual, local spots and larger cognitive spaces (Goulding, 2012: 188).

Be it in imaginary public or private spheres, Carter definitely displays a penchant for conjuring 'affective space' in Henri Lefebvre's sense of the term: 'locations saturated with symbolic connotations, mnemonic vestiges and oneiric residues, and hence resonating with multiple levels of imagery – a fluid, dynamic, and concrete dimension' determined by the body's lived experience of emotionally charged social practices (Lefebvre, 1991: 42 in Cavallaro, 2011: 38). Her examples include a foster child's experience of her new family's home as a 'place replete with other people's unknown lives' (Carter, 1971: 59), or a pedestrian's feel of the metropolis as a malleable microcosm, a 'medium in which we execute our desires' shaped by hypnotically enthralling delusions engulfing the city (Carter, 1972: 42). Dani Cavallaro agrees with critics like Vallorani (1998) and Dimovitz (2016) that the unsettling of the Carterian space as a measurable territory stages both the undoing of socially disciplined, homogenized subjectivity and the postmodernist disruption of linear narrative. It enables a spatial fusion of presences and absences, self and other, inside and outside, retrospective nostalgia and futuristic planning, poeticity and unspeakability. Carter's liminal sites gain their enchanting quality on grounds of individual and collective psychological investment. They become 'portals to an exploration of those special points where perfectly ordinary situations somehow manage to make us sense the power of fantasy as a shadowing of reality by inscrutable forces: energies that may occasionally be glimpsed but never conclusively measured' (Cavallaro, 2011: 6).

The playable space of the open text and the psychogeographer reader

Carter's fictional places – be they associated with heterotopias, affective spaces, or any abjectified Outside constitutive of the normalized Inside – are characterized by tactics of transgression such as the destabilization of boundaries, the preference for haphazard openings, clandestine passageways, sidetracks and detours to official main entrances or obligatory paths. Her conscious project of decentralization relativizes fixed focal points to embrace multi-directionality and pluri-perspectivism in the name of ethical responsibility.

One cannot help noticing the similarity between the Carterian topography and poststructuralist literary criticism's notion of the open 'writerly text'. A 'narrative space' endowed with a 'plurality of entrances, the opening of networks, the infinity of languages' allows for an endless proliferation of meanings generated by a blissful co-productivity of readers who are constantly challenged in their 'historical, cultural, psychological assumptions, the consistency of tastes, values, memories, [and their] relation with language'. The text never ceases to self-reflectively acknowledge its own artifice, to defamiliarize its discourse, and to offer new exits and entries towards an indefinite corpus of other texts with which it is intertextually related (Barthes, 1977: 5).

As many critics – among them Benson (2008), Bacchilega (1999) and Tiffin (2009) – convincingly argued, Carter's fiction lends itself to be interpreted as a postmodernist 'open text' dense with pop and elite cultural references, a rich web of intertextual allusions pointing in an impressive variety of directions (from Hollywood cinema to Sadeian philosophy, surrealist aesthetics, or the semiotics of fashion). Merging different fictional universes, it plays with crossover couplings of iconic figures (like an unlikely match between Wolf Alice and a descendant of Dracula). Characters move and metamorphose between different texts of the authorial corpus (most memorably in her sequence of wolf tales). Endings are ambiguous (resonating with innuendos like Fevvers' spiralling tornado of laughter). Unreliable narrators revel in the double-entendres of their oral performances or showy self-fictionalizations (Dora and Nora's self-stylizing cosmetic beautification matches the making-up of their seducing memoire). Carter's writing style is distinguished by 'a preference for cyclical rhythms and recurring patterns, loops, detours, digressions and veritable flights of fancy' (Cavallaro, 2011: 2). Her work '"writes its way" across the gap that has conventionally divided inside and outside, the public and the private spheres' (Gamble, 2006: 278). These multiple paths of poetic associativity opened up by metaphorical imagery and transverbal musicality correspond to the idea of literary text as a playground of polysemic meanings, as elaborated by critics such as Stanley Fish or Wolfgang Iser (Joosen, 2011: 104).

This textual structure is a literary equivalent of a contemporary design trend of urban planning, the Playable City that toys with temporary architectural experiments to interrupt the metropolitan environment's cold anonymity and utilitarian efficiency, which is void of meaning, by aiming at 'an affectionate re-appropriation of public places' and a collective ludic interaction with our spatial surrounding reinvested with new narratives' (Baggini, 2014). Descriptions of encounters with playable spaces are easily applicable to the experience of an open text. It may offer us new ways of tracing how the implied readers of Carterian fictional worlds turn 'feminist psychogeographer' flâneuses who explore 'a new way of walking [or meaning formation]' that changes our city [or fictional] experience, 'a whole toy box full of playful, inventive strategies for exploring cities [or texts] […] just about anything that takes pedestrians [or readers] off their predictable paths and jolts them into a new awareness of the urban [or literary] landscape' (Bucher and Finka, 2008: 37).

As a woman(writer) Carter acknowledges, besides the pleasures of trespassing the confines of the domestic sphere and 'hunting for the vaguest traces of a storytelling opportunity' (Cavallaro, 2011: 73), the dangers and responsibilities that the exploration of an endlessly open space holds for the solitary female adventurer willing to get lost in the labyrinthine environs. For her, wanderlust is always combined with home-seeking. Instead of uncritically celebrating the endless possibilities of multiple pathways leading to the same spot experienced in a variety of different ways, her heroines testify – in line with Donna Haraway's feminist epistemology – the significance of a limited locatedness' partial perspectives which can yield 'knowledge potent for constructing worlds less organised by axes of domination' (Haraway, 1988: 583). Permeated by sisterly solidarity, these situated knowledges can be connected, shared to gain a politically self-conscious, ethically invested, more nuanced view of the world. Although the Carterian fiction urges readerly interaction, it also problematizes the postmodernist notion of the 'death of the author' (Barthes, 1977: 142) by foregrounding the celebration of the birth of women writers who come into being in texts of their own making which metanarratively reflect upon limits and potentials of their own creative space. I contend that Carter embarks on a strategic mapping of the affective, sensorial, psychological components of both spatial and narrative experience driven by the writer's ultimate enquiry about the origin of stories.

Carter's curious rooms

The topophiliac tendency implied in Carter's fiction traces the affective bonds and environmental interaction between people and places. The emphasis falls on how the curiosity about our surroundings and positionality inspires literary creativity that associates its very own artistic medium, the game space of language with a simultaneously claustrophobic and liberating locatedness. Built environment, and especially the carefully confined space of the house, is particularly challenging to map because it both determines and reflects our consciousness and conduct. In Gaston Bachelard's words, 'the house images are in us as much as we are in them', they trace the topography of our intimate being, and allow for an analysis of the human soul (Bachelard, 1994: xxxvii). In Carter's case, the house is tied to the inner space of the author's mind and an emerging artistic self-awareness coupled with an inquisitiveness concerning sources of narratives.

Spatial imagery is of crucial importance in Carter's non-fiction writing in texts like 'The Mother Lode' or 'My Father's House', where she attempts to gather puzzle pieces of her autobiographical self and family history by tracing what she calls, with a Japanese phrase, 'landscapes of the heart'. This poetic figure of speech refers to 'the Romantic correlation between inside and outside that converts physical geography into part of the apparatus of the sensibility' (Carter, 1998a: 18). Aware of her family's penchant for mythologization and the inaccessible foreignness of past places, she dis/locates home as a 'moveable feast', always already fictionalized, a sequence of sites where the heart is. Her psychogeographical poetics is summed up in the lines 'You don't choose your own landscapes. They chose you' (Carter, 1998a: 19).

In 'The Bloody Chamber' the castle's library serves as the place of epiphany for the bookish narrator heroine, who recognizes her place within the story in which she has become engaged by wedding a Bluebeardish nobleman. The husband's murderous desires permeate both the eponymous secret chambers and the pages of his decadent pornographic book collection she leafs through to mature from passive reader entrapped by a myth into an author of her own destiny aided by a pragmatic maternal revolver on her way to freedom. Martine Hennard Dutheil de La Rochère locates the key to the text in the shifting meaning of the word 'cabinet'. Cabinet denotes just as much the storeroom of treasures where the dandy connoisseur kills his wives into art objects, the ogre's larder replete with fairy-tale lore, the theatre stage of perverted delights fuelled by fin-de-siècle misogyny, and a closet filled with skeletons, which encourage readers to develop an inquisitive mind, while 'rehabilitating female curiosity as a moral function through allusion and intertextual density' (2013: 110).

'The Snow Pavilion' emerges as a fatally feminized space that takes revenge on a womanizer poet. The amateur artist, about to reluctantly return to the claustrophobic love-nest of his older mistress, is caught in a snow storm, and seeks refuge in an old mansion that he believes to have been designed for the indulgence of the flesh. He sexualizes the pavilion as a penetrable feminine space he intends to (ab)use for loveless seduction: he maps it with a poetic imagery, 'a vista like visible Debussy' (Carter, 1997: 431), and associates it with voluptuous caresses of cultured patronesses' pale naked arms. Although the male fantasist plays hide-and-seek with an invisible female entity, which can be attributed to an erotic foreplay, eventually he must realize that he has been ensnared into the pavilion's game-space by a ghastly girl-child and/or an old crone – one not yet and the other no more a woman. Both elude his stereotypical view of femininity and eventually turn him into a doll, covering him with snow. The whiteness of a blank sheet of paper replaces his writing with stories of her silence, telling more than he could ever do.

In 'Alice in Prague *or* the Curious Room', Wonderland is compressed into the titular room, Emperor Rudolph II's late sixteenth-century Curiosity Cabinet. An alchemical homunculus girl child emerges from the crystal ball of court magician Doctor Dee, famed for his quest for the prelapsarian Adamic language, an unmediated means of truly naming reality, lost with the Babelian confusion of tongues. Carter's introduction describes the room as an 'ur-museum [of memories], a manifestation of an omnivorous curiosity, a gluttony for the world, but also a potent image of the unconscious [...] the underworld in which language develops a life of its own' (Carter, 1990: 217). Alice's language games, logical conundrums and mathematical puzzles not only make a mechanical clockwork doll disintegrate into its organic constituents but also stupefy the learned men of the Renaissance, left speechless by her nonsensical reasoning and unanswerable questions. This enigmatically empowered *femme-enfant* storyteller, native of an elsewhere, is headed 'back through the mirror to "time will be", or, even better, to the book from which she had sprung' (Carter, 1997: 408).

This miraculous Alice perfectly fits the eccentric Archduke's collection of curiosities compiled of mandrakes dressed in nightgowns, bottled mermaids, and crystallized angels. Each item manifests the ambiguous meanings nascent from the epistemological crises stimulating the revolutionary cultural movements – mannerism, surrealism, postmodernism – at the root of the short story. The cabinet's chaotic contents represent how the bundle of hypotexts (Lewis Carroll's *Alice* tales, Jan Švankmajer's film *Alice*, *The Surrealist Manifesto*, Dr Dee's and Rudolph II's biographies) bear witness to Carter's perception of 'artistic creation as a true pleasure of confluence rather than an anxiety of influence' (Thomas, 2009: 35). The *Kunstkammer* stores a stuffed dodo, a fallen star and a mechanically anthropomorphized automaton-woman made of fruit: each an embodied intertextual homage – to Lewis Carroll nicknamed for his stutter Dodo-dodgson, to mannerist

John Donne's paradoxical love song about infidelity 'Catch a Falling Star', and to Rudolph's court painter Arcimboldo's fruit composition portraits, respectively; not to mention the numerous allusions to surrealism's emblematic items, including a realization of Lautrémont's beauty ideal of the chance encounter of a sewing machine and an umbrella on the dissecting table. The intertextual play with former artistic works and historical epistemes elicits an experience of *déjà lu*, whereby the multitude of source texts are all regarded (*déjà vu*) as the surrealists' found object composites defamiliarized from their banal use and reprocessed into artistic carriers of metaphorical meanings. This 'alchemy of the word' is defined in spatial terms as 'quotation, the strategy of a sensibility that sees reality slipping away along obscure and tortuous paths' (Carter, 1990: 217) exploring 'shimmering vistas of perhaps yet undiscovered worlds' and words (Frankova, 1999: 131). For Carter, the curious room hides the ultimate question of origins she finds at the kernel of any quest for knowledge: 'In the beginning was … what?' 'Where was I before I was born?' (1997: 401). The room crammed with customized wonders, now forbidden and impossible to remember, in retrospect a utopian place of blissful omniscience forever lost, gains a psychoanalytical significance, representing the maternal womb as much as the creative unconscious. The question of origins 'Where do babies come from?', a topic of kindergarten mischief and existential philosophy alike, is intimately connected to an erotic interest in the textual body constituting a literary theoretical dilemma condensed in the metafictional question about the origins of a story, 'Where do books come from?' and a general enquiry about how social meanings and discursively constituted subjects come into being.

The poetics of the Scarlet House: from unhomely hole of oblivion to self-made sanctuary of stories

'The Scarlet House' is the secret hideout of a sadistic Count obsessed with the chaos he cherishes in its crystallised form in the 'entropic rhetoric of the scream' provoked in his torture chambers (Carter, 1997: 419). He keeps captive young women to perform an occult experiment directed by the chance movement of Tarot cards throughout which prisoners are systematically deprived of their communicational capacities, their memories, identities and eventually their lives. The anonymous female narrator, one of his captives, struggles to keep her sanity, humanity and autonomy by clinging on to memory morsels of her long-lost home. She tries to recapitulate the true story of her origins, and write herself into freedom, into a place of well-being beyond the Scarlet Room designed to be the site of her annihilation.

Despite its suffocating, claustrophobic atmosphere, extradiegetically speaking, the short story invites readers to an open narrative space in so far as the Count ruling over the Scarlet House is intertextually affiliated with many Carterian master villains distinguished by a 'psychic vampirism' (Botelho, 2015: 296) feeding on female victims' bodies and minds emptied of agency. The Count is the evil twin-brother of the anarchist, misogynist poet Zero, who allows mutilated members of his harem to speak only animals grunts, cackles and cries. Another such villain is Christian Rosencreutz, who yearns to sacrifice a winged 'virgo intacta' in order to procure his immortality. Similarly, Doctor Hoffman, who usurps feminized mirages, a glasswoman and a beautiful somnambulist to expand spatial and temporal dimensions and infect the world with simulacra; plus another Count of the same novel is a libertine dedicated to debauchery, self-deprivation and evil.

Like any of the archetypal Bluebeard figures of which Carter was so fond, the Count of the Scarlet House is also strongly connected to the space he dwells in: the ghastly castle, the dark dungeon, the torture chamber. A perverted incarnation of the original genius loci, he functions as an emblem and a 'protective guardian' of a site of gruesome terror and trauma. His pathologically twisted psyche seems to emanate to grant the very ominous spirit of a labyrinthine, unmappable place from which there is no escape. The underground cellar is, of course, a commonplace used by psychoanalysis's spatial modelling of the human mind to represent the unconscious hosting those 'lowly' instinctive, animalistic urges, sexual and aggressive impulses which are meant to be kept hidden by our socialization but which come to light throughout fictionalizations of that bestial otherness lurking deep within ourselves. The Scarlet House is the home of the Count, madness personified as the uncanny double of rational thought.

However, what makes the story truly captivating is not the predictably unpredictable architecture of the Count's demented psyche but the meandering thoughts and imaginative mental mappings of the protagonist, who struggles against her captor's confusion of her sensations and memories. She tries to locate herself in this 'house' – in the literal prison, as well as in his demented fantasies, and her own nightmares – willing to find her way out of it, back to what she has been before descending underground into forgetfulness. Through the focalizer's perspective, the Scarlet House emerges as a patchwork of fleeting impressions. First, its white concrete walls recall a hospital or a large terminal ward, then it is described as a 'rambling, brick-built, red-tiled place, half farmhouse, half country mansion' (421). It evokes mundane institutionalized spaces like an all-girls boarding school along with locales of social deviance and corruption, like an odd combination of brothel and freak-show (featuring in *Nights at the Circus* governed by the same Madame Schreck and her mouthless manservant who appear in the short story too), as well as supernatural sites like a haunted house, the lair of a Gothic monster, an earthly Hell burying people alive.

The narrator's assumption that the entry to the Scarlet House leads through the hole of Madame Schreck, the master-mistress of ceremonies, reflects an atavistic fear of and fascination with the idea of returning to the maternal uterus, constituting the ultimate kernel, the primordial point of origin that equally protects from the outside and entraps within. Magna Mater, mother earth, the womb-tomb is frequently associated in Carterian fiction with houses that symbolize mothers but remain within the property of patriarchal reality, and hence become an arena of fundamentally ambiguous meanings, as Lorna Sage suggests (Sage, 2007: 25). The Scarlet House is a maternal space in so far as the narrator heroine can only survive her tortures provided she can 'birth' (or rather resurrect) herself into being via a narrative reconstruction of her authentic identity the Count aims to shatter. By means of an antidote to the unhomeliness of the Scarlet House bombarding her with amnesia, inducing false-memories, she seeks shelter in her real home she strives to rebuild from memory fragments throughout a creative bricolage of her mnemonic imagination. Aware of the unreliability of her own point-of-view, she also considers the Scarlet House as a product of her own phantasmatic agency – hence an odd empowerment at the heart of complete annihilation. The anatomical catachresis describing the 'subterranean torture-chamber deep at the heart of the maze of my brain' (423) evokes the physical stakes of re-membering. What is an abstract experiment, a stylistic exercise, a cartomantic Tarot game for the Count, a 'Morpholytic Kid who presides over the death of forms' (421) holds fleshly stakes for the narrator for whom it is a matter of life and death to imagine herself into being in the right place.

She desperately tries to reconstruct the moment of her abduction that sealed her fate, as if that adequately captured freeze-frame could reverse time, undo the torture and heal the trauma tormenting her in the Scarlet House. 'If only I could remember everything perfectly, just as it happened, then loaded with the ambivalent burden of my past, I should be free' she says (424). However, all she has are *versions* of reality, with equal un/likelihood of belonging to a possible past, a pseudo-memory artificially implanted in her mind, or a replica of a pain experienced in reality by a fellow sufferer. In one version, she was collecting samples of desolate flora amidst some ruins, and while absorbed in the sight of a hawk plummeting down to capture his prey, was trapped by a leather-clad gang of bikers, the Count's bodyguards. In the second version, she arrived voluntarily on the board of a train, timid but determined to fill a job vacancy advertised in the personal column of *The Times* looking for a governess. According to the third scenario, she was dragged away from the safe shelter of her own home, an afternoon tea enjoyed in the company of her beloved father in a neatly decorated bourgeois sitting-room before he was shot dead and she was raped and kidnapped. Yet these memory-versions all seem suspicious, illusory, fictional, spoilt with an 'inky, overwritten smell' (421). The first stages a post-apocalyptic urban fantasy, the second 'echoes books I might have read', like a nineteenth-century novelette authored by one of the Brontë sisters, while the third 'recapitulates a Middle-European nightmare, an episode from Prague or Vienna seen in a movie, perhaps, or told me by a complete stranger' (424).

These (pseudo)memories share a remarkably spatial quality. They serve to liberate the heroine from the sterile, arid 'wasteland' of the Scarlet House by locating her amidst deserted ruins, on a crowded train, in a stylish parlour. Each place is endowed with private meanings and affective charge because of belonging to a possible past of hers, alternately emerging as a feral-child-like nomad, a Brontëan orphan or a favourite daughter, all identifiable with someone she might have been. She decides to settle with the third memory, the mental image of the bourgeois home, where she can most easily build an imaginative shelter for the self she wants to defend from complete disidentification, from being in a void, and becoming an empty 'void itself' (426). The bourgeois salon represents a clean and well regulated social-space that stands in sharp contrast with the anarchic, taboo-breaking, filthy violence of the Scarlet House and hence becomes ultimately desirable in retrospect. Its sophisticated interior design is rich in subtle sense impression – the scent of carefully arranged potpourri, slices of lemon on a china plate, and geraniums on the balcony, soft summer light flowing through the slatted blinds, birds cheeping audible from the streets, the tactile and visual delights of the slippery horsehair sofa with a paisley shawl thrown over its piles of soft cushions embroidered with flowers and butterflies. These contradict the anti-aesthetics of pain permeating her present dwelling, the Scarlet House. The meticulous description of the decor's details serve to support the veracity of this vision. In this fading memory of home, silence results from cosy intimacy instead of dehumanizing degradation by unspeakable torture. '[E]verything is loved because it is familiar' (422), all the objects of this long-lost homely microcosm constitute extensions of the inhabitants' personality, in a place customized to perfectly fit her, multi-sensually satisfying to match her taste, unlike the 'sensory deprivation unit', the 'hole of oblivion' she crawls in now, alternately suffering from its tightness and vastness, claustrophobic and agoraphobic alike.

The narrator's spatial fantasies about this room echo Gaston Bachelard's insights about the image of the house that emblematizes in the collective cultural unconscious the dream of protected intimacy. They especially resonate with the metaphysical concept of home as an integrating power for the thoughts, memories and dreams of mankind, as a site where one's shattered self can be ordered into a coherent subjectivity. In Sarah Gamble's Bachelardian reading, this is a space that can provide 'a second skin' (Gamble, 2006: 277) for wounded egos like that of the narrator. In *The Poetics of Space* (1994), Bachelard's topoanalytical study of humans' experience of intimate places poses the problem of the 'poetics of the house', arguing that the house is the first universe of any child growing up in a home, the first cosmos that shapes all subsequent knowledge of other spaces, of any larger cosmos. The house is a nest for dreaming, a shelter for imagining. It provides the atavistic consolation of a cave, its secret rooms become abodes for an unforgettable past, so influential that we measure all inhabited spaces in terms of their homeliness or unhomeliness. We comfort ourselves by reliving memories of protection, daydreaming of former dwelling places which allowed us to daydream in peace, in the cradle-like maternal environment of places we chose to call our home.

In the Carterian heroine's hallucinatory reminiscence, the primary comfort zone is associated with an all-embracing 'fleshly' maternal presence, metonymically marked by the eyes of a portrait 'watching over' the parlour. The deceased mother, even in her absence, becomes a ghastly benevolent counterpart of the Scarlet House's evil earthly matriarch, Madame Schreck. For the narrator, the image of the mother's eyes acts as a mnemonic device to recall the room, the locus of origins, and one's authentic self-identity attested by the line 'I have my mother's eyes!' that she keeps endlessly repeating despite punishments from the Count irritated by this relentless commemoration of her affiliation with a matrilinear heritage, and the notion of a traceable past. Via a marvellous spatial metaphor, the mnemonics which assist her in identifying her ego, are compared to odds and ends refugees carry with them, and refuse to leave behind, 'although they're quite insignificant – a spoon with a bent handle, say; or a tram ticket issued by a city that no longer exists. Small items, meaningless in themselves, and yet keys to an entire system of meanings, if only I could remember' (426). In the complex system of mnemonics, a triad of mental images – a hunting hawk, the mother's eyes, and a mouthless face – undergo curious metamorphosis. The preying hawk, first believed to have been seen during her capture amongst the ruins, gradually transforms into a figure of the bird pattern decorating the Persian rug on which she was raped, and eventually gets reinterpreted as the iconic marker of her abduction, as well as a metaphor of her own hunt for words trying to express the inexpressible, fighting forgetfulness, using 'memory [as] the lasso with which capture the past' (419). The watchful maternal gaze she recognizes in her own look represents on the level of iconicity the metanarrative act of 'looking at another looking'. It evokes a relational model of identity defining the self in terms of its interpersonal and communal ties serving as grounds for an empathic solidarity – already emerging in the entanglement of her own and other women's memories 'precipitated into a fugue' (419) resonating the Scarlet House. But it also refers to the possibility of mothering oneself amidst the harshest circumstances by nurturing the idea of a home of one's liking, where one can find refuge via the creative art of storytelling.

The story culminates in the narrator's epiphanic recognition: the puppet can turn against the puppeteer. The rules of the game can be twisted from the inside and turned against themselves. Despite her victimized status she can reach empowerment simply by reinterpreting memory – her only weapon against annihilation by amnesia – as a 'self-spun web' feeding from her own inner core, independent of outside control. Memory is defined again in terms of spatial metaphors, identified as the 'origin of narrative', a 'barrier against oblivion', a 'repository of one's being', and a reservoir of stories where 'delicate filaments of myself I weave, in time into a spider's web to catch as much world in it as I can' (419). The universe is accessible through one's own microcosm mappable by self-narratives embracing forgetfulness, misremembering, and fictionalization within recollections of who one is.

The last lines are both ominous and optimistic: 'I know all that I need to know to enable me to endure [...] This world's a vile oubliette. Yet in its refuse I will find the key to free me' (428). The Scarlet House becomes a dark topographical emblem of existence. The world is pictured as a secret dungeon consigned to oblivion and decay, abandoned by providence. But beyond its ceiling trapdoor, by means of a vague ray of hope shimmering above, reality awaits to be released in words. The detritus of words down-below promises to grant a fragile shelter from forgetfulness and an infinite platform for liberation, too.

'The Scarlet House' encapsulates the essence of Carter's spatial poetics and politics. The fictional explorations of space allow the intradiegetic narrator heroine to escape the abuse and objectification patriarchally assigned to her gender role. Her imaginative re-mappings of a traumatic past facilitate her maturation into a creative storyteller who can invent a narrative space where victims of inequality can coexist together in a space that acknowledges the embodied experience of their pains, affects and voices.

Note

1 Quoted from the inside cover of Susannah Clapp, *A Card from Angela Carter* (London: Bloombsbury, 2012).

References

Bacchilega, Cristina (1999), *Postmodern Fairy Tales: Gender and Narrative Strategies* (Philadelphia: University of Pennsylvania Press).

Bachelard, Gaston ([1958] 1994), *The Poetics of Space*, trans. Maria Jolas (Boston: Beacon Press).

Baggini, Julian (2014), 'Playable Cities: The City that Plays Together Stays Together', *Guardian* (4 September).

Barthes, Roland (1977), *Image, Music, Text* (London: Fontana).

Benson, Stephen (ed.) (2008), *Contemporary Fiction and the Fairy Tale* (Detroit: Wayne State University Press).

Botelho, Inês (2015), 'Destroying and Creating Identity: Vampires, Chaos, and Society in Angela Carter's "The Scarlet House"', in Isabel Ermida (ed.), *Dracula and the Gothic in Literature, Pop Culture, and the Arts* (Leiden: Brill Rodopi,), pp. 293–309.

Bucher, Ulrike and Maro Finka (2008), *The Electronic City* (Berlin: Verlag).

Carter, Angela ([1972] 1982), *The Infernal Desire Machines of Doctor Hoffman* (Harmondsworth: Penguin).

—— (1983), 'Notes from the Front Line', in Michelene Wandor (ed.), *On Gender and Writing* (London: Pandora Press), pp. 69–77.

—— (1990), 'Introduction to "The Curious Room"', in Margaret Bridges (ed.), *On Strangeness: SPELL (Swiss Papers in English Language and Literature)* (Tübingen: Gunter Narr Verlag), pp. 215–17.

—— ([1991] 1993), *Wise Children* (New York: Penguin).

—— ([1984] 1994), *Nights at the Circus* (London: Vintage).

—— (1997), *Burning Your Boats: The Collected Short Stories* (New York: Penguin).

—— (1998a), *Shaking a Leg: Collected Writings* (London: Penguin).

—— ([1977] 1998b), *The Passion of New Eve* (London: Virago).

—— ([1971] 2006), *The Magic Toyshop* (London: Virago).

Cavallaro, Dani (2011), *The World of Angela Carter: A Critical Investigation* (Jefferson: McFarland).

Clapp, Susannah (2012), *A Card from Angela Carter* (London: Bloomsbury).

Dimovitz, Scott A. (2016), *Angela Carter: Surrealist, Psychologist, Moral Pornographer* (New York: Routledge).

Filimon, Eliza Claudia (2014), *Heterotopia in Angela Carter's Fiction: Worlds in Collision* (Hamburg: Anchor).

Foucault, Michel (1984), 'Of Other Places: Heterotopias', *Architecture, Mouvement, Continuité*, 5, 46–9.

Frankova, Milada (1999), 'Angela Carter's Mannerism in Rudolph II's Curious Room', *Brno Studies in English*, 25, 127–33.

Gamble, Sarah (2006), '"There's no Place like Home": Angela Carter's

Rewritings of the Domestic', *Literature Interpretation Theory*, 17, 277–300.
Goulding, Simon (2012), 'Seeing the City, Reading the City, Mapping the City: Angela Carter's *The Magic Toyshop* and the Sixties', in Sonya Andermahr and Lawrence Phillips (eds), *Angela Carter: New Critical Readings* (New York: Continuum), pp. 187–97.
Haffenden, John (1985), 'An Interview with Angela Carter', *Novelists in Interview* (London: Methuen), pp. 76–96.
Haraway, Donna (1988), 'Situated Knowledges: The Science Question in Feminism and the Privilege of Partial Perspective', *Feminist Studies*, 14:3 (Autumn 1988), 575–99.
Hennard Dutheil de la Rochère, Martine (2013), *Reading, Translating, Rewriting: Angela Carter's Translational Poetics* (Detroit: Wayne State University Press).
Joosen, Vanessa (2011), *Critical and Creative Perspectives on Fairy Tales: An Intertextual Dialogue Between Fairy-Tale Scholarship and Postmodern Retellings* (Detroit: Wayne State University Press).
Kérchy, Anna (2008), *Body-Texts in the Novels of Angela Carter: Writing from a Corporeagraphic Point of View* (Lewiston: Edwin Mellen Press).
Kristeva, Julia (1982), *Powers of Horror: An Essay on Abjection* (New York: Columbia University Press).
Lefebvre, Henri ([1974] 1991), *The Production of Space* trans. Donald Nicholson-Smith (Oxford: Blackwell).
Peach, Linden (1998), *Angela Carter* (Basingstoke: Macmillan).
Rushdie, Salman (1995), 'Introduction', in Angela Carter, *Burning your Boats: The Collected Short Stories* (London: Penguin), pp. ix–xiv.
Sage, Lorna (2007), 'Introduction', in Lorna Sage (ed.), *Essays on the Art of Angela Carter: Flesh and the Mirror* (London: Virago).
Thomas, Karima (2009), 'Angela Carter's Adventures in the Wonderland of Nonsense', in Claude Maisonnat et al. (eds), *Rewriting/Reprising in Literature: The Paradoxes of Intertextuality* (Newcastle-upon-Tyne: Cambridge Scholars), pp. 35–43.
Tiffin, Jessica (2009), *Marvelous Geometry: Narrative and Metafiction in Modern Fairy Tale* (Detroit: Wayne State University Press).
Vallorani, Nicoletta (1998), 'The Body of the City', in Lindsey Tucker (ed.), *Critical Essays on the Art of Angela Carter* (New York: Macmillan), pp. 176–90.
Wisker, Gina (2006), 'Behind Locked Doors: Angela Carter, Horror, and the Influence of Edgar Allan Poe', in Rebecca Munford (ed.), *Re-visiting Angela Carter. Texts, Contexts, Intertexts* (Houndmills: Palgrave), pp. 178–99.

3

Bloody chamber melodies: painting and music in *The Bloody Chamber*

Julie Sauvage

IN 1979, WHEN ANGELA Carter published her now famous collection of short stories entitled *The Bloody Chamber*, many feminist writers considered the fairy tale genre to be somewhat obsolete and difficult to handle without reinforcing patriarchal gender stereotypes. Rewriting fairy tales as a feminist meant treading on dangerous ground to appropriate and transform a pervading, controversial legacy.[1] Engaging with the fairy tale, Carter not only dealt with the literary fathers of the genre, like Perrault,[2] but also with its cultural significance and its many pictorial, literary and musical offshoots.

Like most of her works, *The Bloody Chamber* is replete with allusions to literature, painting and music. In this specific case, they mostly lead back to the Golden Age of fairy tales, when the Grimm brothers in Germany, and many other scholars throughout Europe, preoccupied with recovering a folk heritage threatened by massive urbanization, set out to collect folk tales, turning them into written, literary fairy tales. At the time, many writers, composers and painters also adapted fairy tales to painting and music, or for the theatre and the opera.[3] The main artistic movements to which Angela Carter refers in *The Bloody Chamber*, German Romanticism and French Symbolism or Decadence, are marked by the importance of intermedial creation. This involved cooperation between writers, painters and composers, who drew their inspiration from the same stories and used to work together or adapt each other's works for various media.

The Bloody Chamber thus bears testimony to Carter's preoccupation with the relationships between literature, painting and music, which, I would argue, relates to her reflection on the way we tend to conceive of time and space as gendered. In 1979, she had been playing with this idea for a while. Two years earlier, for instance, in her much-debated science fiction and multi-generic novel, *The Passion of New Eve*, Mother, the grotesque leader of the feminist guerrilla group, confidently asserted the following principles:

> Proposition one: time is a man, space is a woman.
> Proposition two: time is a killer.
> Proposition three: kill time and live forever. (Carter, 1977: 53)

Mother's agenda was inspired by William Blake's line: 'Time is a Man, Space is a Woman and her Masculine Portion is Death',[4] which Carter used as an epigraph to the third chapter of *The Sadeian Woman* (Carter, 1993: 78), her equally controversial essay published the same year as *The Bloody Chamber*.

According to W.J.T. Mitchell, the gendering of time and space, together with the resulting gendering of painting and sculpture as female, and literature and music as male, can be traced back to Leonardo da Vinci's *Paragone* or antagonism between the arts of time and space. He shows that it is also implicit in Lessing's influential aesthetic treatise, *Laocoon*:

> The decorum of the arts at bottom has to do with proper sex roles. Lessing does not state this explicitly anywhere in *Laocoon*. Only in the unguarded moments of free association prompted by the contrast between the patrilineal production of ancient sculpture and the monstrous, adulterous maternity of modern art does he allow this figure of the difference to surface. Once we have glimpsed the link between genre and gender, however, it seems to make itself felt throughout all the oppositions that regulate Lessing's discourse, as the following table will show at a glance:
>
> | Painting | Poetry |
> |---|---|
> | Space | Time |
> | Natural Signs | Arbitrary (man-made) Signs |
> | Narrow Sphere | Infinite Range |
> | Imitation | Expression |
> | Body | Mind |
> | External | Internal |
> | Silent | Eloquent |
> | Beauty | Sublimity |
> | Eye | Ear |
> | Feminine | Masculine (Mitchell: 1984, 108–9) |

By such standards, writing a feminist narrative becomes quite a challenge. Carter, however, accepted it, and set out systematically to blur the boundaries between genres and genders.

Focusing first on 'The Bloody Chamber', this chapter shows how she creates literary hybrids including both a pictorial and a musical dimension. This leads to an analysis of how she upsets the hierarchy commonly established between the senses of hearing, sight and touch in the whole collection, and turns the text into a polyphonic score meant for the readers to perform. Finally, the chapter argues that this performative reading aims at changing the readers' relationship to otherness in order to transform them and their perception of the world.

In the first, eponymous short story in the collection, Angela Carter explicitly thematizes the gendering of time and space, together with their related arts. 'The Bloody Chamber' rewrites Bluebeard's story in *fin-de-siècle* France, as the marriage between a murderous aristocrat and a young pianist, entrusted with the keys to his castle. Coupling the Marquis, a collector of books, paintings and wives, with a musician allows Carter to address what Mitchell called Lessing's 'proper gender roles', and shed light on the latent hierarchy and power relationships they usually mask,[5] by operating a series of reversals.

At first sight, the short story seems to invert the conventional gendering of the arts, since it associates the murderous Marquis with sight and the spatial art of painting, whereas hearing and the temporal art of music characterize his young bride, which accounts for the many pictorial and musical references intermingled throughout the text. Debussy, Gounod, Wagner, Czerny, Bach and Verdi keep company with Rops, Odilon Redon, Puvis de Chavannes and an impressive gallery of other famous painters:

> There was Moreau's great portrait of his first wife, the famous *Sacrificial Victim* with the imprint of the lacelike chains on her pellucid skin. Did I know the story of the painting of that picture? [...] He had thought of that story, of that dear girl, when first he had undressed me ... Ensor, the great Ensor, his monolithic canvas: *The Foolish Virgins*. [T]wo or three late Gauguins, his special favourite the one of the tranced brown girl in the deserted house, which was called: *Out of the Night We Come, Into the Night We Go*. And, besides the additions he had made himself, his marvelous inheritance of Watteaus, Poussins and a pair of very special Fragonards, commissioned for a licentious ancestor who, it was said, had posed for the master's brush himself with his own

two daughters ... He broke off his catalogue of treasures abruptly. (Carter, 1995: 123)

This description makes it clear that the association of the Marquis with painting, and his bride with music, does not really amount to a reversal of traditional gender roles. As the passage demonstrates, wives become portraits by Decadent masters, prized possessions to be catalogued. The same fate already struck the first and second wives, respectively an artist's model and opera singer, both literally stilled and framed in the bloody chamber,[6] where the new bride is led by her curiosity and finally realizes she runs similar risks.

Now, Blake and Lessing's conception of time and space as gendered, when applied to their related fine arts, establishes a hierarchy between them. According to W.J.T. Mitchell, if women are supposed to be 'pretty as a picture', conversely, images are treated like women: 'Like the masses, the colonized, the powerless and voiceless everywhere, visual representation cannot represent itself; it must be represented by discourse' (Mitchell, 1994: 163 and 157), male discourse and, in this instance, the Marquis's. The many allusions to paintings and their occasional depictions, or *ekphraseis*, emphasize how pictorial representations objectify women, especially in the historical context Carter chose for the short story.[7] Yet the voice that reports the Marquis's descriptions of those pictures is the bride's, since she is the one who lives to tell her story.

As a consequence, the accumulation of pictorial references seems to be a way for her, as a narrator, ironically to comment on her own failure, as a character, to comprehend blatant clues about the reification and symbolic death such paintings represent, as well as the real violence they foreshadow. Sight and agency remain the Marquis's male privileges during most of the story, so much so that the bride is utterly blind to her own situation. It is hardly surprising, then, that she should be willing to identify with Saint Cecilia, the patroness of musicians, whose portrait by a 'Flemish primitive' (Carter, 1995: 118) receives pride of place in the castle's music room.[8]

Sight and insight are thus clearly linked to gender and power, and definitely seem to be male attributes. Yet, in order to avoid decapitation, the bride can count on being rescued by a quite formidable female figure, her mother, to kill the predator by turning the lethal power of the gaze against him.[9] Charging on horseback, wielding her late husband's revolver, this larger-than-life mother turns the Marquis into his own, grotesque caricature: 'And my husband stood stock-still, as if she had been Medusa, the sword still raised over his head as in those clockwork tableaux of Bluebeard that you see in glass cases at fairs', before putting an 'irreproachable bullet through [his] head' (Carter, 1995: 142).

Faithful to the Decadent imagery the Marquis loves, the narrator compares her powerful mother to Medusa, a mythological figure who both freezes and silences, in a word, *stills* the object of her gaze. As W.J.T. Mitchell has it, Medusa represents the repressed other in temporal arts, even 'the perfect prototype for the image as a dangerous female other who threatens to silence the poet's voice and fixate his observing eye' (Mitchell, 1994: 172). Accordingly, the Marquis is then deprived of the gaze, the agency and the discourse on which his authority relied, which could make the ending of the short story a perfect reversal of power relationships, and the epitome of female empowerment.

Medusa, however, can also be interpreted as an essentially liminal figure, a monstrous synthesis. Studying the significance of the myth in Ancient Greece, Jean-Pierre Vernant underlined Medusa's transgressive aspect, which called into question the very notion of boundaries between femininity and masculinity, youth and age, humanity and animality, beauty and ugliness, life and death.[10] To some extent, this blurring of boundaries may apply to the relationship between narrative and pictorial arts in 'The Bloody Chamber', where the bride uses language to create a monstrous hybrid, a third term, thus resolving the opposition. This Medusean form of literature deliberately combines, not just narrative and painting, but also music into what Liliane Louvel calls 'iconotexts'.[11]

Music is the familiar, reassuring realm to which the distressed bride tries to go back after her visit to the bloody chamber: 'I thought [...] that I could create a pentacle out of music that would keep me from harm for, if my music had first ensnared him, then might it not also give me the power to free myself from him?' (Carter, 1995: 133). As such, it becomes a talisman or even a pentagram, a drawing: in spite of its temporal quality, it delimits a space, a magic area in which she tries to feel safe. She even wishes it could become the net of an enchantress 'ensnaring' the Marquis and freeing her from his grip.[12]

Similarly, the sound of 'the siren sea' (Carter, 1995: 128) seems to give the bride a sense of security, delusive though it may be. Yet the bloody chamber itself is the only place in the castle where it cannot be heard, the place where she realises she is powerless. That the sound of the waves constitutes the magic landscape, or rather soundscape of the castle, is illustrated by a long descriptive passage that artfully blends together painting, narrative and music to create a musical 'iconotext':

> Sea; sand; a sky that melts into the sea – a landscape of misty pastels with a look about it of being continuously on the point of melting. A landscape with all the deliquescent harmonies of Debussy, of the études I played for him, the reverie I'd been playing that afternoon in the salon of the princess where I'd first met him, among the teacups and the little cakes, I, the orphan, hired out of charity to give them their digestive of music. [...]
> No room, no corridor that did not rustle with the sound of the sea and all the ceilings, the walls on which his ancestors in the stern regalia of rank lined up with their dark eyes and white faces, were stippled with refracted light from the waves which were always in motion; that luminous murmurous castle of which I was the châtelaine, I, the little music student whose mother had sold all her jewellery, even her wedding ring, to pay the fees at the Conservatoire. (Carter, 1995: 116–17)

As if trying her hand at various iconotextual techniques, the narrator first sketches a landscape whose 'misty pastels' and 'deliquescent harmonies' suggest a watercolour. Then comes the description of a series of portraits implying that the people they represent all look alike, perhaps because the light reflected on the waves causes the portraits to appear in the manner of an Impressionist or Pointillist painter. However, the musical dimension of the description is also obvious. Beside the explicit mention of Debussy, with his etudes and reveries, 'harmonies' is a term used for both painting and music, and the text 'rustles' with assonances and alliterations, just like the castle does with the 'sound of the sea', while the anaphoric structures create echoes from one paragraph to the next, suggesting the surge of the waves. Such 'luminous murmurous' passages point to a new combination which balances sight and hearing.

Like the theme of sight and blindness, which pervades the short story, this new relationship between sight and hearing, between temporal and spatial arts, is also linked to the Oedipal implications of the fairy tale and its traditional gender roles.

The Oedipal aspects of the fairy tale as a genre have long been documented in psychological approaches, and 'Bluebeard' is a case in point.[13] Carter emphasizes this aspect by constantly drawing attention to the age difference between her narrator and the Marquis, who appears to be a substitute father as well as a predator,[14] while the notion of women seeing what they are not allowed to see takes on sexual overtones, echoing the biblical story of Eve or the myth of Eros and Psyche.

Now, as the psychoanalyst Didier Anzieu puts it in *The Skin-Ego*: 'Like a large majority of phantasies Oedipal scenarios are visual. To move on from the narcissistic problematic to the Oedipal one is to progress from the level of touch, taste, smell, and breathing to that of sight – hearing belongs, in two different forms, to both'[15] (Anzieu, 2016: 216). As a consequence, the overwhelming presence of music in the short story may contribute to question the prominence of sight, but also indirectly to emphasize the importance of 'tasting, smelling and breathing' and, ultimately, the importance of touch.[16]

By rewriting the myth of Demeter and Persephone, which some critics consider to illustrate the ideal bond between mother and daughter,[17] into her version of Bluebeard, Carter hints at the possibility of replacing the relationship to the perverted father figure, for which the Marquis stood, with some idyllic, albeit equally incestuous, pre-Oedipal relationship to the mother. If the Marquis does not abduct his bride, he does take her away from her mother and gives her the key to his '*enfer*'. The French word designates both hell and the erotic books section in a library, which creates a connection between the Marquis and Hades, and underlines the dangerous links between *Eros* and *Thanatos* in his underworld.[18] When the heroine's mother shoots Bluebeard, the traditional, Oedipal situation turns into a new, female order, where the only remaining male is the heroine's blind companion. Logically, this should suggest that it is indeed possible to reverse the hierarchy of the senses, or at least to question the prominence of sight over hearing and touch, which only the Marquis's authority seemed to establish.

When considering the collection as a whole, it does appear Carter tries to ground a new aesthetics, one without power relationships between genres and genders, by offering the sense of touch as an alternative to sight, and then hearing as a way out of the sight/touch dichotomy.

The absence of such power relationships is quite striking in some of Angela Carter's rewritings of Little Red Riding Hood, like 'Wolf-

Alice' and 'The Company of Wolves', as opposed to the traditional Grimm and Perrault versions where, as Jack Zipes notices: 'The gaze of the wolf will consume [Little Red Riding Hood] and is intended to dominate and eliminate her. The gaze of the wolf is a phallic mode of interpreting the world and is an attempt to gain what is lacking through imposition and force' (Zipes, 1987: 258), much like the Marquis's gaze dominates and almost eliminates his young wife. Ironically, most of Carter's wolf-like characters are female, sometimes even short-sighted, like Wolf-Alice who 'can net so much more of the world than we can through the fine, hairy sensitive filters of her nostrils that her poor eyesight does not trouble her' (Carter, 1995: 221). When they possess the traditional devouring gaze of the predator, they are its first victims, like the Duke: 'Those huge, inconsolable, rapacious eyes of his are eaten up by swollen, gleaming pupil. His eyes see only appetite. These eyes open to devour the world in which he sees nowhere, a reflection of himself' (Carter, 1995: 222). Such eyes are monstrous mouths that seem to devour even themselves and make the character literally untouchable to ordinary human beings. In 'The Company of Wolves' too, the Little Red Riding Hood character is faced with a werewolf whose eyes are 'of a beast of prey, nocturnal, devastating eyes as red as a wound' (Carter, 1995: 217). Such images shed a different light on the predators' predicament by taking up the theme of blindness introduced in the opening short story and recalling, once again, the fate of Oedipus. The notion of a wound relates the senses of sight and touch, as if the predatory gaze, when causing the reification of its object, also injured its subject.

Conversely, in 'The Company of Wolves', the young heroine manages to escape the fate of a prey by asserting the prominence of touch over sight, when she decides not to be afraid, burns her own clothes, and finally falls asleep 'between the paws of the tender wolf' (Carter, 1995: 220).[19] In 'Wolf-Alice', a very animalistic Alice manages to restore the Duke's humanity and his reflection in the mirror by licking his wounds, out of mere animal compassion. Such characters establish a relationship to otherness based on openness and vulnerability, in which touch becomes prominent. Truly happy endings are quite rare in the collection but, whenever they occur, in 'The Tiger's Bride', 'The Company of Wolves' and, in some respects, 'Wolf-Alice', they are triggered by intimate, oral and tactile forms of contact, animalistic versions, or rather inversions, of the traditional magic kiss, leading to even more fantastic metamorphoses.

Paradoxically, the importance of touch, linked to orality, accounts for the presence of music in the collection, and contributes to transform its reading process. References to the pictorial arts in *The Bloody Chamber* have generated much criticism, especially focused on the eponymous short story. The fact that music, noise even, pervades the whole collection has drawn less attention. Yet the reader would be hard-pressed to count the musicians, instruments and musical genres mentioned in the volume, ranging from *gavotte* to opera and even concrete music, from the piano to the harp and the violin. Many of them lead to further intersemiotic and intermedial references. To name but a few, specific musical references include Wagner's *Tristan und Isolde* (inspired by a folk tale) with the famous 'Liebestod', Strauss's waltz 'Kennst du das Land wo die Zitronen blühen?', itself an adaptation of Mignon's song from Goethe's novel *Wilhelm Meister*, which the composer included in his opera *The Bat*. Similarly 'The Erl-King' draws from Schubert's Lied, *The Erlkönig*, inspired by Goethe's poem. Puss in Boots, the cunning cat servant, is based on Figaro, a character from a theatre play by Beaumarchais, who is also the hero of Rossini and Mozart's opera adaptations, *The Barber of Seville* and *The Marriage of Figaro*. As to 'The Snow Child', its title definitely evokes Tchaikovsky's *Snow Maiden*.

Such intersemiotic references are bound to affect the reading process and amplify the sound effects of these incredibly polyphonic and sometimes even discordant short stories.[20] Faced with such noisy narratives, some readers may be tempted to look for directions that could guide their interpretation and help them restore some sense of harmony, that is, for the textual equivalents of musical indications like pitch, clef, keynote or signature key.

The sheer number of occurrences of the word 'key' in 'The Bloody Chamber' suggests the pun may be intended: Who better than a pianist could take care of Bluebeard's keys? This short story is also the first in the volume, which suggests a metafictional dimension:[21] it might provide the readers with a key to the collection, or at least deceive them into believing so. Like curious, disobedient brides, they might try to use this key to decipher a secret code and really unlock the deeper meaning of the book they have already opened, a book whose title equates it with the predator's bloody lair and implies reading may be a very dangerous activity.

As Carter's persistent punning suggests, each short story, and even the whole collection, may have to be understood in different ways at the same time. The reading process, which also includes interpretation in the musical sense, as performance, thus becomes incredibly complex and dangerous, yet highly enjoyable.

Some of the voices that resonate off the pages, like both the Marquis's and the piano tuner's in 'The Bloody Chamber', are akin to the sound of the sea. The latter has 'a voice like the soft consolations of the sea' (Carter, 1995: 121) and Jean-Yves's speech 'had the rhythm of the countryside, the rhythms of the tides' (Carter, 1995: 135). Similarly, the lovely vampire of 'The Lady of the House of Love' has a voice with 'the rushing sonorities of the ocean in it' (Carter, 1995: 203). The voice of the Marquis can have the timbre of 'certain great cathedral organs' (Carter, 1995: 138). As to Mr Lyon's voice, it brings 'the terror that the chords of great organs bring' because it comes 'from a cave full of echoes' (Carter, 1995: 149), a phrase also used to describe the lady vampire: 'She is a cave full of echoes' (Carter, 1995: 194). In such voices, harmony seems to dominate melody. Like the music of 'great organs', they are already polyphonic, which may be a key to the composition and interpretation of the collection, suggesting readers can indeed actively try to analyse the polyphony or, alternately, take a more receptive stance and simply be touched, affected by the voices of *The Bloody Chamber*, as by a piece of music. Should they try to analyse each note, to make out a melody in the chords, hear each voice within the voice, they will find echoes of yet more voices from the past, ranging from Perrault to Andrew Lang, from Schubert's Lieder to Carter's voice or, more importantly, their own inner voices.

This contributes further to shift the emphasis from the visual towards the oral/aural dimension of the reading process, which, in turn, reinforces its tactile quality. Indeed, psychoanalysts are not alone in pointing to the similarity between the oral/aural and the sense of touch. As translation theory specialist Henri Meschonnic has it: 'A voice is like a body outside the body. Two voices answering each other almost constitute a bodily contact. You can say a voice is moving, penetrating or caressing. There is gesture in a voice'.[22]

It has been demonstrated that, in *The Bloody Chamber*, Angela Carter's writing simulates the oral quality of the folk tale. All the better to touch her readers.

Conversely, much as touch is reciprocal, Carter's writing urges the readers to perform, to voice, breathe and taste the text.[23] Caroline Webb offers a compelling analysis of 'The Bloody Chamber', demonstrating the prominence of the aural/oral and the tactile in the reading process.[24] She argues that the narrator's command of music allows her to create striking rhymes and rhythms, with 'almost orchestral effects' (Webb, 2009: 197), and concludes:

> First, the conceptual awareness of the sensation of oral reading is centrally important in this very literary narrative. The physical sensation of the movement of tongue, teeth and throat is continually evoked across the story. Critics have taken for granted the idea that the images provided by words on the page may induce sensations such as the erotic, but Carter highlights the extent to which bodily sensation other than the visual can be evoked in the act of reading. (Webb, 2009: 201)

The overall musicality of the collection even makes it impossible for readers to ignore these 'other' sensations, especially when they are faced with passages in the text that compel them to decide on their own interpretation or performance, in terms of rhythm, tempo or intonation. The onomatopoeic knocking on the grandmother's door: 'Rat-a-tap-tap', may sound like a drum roll, for instance. The answer, in 'granny's antique falsetto' (Carter, 1995: 218), must be performed in the reader's inner ear too, not to mention the punctuation marks or typographical effects, with so many ellipses, dashes and blanks functioning like musical signs, or even the narrator's capitalized signature at the end of 'Puss-in-Boots'. Only the ultimate interpreters of the text, its readers, can determine how such signs, or invented musical directions, like '*molto agitato*' (Carter, 1995: 161), will be rendered. They are thus entrusted with the keys to their own *Bloody Chamber*, and the task of performing, like opera singers their own inner stage, a text that reads like a complex, visual, aural, and consequently tactile, musical score.

The Bloody Chamber foregrounds the paradox of reading, as an oscillation between sight and touch. Hence the constant references to painting and music, the tension between the freezing eye of the predator and the kiss of the singer. Psychoanalytic theory closely links orality to the sense of touch, to the first steps of human development, which predate the Oedipus complex and are related to the early mother–child relationship. Yet the mother–daughter relationship is also questioned and shown to be far from idyllic in the collection, in 'The Werewolf' for example. The point, then, is neither to reverse the hierarchy of the senses and establish a matriarchal order, nor to advocate the loss of self with the suppression of all boundaries between self and other, but to create a different relationship to otherness, in which the subject might experience the interconnectedness of the senses, of aural, tactile and visual sensations. It also seeks to resolve these tensions through the creation of visual and musical 'refrains' that can be better perceived when considering the collection as an ensemble.

Paradoxically, this can only be achieved by going against the readers' subconscious tendencies, by fighting their urge to look for a 'still moment' in art, the moment when a stable, fixed and still form can appear at the very heart of temporal arts like literature and music. Murray Krieger calls this general human tendency *ekphrasis*. To him, the term designates much more than a mere rhetorical figure consisting in the description of a work of art (Krieger, 1992: 77). It is akin to the phenomenon Michel Picard describes when he notices our desire 'to dominate the whole of a text', 'to comprehend it'. According to the French critic, this is 'assuming the attitude of a Thomist God who can contemplate it from immobile eternity. It means ... refusing to adopt a mere "traveller's point of view" on the text'.[25] Readers, as well as writers and composers, are prone to this type of fantasy, which the short story is supposed to both trigger and fulfil more easily than the novel.[26]

A reader trying to get a 'bird's eye view' of *The Bloody Chamber* may envisage it as a succession of vignettes making up an irregular triptych. The first four pieces are devoted to tigers and other big cats, the last four to wolves. In the centre, 'The Erl-King' and 'The Snow Child' mirror one another as tales of killing or being killed. In that sense, taking 'god's point of view' on the volume, or getting 'a bird's eye view' of it, may provide a sense of balance, reveal a pattern that a reader can find intellectually rewarding. However, it amounts to stilling the text, in both senses of the word. Angela Carter preferred to play with readers' subconscious desires to 'dominate' either each short story separately or the collection as a whole, and quite systematically thwart it.

In order to get this 'bird's eye view' of the volume, one has to read through a text whose visual, aural and tactile qualities run counter to her readers' 'ekphrastic' tendencies to prevent them from assuming a

God-like point of view on the text, as they are more likely be overwhelmed by its musical quality. They may thus find themselves wandering through strangely familiar fictional woods, yet forced out of the trodden paths of their reading habits, tempted to dawdle through the forest like Little Red Riding Hood, or compelled to descend into an '*enfer*' like Bluebeard's bride. In this respect, the reading process mirrors the trials and tribulations of fairy tale heroes lost in the forest. In traditional fairy tales, this episode constitutes a rite of passage in which the heroes sometimes lose their sense of self, better to reinvent their own identity and overcome obstacles along their way, but such trials become potentially endless for Carter's readers as subjects. It is quite difficult for them to silently pause the reading process in order to enjoy a 'bird's eye view' of the text (aptly, the term 'birdseye' designates a musical sign indicating a silent pause) for the polyphony of discordant voices, jarring instruments and unexpected chords, but also the dizzying host and variety of visual and tactile effects the collection has in store, are quite impossible to ignore.

This is all the more so as Carter keeps dazzling her readers, sometimes juggling with pictures, breaking up scenes or tableaux into smaller pieces in order to reshuffle them into kaleidoscopic compositions, in which images seem to shift and morph into each other. Striking visual elements keep recurring, often with a twist. The caged lark in 'The Lady of the House of Love' mirrors the caged birds in 'The Erl-King'. The traditional woman's portrait in black, white and red, typical of fairy tales, appears in 'The Bloody Chamber' and 'The Snow Child'. Similarly, the scene where a character pricks her finger and bleeds takes place both in 'The Snow Child' and 'The Lady of the House of Love'. Bluebeard's white lilies[27] morph into Beauty's white rose in 'The Courtship of Mr Lyon', which becomes red in 'The Snow Child' and 'The Lady of the House of Love'. Getting a bird's eye view of *The Bloody Chamber* thus means leaving out the mutability and multiplicity of musical and pictorial images, disregarding the way some of them keep recurring, with differences.

Such images tend to take on a formulaic quality, which has become almost incantation-like, and turn into musical and visual 'refrains', as defined by Deleuze and Guattari, who devote a whole section of *A Thousand Plateaus* to this phenomenon. 'Refrains', they write, can be traced throughout the most famous pieces in the history of Western music from Vivaldi to Schuman, as well as in birdsongs. They aim to create a limit, ward off rivals and keep chaos at bay. Sometimes, they can even organize the surrounding chaos and help re-define a territory. If repeating a 'refrain' amounts to defining and defending borders, introducing improvisations and variations into it amounts to venturing outside, going beyond the limits of one's own territory, beyond one's own limits to confront and possibly accept otherness:

> The refrain has [...] three aspects, it makes them simultaneous or mixes them [...] Sometimes chaos is an immense black hole in which one endeavours to fix a fragile point as a centre. Sometimes one organizes around that point a calm and stable 'pace' (rather than a form) [...] Sometimes one grafts onto that pace a breakaway from the black hole [...] Sometimes, one leaves the territorial assemblage for other assemblages somewhere else entirely: interassemblages, components of passage, or even escape.[28] (Deleuze and Guattari, 2004: 344)

That is why they link their 'refrains' to a process of becoming: 'refrains' rely on repetition but cannot lead to anything new if they are just repeated as such. They need difference, variations, to do so. The heroine of 'The Lady of the House of Love', the heir to the curse of her vampire ancestors, thus finds herself trapped in endless repetition, symbolized by the lark she keeps in a cage: Can the caged bird learn a new song, she wonders? Even though she is a prisoner, can her 'refrain' be altered to re-define her world, re-map her territory, liberate and, ultimately, transform her?

The Bloody Chamber's 'refrains' tend to become smaller and smaller, from sentences to words, some of them German or French. In 'The Lady of the House of Love', for instance, the lines '*Suivez-moi, / Je vous attendais/ Vous serez ma proie*' (Carter, 1995: 204, 206) recur, in French in the text; Jack and the Beanstalk's song 'Fi, fi, fo, fum, I smell the blood of an Englishman' is completed one page after it starts (Carter, 1995: 198, 199). In both cases, from one page to the next, is it impossible to determine who is actually supposed to utter them, or even if the same narrative voice is supposed to do so. Similarly, the 'Liebestod' from Wagner's *Tristan & Isolde* appears several times in 'The Bloody Chamber' and in 'The Company of Wolves'. As a German word, it tends to stand out and as a title, it refers to a well-known aria, evoking a specific melody. In 'The Company of Wolves', it is combined with yet another intersemiotic reference, the 'Walpurgisnacht' from both Gounod's opera and Goethe's theatre play, *Faust*, to describe the wolves' howling, which is then compared to a human voice, since the narrator talks about 'an aria of fear made audible' (Carter, 1995: 212), and even compares it to religious hymns with 'the canticles of the wolves' (Carter, 1995: 213), before it becomes 'a threnody' and a 'prothalamion' (Carter, 1995: 219). As the wolves' voices become more and more human, operatic even, human voices become more and more wolfish. This includes the inner voices of the readers who, even if they are trying to dominate the book in their mind's eye, are constantly prompted to change their interpretation, step out of their paths, out of their own selves. They are urged to join the chorus and start howling with the wolves, be they bold enough to lend their own voices to the call of the wild, or just content to 'ineffectually [...] imitate the wolves' chorus' (Carter, 1995: 227), like the parishioners in 'Wolf-Alice'.

Unable to take a good look from the highest tree in order to set a course, like Tom Thumb and so many fairy tale heroes, readers wander through a forest of both auditory and visual symbols. If Angela Carter's 'refrains' did not, precisely, elicit such an uncanny sense of familiarity, they could be compared to the nursery-rhymes scared children sing in the dark to create some illusion of comfort and reassurance, as if creating their own aural zones or soundscapes were sufficient protection against the dangers lurking in the night.

The fact that 'refrains' in *The Bloody Chamber* can be visual, aural or both points to a new type of transaction between the arts and, a new kind of time–space amalgamation. Angela Carter manages to weave them together in such a way that they no longer converge in death, as they did to William Blake, but rather, commingle to open onto new territories. She thus reinvents the tale as the intermedial form allowing for the creation of new relationships between genres and genders.

Images become 'refrains' and create new rhythms with a repetition of striking elements, of fragmented or deconstructed yet recognizable patterns and, at the same time, a wealth of new interpretations that, ultimately, depend on the readers. This brings Carter's written short stories back to the oral, communal roots of the fairy tale. Her ever-shifting narratives have to be told, voiced, in order to move and touch their readers or rather, tellers and audiences. Meant for endless interpretation and re-interpretation, like folk tales, they belong to each and every reader, to everybody and to nobody.

In *The Bloody Chamber*, Angela Carter manages to foreground the repressed, pictorial and musical 'others' of literature, which disrupts readers' habits and the boundaries between the arts. As Michel Thévoz argues, the categorization of the arts according to senses we cannot always spontaneously distinguish or separate may not be related to art itself, nor to perceptions. It rather has to do with 'common sense', with the way we usually make sense of the world (Thévoz, 1996: 106–19). Carter emphasizes the delights and benefits to be derived from calling common sense into question, from creating a breakaway. By writing against the categorization of the arts, she invites her readers to lose themselves in the fictional woods, all the better to see, hear, touch and embrace the otherness that was first repressed by power relationships and social conditioning. Her 'refrains' turn reading into a fully aesthetic experience, in the etymological sense. The performative and, at times, animalistic type of reading that her text calls for appeals to readers' ears, tongues and skins as much as to their eyes and minds. Affected by the text as much as they affect and transform it with their reading, Carter's readers establish a relationship of mutual affection between their own minds and bodies, and the body of the text. They are left to give voice to operatic arias, as well as animal sounds and birdsongs from the forest, literally to perform their own interpretation of the 'refrains' of *The Bloody Chamber*, thus creating new spaces, that is, new songs and new volumes.

Notes

1 See Patricia Duncker (1988: 3–14), as an example of miscommunication between Carter and her readers at the time, as Patricia Duncker herself pointed out, when asked about her appreciation of Carter's use of the fairy tale genre during a conference at University Michel de Montaigne-Bordeaux III, on 26 November 2004.
2 Carter translated the fairy tales of Charles Perrault (Carter, 1977). For an in-depth analysis of her translations and the crucial role translation played in her literary creation, see (Hennard Dutheil de la Rochère, 2013).
3 A striking example would be Robert Schumann's *Märchenbilder* or *Fairy Tale Pictures for Viola and Piano*, Op. 113, written in 1851.
4 *A Vision of the Last Judgement* (Blake, 1974: 614).
5 This would be in keeping with the general strategy she mentioned in a later interview, when she explained that she wanted to use the 'latent

content' of the fairy tales to write *The Bloody Chamber* (Goldsworthy, 1985: 6).

6 It is worth noting that the model's body is finally reduced to what the narrator describes as her 'still so beautiful' skull (Carter, 1995: 132).

7 Martine Hennard Dutheil de la Rochère has brilliantly desmonstrated this, analysing, for instance, how the inaccurate description or invention of a Rops engraving, earlier in the short story, is meant to enhance the sense of objectification created by the Marquis's predatory gaze (Martine Hennard Dutheil de la Rochère, 2006: 193–5).

8 Cecilia is often represented as blind because her name was believed to derive from the Latin word *cecus*, which seems to be a traditional theme for painters. This can be seen to connect with the blind piano tuner in the story. Waterhouse's 1895 *Saint Cecilia*, for instance, depicts the saint as reclining with her eyes closed.

9 To Martine Hennard Dutheil de la Rochère, it shows that 'While providing ample evidence of patriarchal visual traditions, it [the story] nevertheless refuses to see the gaze as necessarily male and therefore rejects visual representation as intrinsically sexist' (Martine Hennard Dutheil de la Rochère, 2006: 186). This is undeniable. Visual representation, however, remains linked to power, and the figure of Medusa could even point to the essentially female nature of such power, which has to be repressed and concealed in a patriarchal context. This would square with feminist analyses of the mythological figure, like Marina Warner's (Warner, 2000: 110–15) and, as demonstrated later, relate to the latent orality of pictures, as explored by W. J. T. Mitchell in *What do Pictures Want?* (Mitchell, 2005).

10 Monstrous by definition, Medusa's face violated the rules of nature as well as culture, so that, in the ancient myth, her murder was supposed symbolically to assert the primacy of order against the chaos she stood for. In the ancient Greek context, the order in question was, of course, patriarchal (Vernant, 1985: 80).

11 The term, Liliane Louvel writes, 'illustrates perfectly the attempt to merge text and image in a pluriform fusion, as in an oxymoron [...]. It is therefore the perfect word to designate the ambiguous, aporetic and in-between object of our analysis' (Louvel, 2013: 15).

12 Much more complex 'pentacles' are also to be found in *The Key of the Mysteries*, a book by Eliphas Levi, a French nineteenth-century occultist, which the bride finds in the Marquis's library, a few pages earlier in the short story (Carter, 1995: 120). One of them, the 'Great Pentacle from the Vision of Saint John' ('Grand Pantacle de la Vision de Saint Jean'), even represents the author of the revelation (Levi 1861: 77), which is

worth noticing since, as will be discussed, the narrator of 'The Bloody Chamber' also resorts to apocalyptic imagery to describe her mother as a *dea ex machina*.

13 See Bruno Bettelheim, *The Uses of Enchantment: The Meaning and Importance of Fairy Tales* (London: Thames & Hudson, 1976).

14 The Marquis's 'licentious ancestor' who posed for Fragonard 'with his daughters' in the previously quoted passage also suggests incest.

15 My translation of: 'Les scénarios œdipiens, comme la grande majorité des fantasmes, sont visuels. Passer de la problématique narcissique à la problématique œdipienne, c'est passer du gustatif, du tactile, de l'olfactif, du respiratoire, au visuel (le sonore faisant, sous deux formes différentes, partie de ces deux niveaux)' (Anzieu 1995: 217). The latest translation by Naomi Seagal still offers 'hearing' as an English equivalent for 'le sonore', which does not seem to render the polysemy of 'le sonore', nor account for the precision Anzieu adds ('under two different forms', i.e. oral and aural).

16 Of course, this goes beyond the psychoanalytical interpretations of Carter's short stories: At the individual level, the sense of touch is of paramount importance in the development of the subject, as the title of Anzieu's book indicates. While at the collective, social level, as W. Ong demonstrated in *Orality and Literacy*, the prominence of sight over hearing and touch has historical roots. It dates back to the invention of writing, and was later reinforced by the invention of the printing press and subsequent generalisation of reading (Ong, 1988).

17 See Donovan (1989), for instance.

18 From the beginning of the story, the bride uses religious imagery to hint at her mother's supernatural powers. 'My eagle-featured, indomitable mother; what other student at the Conservatoire could boast that her mother had outfaced a junkful of Chinese pirates, nursed a village through a visitation of the plague, shot a man-eating tiger with her own hand, and all before she was as old as I?'(Carter, 1995: 111) While her physical appearance recalls Saint John's eagle, she thus seems to have defeated three of the Four Horsemen of the Apocalypse, War, Pestilence and possibly Famine on her own, at an early age. This use of Christian imagery may seem strange but, besides establishing the narrator's mother as a female figure of divine power and authority, it also conveys the notion that Death itself – or rather, Hades himself – should come next.

19 Commenting on the script that Angela Carter wrote for the 1984 film directed by Neil Jordan, *The Company of Wolves*, Catherine Lappas notes that 'touch acts as a metaphor for Carter's incorporation of the patriarchal into herself' (Lappas, 1996: 130).

20 There now seems to be reliable neurological evidence that the same

areas of the brain respond when subjects perform an action and when they are shown a representation of it, or when they listen to an actual sound and when they imagine it: 'When we read the verbs *throwing* or *kicking*, for example, the cortical areas associated with those actions fire' (Armstrong, 2013: 54).
21 I counted sixty-seven occurrences over the thirty-one pages of the short story (Carter: 1995, 112–43).
22 My unsatisfactory translation of: 'Une voix, c'est du corps hors corps. Deux voix qui se répondent, c'est un peu du corps à corps. On dit bien qu'une voix est touchante, ou pénétrante, ou caressante. Il y a du geste en elle, sous une forme sonore' (Meschonnic, 1988: 28). '*Corps à corps*' is an ambiguous phrase, with either erotic or aggressive connotations (it can be used as a French equivalent to 'close combat').
23 Carter suggests similarities between bodies and musical instruments: the narrator of the Erl-King plans to use his hair to string his fiddle once she has killed him (Carter, 1995: 192); Wolf-Alice, who did not learn to speak, has 'unused chords [sic] in her throat', 'like a wind-harp that moves with the random impulses of the air' (Carter, 1995: 223); 'organ', a recurring word, may sometimes be read as a multilingual pun, since the French *organe* (which does mean biological 'organ') can refer to voices too, especially those of opera singers.
24 Caroline Webb comments on a passage in 'The Bloody Chamber' which ends with: 'His kiss, his kiss with tongue and teeth in it and a rasp of beard, had hinted to me, though with the same exquisite tact as this nightdress he'd given me, of the wedding night' (Carter, 1995: 111). Although she does not comment on this, it is revealing she should focus on the description of a kiss, a most intimate combination of touch and orality, rendered by a strikingly alliterative passage to bolster her demonstration. Interestingly, the first answer J.W.T. Mitchell gives to his own question ('What do pictures want?') is also: 'Pictures want to be kissed. And of course, we want to kiss them back' (Mitchell, 2005: xvi). The sense of touch, which most arts – painting, music and literature included – usually tend to repress, thus seems to be linked to both the visual and the oral/aural.
25 My translation of: 'Dominer le texte dans son ensemble, com-prendre, c'est se placer en quelque manière hors du temps, comme le Dieu tho miste qui l'envisage depuis l'éternité immobile. C'est refuser le simple 'point de vue du voyageur' dans la lecture" (Picard, 1989: 43). Here, Picard reformulates what Iser before him had called the 'wandering viewpoint' of the reader (Iser, 1978: 111).
26 Critics like Liliane Louvel have pointed out the presence of the pictorial metaphor – the notion that, because of its brevity, a short story ought to

be immediately intelligible for the reader like a painting – as a 'cognitive fantasy' to be found in many theories of the short story (Louvel and Verley, 1995: 37).

27 In 1911, Béla Bartók composed *Duke Bluebeard's Castle*, an opera with a libretto by Béla Balász, from whom Carter may have borrowed the image of the lilies ('lilies tall as men' in the English translation by Christopher Hassall available here: www.powell-pressburger.org/ Reviews/64_Bluebeard/Words.html, last accessed 29 August 2016). Carter must have seen Michael Powell's filmed version of the opera, shot in Germany in 1963, but released in the United Kingdom only in 1978. In this version, Bluebeard's new wife, whose name (Judith) evokes a famous beheading from the Old Testament and who, in the last scene, wears a diadem on her bent head, recalls Moreau's *Salome*. She also becomes his 'Night wife', which may account for the similarities Martine Hennard Dutheil de la Rochère (2006: 201) finds between Moreau's *La Nuit* and the fictional painting entitled *The Sacrificial Victim* mentioned by the narrator in 'The Bloody Chamber' (Carter, 1995: 122).

28 Brian Massumi's translation of: 'On les retrouve dans les contes, de terreur ou de fées, dans les *lieder* aussi. La ritournelle a les trois aspects [...]. Tantôt le chaos est un immense trou noir, et l'on s'efforce d'y fixer un point fragile comme un centre. Tantôt l'on organise autour du point une "allure" (plutôt qu'une forme) calme et stable: le trou-noir est devenu un chez-soi. Tantôt on greffe une échappée sur cette allure, hors du trou noir' (Deleuze and Guattari, 1980: 383).

References

Anzieu, Didier (1995), *Le Moi-Peau* (1985, Paris, Dunod).
—— (2016), *The Skin-Ego: A New Translation by Naomi Seagal* (London: Routledge).
Armstrong, Paul B. (2013), *How Literature Plays with the Brain: The Neuroscience of Reading* (Baltimore: Johns Hopkins University Press).
Blake, William (1974), *Complete Writings*, ed. G. Keynes (Oxford: Oxford University Press).
Carter, Angela (1977), *The Fairy Tales of Charles Perrault* (London: Gollancz).
—— ([1977] 1992), *The Passion of New Eve* (London: Virago Press).
—— ([1977] 1993), *The Sadeian Woman* (London: Virago Press).
—— (1995), *Burning Your Boats* (London: Chatto & Windus).
Deleuze, Gilles and Félix Guattari, *Mille Plateaux* ([1980]), trans. Brian Massumi, *A Thousand Plateaus* (1988, London: Continuum).
Donovan, Josephine (1989), *After the Fall: The Demeter-Persephone Myth*

in Wharton, Cather and Glasgow (Philadelphia: Pennsylvania State University).
Duncker, Patricia (1988), 'Re-imagining the Fairy Tales: Angela Carter's Bloody Chambers', *Literature and History*, 10, 3–14.
Goldsworthy, Kerryn (1985), 'Angela Carter', *Meanjin*, 44, 4–13.
Hennard Dutheil de la Rochère, Martine (2006), 'Modelling for Bluebeard', in Beverly Maeder, Jürg Schwyter, Ilona Sigris and Boris Vejdovsky (eds), *The Seeming and the Seen: Essays in Modern Visual and Literary Culture* (Bern: Peter Lang, 2006), pp. 183–208.
—— (2013), *Reading, Translating, Rewriting: Angela Carter's Translational Poetics* (Detroit: Wayne State University Press).
Iser, Wolfgang (1978), *The Act of Reading: A Theory of Aesthetic Response* (Baltimore: Johns Hopkins University Press).
Krieger, Murray (1992), *Ekphrasis: The Illusion of the Natural Sign* (Baltimore: Johns Hopkins University Press).
Lappas, Catherine (1996), 'Seeing is Believing, but Touching is the Truth: Female Spectatorship and Sexuality in *the Company of Wolves*', *Women's Studies*, 25, 115–35.
Levi, Eliphas (1861), *La Clef des grands mystères* (Paris: Alcan). Digitalized version freely accessible on the French National Library website: http://gallica.bnf.fr/ark:/12148/bpt6k5510884x/f90.item.r=grand%20penta (accessed 29 August 2016).
Louvel, Liliane (2013), *Poetics of the Iconotext* (London: Routledge).
—— and Verley, Claudine (1995), *Introduction à l'étude de la nouvelle* (Toulouse: Presses Universitaires du Mirail).
Meschonnic, Henri (1988), 'Le théâtre dans la voix', in Gérard Dessons (ed.), *La Licorne, penser la voix*, 41, 25–42.
—— (1989), *La Rime et la vie* (Paris: Verdier).
Mitchell, W.J.T. (1984), 'The Politics of Genre: Space and Time in Lessing's *Laocoon*', *Representations*, 6 (Spring), 98–115.
—— (1994), *Picture Theory* (Chicago: University of Chicago Press).
—— (2005), *What do Pictures Want?* (Chicago: University of Chicago Press).
Ong, Walter J. ([1982], 1988), *Orality and Literacy* (London: Routledge).
Picard, Michel (1989), *Lire le temps* (Paris: Minuit).
Thévoz, Michel (1996), *Le Miroir infidèle* (Paris: Minuit).
Vernant, Jean-Pierre (1985), *La Mort dans les yeux: figures de l'Autre dans la Grèce ancienne* (Paris: Hachette).
Warner, Marina ([1985] 2000), *Monuments and Maidens: The Allegory of the Female Form* (Berkeley: University of California Press).
Webb, Caroline (2009), 'The Language of the Senses: Angela Carter's "The Bloody Chamber" and the Seduction of the Reader', in Anthony Uhlman,

Helen Groth, Paul Sheehan and Stephen McLaren (eds), *Literature and Sensation* (Newcastle: Cambridge Scholars).

Zipes, Jack (1987), *Don't Bet on the Prince: Contemporary Feminist Fairy Tales in North America and England* (Abingdon: Routledge).

4

Angela Carter's poetry

Sarah Gamble

Angela Carter was an assiduous fashioner of her own autobiographical narrative, which became ever more stylized and repetitive as the years went by. Twenty-five years after her death, her own life-account has not been substantially challenged: following the script that she herself set out, we talk of Carter the novelist, the short story writer and the cultural commenter; Carter as feminist, socialist and demythologizer. Not until recently, however, has she also been identified as a poet. This is not surprising, as none of the Chatto & Windus anthologies that were published immediately after her death – which played an important part in making more obscure aspects of her oeuvre accessible to the general reader – include any poetry written by her. Moreover, it was an aspect of her career that she herself chose not to mention, neatly excising it from her artistic autobiography. It was not until 2015 that this aspect of her work began to be openly discussed, when an anthology of her poetry, *Unicorn: The Poetry of Angela Carter*, appeared. A year later, Edmund Gordon published the first authorized biography of Carter, which also makes reference – albeit briefly – to her small poetic output.

It is the purpose of this chapter to begin a more detailed investigation into Carter's verse by, firstly, situating her work within the context of general poetic activity in Britain in the mid-1960s; and, secondly, to examine whether any links can be established between her poetry and her far better-known prose writing. Should this work be considered purely as a curiosity, a minor footnote in the narrative of her illustrious career, or does it have a more pivotal part to play in helping us to understand her art?

Carter's poetic career was, admittedly, extremely short, and can be roughly dated as lasting only for the duration of her period as an English undergraduate at Bristol University between 1962 and 1965, although some of her earlier work, including 'Unicorn', was republished in 1966.[1] This means that she was working on poetry at the same time as she was writing what was to become her first novel, *Shadow Dance*, the first draft of which was written during the 1963–64 academic year. What this suggests is that at this period in her life Carter saw herself as a poet as well as a prose writer – perhaps even *more* of a poet than a prose writer – and her correspondence reveals her determination to be recognized as such. In her endeavour to get her poetry into print she entered into regular communication with at least two editors of literary magazines – Father Brocard Sewell, editor of *The Aylesford Review*, and Cavan McCarthy, who set up *Tlaloc* in 1964 – and it is this correspondence, alongside the published poetry and the manuscripts of unpublished pieces preserved in the archives of both magazines, that forms the main body of research for this chapter.

It is obvious from Carter's letters that she had real ambitions for her verse, bombarding both Father Brocard and McCarthy with unsolicited samples of her poetry, some of which was published, and a lot of which was not. In addition, along with a fellow undergraduate in the English department at Bristol, Neil Curry, Carter also tried setting up her own poetry magazine, *Vision*, in order to, in her own words, 'nudge some sort of literary activity out of the predominantly apathetic students' (AC to FB, 2 September 1965). Unfortunately, the attempt failed ignominiously, and *Vision* did not survive beyond a single issue, which appeared in 1964. As Carter rather grumpily wrote to Father Brocard: 'Much of the material in our unique edition came from non-students anyway. But we got no further contributions of any standard whatsoever, and so we shut up shop. It was, all round, a depressing experience' (AC to FB, 3 September 1965). Two poems in that issue, 'Unicorn' and a three-line piece entitled 'Through the Looking Glass', were written by Carter herself, submitted under a pseudonym, Rankin Crowe. To Father Brocard, she claimed to have regretted the decision to hide her identity as 'cowardice' (AC to FB, 3 September 1965), but when she sought to get 'Unicorn' republished in Cavan McCarthy's *Tlaloc* in 1966, she made out that her choice was rather more deliberate:

> My pseudonym is a big secret, so I trust you will keep as quiet as the grave about it; I have adopted it for the reasons most women who write sooner or later find themselves using masculine names, unless they are those quivering-sensibility-type females who trade on being a woman. Unfortunately I do not really write like a woman and some men get upset. (AC to CM, 20 October 1965)

Whether Carter really was trying to surmount misogyny as she claimed, or whether she was simply rather embarrassed at publishing her verse in what was effectively her own magazine, is unclear. What this declaration does illustrate is that at this stage in her career, Carter was very concerned not to be seen to be writing as a woman – indeed, much of her poetry, like her early prose, resolutely avoids an explicitly female voice or subject-matter. This may, of course, be due to the fact that she was writing before feminism's second wave had properly got underway in Britain: as Jane Dowson and Alice Entwistle say in *A History of Twentieth-Century Women's Poetry*, avowedly feminist verse was 'Mostly written or first published in magazines, pamphlets and anthologies soon after 1968' (Dowson and Entwistle, 2005: 139) – a date with which other critics of twentieth-century poetry concur.

Given that Carter had written most of her poetry by the end of 1965, we can regard her as pre-dating the real upsurge of feminism's Second Wave in Britain and its resulting influence upon women's poetry. Indeed, Carter herself was later to claim in 'Notes from the Front Line', published in 1983, that she did not fully consider herself to be a feminist until the end of the 1960s:

> I can date to that time and to some of those debates and to that sense of heightened awareness of the society around me in the summer of 1968, my own questioning of the nature of my reality as a *woman*. How that social fiction of my 'femininity' was created, by means outside my control, and palmed off on me as the real thing. (Carter, 1997a: 37–8)

The poetry supports this, lacking the interest in the socio-cultural construction of femininity that was to become the hallmark of much of Carter's later work.

Carter was striving to invent herself as a poet in the midst of a general explosion of poetic activity in Britain. 1965 saw the Royal Albert Hall Poetry Incarnation, in which the American beat poet Alan Ginsberg participated: it was a four-hour poetry reading that was attended by over 7,000 people. What subsequently become known as the British Poetry Revival saw an enormous increase in publication outlets: according to Andrew Duncan, 'there were 2,000 poetry magazines during the Sixties; poetic activity went to an unheard-of height' (Duncan, 2003: 76). Carter's poems appeared in just such publications – principally *The Aylesford Review* (1955–68) and *Tlaloc* (1964–70). She also had three poems published in *Universities' Poetry*, one in the Leeds University student magazine *Poetry and Audience*, and five poems in a pamphlet anthology entitled *Five Quiet Shouters*, published by Poet & Printer Press.

How far Carter saw herself as part of the British Poetry Revival is unclear. She did have fairly definite ideas concerning her poetic intentions, being very dismissive about what she called 'the sort of poetry which is really nothing more than one fog-bound intellectual semaphoring elaborately to another, occasionally sending up S.O.S.'s' (AC to CM, 18 May 1965). Instead, she said to Cavan McCarthy,

> It is terribly important (to me at least) that people read what I write; and it is also important, to me, that I make them laugh; and as my slapstick is usually about them [sic] more horrible aspects of life, that it should be funny is very, very important, because I don't want to bore you with trite, pretentious and self-conscious observations on the nastiness of being human (see George Macbeth), do I? (AC to CM, 18 May 1965)

Perhaps as part of her desire to set herself apart from pretentious intellectualism, in the letters to Father Brocard and Cavan McCarthy she repeatedly expresses only peripheral knowledge of what was going on in the world outside Bristol – but this was also due to the fact that she had a true Londoner's contempt for the provinces. Interviewed by Lorna Sage in 1977, she described herself at this time in her life as 'a wide-eyed provincial beatnik' (Sage, 1977: 54), and this accords with the tone of the letters. For example, in *The Poetry of Saying* Robert Sheppard says that the term 'British Poetry Revival' 'was first proposed by Tina Morris and Dave Cunliffe in the eighth edition of their underground magazine *Poetmeat* around 1965, which presented an anthology of such work' (Sheppard, 2005: 35). Soon after this issue's publication, Father Brocard appears to have queried whether Carter had read it, to which she responded:

> I don't know 'Poetmeat' except by name. Such things don't get this far West, I'm afraid. I'd like to see their anthology, though; I'll go

foraging for it in 'Better Books' next time I go to London to see my mum, it's sure to be in 'Better Books'. (AC to FB, 6 July 1965)

This rather dismissive attitude towards the Bristol arts scene does not reflect what was actually going on in the city at the time. Andrew Duncan argues that one of the hallmarks of the British Poetry Revival was the fact that it was disseminated across the country: because, he says, it 'took place everywhere, we will not mention the provinces again; the distinction has vanished. "Everywhere" means, more likely, towns with universities or art colleges' (Duncan, 2003: 76–7). Bristol, of course, has both, and in an essay included in the anthology *The 60s in Bristol*, A.C.H. Smith recalls it as the centre of a hive of artistic activity, with 'much more than [its] share of the country's rich creative surge in the early 1960s' (Belsey, 1989: 40). Bristol was home to the playwrights Tom Stoppard and John Arden, and the Art College fostered the talents of many painters (Smith names artists such as Paul Feiler, Derek Balmer and Anne and Jerry Hicks). In terms of poetry, although Bristol never gained its own small publisher to perform the same function as, for example, Northern House in Leeds and Bloodaxe Books in Newcastle, there was a great deal going on in terms of poetry. The poet Charles Tomlinson ran a poetry group in the city from the early 1960s, and a poetry reading group that became known as 'the circle in the square', based at the Bristol Arts Centre, was established around 1962. In 1964, Bill Pickard was appointed Director of Poetry and Literature at the Arts Centre, and was given a budget to set the group up on a more official footing.[2] Intriguingly, A.C.H. Smith comments that Carter herself 'was involved in a brief attempt to set up a writers' group' (Belsey, 1989: 40) in the city. This may either be a reference to the short-lived magazine *Vision*, or to another, similarly doomed, attempt, but it does suggest that Carter may have been more interested in participating in the city's art scene than she was later to make out, saying to Lorna Sage that a possible sighting of 'Tom Stoppard across a crowded room once' was as close as she ever got to the 'provincial glamour circuit' (Sage, 1977: 54).

From this it is clear that Carter only ever hovered on the outskirts of the British Poetry Revival, although her work was published in some of the foremost of the little poetry magazines. She tried to get some of it into Ken Geering's *Breakthru New International Poetry Magazine*, but was rejected, and in 1965 she was delighted to receive a fan letter from the concrete poet Ian Hamilton Finlay (AC to FB, 2 May 1965). By the end of 1966, she had garnered enough recognition to be included in Barry Tebb's pamphlet collection *Five Quiet Shouters*. The self-proclaimed intention of this publication, as stated in Tebb's introduction, was 'to present to serious readers of contemporary poetry a selection of poems [...] by five young poets. [...] The criterion for selection was *aliveness* – not verbal pyrotechnics but proof of having followed Pound's dictum to MAKE IT NEW' (Tebb, 1966: no page no.). Carter's contributions in particular were singled out as possessing 'a directness which at times is dizzying' (Tebb, 1966: no page no.). This was quite a coup for her, as the collection was published by Poet & Printer, one of the foremost small presses of the period, which also published the early work of such luminaries as Ted Hughes, Peter Redgrove and Michael Longley.

In reality, though, Carter had published very little: by my calculation her total stands at around nine poems, not including reprints – 'Unicorn' was published twice, in *Vision* in 1964, and *Tlaloc* in 1966, and of the five poems in *Five Quiet Shouters*, four had definitely appeared elsewhere. 'My Cat in her First Spring', 'Life-Affirming Poem About Small, Pregnant White Cat' and 'The Horse of Love' had been published in *Universities' Poetry* and 'Poem for a Wedding Photograph' in *The Aylesford Review*. This latter poem, however, demonstrates Carter's tendency to rewrite her poems between publications, since, although recognizably linked, the two pieces are substantially different. In a letter to Barry Tebb, Carter claimed that the shorter, second version 'is now very, very much better' (AC to BT, 15 June 1966).

The reasons for this rather limited output can be attributed to two significant factors. Firstly, Carter was already venturing into prose fiction, working as she was on *Shadow Dance*, and was also buzzing with ideas for other novels. In a letter written to Father Brocard some time towards the end of 1965 (the date November 9 has been written and crossed out), Carter somewhat diffidently mentions her soon-to-be published novel:

> By the way, it seems as though I'll be having a novel published in the new year. It's a sort of fantasy. Basically it is an apprentice work, but the publishers are quite happy with it, I think. I'm working on two and a half others at the moment [...] Anyway, my 'prentice piece will add a bit of ballast to my work record & I thought you would like to know'. (AC to FB, 9 November [?] 1965)

Secondly, her letters reveal that she was working extremely hard at her university studies, which she claims to have found somewhat of a burden. Although it is true that she wrote *Shadow Dance* while at university, it is obvious that she found it difficult to write imaginatively while also being occupied with the demands of exam revision and essay writing. She had a particular reason for wanting to distinguish herself academically, since she harboured ambitions to remain at Bristol as a postgraduate – telling Father Brocard, for example, that 'the reason why it behoves me to work very hard for my exams is that I want to be invited to stay on and study some more' (AC to FB, 18 May 1965). But, particularly with that added pressure, she found the process of examination and assessment stressful. Early in her final year, she informed Cavan McCarthy that 'a first degree course is solely designed for the production of neurosis on a vast scale among poor defenceless students' (AC to CM, 20 January 1965); and by the time her finals were upon her, she was opining to Father Brocard that:

> Exams are nothing but an ordeal, they are designed to turn you into a zombie, so you can go down to the shades and communicate with the spirits of your ancestors (i.e. Shakespeare, Milton and the rest of the boys) and this is your initiation into adult-hood [...] It is a middle-class puberty rite, examinations. (AC to FB, 22 June 1965)

Consequently, she said, 'doing my exams has more or less cauterized my imagination, temporarily, I trust' (AC to FB, 22 June 1965).

She did find some way to accommodate both her verse and her study, to some extent at least, as her best poetry is directly connected to her university reading. Reflecting her degree specialism in literature of the medieval period, several of her pieces consist either of translations or broader adaptations of medieval verse, or are clearly influenced by medieval models. Writing poetry – and particularly poetry that translated or adapted the medieval literary texts she most enjoyed – thus enabled her 'to keep her hand in' (AC to FB, 22 June 1965), while not removing her completely from the academic realm.

'Unicorn' (*Vision*, 1964 and *Tlaloc*, 1966), 'William the Dreamer's Vision of Nature' (*The Aylesford Review* 7/3, 1965), 'The Thirteenth Key of Basil Valentine' (*Tlaloc* 7, April 1965) and 'Two Wives and a Widow' (*The London Magazine*, March 1966), all have medieval antecedents. 'Two Wives and a Widow' is a fairly straightforward translation of William Dunbar's early sixteenth-century poem 'The Tretis of the Twa Marrit Wemen and a Wedo'. 'William the Dreamer's Vision of Nature' is based on William Langland's fourteenth-century work *Piers Plowman*. 'The Thirteenth Key of Basil Valentine' was inspired by medieval alchemical texts, as 'Basil Valentine' was the nom-de-plume of an unknown fifteenth-century alchemist, whose work 'Duodecim Claves' or 'Twelve Keys' appeared in print around the end of the sixteenth century. 'Unicorn', meanwhile, may not have a single source text, but is a more original composite of medieval imagery, utilizing – and subverting – the traditional allegory of the virgin and the unicorn.

It is 'Unicorn' that best illustrates Carter's own description of her poetic technique as 'a kind of pop poetry, with images from Ian Fleming, off the back of corn-flake packets, women's magazines, strip cartoons etc.' (AC to CM, 18 May 1964). The piece is presented to the reader from the outset as a kind of pop-art collage, summed up in the early line 'Let us cut out and assemble our pieces'. It opens with the following quotation: 'Unicornis the unicorn. No hunter can catch him but he can be trapped by the following stratagem. A virgin girl is led to where he lurks and there is sent off by herself into the wood. He soon leaps into her lap when he sees her and hence he gets caught' (1966b: 1–5). In the poem, this passage is attributed to the seventeenth-century critic Sir Thomas Browne, who did indeed devote a chapter of his *Vulgar Errors* of 1646 to exploding the unicorn myth, but he did not write these lines, which actually come from T.H. White's 1954 translation of a medieval bestiary *The Book of Beasts*. This misattribution is in no way highlighted or acknowledged, but this need not necessarily be read as an error on Carter's part: she was, after all, a would-be academic, fully aware of the importance of verifying her sources. Instead, it is linguistically reproducing one of the trademark techniques of 1960s pop art – the incongruous mixing of references from different sources. The 'Young Contemporaries Exhibition' of 1961 at the Royal Society of British Artists, for example, was described as follows:

> For these artists the creative act is nourished on the urban environment they have always lived in. The impact of popular art is present, but checked by puzzles and paradoxes about the play of signs at different levels of signification in their work, which combines real objects, same-size representation, sketchy notation, and writing. (Alloway, 1966: 53)

Taken out of a visual context, this could stand as a pretty good description of 'Unicorn', which forsakes veracity or accuracy in favour of the assembling of a seemingly random montage of references drawn from a variety of sources – medieval allegory, film, Romantic poetry and pornography, among other things. The poem is divided into three parts: 'a) *The Unicorn*', 'b) *The young girl*', and 'c) *Lights, action*'. The lines themselves often further subdivide, breaking down into fragments that resist the impulse to read the piece as a narrative sequence:

> As with the night-scented stock, the full
> splendour of the unicorn manifests itself most potently
> at twilight. Then the horn sprouts, swells, blooms
> in all its glory. SEE THE HORN
> (bend the tab, slit in slot
> marked 'X')
> SEE THE HORN SEE THE HORN SEE THE HORN (8–14)

In these lines, the unicorn appears as a type of what might be termed a 'montage-effect', possessing no existence beyond that which we construct. Instead he is a flimsy model assembled from pieces that appear as if they might have been cut out from the back of a cereal packet. The virgin, meanwhile, is positioned in diametrical opposition to him: where he is flat and one-dimensional, with only a tenuous existence, she is portrayed as resolutely earthy and robust: 'raw and huge' with 'breasts ... like carrier bags'. Ironically, though, this rather vulgar fleshiness contradicts her own pathetic desire to etherealize herself as a universal romantic heroine:

> she is comforting herself
> with the pathetic fallacy, 'even
> the trees weep for me
> in my predicament.' (25–8)

However, the inclusion of the directorial instruction, '*lights, action*' (15), reminds us that neither the virgin nor the unicorn have an independent existence beyond the mere fact of their representation. Instead, both are emptied of significance in a poem that, while it certainly can be read as a critique of sexual politics, does so through the play of surface, rather than in-depth and sustained exposition. As Andrew Duncan says, 'Montage can act like the conscious artificiality in Brechtian plays, anti-realistic gaits and gestures, which makes us conscious of the rules of genre, directing attention away from the poet and towards the way social institutions and symbolism are constructed' (Duncan, 2003: 86).

While Carter did not base all her poetry around medieval references, the effect remains the same: as in, for example, 'Venus Testudo Graeca' (1965), which imagines tortoise sex. It does not seem to be much fun: the male tortoise performs his 'drab genetic chore' on the female only because 'She is a challenge, to mount/her a gesture because she's there'. The poem resembles 'Unicorn' in both its deliberate demystification of romantic discourses surrounding sexuality and its determination to empty the subject (in this case, the male tortoise) of meaning:

> The chill blood sparks; the pulsing heart beat tolls,
> clangs in the tortoiseshell echo chamber (ah, inside –
> what pin-ups on the walls (as in other tanks); 'mother'
> in a heart tattooed on a flipper under a hem of sheer shell;
> a crouched lever-puller munches sardine sandwiches, throws
> the switch marked 'sex' setting all in unimagineable
> slow motion as he bites the top off a light-ale bottle. (1965: 5–11)

Although more cohesive than 'Unicorn', there is a similar process of deconstruction at work in this poem. The 'blood' and 'heart' mentioned in the first line are then contradicted by the notion of the tortoise as a machine, literally emptied out in order to become an 'echo chamber' containing 'a crouched lever-puller', who sets into motion a robotic copulation bereft of pleasure – indeed, bereft of any kind of feeling at all.

In many ways, much of Carter's poetry conforms to Robert Pinsky's description of the kind of surrealist tone adopted by the poets of the 1960s and early 1970s as:

> cool [...] a matter of dazzlingly, eloquently manifold surfaces, rather than depth: wild event or anecdote, rather than dream; inchoate, self-enclosed events rather than disclosed junctures; above all a daffy or sinister absurdity in this one reality, rather than a more profound realm beyond. (Pinsky, 1978: 82)

Carter was certainly reading surrealism at this time, translating poetry by Pierre Reverdy and André Breton which she was also (unsuccessfully) trying to get published in the little poetry magazines. Yet Pinsky's description of the surrealist sensibility of the 1960s poets is knowingly at odds with the idea, so central to surrealism, that its art should create 'a world transformed by imagination and desire' (Carter, 1997b: 509) and full of 'images or objects that are enigmatic, marvellous, erotic – or juxtapositions of objects, or people, or ideas, that arbitrarily extend our notions of the connections it is possible to make. In this way, the beautiful is put at the service of liberty' (Carter, 1997b: 512).

These are, in fact, Carter's words, taken from an article on surrealism she wrote for *Harpers & Queen* in 1978; but they are also ironic ones. In the 1960s, her love affair with surrealism was in full swing, but by 1978, she had 'got bored with it and wandered away' (Carter, 1997b: 512). She did so, she said, because she felt alienated by the movement's inability to regard women in anything other than symbolic terms, but the poems suggest that she was never *really* taken in by it, since none of them, no matter how 'surreal' in form, subscribe to this surrealist ideal of transformation.

Whatever she was to retrospectively claim, it does not seem that at this point in her career Carter was particularly concerned with deconstructing misogynistic images of women, although this was, of course, to become a central motivation in her later work. This is illustrated by one of her other medieval source poems, 'Two Wives and a Widow', which reproduces medieval anti-feminist rhetoric more or less word-for-word. The setting of the poem is a beautiful garden on Midsummer's Eve, in which the poet comes across three women discussing marriage. Although the backdrop lures the audience into thinking they are going to hear a narrative of courtly love, they are soon disabused of this notion once the women get into their narrative stride, drunkenly disparaging the sexual shortcomings of their husbands, both living and (in the case of the widow, of course) dead. Carter admiringly described this poem as 'one of the most obscene poems in the language': the women, in her words, 'none of them have the slightest bit of kindness or charity in their hearts – they're just randy bitches' (AC to CM, 19 June 1965). Carter's piece is a more or less straight translation of Dunbar's poem into contemporary idiomatic English, and although it is certainly possible to align her admiration for the protagonists of Dunbar's poem with her later support for what she was to term 'wayward girls and wicked women' rather than the virtuous and the virginal, in Carter's ventriloquization of a male poet's view of womanhood, it can also be read as exemplifying the extent to which she tended to veer away from an explicitly female point of view in her early writing. In 'Notes from the Front

Line', she critiqued her past self: 'that confused young person in her early twenties' who tended 'quite unconsciously – [to] posit a male point of view as a general one' (Carter, 1997a: 38). 'Two Wives and a Widow' certainly possesses the 'element of the male impersonator' (1997a: 38), from which Carter was to subsequently distance herself.

Instead, Carter's principal preoccupation in many of these poems – as the examples already cited illustrate – is with a more general deconstruction of the sentimental ideal of romance. Later, she was to specifically gender this critique by demonstrating the extent to which romantic discourse codifies and confines women, but here her concern is to divest the romantic myth of its glamour. This is exemplified by 'The Horse of Love', which echoes 'Unicorn' and 'Venus Testudo Graeca' in its hollowing out of the central subject – in this case, both literally *and* metaphorically. The poem opens in a fantasy world infused with colour and light:

> The colour of the round moon is yellow, yellow
> as lemons (old lemon slice moon) tumbling in
>   dark leaves.
> Sharp, clean and pleasing yellow; and
> This is the land where the lemon trees grow.
> The Horse of Love jumps over the moon, shaking
> out blue mythopaeic dust from mane, from tail,
> from fringed anemone eyes.
> Horse (of Love) bearing
> this clasped, amorous couple. (1966c: 1–10)

By the next stanza, however, the Horse of Love has become nothing but a moth-eaten 'hide' (17) under which the couple huddle, as their relationship becomes submerged under a deluge of bleak reality, listed with brutal directness:

> contraceptives, gas bills, curlers, pimples, body odour,
> face cream, stained vests, sanitary towels skulking
> rat-like under beds full of no rose petals but crumbs
> of last night's fish-paste sandwiches and the fecund
> milk bottles breeding under the sink
> etc. etc. etc. (1966c: 25–30)

And in the poem's last few lines, romance has become reduced to mere nursery-rhyme status, the equivalent of riding a 'pantomime horse' (33) upwards to a moon made of 'green cheese' (35).

The same cynicism can be detected in 'Poem for a Wedding Photograph'[3] in which the bride and groom become sundered from their individual and particular selves and cast adrift in the impersonal paraphernalia of the marriage ceremony:

> Dressed up, they are strangers to one another.
> They move awkwardly, smile
> the shy, nervous smiles of shipwrecked voyagers,
> never met on the crowded liner until now. (1966d: 4–7)

Subsequently, the click of the photographer's camera immobilizes the couple, who are

> ... taken. Frozen in this eternal moment,
>   forever.
> Scissored out of the fabric of their time,
> an icon of marriage [...] (18–21)

Absorbed into the marriage institution, the couple cease to be individuals, and are forced instead into a cultural template derived from 'the first man and wife of all and ever' (25). The photograph, stuck in 'a silver frame, for life' (26), does not represent a treasured memory, but the restrictions of a prison sentence. The protagonists of this poem have indeed been 'taken' by the sugar-coated blandishments of a romance narrative that exists to corral individuals into neatly classifiable pairs.

Not all of Carter's poetic work is concerned with abstract ideas – there are a few poems that could be classified as 'observational', their source material drawn from the everyday world around her. The cat poems, 'My Cat in Her First Spring' and 'Life-Affirming Poem About Small, Pregnant White Cat', published together in *Five Quiet Shouters*, as well as the unpublished 'Black Panther', not only signal the beginning of a long-standing fascination in Carter's writing with felines of all kinds – such as the tigers of *Nights at the Circus* and the short story 'Lizzie's Tiger'; the gentlemanly and savage beasts from *The Bloody Chamber* – but also demonstrate her drawing on scenes from her own life rather than from literary or wider cultural sources. Carter and her husband owned the cat, while the panther lived in Bristol Zoo. Carter had spotted it while working there as a washer up in the zoo café: she was attracted to it, she told Father Brocard, because she thought it 'looked as though it was a bit of a swine, on the quiet' (AC to FB, 1 March 1965).

The cat poems, first published in *Universities' Poetry* in 1965, then reproduced in *Five Quiet Shouters* in 1966, are particularly interesting to consider in view of my argument that Carter's separate poems are linked by their determination to empty the subject of meaning, reducing them to an emotionless play of surfaces. In 'My Cat in Her First Spring', the cat is full of sensual possibility, 'beginning to bud,/sprouting nipples all along her long, white breast'. Inside 'the rich fruit-cake of her dark recesses [...] wrinkled/intuitions of her summer roses stir and tremble in her sleep'. In 'Life-Affirming Poem About Small, Pregnant White Cat', that promise has come to fruition, and she is now a 'bulging sack of life', who, rather uncomfortably, is:

> [...] Stuffed full,
> brim-full
> FULL
> (to the teeth)
> with kittens, she yowls – and you fear an incontinent
> brindled kitten will burst wrongways, out of the pink
> front door. (1966f: 4–10)

As a result, the cat becomes a symbol of possibility:

> [...] (Miracle of Everyday Things) – inside her
> all the little furry commas lie blindly,
>   futurity in futurity
> stirring shifting waiting
>   to be born (1966f: 25–9)

But this was all imaginative speculation: Carter revealed to Barry Tebb that the idea of the cat's fecundity was a private joke because it was actually, she said, 'frigid. It won't go near other cats, even when its [sic] on heat, which is relatively often, shows no inclination whatsoever towards the sex act and seems likely to die a virgin' (AC to BT, 15 June 1966). This poem is not 'life-affirming' in the least – instead fertility remains mere supposition; a heavily ironic fantasy imposed upon a neurotic pet.

Carter's venture into poetry appears to have stopped quite abruptly in 1966. Apart from a single poem, 'The Dark Tower', published in *Triquarterly* in 1976, *Five Quiet Shouters*, scathingly dismissed in a review published in *The Aylesford Review* as 'mediocre' (VII/3, 196), marked both the climactic moment and the culmination of Carter's poetic phase. In fact, her momentum had already begun to flag towards the end of the previous year. In January 1966, she told Cavan McCarthy that 'I just can't kick any poetry or pseudo-poetry out of the bat-haunted recesses of my mind' (AC to CM, 4 January 1966), and by the time she was communicating with Barry Tebb about *Five Quiet Shouters* in June she was talking about her poetry in the past tense: 'I wrote a fair amount of pop art poetry like the first two and then got bored with it and stopped, and am feeling around as to where and how to go on' (AC to BT, 15 June, 1966). *Shadow Dance* was published the following month, on 4 July, and with the inception of her career as a novelist Carter's impulse to write poetry disappeared. In one of her final letters to Cavan McCarthy, she confessed: 'I've more or less dried up poetry-wise, and am contemplating writing a novel about Old Tyme Music Hall. I just found I was getting weaker & softer & softer & weaker, so will rest a while' (AC to CM, 5 May 1966).

While the novel about 'Old Tyme Music Hall' never appeared, in accordance with her belief in 'not wasting anything' (AC to FB, 11 January 1966), elements of her poetry were recycled in her subsequent prose. Of all Carter's books, *Several Perceptions*, which was written in 1967, but not published until 1968, is most obviously influenced by Carter's poetic interests. She told Father Brocard in 1966 that, following the publication of *Shadow Dance*, her next novel would be 'a metaphysical Merlin one, which is going to have great chunks of poetry in it which I won't be mature enough to do properly for about five years, so am mainly amassing material' (AC to FB, 9 November (?) 1966). That novel never appeared, and Carter went on to write *The Magic Toyshop*, but there are grounds for arguing that *Several Perceptions* constituted a kind of swansong to Carter's poetic ambitions, since it both begins and ends with allusions to her published verse. Old Sunny, the tramp who, on the novel's first page, is described playing an imaginary fiddle on the Down above Bristol originates from the poem 'On the Down', published in *The Aylesford Review* in 1965. Passages such as: 'Grave-clothes small-clothes flapped around his legs like small brown dogs [...]. Raptly he serenaded the tree, which dropped leaves on his head from time to time as if tossing contemptuous pennies' (Carter, 1995: 1) constitute more or less direct quotations from the earlier work, in which the tramp wears 'Grave-clothes small-clothes' which 'flap / around his ankles / like little brown dogs' (3–5), while:

> The tree drops
> leaves
> around him
> as if throwing
> contemptuous pennies. (12–16)

The white cat, who in the carnivalesque climax to the novel, gives birth 'to five kittens all as white as snow and beautiful as stars' (Carter, 1995: 148) is the 'small pregnant white cat' of the poem included in the *Five Quiet Shouters* anthology, finally delivered of her little furry commas.

So, what is the significance of Angela Carter's poetry: this slight collection of verse written on the periphery of the arts scene of the 1960s by an as yet anonymous Bristol undergraduate? Certainly, it lacks the dazzling inventiveness of her prose; although that is not to say that it is without merit. Both Rosemary Hill and Edmund Gordon agree that the poetry enables the honing of what was to become a powerful voice: Hill claims that Carter's poetry 'shows an extraordinary imagination finding its expression' (Hill, 2015: 49), while Gordon states that for most of the 1960s 'Poetry was [...] the form in which she explored ideas and indulged in her penchant for the fantastical' (Gordon, 2017: 78). The value of this small body of work, therefore, might not necessarily be found in the quality of the poetry itself, but, placed in the context of Carter's career as a whole, it provides us with a valuable body of juvenilia. *Shadow Dance* is a remarkable first novel because it delivers an artistic vision that is more or less fully formed: its central preoccupations with sexuality, dandyism and bricolage are ones that would continue to preoccupy its author more or less throughout her career. It was through the poetry written concurrently with *Shadow Dance* that Carter experimented with and honed the artistic concerns that were to become her literary hallmarks – her intertextuality, her polemicism, her refusal to condone mythologizing of any kind, no matter how consolatory. Interestingly, the poetry also reproduces, to a great extent, the tendency towards 'male impersonation' that she was later to identify as a hallmark of her early novels.

This chapter began with the observation that when she became a well-known writer, Carter herself never mentioned that she once had poetic ambitions. Her foray into the poetic world might have been intense, but it was also short-lived and, ultimately, something that she chose to erase from her autobiography. Why? I would hazard that, ever-zealous guardian of her own reputation that she became, Carter did not bring her early poetry to the attention of her readership because she suspected that it was, ultimately, a failure. Her final original poem of the sixties (that is, a poem that was not published later elsewhere) was 'Two Wives and a Widow', published in March 1966. But it could be argued that at this point Carter was still four months away from the launch of her real literary career; for her authentic voice – her distinctive, challenging and utterly individual voice – may not be found in her poetry, but her prose.

Notes

1 Although the main body of Carter's poetic output was published in the 1960s, she continued – very – occasionally to venture into verse. Three poems entitled 'Japanese Snapshots' (anthologised in the *Unicorn* collection) were published in *The Listener* in 1971, and a poem based on *The Sadeian Woman*, 'The Dark Tower', appeared in *Triquarterly* in 1976.
2 These details were provided by the poet Fred Beake in private email correspondence (13 March 2009).
3 This poem exists in two very different versions. The longer can be found in *The Aylesford Review* VII/4 (Winter 1965/Spring 1966), p. 272, but it is the second, abridged, version from *Five Quiet Shouters* that is being discussed here. (For publication details, see References.)

References

Alloway, Lawrence (1966), 'The Development of British Pop', in Lucy R. Lippard (ed.), *Pop Art* (London: Thames & Hudson) pp. 27–67.
Carter, Angela (1965), 'Venus Testudo Graeca', *Tlaloc* 3 (January): no page no.
—— (1966a), 'Two Wives and a Widow', *The London Magazine* (March), 31–40.
—— (1966b), 'Unicorn' (Leeds: Location Press).
—— (1966c), 'The Horse of Love', in Barry Tebb (ed.), *Five Quiet Shouters: An Anthology of Assertive Verse* (London: Poet & Printer), pp. 25–6.
—— (1966d) 'Poem for a Wedding Photograph', in Barry Tebb (ed.), *Five Quiet Shouters: An Anthology of Assertive Verse* (London: Poet & Printer), p. 27.
—— (1966e), 'My Cat in Her First Spring', in Barry Tebb (ed.), *Five Quiet Shouters: An Anthology of Assertive Verse* (London: Poet & Printer), p. 24.

—— (1966f) 'Life-Affirming Poem About Small, Pregnant White Cat', in Barry Tebb (ed.), *Five Quiet Shouters: An Anthology of Assertive Verse* (London: Poet & Printer), p. 24–5.

—— Carter, A. ([1968] 1995) *Several Perceptions* (London: Virago Press).

—— (1997a) 'Notes from the Front Line', in *Shaking a Leg: Collected Journalism and Writings*, ed. Jenny Uglow (London: Chatto & Windus), pp. 36–43.

—— (1997b) 'The Alchemy of the Word', in *Shaking a Leg: Collected Journalism and Writings*, ed. Jenny Uglow (London: Chatto & Windus), pp. 507–12.

Dowson, Jane and Alice Entwistle (2005), *A History of Twentieth-Century Women's Poetry* (Cambridge: Cambridge University Press).

Duncan, Andrew (2003), *The Failure of Conservatism in Modern British Poetry* (Cambridge: Salt Publishing).

Gordon, Edmund (2017), *The Invention of Angela Carter: A Biography* (London: Vintage).

Hill, Rosemary (2015), 'A Splinter in the Mind: The Poems of Angela Carter', *Unicorn: The Poetry of Angela Carter* (London: Profile Books), pp. 47–70.

Pinsky, Robert (1978), *The Situation of Poetry* (Princeton: Princeton University Press).

Sage, Lorna (1977), 'The Savage Sideshow: A Profile of Angela Carter', *The New Review*, 4 (39/40), 51–7.

Sheppard, Robert (2005), *The Poetry of Saying* (Liverpool: Liverpool University Press).

Smith, A.C.H. (1989), 'Arts Page', in James Belsey (ed.), *The 60s in Bristol* (Bristol: Redcliffe Press), 39–45.

Barry Tebb (ed.) (1966), *Five Quiet Shouters: An Anthology of Assertive Verse* (London: Poet & Printer).

Archive material

Correspondence between Angela Carter and Father Brocard Sewell (1 March 1965–5 July 1966). Unpublished letters. Aylesford Msss. Lilly Library, Indiana University, Bloomington.

Correspondence between Angela Carter and Cavan McCarthy (18 May 1965–undated 1966). Unpublished letters. *Tlaloc* archives, Special Collections, University College London.

Correspondence between Angela Carter and Barry Tebb (12 June 1966–13 July 1966). Unpublished letters. *The Review* archive, Folder 18. Northern Illinois University Libraries, DeKalb, Illinois.

5

Angela Carter's *objets trouvés* in translation: from Baudelaire to *Black Venus*

Martine Hennard Dutheil de la Rochère

> Translating someone else's writing can be a way of easing oneself back into one's poetry, using the other writer's work as a point of inspiration. (Bassnett, 2011: 166)

AN ENTHUSIASTIC, IF SLIGHTLY baffled, review of *The Infernal Desire Machines of Doctor Hoffman* aka *The War of Dreams* (1972), published 14 August 1974 in *Kirkus Reviews*, stresses the translated character of Angela Carter's surrealist-picaresque novel in an effort to reconcile the author's Englishness with the South American setting, hybrid form and extravagant style of this 'philosophico-magical phantasmagoria of a novel [that] reads, in the best sense, *as if it had been translated from the Spanish*. It is Borgesian but brisker, full of linguistic and logical games but never bogged down in them, borne along on a current of adventure' (*Kirkus Reviews*, emphasis added).

I propose to elaborate on the reviewer's grappling with the foreign feel of Carter's speculative fiction by arguing that the author evolved her unique, multi-layered, densely intertextual, punning and baroque style by actively engaging with foreign tongues, authors and movements, notably through her activity as a translator from the French – a long-overlooked aspect of her work that nevertheless played a crucial role in fashioning her own, distinct, voice.[1] From adolescence onward, Carter was an avid reader of French poetry. An integral part of foreign language acquisition, translation develops close reading skills and a keen awareness of linguistic and cultural difference, and so Carter acquired a deep and intimate knowledge of other texts, works and world-views that she responded to in dialogic or, as I have argued elsewhere, contrapuntal fashion.[2] Translation stimulated

Carter's imagination, reflection and creativity. From her early efforts to translate French and obscure middle-English poets in the mid-1960s, to her fully developed, systematic and comprehensive method of revisiting the fairy tale tradition in translating and rewriting Charles Perrault's *contes du temps passé* in *The Fairy Tales of Charles Perrault* (Perrault, 1977), from which *The Bloody Chamber and Other Stories* (Carter, 1979a) evolved, Carter used translation as a laboratory of creation, and so shared Henri Meschonnic's view that 'If translation is writing ... Translating is translating only when translation is a laboratory for writing' (Meschonnic, 1999: 459).[3]

During her studies at Bristol University, Carter jotted down in her journal: 'I am very, very weary of English literature' (Carter, MS 1962–63).[4] To get away from the Leavisite great tradition that she comically described as the '"eat up your broccoli" approach to fiction' (Carter, 1998a: 490), Carter developed an interest in medieval literature, and read extensively in French – especially Charles Baudelaire and other authors associated with the surrealist movement. Already as a teenager she 'used to sing along to a record of Baudelaire's poems as if they were pop songs' (Carter quoted by Tonkin 2012: 113; see also Gordon 2016: 36). A few years later, she referred to Baudelaire's *Les Fleurs du mal* (Baudelaire, 1857) in a diary entry dated 1 November 1961, looking back on her adolescent passion for the poet with abrasive humour and a good dose of self-mockery, but returning to his poetry all the same:

> When I was young & inexperienced, I adored Baudelaire because he was such a luscious, juicy phony; re-reading 'Spleen,' I got scared – not because of the terrifying vision, it still seems over-done & melodramatic ('plante sur mon crâne son drapeau noir' indeed) but because a man who will go to these lengths simply to frighten himself is indeed in a horrifying state of mind. (Carter, MS 1961)[5]

This quotation is preceded by a reference to Edgar Allan Poe's 'Annabel Lee', which suggests that Carter was keenly aware of the role played by translation in Baudelaire's own poetry, as well as his borrowing of the English word *spleen* to capture its dominant mood.[6] Baudelaire's name often crops up in her notebooks, usually in connection with surrealism. Carter read widely in this area, including critical studies on poetry, art and cinema that had a profound impact on her work. Marcel Raymond's *De Baudelaire au surréalisme* (Raymond, 1933), read in the original language in late 1964 or early 1965 (see Watz, 2017: 45), notably influenced her perception of the role of Baudelaire as a precursor of surrealism.[7] In her correspondence to Father Brocard Sewell, editor of the literary journal *Aylesford Review*, Carter enclosed 'bits of translations' from a book she was reading at the time 'about the inter-war surrealists' which, Watz surmises, is probably Marcel Raymond's study.[8] She reports that 'In a letter to Sewell, dated 1 March 1965, Carter quotes verses from a poem by Pierre Reverdy which, she claims, "knocked [her] out", and one by Andre [sic] Breton, intending "to show you", as she explains in another letter, "What I was liking then" (pers. comm.)' (Watz, 2017: 14–15). Watz also refers to another letter addressed to Cavan McCarthy, founder of the poetry magazine *Tlaloc*, who published some of her poetry in the mid-1960s, about her plans to translate 'some Andre [sic] Breton this summer' which she hopes *Tlaloc* will publish, 'an indication of an early interest in the possibility of establishing herself as a translator of French (pers. comm.) (Letter dated 11 May 1965)' (Watz, 2017: 15).[9] Later on that year, she jots down in her blue diary: 'I don't know about poetry. Maybe try some more translation'. And near the end, in a to-do list ('What I want to do'): 'Learn French well enough to translate it' (Carter, MS 1965–66).[10]

Carter even placed Japan, where she resided from 1969 to 1971, under the sign of Baudelaire.[11] The Japan notebooks record the dense interweaving of Carter's love life with reading foreign literature and writing surrealism-inspired fiction. The writer had a passionate love affair surrealist-style with Sozo Araki, upon whom she seems to have projected the erotic and poetic principles of Breton's *hasard objectif* (objective chance).[12] Breton's autobiographical writings in *Nadja* (1928/1962), *Les vases communicants* (1932) and *L'Amour fou* (1937) are thus echoed in Carter's semi-autobiographical pieces in *Fireworks* (Carter, 1974), down to the erotic encounters and aimless wanderings of the *flâneuse* in Tokyo.

Carter saw her Japanese lover as a 'Baudelairian dandy', and an extension of the wonderful city of Tokyo itself.[13] Their relationship, which was transmuted in 'A Souvenir of Japan' and 'Flesh and the Mirror', parallels the trajectory of the high hopes of surrealism turning into an 'amour déçu' (disillusioned love) in *Surréalisme et sexualité* (Gauthier, 1971). Carter expressed her own disenchantment with the movement in her 1978 essay 'The Alchemy of the Word':

'The surrealists also fell in love. Love, passionate, heterosexual love, together with freedom, from which it was inextricable, was their greatest source of inspiration'. But she remarks that 'their women live vividly on the page at second hand. Gala, who left Eluard for Dali. Elsa Triolet [...] Youki Desnos. The three wives of Breton' (Carter, 1998b: 512). In short, 'The surrealists were not good with women', so she 'had to give them up in the end' (Carter, 1998b: 512). And yet, she adds that 'the old juices can still run' when she hears the old slogan 'The marvellous alone is beautiful' (Carter, 1998b: 512).[14] In a sense, Sozo Araki crystallized Carter's attraction to the surrealist movement as promising erotic liberation and female creativity, and he became a male muse of sorts in a characteristic reversal of the traditional pattern exemplified by Baudelaire and the surrealists, as Carter reinvented herself as a writer and a woman in Japan.

In her 1970 notebook, she describes the summer *hanabi* festival, after which *Fireworks*, her collection of semi-autobiographical short fiction, is named, as the epitome of Japanese culture and aesthetics as follows:

> The word for firework is 'hannabi', 'fire-flower'; they are the morning glories of the night and possess that quality of evanescence which gives Japan its unquestionable tragic style and its amazing, death-defying elegance, that of a Baudelairean dandy, who has made of artifice a kind of heroism. For this is a great country for appearances and it is often hard to tell what is real and what is not. [...] goodbye, Plato; au revoir, Descartes; auf wiedersehen, Hegel, you did swell. (Carter, MS 1969–74)

In her journal, Carter sums up the 'cardinal virtues' of the surrealist movement according to André Breton as 'a) convulsive beauty b) objective chance c) black humour d) amour fou' (Carter, MS 1969–70).[15]

These key features of the movement shed light on Carter's love life as inseparable from her reading, translating and writing during these years. In her blue and grey notebook for 1972, she praises the beauty of another lover among quotes from Breton, Baudelaire and Gauthier, and ponders alternative translations of Breton's ode to sex in *L'Amour fou*:

> amour, seul amour qui soit, amour charnel, j'adore, je n'ai jamais cessé d'adorer ton ombre vénéneuse, ton ombre mortelle

> Carnal love, the only one I love there is, I've never ceased to adore your venomous shadow, your mortal shade
> Carnal love, the unique form of love how I adore, how I've always adored! your poisoned shadow, your mortal shadow. (Carter, MS 1972)

Further on, she quotes the same passage from Breton's exaltation of love more fully, including its 'mysterious perversions' catalogued by Gauthier in *Surréalisme et sexualité*: 'amour, seul amour qui soit, amour charnel, j'adore, je n'ai jamais cessé d'adorer ton ombre vénéneuse, ton ombre mortelle. Un jour viendra où l'homme saura te reconnaître pour son seul maître et t'honorer jusque dans les mystérieuses perversions dont tu t'entoures' (Breton, 1937). ('Love, only love that you are, carnal love, I adore, I have never ceased to adore your lethal shadow, your mortal shadow. A day will come where man will be able to recognize you for his only master, honoring you even in the mysterious perversions you surround him with' (Breton, 1987: 76)).[16]

Shortly after her stay in Japan, translation offered Carter another opportunity to renew her intimacy with surrealist poetry. She embarked on an ambitious translation project when she decided to turn *Surréalisme et sexualité* into English.[17] Even though she chose not to publish her translation after an anonymous reviewer faulted it for being 'a hopeless garble of jargon and isms' (quoted by Watz, 2017: 2), Gauthier's study sensitized her to the problematic sexual politics of the surrealist movement, and revived her interest in translation as a creative method. *The Infernal Desire Machines of Doctor Hoffman*, written during her transformative years in Japan, already reflects Carter's growing dissatisfaction with the liberating potential of surrealism for women, but the Gauthier translation project gave her an opportunity to explore the contradictions of the movement while sharpening her own 'feminist-surrealist idiom' (Watz, 2017: 177). It is interesting to note that on the first page of her translation of Gauthier's study, Carter criticizes the French feminist scholar's indictment of the sexual politics of surrealism for failing to acknowledge the very different positions of the writers and artists associated with the movement:

> Here, a first question. The author of this book regards as an internal contradiction or, worse, an unpardonable weakness, what seems to us a simply [sic] divergence of idiosyncrasies. The Andre Breton's mythology of love, centred around the marvellous meeting with the

'only woman,' the lost segment of the primordial androgyne, is very distant from Max Ernst's 'woman with a hundred heads' or Bellmer's doll. And she may herself be accused of artifice to have accused all the surrealists [sic] artists, with but few exceptions, of the crime of androcentricism [sic]. Breton's repugnance on the subject of perversion is hardly the signed [sic] of a shared ideology. I think myself that Breton, like all leaders of groups, tried to claim his own convictions were common to all. But that does not justify the contradictory attitudes of the surrealists to sexuality. (Carter, MS 1973)

Moreover, Carter would keep on emulating surrealist poetic devices, including collage, *cadavre exquis*, wordplay, analogies and black humour as a means to stimulate her creativity, including the technique of *objets trouvés* in translation.[18] Carter's method of reading across languages, genres and art forms thus highlights the *translational poetics* that characterizes her fiction during this period.

Found in translation: Xavière Gauthier's *Surréalisme et sexualité*

Several elements from Xavière Gauthier's study percolated in Carter's fiction, first and foremost the theme of androgyny central to *The Passion of New Eve* (Carter, 1977).[19] *Surréalisme et sexualité* also found an echo in Carter's polemical essay on Sade, *The Sadeian Woman: An Exercise in Cultural History* (Carter, 1979b), while emulating Gauthier's feminist cultural critique in contrapuntal fashion: written in a simple, easy, non-academic style with no footnotes (in marked contrast with Gauthier's study), *The Sadeian Woman* provocatively proposes to rehabilitate Sade as a 'moral pornographer' in the service of women, which unsurprisingly triggered outraged reactions from radical feminists.[20] This polemic has been well documented, and my interest lies elsewhere: translating Gauthier's study also meant translating a number of poems (or excerpts) that Gauthier liberally quotes from, including verse by René Crevel, André Breton, Louis Aragon, Paul Eluard, Jacques Prévert, Joyce Mansour and Antonin Artaud, as well as passages from Breton's *L'Amour fou, Les vases communicants, Arcane 17* and *Nadja* among others.[21]

In an oft-quoted passage from 'Notes from the Front Line', Carter encourages 'the reader to construct her own fiction for herself from the elements of my fictions' (Carter, 1998c: 37), and memorably associates intellectual development with critical and creative reading: 'Reading is just as creative an activity as writing and most intellectual development depends upon new readings of old texts. I am all for putting new wine in old bottles, especially if the pressure of the new wine makes the old bottles explode' (Carter, 1998c: 37). The potent 'new wine in old bottles' image, which Carter had already used in the conclusion to her BA thesis, took on a new significance in the light of surrealist imagery that Gauthier's study analyses from a feminist perspective in *Surréalisme et sexualité*.

In particular, Gauthier elaborates on the 'femme-fruit' (fruit-woman) as an object to be enjoyed and consumed (Gauthier, 1971: 115), and even reproduces a painting by René Magritte entitled *La Dame* (1936) representing a woman in a bottle.[22] She observes that Magritte puts a woman in a bottle, where others would put wine ('Magritte met la "femme en bouteille" comme d'autres y mettent le vin' (Gauthier 1971: 117)), and mentions Meret Oppenheim's surrealist installation *Le Festin* displaying a woman covered with food at the international surrealist exhibition of 1959–60.[23] Xavière Gauthier's critique of surrealist imagery, however, is nuanced, as it recognizes the ironic dimension of the surrealist approach to the portrayal of women in Western art, underlines the subversive potential of the aesthetics of perversion, and refers to the contribution of female artists like Meret Oppenheim, Dorothea Tanning and, especially, Joyce Mansour. Another quote that resonates with Carter's turning of the biblical parable against putting new wine in old bottles upside down is René Crevel's ode to sexual desire and release in *Le clavecin de Diderot* (Diderot's harpsichord) (Crevel, 1932), quoted in the first chapter of Gauthier's study:

> Mais on a beau être conservateur, le foutre ne veut
> Pas se laisser mettre en bouteille
> tandis qu'un cerveau,
> Si on ne le porte que le Dimanche, jour de repos,
> pour ne pas l'user trop vite
> la semaine, on le range ... (Crevel, 1932: 58, quoted by Gauthier, 1971: 29)

Carter translates Crevel's quote as follows:

> But it's a fine thing to be conservative, the come doesn't want
> To be bottled

whereas a brain,
If only worn on Sunday, the day of rest,
So you don't use it up too quickly,
and keep it in check during the week… (Carter, MS 1973)

The juxtaposition of Magritte's picture of the bottled woman and Crevel's imagery draws attention to the contentious sexual politics of the surrealist movement, and inevitably raises the question of its emancipatory potential for women, a concern that Angela Carter and Xavière Gauthier both shared. Translating *Surréalisme et sexualité* thus fed into the 'experiments of thought' carried out in Carter's laboratory of literary creation, giving a new impulse and direction to her fiction, which Carter herself described later (with some misgivings) as a form of 'literary criticism' (Haffenden, 1985: 79).

The first chapter of Gauthier's study, titled 'L'espoir surréaliste' (surrealist hope), is filled with erotic-lyrical poems by Breton, including the famous surrealist ode to free love, 'L'Union libre' ('Free Union'), celebrating his wife's body in striking images, as well as excerpts from Aragon's cycle of poems to Elsa, melancholic woman-centred poems by Prévert, and several exalted love poems by Eluard, which all celebrate the magical encounter and sexual union of the lovers. In stark contrast, chapter two opens with Baudelaire's misogynistic declaration in *Mon coeur mis à nu* (*My Heart Laid Bare*): 'Woman is natural – that is, abominable' (Gauthier 1971: 42). Further on, Gauthier quotes another sarcastic jibe by the same author: 'Aimer les femmes intelligentes est un plaisir de pédéraste' in *Fusées* (Baudelaire, 1897) ('To love an intelligent woman is a pleasure for pederasts' in *Rockets*) (Carter, MS 1973). In the chapter dealing with sexual perversions, Gauthier also reports the anecdote of Baudelaire seeking sexual relief from one of his muses, Mme Sabatier, who 'gets nowhere' with him, and so he ends up returning to Jeanne Duval as his 'bordel à domicile' (stay-at-home whore) where he can feel superior to a woman, according to René Crevel (quoted by Gauthier, 1971: 236).

Carter not only translated Breton's famous poem 'L'Union libre', but also lesser-known lines from Breton's 'Le Marquis de Sade a regagné' ('The Marquis de Sade Recovered') which echo her own interest in the revolutionary potential of Sade's writings:

> He never ceased to issue mysterious orders
> Which open a breach in the moral night

Through that breach I see
Great shadows breaking the old undermined bark
Dissolve. (Carter, MS 1973)

Il n'a cessé de jeter les ordres mystérieux
Qui ouvrent une brèche dans la nuit morale
C'est par cette brèche que je vois
Les grandes ombres craquantes la vieille écorce minée
Se dissoudre. (Gauthier, 1971: 51 and quoted again 1971: 205)

Although Gauthier only marginally refers to female surrealists, she reproduces several poems by the Paris-based Egyptian-British poet Joyce Mansour, whose self-portrayal as a praying mantis, and provocative use of violent sexual imagery, may have intrigued Carter, and perhaps even spurred her own reclamation of Sade. Chapter two of Gauthier's study, titled 'Perversions', opens with a lengthy quote from Sade's *La philosophie dans le boudoir* (Gauthier, 1971: 207) and details various transgressive sexual practices represented in surrealist art.[24] Gauthier also liberally quotes from Mansour's candid and incandescent lesbian poems with their disturbing association of love, pleasure and violence:

In the red velvet of your belly
In the blackness of your secret cries
I've penetrated ...
And the earth balances turning and singing
And my head bursts apart with joy
I am the whirlwind of Gomorrah. (Carter, MS 1973)

Dans le velours rouge de ton ventre
Dans le noir de tes cris secrets
J'ai pénétré...
Et la terre se balance en tournant en chantant
Et ma tête se dévisse de joie,
Je suis le tourbillon de Gomorrhe. (Gauthier, 1971: 244)

Mansour's brazen poetry is also abundantly quoted in the chapter devoted to 'L'Echec surréaliste' ('The Surrealist Failure') in Gauthier's study, followed by an account of the descent into madness of Leonora Carrington and Antonin Artaud (Gauthier, 1971: 301). Chapter XVII of *Surréalisme et sexualité* ends on a lighter note with a section on language games such as 'Anagrammes, jeux de mots, contrepétries' (Gauthier,

1971: 328) ('Anagrams, wordplay, spoonerisms' in Carter's typescript) that also figure prominently in Carter's fiction.

From *The Infernal Desire Machines of Doctor Hoffman* to Surrealism and Sexuality: 'new wine in old bottles' surrealist style

The Infernal Desire Machines of Doctor Hoffman (Carter, 1972), which uncannily anticipates Gauthier's critique of surrealist aesthetics in fictional form, revisits the speculative fiction of the Enlightenment epitomized by Jonathan Swift's *Gulliver's Travels* surrealist-style, as it maps Carter's self-estrangement in Japan onto a fantasized South America.[25] Told by the 'mestizo' narrator Desiderio, who observes the European movement embodied by the mad Doctor Hoffman from a wry, ironic distance, the picaresque novel mocks the surrealist utopianism that Frida Kahlo would dismiss with a laugh. Kahlo, a Mexican artist associated with surrealism, was free of the fascination exerted by its famous male proponents whom she described as 'parasites of the bunch of rich bitches who admire their work', which Carter gleefully (mis)quoted in her notes for a review on the painter.

Angela Carter not only experimented with translation across languages and cultures, but also across genres and media, and this informs the creative dynamic that brings together *The Infernal Desire Machines of Doctor Hoffman, Surrealism and Sexuality* and Carter's polemical essay *The Sadeian Woman: An Exercise in Cultural History*, which she was also working on at the time.[26] The notion of the hybrid, metamorphic text so central to her literary practice therefore challenges traditional boundaries between critical and creative writing, visual and narrative art, as well as fiction and life, since Carter's disillusionment with surrealism echoed the end of her affair with her Japanese lover whom she had so heavily invested with surrealist hopes. Carter thus drew creative and subversive (even explosive) energy from productive differences between art forms whose material she transposed, transformed and *transcreated* in her own writing. This complex and dynamic process takes place *across* genres and discourses (including philosophy, psychoanalysis and literary criticism), as well as media (paintings, drawings, installations, photographs, films, critical studies ...).[27]

As Anna Watz has well demonstrated, Carter's response to the surrealist movement is indebted to Xavière Gauthier's study, which according to the French psychoanalyst, writer and philosopher Jean-Bertrand Pontalis reflects a fundamental ambivalence that he attributes to Gauthier's disillusionment with the revolutionary promise of the movement akin to an 'amour déçu' (Gauthier, 1971: 9) (a lost or disillusioned love). Even though Carter dismisses Pontalis's preface as 'a piece of Fr. academic infighting' in her covering letter to Marion Boyars (of the publishers Calder and Boyars), and recommends that it should not be included in the new publication, Pontalis captures the significance of Gauthier's nuanced assessment of the sexual politics of surrealist art and thought, and aptly refers to the 'ready-made' in terms of 'translation' (Gauthier, 1971: 15). In her turn, Carter used Gauthier as a kind of 'ready-made' that she would 'decant' into her own work, as she found inspiration in Gauthier's exploration of a fundamental contradiction between the glorification of monogamous and idealized love or *amour fou* in Breton, Aragon and Dali on the one hand, and a fascination for free, polymorphous and transgressive forms of sexuality in Bellmer, Ernst and Trouille on the other. The originality of Gauthier's thesis, Pontalis argues, indeed lies in diagnosing these antagonist myths of the 'eternal feminine' as child-bride ('femme-enfant') or debauched whore as two sides of the same coin, both deriving from male sexual fantasies and androcentric culture – which would inform Carter's own 'demythologizing' project.

Gauthier wittily used a spoonerism by Robert Desnos as an epigraph to her study: 'Rrose Sélavy demande si les Fleurs du Mal ont modifié les moeurs du phalle: qu'en pense Omphale?' ('Rrose Sélavy asks if *The Flowers of Evil* has changed the mores of the phallus: what do you think, Omphale?')[28] (Desnos, 1930). In turn, Carter reproduced the French quote in her 1971 notebook among other references to the surrealist movement and its legacy, and placed *The Infernal Desires of Doctor Hoffman* under the aegis of another spoonerism by Desnos: 'Les lois de nos désirs sont des dés sans loisir' (Desnos, 1930) ('The laws of our desires are dice without leisure').[29] Rrose Sélavy, one of Marcel Duchamp's personas, whose name punningly celebrates *eros* (libido) as the principle of life, is also associated with a famous photograph series of the author in drag taken by Man Ray. This sexual ambiguity, echoed in Carter's first speculative novel, holds centre-stage in *The Passion of New Eve* (Carter, 1977), which freely borrows from Desnos's *La Liberté ou l'amour* (1927) among other sources, as Susan Rubin Suleiman has pointed out (Suleiman, 1990: 137). Gauthier's study discusses the surrealists' passion for Sade and sexual transgression throughout her work, especially in the second part of chapter two, which lists various perversions, including sado-masochism. Several surrealists notoriously referenced Sade as a radical revolutionary in their work, like Clovis Trouille in *Luxure* (*Dolmancé au château de la Coste*)[30] (1959) (reproduced in Gauthier, 1971: 257). The painting by Trouille represents half-naked women in bondage with chubby buttocks and breasts bared, about to be whipped by a pensive (but visibly roused) Marquis. The artist embedded it as a poster 'interdit aux moins de 50 ans' (forbidden for men and women below 50) in another painting, 'Voyeuse', which depicts a young woman in a yellow dress peeping through a purple curtain that Carter chose for the original cover of *The Sadeian Woman* published by Virago in 1979 (see figure 1).

1 Original cover of *The Sadeian Woman* published by Virago in 1979.

Needless to say, the book outraged some puritanical feminists, which greatly amused Carter: 'If I can get up Susanne Kappeler's nose, to say nothing of the Dworkin proboscis', she observed, 'then my living has not been in vain' (quoted by Gordon, 2016: 292). Carter's close friend and Virago editor, Carmen Callil, courageously defended this choice of cover.

Carter's description of the Count's dress in 'The Erotic Traveller' chapter of *The Infernal Desire Machines*, his 'black cloak' and 'diabolical elegance' (Carter, 1972: 122), and his obscene outfit in the 'bestial room' episode during his visit to 'The House of Anonymity' (down to the 'hood-like masks' – Carter, 1972: 129), are modelled on the surrealist artist Jean Benoît's costume for his sculpture, *Execution of the Testament of the Marquis de Sade* (1950). Carter reproduced a picture of the outlandish costume in her 1971 notebook (Carter, MS 1969–70), and transposed it in her own narrative with a comic, deflating twist. She also pasted a cutout of 'The Necrophile' (dedicated to Sergeant Bertrand) (1965) in the same notebook entry, both taken from Sarane Alexander's *Surrealist Art* (1970).[31] The image evokes a number of emblematic figures in Carter's fiction, from the cruel but grotesque Count in *The Infernal Desire Machines* to the sadistic Marquis of 'The Bloody Chamber' and the sinister Duke in 'Wolf-Alice' (Carter, 1979a), who dwells in a ruined castle and feeds on corpses (literalized *cadavres exquis*) dug up in the graveyard of the neighbouring village. Carter's treatment of the legacy of surrealism is therefore humorous, ironic and parodic, as it turns the black humour injunction against the movement itself in an ambivalent gesture of appropriation, homage, emulation and derision.

In her fictional reworking of the sado-masochistic costuming in *The Infernal Desire Machines of Doctor Hoffman*, Carter does not glamorize the Sadeian figure, but emphasizes his grotesqueness, existential vacuity and inability to relate to other human beings instead.[32] The brothel scene focalizes on the prostitutes' pain and degradation as they are reduced to objects of the Count's mindless, brutal and destructive desire, mediated by her male but empathetic narrator. Pontalis had already noted what he calls 'the inexhaustible bestiary of the female body in surrealist imagery' ('cet inépuisable bestiaire du corps féminin qu'est l'imagerie surréaliste') (Gauthier 1971: 12), which Carter literalizes in the episode of the brothel.[33] The dense intertextuality characteristic of her writing style accordingly reflects her engagement not only with her literary and visual sources but also with the reception of surrealism in critical discourse, and brings a fuller understanding of Carter's position in feminist debate.

Carter went on to transpose, rework and fictionalize elements of Gauthier's study in *The Passion of New Eve* as part of a process of *transcreation* that characterizes her work, picking up on Gauthier's discussion of the figure of the *androgyne* central to surrealist art and thought, which concludes her study. Likewise, she both reclaims and critiques Sade from a woman's perspective in *The Sadeian Woman*, not unlike Joyce Mansour before her. Carter would also contribute to the (re)discovery of female figures associated with the movement, such as Frida Kahlo, Meret Oppenheim and Leonora Carrington among others. Her English translation of Carrington's short story 'La Débutante' for her anthology *Angela Carter's Book of Wayward Girls and Wicked Women* (Carter, 1986) testifies to this. However, this interest in the contribution of female surrealists did *not* lead her to simply reject or condemn surrealist art by male authors. Just as she would use Sade to intervene in the feminist debate on pornography by polemically presenting him as a 'moral pornographer' in *The Sadeian Woman*, Carter would investigate the contradictions of the movement as well as the different strategies, productions and positions of the figures associated with it, reflecting on their contemporary relevance and responding to them in her own fiction (see Sheets, 1991). The shock tactics of surrealist art made it a good tool to think with, and *The Infernal Desire Machines of Doctor Hoffman* presents a repertoire of images that encourage the questing hero Desiderio to sharpen his critical faculties as a fundamental tool for emancipation (and through him the reader), bearing out Anna Watz's point about Carter's 'libertarian aesthetics'. The power of visual and verbal images celebrated by surrealists also owes a lot to Baudelaire, a figure both admired and demystified by Carter in her later work.

Baudelaire goes viral: from the ode to Venus to the price of (venereal) love, 'Black Venus' or writing in prosaic counterpoint

Carter's teenage infatuation with Baudelaire still resonates in *The Bloody Chamber and Other Stories* (Carter, 1979a), in connection with the Sadeian figure haunting the eponymous story. Two quotes from Baudelaire's journals are even used as epigraphs in Carter's working notes for 'The Bloody Chamber':

Il y a dans l'acte de l'amour une grande resemblance avec la torture ou avec une opération surgicale [sic].
(The act of love strongly resembles torture or a surgical operation)

Quand j'aurai inspiré le dégout [sic] et l'horreur universels, j'aurai conquis la solitude.[34] (Carter, MS BL 2018)
('When I have inspired disgust and universal horror, I will have conquered solitude)

In characteristically ambiguous and ironic fashion, the perverse Bluebeard-like Marquis quotes his favourite poet to justify the cruel treatment of his young bride on aesthetic grounds: '"There is a striking resemblance between the act of love and the ministrations of a torturer," opined my husband's favourite poet' (Carter, 1979a: 27). He also recites the opening lines of the erotic poem 'Les Bijoux' ('The Jewels', one of the censored pieces from the Jeanne Duval cycle) before raping her (Carter, 1979a: 17): 'Rapt, he intoned: "Of her apparel she retains / Only her sonorous jewellery"' ('La très-chère était nue, et, connaissant mon cœur / Elle n'avait gardé que ses bijoux sonores') (Baudelaire, 1857). The play on rape-rapt, two words linked etymologically, captures the Marquis's aestheticization of sexual violence and death, symbolized by his decision to have his bride wear a ruby choker that painfully bites into her skin during sex. This motif is derived from Baudelaire, Carter jotting down in her notes that objects and jewels 'become so many symbols of wickedness, lust or cruelty' in his poetry (Carter, MS BL 2018). 'The Bloody Chamber' thus marks a shift of point of view to explore the woman's perspective.

Baudelaire is even more openly referenced in *Black Venus's Tale*, which appeared shortly after in Next Editions (Carter, 1980). Centring on Baudelaire's creole mistress, 'Black Venus' was later included in the eponymous collection of short fiction in 1985.[35] In an interview with Anne Smith, Carter described Baudelaire's cycle of poems devoted to Duval in *Les Fleurs du mal* as 'incredibly beautiful and also terribly offensive' (quoted by Tonkin, 2012: 114), and she responded to them accordingly. As Rebecca Munford has also noted (Munford, 2004), allusions to Baudelaire are scattered throughout Carter's work, from *Shadow Dance* (Carter, 1966) to *Nights at the Circus* (Carter, 1984) and onto *Wise Children* (Carter, 1991), but they most fully come to fruition in *Black Venus's Tale*.[36] Designed by Julian

2 Cover of *Black Venus's Tale* published by Next Editions in 1980.

Rothenstein, the booklet contains three woodcuts by Philip Sutton, aside from the front cover (see figure 2).

Carter's text is supplemented with Baudelaire's poem 'Sed non satiata' facing a black-and-white reproduction of Edouard Manet's oil painting of Baudelaire's creole mistress (*La Dame à l'éventail ou La Maîtresse de Baudelaire*, 1862).[37] We recall that Manet's iconic *Le Déjeuner sur l'herbe* illustrates John Berger's point about men as active subjects and women as passive objects of the male gaze in Western art in *Ways of Seeing* (Berger, 1972), to which Carter in turn responds: 'He is artful, the creation of culture. Woman is: and is therefore, fully dressed in no clothes at all, her skin is common property, [...] that, he insists, is the most abominable of artifices' (Carter, 1980: 10).[38] The blurb gives the gist of the tale as follows:

> Black Venus's Tale is a description of a woman forced, involuntarily, to become a muse, done mostly from her own point of view, because you can only make a real person into a muse by ignoring the reality of them. The characters in this story bear an imaginative relation to the great poet, Charles Baudelaire and his mistress, Jeanne Duval aka Jeanne Prosper aka Jeanne Lemer; the story is about romanticism, negritude, colonialism, syphilis and contingency. (Carter, 1980)

Carter's tale is part of a series of 'New Tales' by contemporary poets and writers including Ted Hughes, J.G. Ballard and Sara Maitland, and poetry by Ossip Mandelstam, Elaine Feinstein, Tom Nairn and Liz Lochhead.[39]

The story of Black Venus notoriously shifts the focus from the poet to his creole mistress and imagines the miserable childhood and the harsh material conditions in which Baudelaire's muse made a living in Paris, as well as the nature of their relationship that she imaginatively reconstructs from Jeanne Duval's perspective: no longer the eroticized and exoticized muse, she is struggling against destitution, disease and old age, but somehow manages to put her famous lover's legacy to good use. Carter's optimistic alternative version thus deliberately departs from Nadar's poignant visual testimony of spotting Duval in the street, toothless, hairless and hobbling on her way to the pawnshop. In short, Carter invents a happy ending for Jeanne (fairy-tale fashion), using Baudelaire's poetry as the wings that carry the muse back to Martinique where she can prosaically settle as a respectable and fairly well-to-do whore ('she had come down to earth') (Carter, 1980: 13).

The short story reads like a prosaic, feminist materialist counterpoint to Baudelaire's exalted ode to his beloved as an exotic ship-like vessel capable of carrying him away from the *spleen* that brings him down, and yet threatening to exhaust him with her insatiable lust. Carter problematizes the double idealizing/demonizing movement of Baudelaire's representation of his muse and ironizes his sexual anxiety at not being able to satisfy her. She focuses on Jeanne's precarious existence as a stranger in Paris triply marginalized by her class, race and gender (she is from the French colony of the Antilles and can barely make herself understood in the capital), owing to her status as a kept woman whose body is her sole commodity. Thanks to Baudelaire, however, she manages to reverse the situation after his death, when she makes a comfortable living by selling a few manuscripts and memorabilia of the poet in Carter's imaginary vindication of the creole muse – including 'the veritable, the authentic, the true Baudelairean syphilis' (Carter, 1980: 14). This revisits, appropriates and reinterprets the famous line at the end of one of the 'pièces condamnées' (condemned poems), 'A celle qui est trop gaie' ('To she who is too gay'), when the poetic persona addresses his pretty, young and light-hearted lover. He wants to wound her for being carefree and immune from the spleen that affects the poet-lover, and threatens to instil his 'venom' into her ('T'infuser mon venin, ma soeur!') (Baudelaire, 1857) ('Inject my venom, O my sister!', online translation by Geoffrey Wagner, 1974). The image was deemed blasphemous by the judges who, sensing an allusion to the poet's syphilis, censored the volume. Carter, on the contrary, activates the obscene, physical meaning, but imagines how the woman turned the disease into a selling asset and thrived on it, as an optimistic alternative to the historical record (Jeanne as a prematurely aged and toothless destitute in Paris) in a kind of feminist-surrealist *humour noir* gesture of reclamation and remediation of the exotic muse.

Characteristically, Carter modernizes the style of the poem which she translates as though to adapt it to the woman who inspired it, and accordingly her entire text enacts the casual gesture of Jeanne using 'another spill out of a dismantled sonnet to ignite a fresh cheroot' (Carter, 1980: 7) as its main creative principle, since it is woven through with fragments of *Les Fleurs du mal*, especially the poems to Jeanne in *Spleen et idéal* and the famous condemned poems. Carter translates the first stanza of 'Sed non satiata' as follows:

> Weird goddess, dusky at night,
> reeking of musk smeared on tobacco,
> a shaman conjured you, a Faust of the savannah,
> black-thighed witch, midnight's child … (Carter, 1980: 7)

> (Bizarre déité, brune comme les nuits,
> Au parfum mélangé de musk et de havane,
> Oeuvre de quelque hobi, le Faust de la savane,
> Sorcière au flanc d'ébène, enfant des noir minuits, …) (quoted in full by Carter, 1980: 14)

The translation sheds all the ornaments (or 'jewels'?) of Baudelaire's style to portray the mulatto woman in the fleshy materiality of her odorous body, and so echoes the unconventional blazon of the dark beloved in Shakespeare's sonnet 130, creating new intertextual resonances between Baudelaire and the English poetic tradition that he returns to (we remember Poe's impact on his own poetics). The venereal imagery is thus reinterpreted from a woman-friendly, unabashed and darkly comic perspective as it spills over into a new narrative that vindicates the muse. In short, it gives Jeanne Duval a new (if fictional) lease on life in a bold variation on the 'new wine in old bottles' image (a kind of elaborate joke on the 'anti-fleurs du mâle'?), as Baudelaire's exalted poem turns into its prosaic counterpart, down to the idea of afterlife as venereal disease passed on from one partner to the next.

Studying the intricate and complex connections that link Carter's fiction with her numerous intertexts demonstrates that, as she put it herself, 'Reading a book is like re-writing it for yourself. And I think that all fiction should be open-ended. You bring to a novel, anything you read, all your experience of the world. You bring your history and you read it in your own terms' (Carter, 1985a).[40] The creative dimension of reading that is realized in its highest form in translation is a key to Carter's fiction. Discarding any simple idea of authorship, authority and original creation, Carter promoted the active, free and bold engagement with the artworks of the past, since every reader is a potential author who can tease out new meanings in old texts. In this sense, every book becomes an *objet trouvé* that can be re-contextualized, reworked and reinterpreted in a bold and original fashion, in the hope that the ferment of the new wine will liberate energies that shatter the container itself (including Magritte's bottle). Carter's approval of the explosive effects of the decanting experiments carried out in the laboratory of fiction thus draws attention to the profoundly transformative impact of the reading, translating and rewriting process as it frees up anti-conventional readings of old texts, and challenges expectations, certainties and comfortable beliefs (including feminist pieties), undermining all efforts to contain interpretation and bound creativity – let alone bodily fluids.

Notes

1 On the dynamic interplay of Carter's translating and retelling fairy tales, see Hennard Dutheil de la Rochère, 2013. On Carter's *transcreative* method across languages, literatures, genres and media, see Hennard Dutheil de la Rochère, 2016.

2 Carter described her method of writing in *counterpoint* in the Japan notebooks: 'Fictions Written in a Certain City' is 'a polyphonic composition ... harmonized according to the laws of counterpoint and introduced from time to time with various contrapuntal devices' (Carter, MS 1969–74). See Hennard Dutheil de la Rochère (2013).
3 My translation of 'Si traduire est écrire ... Traduire n'est traduire que quand traduire est un laboratoire d'écrire' (Meschonnic, 1999: 459).
4 The quotation appears in an entry dated 3 June, probably 1963, since the journal starts in November 1962, when Carter was preparing for her end-of-year examinations. In the 1960s, she published two translations-adaptations from Middle English, 'William the Dreamer's Vision of Nature', 'freely translated from passages in William Langland's Middle English alliterative poem "Piers Plowman"', and 'Two Wives and a Widow', subtitled 'A modern version from the Middle Scots of William Dunbar', recently anthologized in *Unicorn* (Carter, 2015). Carter's poetic practice reveals the hidden role that translation often plays in the development of individual works and styles.
5 (Plants on my bent skull its flag of black). I am grateful to Marie Emilie Walz for drawing my attention to this quotation (Carter, MS 1961). Maggie Tonkin notes that 'Carter's fascination with Baudelaire is well charted, and goes back to her school days' (Tonkin, 2012: 113), although this youthful enthusiasm was to give way to a more ambivalent response informed by her feminist sensibility. Edmund Gordon stresses the influence of Carter's 'wonderful French teacher', Miss Syvret, who lent her a record of Baudelaire and Rimbaud's poems which had an epiphanic effect and prompted her to become a writer: 'That record was my trigger. It was like having my skull opened with a tin opener and all its contents transformed' (quoted by Gordon, 2016: 36). The striking metaphor of the opened skull itself may owe something to Baudelaire's mindscape imagery in 'Spleen'.
6 When Baudelaire discovered Poe, he was so thrilled to have found a kindred spirit (even an uncanny double), that he decided to translate his works into French as *Histoires extraordinaires, Nouvelles histoires extraordinaires, Histoires grotesques et sérieuses, Aventures d'Arthur Gordon Pym, Eurêka,* and a few poems including 'The Raven' (into prose), which greatly contributed to establishing Poe's fame in France and America. These translations became the crucible for Baudelaire's experiments in genre in the *Petits poèmes en prose* (aka *Le Spleen de Paris*). Mallarmé's own translation project of rendering Poe's poetry in prose after Baudelaire further undermines the conventional separation between translator, editor and author.
7 In his influential study, Marcel Raymond expressed a sense of

disillusionment with the surrealist movement (Raymond, 1933: 335), which Xavière Gauthier echoes in *Surréalisme et sexualité*, albeit from a feminist perspective. While, as Gauthier observes, surrealist poets tended to exalt love and women, visual artists developed more radical tactics and explored sexual perversion to subvert dominant norms and 'bourgeois' values. Anna Watz convincingly argues that Carter's critique of the masculine bias of the surrealist movement was sharpened by her (unpublished) translation of Xavière Gauthier's *Surréalisme et sexualité*, but she also cautions against taking her rejection of the movement in 'The Alchemy of the Word' at face value (Watz, 2017). The idea of the modern poet as an alchemist 'turning mud into gold' comes from Baudelaire via Breton (see Carter, 1998b): not only did Carter's love of 'verbal magic' and taste for wonder remain throughout her life, but she continued to resort to surrealist techniques in her own work (see Hennard Dutheil de la Rochère, 2016).

8 Raymond locates the origin of the surrealist movement in Baudelaire's *Les Fleurs du mal*, which endowed poetry with the capacity to gain metaphysical knowledge and transform life (Raymond, 1933: 11): 'From then on poetry tended to become an ethic or some sort of irregular instrument of metaphysical knowledge. Poets were obsessed by the need to "change life"' (Raymond, 1957: 5). Raymond describes the poetic experiments carried out by the French poet and his followers as a 'verbal alchemy', which centrally draws on analogies and correspondences materialised in bold metaphors, symbols, comparisons and allegories. Echoing Breton, he defines the movement as a poetics and a philosophy of life (even a mystique) that seeks to re-enchant reality and transform society. Carter self-consciously reclaimed and revisited this heritage in the 1970s. Her characteristic strategy of mixing images, registers, styles, genres and media thus echoes Pierre Reverdy's own poetic method (Raymond, 1933: 286): 'The characteristic of the strong image is that it derives from the spontaneous association of two very distant realities whose relationship is grasped solely by the mind' Raymond, 1957: 288).

9 Written in 1969 and published in 1971, Carter's novel *Love* is also informed by her extensive reading in French and interest in the *Nouvelle Vague*, as a letter to Carole Roffe confirms: 'This novel, as promised, remains in the French style, but technically is turning into a film de Alain Resnais' (quoted by Gordon, 2016: 128).

10 It may be around that time that Carter translated twelve poems in prose from Baudelaire's *Le Spleen de Paris* (1869), collected in an undated notebook and as yet unpublished (see Hennard Dutheil de la Rochère, forthcoming).

11 Carter's notebooks suggest that much of her experience of Japan was

filtered through surrealist literature, visual art, film and criticism, mostly mediated in French: the first Japan notebook opens with a quotation from Luis Buñuel's anti-clerical and anti-bourgeois film *L'Âge d'or* (*A Idade do Ouro*, 1930), complete with Sadeian echoes: 'Modot. Quelle joie, quelle joie que nous assassîmes ensemble! / Lyalys: Mon amour! Mon amour!' (Modot. What joy, what joy it is to kill together! / Lya Lys. My love! My love!), while the second opens with an aphorism by the Dada poet Tristan Tzara (from his 1918 *Manifeste Dada*): 'Tout ce qu'on regarde est faux' (Everything we see is false) (Carter, MS 1969–74).

12 Edmund Gordon's fine biography memorializes their relationship, including the months spent at a beach house where Angela wrote *The Infernal Desire Machines of Doctor Hoffman*, and Sozo Araki's tender recollections of 'a 40-year-old love affair' (Gordon, 2016). Testimonies of Carter's sexual temperament also shed light on her sex-positive feminism and identification with sensuous figures like Mae West and Jeanne Duval among others.

13 See (Murai, 2005) and (Hennard Dutheil de la Rochère, 2016) in particular.

14 Watz points out that 'The marvellous alone' quote from Breton's *Manifeste du Surréalisme* (1924) appears no less than three times in Carter's journal for 1965–66. She speculates that Carter first read Breton's manifesto in translation before seeking out the French original (Watz, 2017: 14).

15 Carter lists Japanese classics such as Sei Shōnagon's *The Pillow Book*, Bashō's *The Narrow Road to the Deep North*, Richard M. Dorson's *Folk Legends of Japan* and *The Tale of Genji* in Arthur Waley's translation, followed by a quote from Wittgenstein that reflects her awareness of each language shaping reality in its own way: 'The limits of my language means the limits of my world' (Carter, MS 1969–70). Carter also records the uncanny experience of hearing her name echoing back in translation, as it were, while making love with Sozo Araki. Aside from several references to 'Japan's death-defying dandies', she quotes Baudelaire's 'Le Revenant' in full, an erotically charged poem where the I-speaker comes back as a ghoul to visit his youthful beloved at night (Carter, MS 1969–70).

16 It is to be noted that in this autobiographical and lyrical essay Breton pays homage to Baudelaire as one of the writers 'whose wording has transfixed [him] some time or other' (Breton, 1987: 9). Breton's imagination is also sprinkled with references to fairy tales, first and foremost to Cinderella and the glass slipper, but also punningly to Bluebeard in the passage on carnal love quoted by Carter.

17 Watz has reconstructed the chronology of the translation as unfolding

from 1972 to August 1973, when Carter submitted the typescript to Calder and Boyars, and eventually decided against publishing it.
18 This supports Watz's nuanced assessment of Carter's disillusionment with the surrealist movement.
19 A blue and grey notebook recording the last months of her stay in Japan (Carter, MS 1972) includes 'Notes for *Hermaphrodite* from Xavière Gauthier'.
20 Watz notes that Carter obliquely acknowledged her debt to Raymond's and Gauthier's study among others: 'When asked in a 1987 interview what had led her to Sade and what had inspired her to think about him in the light of feminism, Carter answered that it was "really, surrealists. Baudelaire ... I think it may even have been a book by Mario Praz ... but really, the surrealists treating him as this great architect of liberation, if you like"' (Appignanesi, 1987 cited by Watz, 2017: 113).
21 Baudelaire's iconic poem 'Correspondances' is reproduced in full in Marcel Raymond's *De Baudelaire au surréalisme*, along with verse from Breton, Soupault, Vitrac, Eluard, and Tzara quoted liberally in the chapter devoted to surrealist poetry.
22 Both Watz and Dimovitz refer to several paintings by Magritte that manipulate and 'deface' the female body (with a focus on *Le Viol*, 1947), but not *La Dame*.
23 This type of imagery would outrage Anglo-American feminist critics, including Mary Ann Caws, whose book on *The Poetry of Dada and Surrealism* (1970) is mentioned in Carter's 1977 notebook (Carter, MS 1977), although Caws would subsequently translate Breton, Char, Eluard and many other poets of the period and become a renowned scholar of surrealism in the US. Carter explores the idea of flesh as meat (and female sex as fig etc.) in 'The Bloody Chamber' and throughout *The Bloody Chamber* collection. The fruit dummy in 'Alice in Prague *or* The Curious Room' comically nods at the work of the female surrealist artist Meret Oppenheim, who literalized this imagery in 'Le Festin', an ironic and irreverent installation shown at the E.R.O.S. exhibition – Exposition inteRnatiOnale du Surréalisme (1959) in the Galerie Cordier.
24 Gauthier notably reproduces a scatological poem that Antonin Artaud 'howled' on the scene of the Vieux-Colombier theatre about sex with a urinating servant infected with syphilis (Gauthier, 1971: 214).
25 It is to be noted that Breton founded the International Federation of Independent Revolutionary Art with Leon Trotsky in Mexico, where he had travelled with the heroine of *L'Amour fou*, the artist Jacqueline Lamba.
26 Gauthier devotes several pages of her study to Sade as a problematic 'surrealist hero' (Gauthier, 1971: 50–7).

27 See Watz and Dimovitz for a thorough examination of Carter's intertextual and visual references to surrealism.
28 Literal translation mine. See Genette's analysis of the phonic and semantic games (Genette, 1995).
29 The literal translation proposed by Susan Suleiman inevitably fails to convey the spoonerism. However, she points out the fact that Desiderio is not only a popular name in Spanish and Portuguese, but a translingual pun (French/Italian) when she states parenthetically that '*dés* can also be read as a short name for Desiderio' (Suleiman, 1994: 112).
30 ('Lust (Dolmancé at the Lacoste castle)'). Dolmancé is a character from Sade's *Philosophy in the boudoir*.
31 In her translation notes, Carter refers to Jean Benoît 'wearing an extraordinary, terrible and diabolical costume with wandering hoods, masks and?' (Carter, MS 1969–70). She also sharply queries the implicit assumptions governing Gauthier's views of male and female sexuality: 'In general, you use the word "virile" meaning "active" and the word "feminine" meaning passive. I am not sure, however, that by doing so you have discovered something essential' (Carter, MS 1969–70).
32 In *The Sadeian Woman*, Carter diagnoses the Sadeian pathology as an inability to love.
33 Man Ray's portrait of Sade merging with the walls of the various prisons (and mental asylum) in which he spent 30 years of his life, in Man Ray and Paul Eluard's collaborative *Les Mains libres* (1937) is also reminiscent of Carter's representation of the 'stony' look of the Marquis as a new Bluebeard in *The Bloody Chamber* (see Hennard Dutheil de la Rochère, 2006: 132–6). The narrator's description of the perverse Marquis as a phallic tiger-lily or 'mâle fleur' (male flower) evokes both Dali and Fini (Gauthier, 1971: 101).
34 The correct words are 'chirurgicale' and 'dégoût' respectively, and the quotes are from Baudelaire's *Journaux intimes* (first published in *Œuvres posthumes* in 1887), including notes, aphorisms and fragments in preparation for *Fusées*, *Hygiène* and *Mon Cœur mis à nu*, whose title was inspired by Edgar Allan Poe.
35 See Maggie Tonkin's insightful analysis of Carter's 'highly subversive structural inversion by which Baudelaire is displaced from his position as *poète maudit* and recast as Carter's muse' (Tonkin, 2012: 117), just as Poe functioned as Baudelaire's own dead beloved/muse. Tonkin interprets the spirochaete as a Baudelairean synecdoque that Jeanne Duval turns into a saleable commodity after the poet's death. In my reading, the venereal disease serves as an ironic metaphor for Carter's fascination with Baudelaire, the viral imagery renewing our understanding of the translation-rewriting process. 'Black Venus' proposes an alternate

ending to Nadar's poignant testimony of the last years of Duval's life that vindicates the exoticized, eroticized and abjected muse muted by circumstances and maligned by Baudelaire's mother, friends, and biographers. Carter seems to project herself in Jeanne as an exotic, monstrous, foul-mouthed and desiring/eroticized beast waiting to depart with her Japanese lover, whom she referred to on several occasions as a Baudelairian dandy: 'The black Venus lies on the bed, waiting for a wind to rise: the sooty albatross hankers for the storm. Whirlwind!' (Carter, 1980: 25). She may also be recalling the cruel lines in *Mon cœur mis à nu* (1887): 'La Femme est le contraire du Dandy. Donc elle doit faire horreur. / La femme a faim, et elle veut manger; soif, et elle veut boire. / Elle est en rut, et elle veut être f… / Le beau mérite! / La femme est *naturelle*, c'est-à-dire abominable' (Woman is the opposite of the Dandy. That is why she should be regarded with disgust. Woman is hungry, and she wants to eat; thirsty, and she wants to drink. / She feels randy, and she wants to be fucked. / Fine characteristics! / Woman is 'natural' – that is to say, abominable) (Baudelaire, 1995: 31).

36 Carter's notes for *Black Venus*, collected in an undated lined notebook, begin with Yeats's 1895 poem 'The Indian to His Love'. They contain biographical information about Baudelaire's sartorial style (including the pale pink gloves) and apartment, Jeanne Duval, and her relationship with the poet. She also ponders on the role of woman as muse in Baudelaire's poetry, underlining 'Woman is a perpetual metaphor' twice, and refers to Baudelaire's belief in the 'satanic' aspect of love and sex ('a damned venereal sun').

37 In scholarly fashion, Carter reproduces the full poem quoted in her own text in French, and lists other poems inspired by Jeanne Duval.

38 Based in London, Next Editions Limited published spiral bound notebook-like collections of short illustrated texts in collaboration with Faber & Faber in the early 1980s.

39 Carter introduced minor changes between the 1980 and the 1985 editions that shift the focus to Jeanne's own point of view: her 'atrocious accent of the Antilles' (Carter, 1980: 21) becomes her 'dawdling accent of the Antilles' (Carter, 1985b: 7), and the smell of coconut oil in her hair turns from 'this faintly rancid odour' (Carter, 1980: 27) into 'this homely odour of the Caribbean kitchen' (Carter, 1985b: 10); Jeanne also comes to embody colonial relations, from 'There were no fathers in her family although there must have been a white one somewhere' (Carter, 1980: 24) to 'The colony – white, imperious – had fathered her' (Carter, 1985b: 8). In her exploration of the complex intersections of gender and race in the colonial context, but also artistic, subject–object relations, Carter seems to be projecting herself in Jeanne. Displaced and

exotic in Japan, 'so tall and witchy' (Carter, 1980: 8) and bearing a wild mane of hair (both out-of-place and eroticized), and unable to speak the language properly, 'It was as though her tongue had been cut out and another one sewn in that did not fit well' (Carter, 1980: 9).

40 Re-reading extended to Carter's own work as a form of internal translation or rewriting. The Carter Papers archive (notebooks, drafts etc.) confirms that writing involved important revisions, annotations, and even generic shifts, which resulted in significant transformations of the 'original' version, even in the last stages of the editorial process.

References

Quotations are from the Angela Carter Papers in the British Library. Copyright © The Estate of Angela Carter. Reproduced by permission of the author's Estate, c/o Rogers, Coleridge & White Ltd., 20 Powis Mews, London W11 1JN.

Anonymous (1974), www.kirkusreviews.com/book-reviews/angela-carter-3/the-war-of-dreams/ (last accessed 17 August 2016).
Bassnett, Susan (2011), *Reflections on Translation* (Bristol, Buffalo, Toronto: Multilingual Matters).
Baudelaire, Charles (1857), *Les Fleurs du mal* in *Oeuvres complètes* (Paris: Gallimard Bibliothèque de la Pléiade) ed. Claude Pichois 1975, tome 1. English translations: https://fleursdumal.org/poem/138, accessed 26 November 2018.
—— (1897), *Journaux intimes. Fusées. Mon coeur mis à nu* (Paris: Gallimard Bibliothèque de la Pléiade) ed. Claude Pichois 1975, tome 1.
—— (1995), *Intimate Journals*, trans. Norman Cameron (Madison: Syrens).
Berger, John (1972), *Ways of Seeing* (London: Penguin).
Breton, André (1937), *L'Amour fou* (Paris: Gallimard).
—— (1987), *Mad Love*, trans. Mary Ann Caws (Lincoln and London: University of Nebraska Press).
Carter, Angela (1966), *Shadow Dance* (London: William Heinemann).
——(1972), *The Infernal Desire Machines of Doctor Hoffman* (London: Rupert Hart-Davis).
—— (1974), *Fireworks: Nine Profane Pieces* (London: Quartet Books).
—— (1977), *The Passion of New Eve* (London: Victor Gollancz).
—— (1979a), *The Bloody Chamber and Other Stories* (London: Victor Gollancz).
—— (1979b), *The Sadeian Woman: An Exercise in Cultural History* (London: Victor Gollancz).
—— (1980), *Black Venus's Tale*, with woodcuts by Philip Sutton (London: Next Editions and Faber & Faber).

—— (1984), *Nights at the Circus* (London: Chatto & Windus).
—— (1985a), 'The Company of Angela Carter: An Interview', *Marxism Today*, January 1985, pp. 20–2.
—— (1985b), 'Black Venus', in *Black Venus* (London: Chatto & Windus) pp. 121–39.
—— (1986), (ed.), *Angela Carter's Book of Wayward Girls and Wicked Women* (London: Virago).
—— (1991), *Wise Children* (London: Chatto & Windus).
—— (1998a), 'Milorad Pavic: Dictionary of the Khazars (1989)', in *Shaking a Leg: Collected Journalism and Writings*, ed. Jenny Uglow (London: Vintage) pp. 490–6.
—— ([1978] 1998b), 'The Alchemy of the Word', in *Shaking a Leg: Collected Journalism and Writings*, ed. Jenny Uglow (London: Vintage) pp. 507–12.
—— (1998c), 'Notes from the Front Line (1983)', in *Shaking a Leg: Collected Journalism and Writings*, ed. Jenny Uglow (London: Vintage) pp. 36–43.
—— (2015), *Unicorn: The Poetry of Angela Carter*, with an essay by Rosemary Hill (London: Profile).
—— (MS BL 2018), Angela Carter Papers, The British Library, https://www.bl.uk/collection-items/manuscript-notes-and-drafts-of-the-bloody-chamber-by-angela-carter, accessed 24 March 2018.
—— (MS 1961), *Journal 1961* Add. MS 88899/1/86. Angela Carter Papers, The British Library.
—— (MS 1962–63), *Journal 1962–1963?* Add. MS 88899/1/88. Angela Carter Papers, The British Library.
—— (MS 1965–66), *Journal 1965–1966* Add. MS 88899/1/90. Angela Carter Papers, The British Library.
—— (MS 1969–70), *Journal 1969–1970* Add. MS 88899/1/93. Angela Carter Papers, The British Library.
—— (MS 1969–74), *Japan 1–2 1969–1974* Add. MS 88899/1/80–81. Angela Carter Papers, The British Library.
—— (MS 1972), *Journal 1972* Add. MS 88899/1/94. Angela Carter Papers, The British Library.
—— (MS 1973), *Surrealism and Sexuality 1973* Add. MS 88899/1/83. Angela Carter Papers, The British Library.
—— (MS 1977), *Journal 1977* Add. MS 88899/1/96. Angela Carter Papers, The British Library.
—— Review of Frida Kahlo, 'A Ribbon around a Bomb', with manuscript note from 'Tony' (May 1989), Add. MS 88899/1/68. Angela Carter Papers, The British Library.
Crevel, René ([1932] 1960), *Le Clavecin de Diderot*, ed. Pauvert (Paris: Éditions surréalistes).
Desnos, Robert (1930), *Corps et biens* (Paris: Gallimard, 1968).

Dimovitz, Scott A. (2016), *Angela Carter: Surrealist, Psychologist, Pornographer* (London and New York: Routledge).
Gauthier, Xavière (1971), *Surréalisme et sexualité*, intro. Jean-Bertrand Pontalis (Paris: Gallimard, coll. Idées).
Genette, Gérard (1995), *Mimologics* (Lincoln and London: University of Nebraska Press), trans. Thaïs E. Morgan, with a foreword by Gerald Prince.
Gordon, Edmund (2016), *The Invention of Angela Carter: A Biography* (London: Chatto & Windus).
Haffenden, John (1985), '*Angela Carter*': *Novelists in Interview* (London: Methuen) pp. 76–96.
Hennard Dutheil de la Rochère, Martine (2006), 'Modelling for Bluebeard: Visual and Narrative Art in Angela Carter's "The Bloody Chamber"', in Beverly Maeder et al. (eds), *The Seeming and the Seen: Essays in Modern Visual and Literary Culture* (Bern: Peter Lang), pp. 183–208.
—— (2013), *Reading, Translating, Rewriting: Angela Carter's Translational Poetics* (Detroit: Wayne State University Press).
—— (2016), 'From the Bloody Chamber to the *Cabinet de Curiosités*: Angela Carter's Curious Alices Through the Looking Glass of Languages', *Marvels and Tales: Journal of Fairy-Tale Studies*, 30:2, 284–308.
—— (In progress), '*Mud into Gold*': *Angela Carter and Charles Baudelaire.*
Mansour, Joyce (1960), 'Déchirures', in *Rapaces* (Paris: Seghers).
—— (1965), 'L'amoureuse guerrière', in *Carré blanc* (Paris: Le soleil noir).
Meschonnic, Henri (1999), *Poétique du traduire* (Paris: Verdier).
Munford, Rebecca (2004), 'Re-presenting Charles Baudelaire/Re-presencing Jeanne Duval: Transformations of the Muse in Angela Carter's "Black Venus"', *Forum for Modern Language Studies*, 40:1, 1–13.
Murai, Mayako (2005), 'Passion and the Mirror: Angela Carter's Souvenir of Japan' (revised paper presented at the University of Wolverhampton). https://fr.scribd.com/document/125743827/Mayako-Murai-Passion-and-the-Mirror-Angela-Carter-s-Souvenir-of-Japan, accessed 26 November 2018.
Perrault, Charles (1977), *The Fairy Tales of Charles Perrault*, trans. Angela Carter; illus. Martin Ware (London: Victor Gollancz).
Raymond, Marcel (1933), *De Baudelaire au surréalisme* (Paris: Correa).
—— (1957), *From Baudelaire to Surrealism* (London: Peter Owen Limited) translator's name not given.
Sheets, Robin Ann (1991), 'Pornography, Fairy Tales, and Feminism: Angela Carter's "The Bloody Chamber"', *Journal of the History of Sexuality*, 1:4, 633–57.
Suleiman, Susan Rubin (1990), *Subversive Intent: Gender, Politics and the Avant-Garde* (Cambridge, MA: Harvard University Press).

Tonkin, Maggie (2012), *Angela Carter and Decadence: Critical Fictions/Fictional Critiques* (New York: Palgrave Macmillan).

Watz, Anna (2017), *Angela Carter and Surrealism: 'A Feminist Libertarian Aesthetic'* (London and New York: Routledge).

6

Myths, meat and American Indians: Angela Carter and Claude Lévi-Strauss

Heidi Yeandle

IT IS NOT SURPRISING that Angela Carter was interested in Claude Lévi-Strauss's work. An eminent anthropologist, Lévi-Strauss (1908–2009) was fascinated with primitive communities, and dedicated years of research to studying South American Indian tribes. His works challenge the 'savage' portrayal of Native American societies, and primitive tribes more broadly, questioning 'the supposed ineptitude of "primitive people"' (1962: 1). Arguing that the social arrangements and languages of such native cultures are much more complex than his predecessors and contemporaries had assumed, Lévi-Strauss examines the kinship systems and languages of a range of South American Indian cultures, while also analysing the myths that underpin these communities, and discussing what these myths reveal about their social systems. Thus, his research blurs the supposed distinction between 'primitive' and 'civilized' communities. As Lévi-Strauss argues in *Structural Anthropology* (1958), 'a primitive people is not a backward or retarded people; indeed it may possess, in one realm or another, a genius for invention or action that leaves the achievements of civilized peoples far behind' (1963: 102).

Carter's work similarly shows a keen interest in 'primitive' or 'savage' communities, from her portrayal of the Barbarians in *Heroes and Villains* (1969) to the South American River People in *The Infernal Desire Machines of Doctor Hoffman* (1972). What is more, like Lévi-Strauss, Carter is pre-occupied with the power of mythology. Lévi-Strauss argues that in a primitive context, 'myths operate in men's minds without their being aware of the fact' (1970: 12), and Carter similarly states that, from a more contemporary ideological perspective, 'all myths are products of the human mind' and claims – as is often quoted – that she is 'in the demythologising business' (1998a: 38). Carter's concern with how myths shape human consciousness, and her aim to expose 'social fictions' as myths (1998a: 38), illustrate her view that myths restrict and regulate people, and her belief that exposing myths is a liberatory exercise.

The literary manifesto 'Notes from the Front Line' (1983) focuses on the myths that operate in Western civilizations, but elsewhere Carter discusses the myths surrounding American Indians. In 'That Arizona Home' (1977), she discusses the 'myth of the Noble Red Man' that has been 'thrust upon' American Indians, saying that 'this is a myth on which, like many Europeans, I was raised' (1998b: 276). She contrasts this with the 'alternative myth – that of Murderous Brute', depicting dichotomous myths related to American Indian communities (276), as well as portraying the geographical distance between the Europeans with such assumptions and the American Indians to whom the myths correspond. Thus, as Carter notes, like a number of ethnic minority groups, American Indian communities are 'a screen for projective fantasies, rather than a phenomenon of reality' (277). In this light, this chapter will examine Carter's portrayal of native, 'primitive' societies, and how she simultaneously engages with and debunks the myths, or 'projective fantasies', surrounding them. I discuss how Carter's representation of American Indian tribes (both North and South American), as well as of primitive communities more broadly, is shaped by her extensive reading of Claude Lévi-Strauss's work.

As part of her discussion of Desiderio's time with the River People in *Doctor Hoffman*, Lorna Sage says that 'like Angela Carter, he [Desiderio] has read his Lévi-Strauss' (2007: 35). Likewise, Joseph Bristow and Trev Lynn Broughton note that *Doctor Hoffman* demonstrates Carter's engagement with 'Lévi-Strauss's anthropological research' (1997: 3). Chiharu Yoshioka also discusses Carter's portrayal of the River People in this novel, saying that they represent 'a parable about Lévi-Straussian mythology' (2001: 96). The research journals that comprise the Angela Carter Papers Collection, an archive of Carter's notes held at the British Library, show that Carter was reading Lévi-Strauss's work as research for *Doctor Hoffman*, especially *The Raw and the Cooked: Introduction to a Science of Mythology Volume 1* (1964), the first instalment of his *Mythologiques* series, as well as his 1962 work *The Savage Mind* (Carter 1969–70). However, Carter's research on Lévi-Strauss is much more wide-ranging than this, and is central to her notebooks from the mid-1960s to the early 1990s, thus spanning her writing career. Her archived notes suggest that her initial reading of Lévi-Strauss was in 1966–67 when she read *The Savage Mind* – a text that was first published in English in 1966 – as research for *Heroes and Villains* (Carter, 1966–68). She then went on to read *Tristes Tropiques* (1955 in French, 1961 in English) in 1968–69, and included *Structural Anthropology* (1958 in French, 1963 in English) in a reading list for *Heroes and Villains* (Carter, 1968–69). Carter returned to *The Savage Mind* in 1970–72, but during this time her research on Lévi-Strauss was mostly dedicated to *The Raw and the Cooked* (first translated into English in 1969), research that is central to *Doctor Hoffman* as well as her 1974 collection of short stories, *Fireworks: Nine Profane Pieces* (Carter, 1969–70; Carter undated). Carter's notebooks suggest that her research on Lévi-Strauss was at its peak from 1970–72, the period when she was living in Japan; she made over 2,500 words of notes on *The Raw and the Cooked* during this time. But she continued to read Lévi-Strauss's work after this, including *From Honey to Ashes* (1966 in French, 1973 in English) and *The Origin of Table Manners* (1968 in French, 1978 in English) between 1977 and 1979 (Carter, 1977), while also referring to Lévi-Strauss in 1990 as part of her plans for her final novel, *Wise Children*, published in 1991 (Carter, 1989–90).

This overview illustrates the prolonged and extensive nature of Carter's research on Lévi-Strauss; while current criticism suggests that her engagement with Lévi-Strauss is limited to *Doctor Hoffman*, her reading of Lévi-Strauss inspired a number of her novels and short stories, and also feeds into her journalism.[1] As Carter's reading of Lévi-Strauss is so vast, this chapter does not provide an exhaustive discussion of this area of her research. Rather, it explores some of the most fruitful areas of her engagement with Lévi-Strauss, examining the more explicit and most overlooked aspects of her research on him. As such, this chapter focuses on Carter's texts that were published between 1969 and 1974: *Heroes and Villains* (1969), *Doctor Hoffman* (1972) and *Fireworks* (1974), paying particular attention to 'Master', a short story that has received limited critical attention (Artt, 2012: 176). This period of Carter's work encompasses her initial engagement with Lévi-Strauss as well as the time when her research on Lévi-Strauss was at its most concentrated, from 1970–72. I discuss Carter's depiction of primitive communities in these three texts, and explore how Carter's portrayal of the River People in *Doctor Hoffman* and the American Indian community in 'Master' is shaped by Lévi-Strauss's research on mythology in American Indian cultures, especially his analysis of myths surrounding the origin of fire, particularly for cooking meat, in such primitive tribes.

Heroes and Villains

Carter's post-apocalyptic novel *Heroes and Villains* portrays a world divided into Professors and Barbarians. As the names of these groups suggest, the Professors value education and their knowledge stems from books, while the Barbarians focus on surviving in the hostile landscape, under the leadership of the renegade Professor Donally. In the first of Carter's texts to be influenced by Lévi-Strauss, she explicitly signals his relevance to the novel: Donally's library includes books by 'Teilhard de Chardin, Lévi-Strauss, Weber, Durkheim and so on' (1972: 62). Marianne – the protagonist and daughter of the Professor of History, who has been 'rescued' by the Barbarians – notices this, as 'she looked over his [Donally's] books and saw names she remembered from the spines in her father's study' (61–2). Thus, both Donally and Marianne's father are depicted as being at least familiar with Lévi-Strauss's work. But Carter also embeds a short quotation from Lévi-Strauss's work into *Heroes and Villains*. While Lévi-Strauss stresses the importance of 'mistrusting appearances' of primitive peoples and carrying out ethnographic research (2011: 280), Donally urges Marianne to do the same, writing 'MISTRUST APPEARANCES' as an aphorism on the wall (Carter, 1972: 60). Questions surrounding the 'reality' of the Barbarians and native tribes are therefore raised via Carter's engagement with Lévi-Strauss.

Like Lévi-Strauss, Marianne's father and the rest of the Professors are fascinated with 'primitive' communities – the Barbarians in this instance. When Donally asks Marianne how the Professors would react if she returned to them with Jewel, the Barbarian who rescued her, she says they would put Jewel 'in a cage so everyone could examine' him (1972: 123). He would be an 'icon of otherness' (123), subjected to a range of tests and 'studied and annotated until you were nothing but a mass of footnotes with a tiny trickle of text at the top of a page' (124). Jewel, as his name suggests, is a 'curiously shaped, attractive stone' (82): an object to be subjected to the Professors' scrutinizing gaze. Marianne's portrayal of the Professors' studies is revealing as their hypothetical examination of Jewel is reductive – as a museum exhibit, Jewel is reduced to a 'tiny trickle of text' and remains a 'perfect stranger' (124) to the Professors. The Professors' savage beliefs about the Barbarian outsiders are apparent here as well, as they are thought to cage Jewel – treating him 'like a talking beast' – and 'walk around you [Jewel] carefully in case you bit them' (123), which ties in with the brutish myths the Professors' circulate about the Barbarians; Marianne is told that the Barbarians are uneducated cannibals who rape and 'sew up cats inside' women (10).

Carter's portrayal of the Professors' beliefs about the Barbarians, and their method of examining Jewel, voices Lévi-Strauss's call for primitive communities to be studied properly, by respecting and giving voices to the natives, and not embellishing accounts of primitive tribes with falsehoods. In *Tristes Tropiques*, Lévi-Strauss talks about the 'manipulation' of travel books, where 'actual experience is replaced by stereotypes', and where the presence of the observer is 'glossed over' (2011: 39). Marianne's depiction of the Professors' excessive examination of the caged Jewel, who remains a 'perfect stranger', suggests that their studies do not yield a real understanding of the Barbarian, and do not take into consideration the fact that Jewel is not being studied in his normal environment. Marianne, however, discovers what the Barbarians are actually like, dispelling the myths she was told in her childhood and challenging her father's assumptions about them. After living with them for just a short period of time, she 'wished she could tell her father about the true nature of the Barbarians' (1972: 53), noting the differences between the Professors' view of the Barbarians and her own first-hand encounter. Marianne discovers that Jewel contradicts the expectations she had of his community based on her education: 'not even in pictures had I seen anything like you, nor read your description in books' (137). Her research reveals the 'remote resemblance' the Barbarians have to the 'false picture' the Professors had of them (Lévi-Strauss, 2011: 19). But, like her father, Marianne wants to keep Jewel 'in preserving fluid in a huge jar on the mantelpiece', keeping him as 'an exhibit for intellectuals to marvel at' (Carter, 1972: 137). She also objectifies Jewel, but differs from her father in that she does not envisage treating him like an animal; rather, Jewel is an object that Marianne admires.

As well as parodying the Professor's supposed knowledge of the Barbarians, Carter uses her reading of Lévi-Strauss to show the differences between the Professors and Barbarians in terms of language. In the opening chapters of *The Savage Mind*, Lévi-Strauss discusses the languages used in primitive communities. He condemns the speculations made by earlier ethnologists about primitive social groups, arguing that they made assumptions 'about the simpleness and coarseness of "primitives"' (1962: 40). He particularly focuses on the vocabulary of 'primitive' peoples, and the 'fashion' of believing that the absence of certain terms in a given language 'prove[s] the intellectual poverty of Savages' (1). Using botany as an example, Lévi-Strauss notes the extensive vocabularies that a range of primitive communities have for plants and their properties in relation to food and medicine, and says that their 'extreme familiarity' and 'precise knowledge' of this field 'has often struck inquirers as an indication of attitudes and preoccupations which distinguish the natives from their white visitors' (5). Thus, Lévi-Strauss calls for a change in 'our traditional picture of this primitiveness' (42).

Lévi-Strauss's discussion of the vocabulary used by supposedly savage groups is central to Carter's depiction of the Barbarians. Marianne is shocked to hear Jewel use the word 'intellectual' when she first meets him, saying 'I never thought you'd know such a word!' (Carter, 1972: 19). On her way to the Barbarians' current base, Marianne is bitten by a snake and saved by Jewel who notes that it was 'lucky it was only an adder. *Viperus berus*', but Marianne 'did not believe she had heard him give the snake its zoological name' (28). The Professors' limited assumptions about the Barbarians in terms of language are apparent here, and, like Lévi-Strauss, Carter dispels such assumptions, mocking the Professors in doing so. Not only do the Barbarians have a more extensive vocabulary than anticipated by the Professors, but the Professors' language is endangered, as a number of terms are becoming obsolete. Marianne's misunderstanding of the word 'city' – which she thinks means 'ruins' (7) – is one example of this, a misunderstanding that leads her father to instruct her to consult a dictionary. Marianne, however, recognizes that the dictionary is now a defunct relic: 'the dictionaries contained innumerable incomprehensible words she could only define through their use in his other books' (7). Thus, as well as debunking myths 'about the simpleness and coarseness of "primitives"' (Lévi-Strauss, 1962: 40), Carter provides a satirical representation of the Professors' knowledge,[2] by depicting their language rewinding. In doing so, like Lévi-Strauss, Carter blurs the distinction between the civilized and the primitive – in comparison to the Barbarians, the scholarly 'civilized peoples [are] far behind' (Lévi-Strauss, 1963: 102).

The Infernal Desire Machines of Doctor Hoffman

Published three years after *Heroes and Villains*, *Doctor Hoffman* is the next text in which Carter engages with the ideas of Lévi-Strauss. This novel depicts a reality war in a South American city into which the eponymous Doctor Hoffman is beaming apparitional images, causing the residents to be uncertain as to what is real or not. The text takes the form of a memoir written by Desiderio fifty years after killing Doctor Hoffman and ending the war. On his journey, Desiderio encounters a community of River People in South America – a location that recalls one of Lévi-Strauss's primary focuses – which gives him an escape from Doctor Hoffman, as they 'seemed relatively unaffected by the war' (Carter, 2010: 85). Similarly to Marianne's first-hand experience with the Barbarians, Desiderio lives with the River People, and during his time with them he learns about their language, marriage traditions and eating habits, as well as about the 'folkways and the mythology of the past' (2010: 88) which their culture is founded upon. Unlike Marianne, who seemingly takes on the role of the Barbarians' leader at the end of *Heroes and Villains*, Desiderio becomes an almost fully integrated member of the River People's tribe, learning their language to the extent that 'my new language came to my tongue before my former one' (84).

One of the main reasons as to why Desiderio blends in so well with the River People is that he 'was of Indian extraction' (Carter, 2010: 10) – he has 'hair black enough and cheekbones high enough to pass among the river people for one of their own' (77). While Desiderio hints at the stigma associated with his ancestry at the beginning of his memoir, saying that his 'colleagues always contrived politely to ignore' his 'genetic imprint' and noting that the 'word "indigenous" was unmentionable' in the city (10), the ignorance and disregard towards the Amerindian communities comes to the fore in the chapter dedicated to 'The River People' (73–105). Carter opens this chapter by explaining that the River People – a fictional version of the South American Indian tribes that Lévi-Strauss researched – were discovered in the sixteenth century by Portuguese explorers. The Jesuits, who sailed with the conquistadors, kept records of 'attempted conversions' to Catholicism, and Desiderio notes that it is to 'the journals of those indefatigable storm-troopers of the Lord that we owe most of our knowledge of the aborigines' (75). This 'knowledge', however, is false: Desiderio accuses the Jesuits of writing 'fallacious' accounts of tribes and their customs (75). But as well as being false, because of their remote location there is limited documentation about the River People; Desiderio 'found very few of their customs in the writings of the Jesuits' (77). As a result, in the urban areas of South America that Desiderio refers to, they 'know little if anything of the Indians' (76), who are seen to be 'resident aliens' (74) or 'bogeymen with which to frighten naughty children' (76), recalling the savage myths that Marianne is told about the Barbarians in *Heroes and Villains*.

This aspect of Carter's portrayal of the River People is inspired by her reading of *Tristes Tropiques*. Similarly to her critique of falsified accounts of the Barbarians, Carter draws attention to the biased and deceptive nature of travel writing in *Doctor Hoffman*. The 'manipulation' and 'falsified' (Lévi-Strauss, 2011: 39) depiction of American Indian tribes is central to the opening pages of the chapter on the River People but, in contrast to the Barbarians in *Heroes and Villains*, in *Doctor Hoffman* Carter's representation is grounded in Lévi-Strauss's account of the Brazilian Ambassador's view of the native Indian communities, which he documents in *Tristes Tropiques*. Reflecting on meeting the Ambassador in 1934 and hearing the 'official view' of the natives, Lévi-Strauss recalls the Ambassador telling him that the 'Indians […] all disappeared years ago' and that 'this is a very sad, very shameful episode in the history of my country' (2011: 48). Looking back, Lévi-Strauss says that he finds it 'quite incredible' that 'the Brazilian elite […] could not bear any allusion to Indians or more generally to the primitive conditions of the interior, except to admit – or even suggest – that an Indian great-grandmother might be responsible for their slightly exotic cast of countenance' (48). He also goes on to note that 'there could be no doubt about his [the Ambassador's] Indian ancestry' (48), which the Ambassador has opted to forget.

The urban and elitist belief that the Indians are now non-existent and an ignorance of their conditions is apparent in *Doctor Hoffman*, with the River People living 'secret, esoteric lives, forgotten, unnoticed' (Carter, 2010: 76). While Carter introduces the River People in relation to the Portuguese Jesuits, she also suggests that Doctor Hoffman's Ambassador comes from Indian descent, which further links Carter's novel to Lévi-Strauss's account of the Brazilian Ambassador's appearance. Doctor Hoffman's Ambassador is described as having 'vestigial' eyelids, 'unusually high' cheekbones and 'luxuriantly glossy hair so black it was purplish' (30), and is thus depicted as having similar features to Desiderio. As Desiderio reflects, 'presumably he was either of Mongolian extraction or else he numbered among his ancestors, as I did, certain of the forgotten Indians' (30). As well as demonstrating a more subtle engagement with Lévi-Strauss's work, this adds to the blurring of the distinction between the native Indians and the civilized elite in *Doctor Hoffman*, as both Desiderio and the Ambassador are portrayed as coming from Indian descent.

A significant aspect of Carter's portrayal of the seemingly Brazilian River People *vis-à-vis* Lévi-Strauss is Desiderio's account of the origin of fire in the tribe, from a myth that Nao-Kurai, the leader, drunkenly tells him. Nao-Kurai tells Desiderio that 'a very long time ago' the tribe 'didn't know how to make fire' (Carter, 2010: 99), which meant that their diet consisted of foods such as 'raw slugs and snails' (101). Their first experience of fire was when a snake spat venom into a woman's womb, leading to the woman conceiving a snake, which can make fire: 'so out pops Snake from her hole with a bit of fire in his jaws and she rubs her hands to feel the glow and jumps for joy', teaching her 'the word for "warm"' (100). This leads to the snake encouraging the woman to try cooked food which is 'ever so much more tasty', so 'she toasted and roasted her dinners' whenever she was eating alone (101). Her family were enticed by the 'lovely savoury smells' in her hut, but when the youngest brother saw the snake cook a meal it 'vanished up the sister', which meant that the woman was unable to share fire with her tribe 'because *she* didn't know how to make fire' (101, original emphasis). This results in the brother chopping the sister up to get to the snake, who eventually agrees to teach them how to make fire using two sticks, 'but they couldn't learn, no matter how they tried' (102). Due to their inability to produce fire they believe that the snake uses magical powers to do so, leading them to kill and eat the snake, thus digesting the 'magical' ability. This myth leads to Desiderio's realization that the tribe are planning to kill him to obtain his ability to write, a skill which Nao-Kurai was unable to learn from Desiderio.

The River People's myth of the snake as the Fire-Bringer is inspired by Carter's reading of *The Raw and the Cooked* (Carter, 1969–70; Carter undated). In this first volume of his *Mythologiques* series, Lévi-Strauss catalogues and analyses a range of American Indian myths, examining their variations and connections and discussing what these reveal about the social systems and territories they correspond to, as well as about mythology more generally. One area of analysis is myths about the origin of fire, particularly fire used for cooking. Fire allows the hero of Myth 7 (M7) to experience 'his first meal of cooked meat' courtesy of the jaguars (Lévi-Strauss, 1970: 67), whereas in M54 a woman uses fire from a swallow's beak to 'cook the manioc' (126). Lévi-Strauss discusses the similarities between a range of such myths, noting that 'they attribute the origin of fire to an animal, who gave it to man or from whom man stole it' – usually a jaguar or a vulture – and that 'each species is defined in terms of the food it eats', whether raw, rotten or cooked (142). Lévi-Strauss goes on to identify 'the truly essential place occupied by cooking in native thought' noting that 'not only does cooking mark the transition from nature to culture, but through it and by means of it, the human state can be defined with all its attributes' (164). With raw food being associated with nature, and cooked food marking the change to culture, it is clear that animals enable humans to progress in the realm of gastronomy, as well as culturally.

While the animal responsible for the origin of fire and the introduction of cooked food in *Doctor Hoffman* is a snake – rather than a jaguar, in line with most of the myths related to fire in *The Raw and the Cooked* – the same similarities apply: the River People 'steal' fire from the snake, by killing it and inheriting the ability to create fire, and the River People are restricted to eating raw food until the snake arrives. The River People's inability to make fire following the snake's instructions demonstrates not only their desire for warmth and cooked food but also, in line with the myths Lévi-Strauss examines, the snake's role in the cultural progression of the River People. Although the snake is not normally associated with the origin of fire, there are some myths in *The Raw and the Cooked* which depict the snake residing in a womb and providing natives with tobacco (Lévi-Strauss, 1970: 103–4), or stopping humans from being immortal

(156). In a myth about the origin of tobacco (M26), for instance, a snake fertilizes a woman and then helps her to collect fruit, before retreating to the womb; upon discovering this, the brothers kill the snake when he appears, and tobacco sprouts from the ashes (103–4). Thus, the snake's uterine role as the Fire-Bringer in *Doctor Hoffman* shows an engagement with and blurring of a range of myths discussed in *The Raw and the Cooked*, as well as illustrating the River People's reliance on the snake to progress from raw to cooked food, a skill that marks a cultural transition.

Carter's reading of *The Raw and the Cooked* goes beyond the chapter on the River People, though, as this text also heavily influenced her depiction of Doctor Hoffman's methodology. Lévi-Strauss opens *The Raw and the Cooked* with a discussion of the aims of this book and subsequent volumes in the *Mythologiques* series, and outlines his method of analysing mythology. He starts with one myth, called the 'key myth' (1970: 2), which he interprets in relation to other myths, examining how they adapt and what patterns are apparent. He 'work[s] outward from the center' (4), analysing the key myth in relation to other myths, a process which continues to expand outwards. Thus, as Carter notes in a journal dedicated to *Doctor Hoffman* (undated), for Lévi-Strauss's mythological analysis:

> as the nebula gradually spreads, its nucleus condenses [...] and something resembling order is to be seen emerging from chaos. Sequences arranged in transformation groups, as if around a germinal molecule, join up with the initial group and reproduce its structure and determinative tendencies. Thus is brought into being a multidimensional body, whose central parts disclose a structure, while uncertainty and confusion continue to prevail along its periphery. (Lévi-Strauss, 1970: 3)

This is the inspiration for Doctor Hoffman's 'reality modifying machines' (Carter, 2010: 250), the machines that create apparitional images using 'eroto-energy' (251) from 'secretions of fulfilled desire' (250). Doctor Hoffman's discussion of how these machines work uses the same terminology as Lévi-Strauss's account of analysing myths:

> inside the reality modifying machines, in the medium of essential undifferentiation, these germinal molecules are agitated until, according to certain innate determinative tendencies, they form themselves into divergent sequences which act as what I call 'transformation groups'. Eventually a multi-dimensional body is brought into being which operates only upon an uncertainty principle. (Carter, 2010: 251–2)

While on the one hand this intertextual reference positions Doctor Hoffman's work as a myth, something that Carter constantly seeks to debunk, the link to Lévi-Strauss also illustrates the vast nature of Doctor Hoffman's machinery, and the 'ordered chaos' it creates. Lévi-Strauss's discussion focuses on the 'order [...] emerging from the chaos' in relation to the key myth, but when analysing the structure of the myths as a whole body, 'uncertainty and confusion continue to prevail'. Likewise, inside Doctor Hoffman's machines the initial molecules fit into sequences and patterns are identified, but the 'multi-dimensional' being created as a result 'operates only upon an uncertainty principle'. Just as Lévi-Strauss claims that a community's mythology can never be known in its 'entirety' because mythology is constantly in flux – it is a 'shifting reality' (1970: 3) – one of the key aspects of Doctor Hoffman's reality war is mutability. As the peep-show proprietor, who once taught the Doctor, says: 'nothing [...] is ever completed; it only changes' (Carter, 2010: 113). The work of both Doctor Hoffman and Lévi-Strauss is founded upon limitlessness, with the Doctor using Lévi-Strauss's claim that 'the analysis of myths is an endless task' (1970: 5) as the inspiration for his endeavour to, as Lévi-Strauss says, shift reality.

Carter alludes to this aspect of Lévi-Strauss's work – his argument that 'there is no real end to mythological analysis, *no hidden unity* to be grasped once the breaking-down process has been completed' (Lévi-Strauss, 1970: 5 – emphasis mine) – when the peep-show proprietor murmurs 'no hidden unity' (Carter, 2010: 113). Lévi-Strauss's notion that 'multiplicity is an essential characteristic' of mythology and that 'mythological thought never develops any theme to completion: there is always something left unfinished' (1970: 6) is therefore the basis for Doctor Hoffman's reality war. What is more, Carter makes a note of these quotations from *The Raw and the Cooked* in her plans for *Doctor Hoffman* under the heading 'Dr Hoffman's Methodology' (undated: 122),[3] illustrating the extent to which this novel is inspired by her reading of Lévi-Strauss's work. Thus, not only did Lévi-Strauss influence Carter's portrayal of the River People, particularly their myth of the snake as a Fire-Bringer, which is based on myths related to the origin of fire and cooked food in *The Raw and the Cooked*, but the methodology behind Doctor Hoffman's reality war is also guided by Lévi-Strauss's work, positioning Lévi-Strauss as a key intertext for this novel.

'Master': *Fireworks*

Carter wrote the short stories collected in *Fireworks* between 1970 and 1973, the time when she also published *Doctor Hoffman* and was extensively researching Lévi-Strauss. In line with *Doctor Hoffman*, the myths collected and discussed in *The Raw and the Cooked* inspired some stories in *Fireworks*, particularly 'Master', which depicts an explorer – the eponymous Master – discovering an American Indian tribe in 'the world whose fructifying river is herself a savage woman, the Amazon' (Carter, 2006: 76), and situates the tribe in the South American region researched by Lévi-Strauss. In contrast to Marianne and Desiderio, who are interested in and research the tribes they encounter, the Master is motivated by killing animals; he also purchases a girl from the Indian primitives, whom he names 'Friday' (77) and refers to as 'brown meat' (76). A much more hostile relationship between the natives and the 'civilized' new arrival is portrayed here: the hunter asserts his authority over his prey, as well as over the woman he objectifies and rapes. His identity as 'Master' is suggestive of this, implying a master/slave relationship.

As part of her portrayal of the Master and the native, Carter revisits South American Indian myths related to fire and the transition from raw to cooked food that she initially engaged with in *Doctor Hoffman*, but this time her main focus is the jaguar, the animal Lévi-Strauss calls the 'master of fire' (Lévi-Strauss, 1970: 190). This suggests a conflict between the jaguar and the Master in terms of their mastery. Rather than the jaguar being responsible for the origin of fire and the primitives' transition to cooked food, the Master brings fire with him and introduces the herbivorous woman – her tribe 'only ate roots' – to meat; 'he taught her to eat the meat he roasted over his camp fire' (Carter, 2006: 77). The Master slaughters jaguars on a daily basis, leading the woman, who 'had been born into the clan of the jaguar', to want to 'learn a little of Master's magic' (78) and learn to kill as well. While the woman sees the Master as 'death itself' (77), she thinks that 'since he had taught her to eat meat [...] she must be death's apprentice' (79), suggesting that progressing from natural, raw food to culture – represented by cooked food for Lévi-Strauss – is not necessarily a positive transition in terms of the brutal depiction of the supposedly civilized 'white hunter' (75).

At the end of the short story, though, the woman gradually transforms into a jaguar, growing claws, a pelt and whiskers, while still walking on two legs. In this state 'she could no longer tolerate cooked meat but must tear it raw between her fingers off the bone before Master saw' (Carter, 2006: 80). This inversion of the transition from raw to cooked food suggests, in relation to Lévi-Strauss, a rewinding of the progression from nature to culture, in line with the transformation from woman to jaguar. The story ends with the jaguar woman killing the Master as 'his prey had shot the hunter' (80) and then losing the ability to hold a gun, completing her metamorphosis into a jaguar and rejecting the cultured end of the nature–culture spectrum. As Sarah Artt notes, Carter 'ascribes agency to [...] previously silent and powerless female figures'; 'the woman in "Master" becomes the jaguar and undergoes a magical transformation in order to escape the brutal power of patriarchy – a trope that Carter revisits in many of the stories originally published in *The Bloody Chamber*' (2012: 176).[4]

However, there is much more to this short story than the liberation of the primitive woman, as Carter's portrayal of the jaguar woman stems from her reading of the myths in Lévi-Strauss's *The Raw and the Cooked*. This manifests itself when Carter includes a 'picturesque folk-tale' (2006: 77) that is central to the American Indian tribe the woman belongs to, in which the:

> jaguar invited the anteater to a juggling contest in which they would use their eyes to play with, so they drew their eyes out of the sockets. When they had finished, the anteater threw his eyes up into the air and back they fell – plop! in place in his head; but when the jaguar imitated him, his eyes caught in the topmost branches of a tree and he could not reach them. So he became blind. Then the anteater asked the macaw to make new eyes out of water for the jaguar and, with these eyes, the jaguar found that it could see in the dark. So all turned out well for the jaguar; and she, too, the girl who did not know her own name, could see in the dark. (Carter, 2006: 78)

This myth, which stresses the connection the woman from the jaguar clan has to jaguars in portraying their shared ability to see in the dark, is collected in *The Raw and the Cooked* as M119, a myth about 'the jaguar's eyes' (Lévi-Strauss 1970: 190), which Carter makes a note of in her journal (1969–70). The myth depicts conflict between the jaguar and the anteater:

> the jaguar invited the anteater to a juggling contest, using their eyes removed from the sockets: the anteater's eyes fell back into place, but the jaguar's remained hanging at the top of a tree, and so it became blind.

> At the request of the anteater, the macuco [macaw] bird made the jaguar new eyes out of water, and these allowed it to see in the dark.
> Since that time the jaguar only goes out at night. Having lost fire, it eats its meat raw. (Lévi-Strauss, 1970: 190)

Carter's recycling of the myth from *The Raw and the Cooked* illustrates her well-noted strengths in intertextuality, where the rewritten myth is faithful to the version noted by Lévi-Strauss, while also seamlessly embedded into Carter's prose. Not only does Carter's reading of Lévi-Strauss situate the tribe portrayed in 'Master' as a 'real' South American Indian community, but she has also added something to the myth about 'the jaguar's eyes' – the woman and her similarity to the jaguar. Both the woman and the jaguar can see in the dark in Carter's short story but, in addition, following on from the fact that the jaguar 'lost fire' and now 'eats its meat raw' in M119 (Lévi-Strauss, 1970: 190), the jaguar woman similarly rejects cooked meat at the end of 'Master' as part of her bestial transformation.

While Carter has added the woman to the myth about the jaguar's eyes, an addition which is central to the woman's metamorphosis at the end of the story and the inversion of the 'hunter' and 'prey' roles, I would argue that the inspiration for the jaguar woman also stems from a myth in *The Raw and the Cooked*. In M22, a myth about 'the origin of the jaguar', a woman kills her husband, returns home, and overnight 'she ate her children and ran away to the bush. She changed herself into a jaguar. Jaguars are women' (Lévi-Strauss, 1970: 99). In 'Master', the woman murders the savage explorer rather than a husband, but like the woman in the myth, the killing of the male counterpart and transformation into a jaguar is synonymous with freedom, particularly a freedom from patriarchal power, as Artt argues. Carter's reading of Lévi-Strauss's *The Raw and the Cooked* adds authenticity to her portrayal of the American Indian tribe in 'Master', but Carter also blurs the 'real' myths together – the myth of 'the jaguar's eyes' and of 'the origin of the jaguar' – enabling her to portray the woman's escape from the Master as well as her transformation into a jaguar and the implications this has for the tribe in terms of the progression from nature to culture. Rather than sharing cooked food with the rest of the tribe and thus making the successful transition to culture, the woman's transformation and preference for raw meat shows a rejection of culture in favour of nature.

Thus, Carter's engagement with Lévi-Strauss in *Heroes and Villains*, *Doctor Hoffman* and 'Master' serves to parody communities that are seen to represent culture and civilization. The Professors' language is unwinding and their 'knowledge' of the Barbarians is false, while the colonizing Master is killed by his prey, the jaguar woman. Similarly, Carter's portrayal of Portuguese explorers and their disregard for the River People in *Doctor Hoffman*, as well as of the stigma the Brazilian elite associate with American Indian communities, voices the manipulated and biased portrayal of primitive tribes in travel books written by explorers and anthropologists. Carter's reworking of Lévi-Strauss's work, with Doctor Hoffman's methodology as well as the American Indian myths in 'Master' and *Doctor Hoffman* being heavily influenced by *The Raw and the Cooked*, illustrate the extent to which Lévi-Strauss inspired a range of her works and ideas. While Carter claims that before *The Bloody Chamber and Other Stories* (1979), she 'used bits and pieces from various mythologies quite casually, because they were to hand' (1998a: 38), her engagement with Lévi-Straussian myth in *Doctor Hoffman* and 'Master', in particular, shows that her use of myth is far from 'casual'. Instead, Carter consciously uses myths from *The Raw and the Cooked* to shape her portrayal of American Indian tribes, while also debunking or 'demythologising' myths about such tribes being 'savage' or 'primitive'.

Notes

1 A number of Carter's articles make reference to Lévi-Strauss, often in relation to food. In 'Jessica Kuper (ed.), *The Anthropologist's Cookbook*' (1977), for instance, Carter refers to Lévi-Strauss's discussion of cookery in 'the Amazonian tribes with which he worked' (1998c: 87), and she references his work on 'raw and rotten foods' in 'Munch and Antibiotics' (1998d: 223), published in 1982. Carter also recycles the 'to eat is to fuck' phrase in association with Lévi-Strauss in her 1984 article 'An Omelette and a Glass of Wine and Other Dishes' (1998e: 98).
2 For a further discussion of Carter's satirical depiction of the Professors' knowledge (or lack of), see my chapter on Carter's engagement with Jean-Jacques Rousseau and Thomas Hobbes in *Imagining the End: Interdisciplinary Perspectives on the Apocalypse* (Yeandle, 2015: 55–82).
3 In fact, Carter copies down a 300-word quotation from pages 5–6 of *The Raw and the Cooked* (undated), a lengthy quotation which includes the shorter quotations cited here.

4 In 'The Tiger's Bride', one story in *The Bloody Chamber* collection, the woman transforms into a tiger at the end of the narrative.

References

Artt, Sarah (2012), '"Ambulant Fetish": The Exotic Woman in "Black Venus" and "Master"', in Sonya Andermahr and Lawrence Phillips (eds), *Angela Carter: New Critical Readings* (London: Continuum), pp. 176–86.

Bristow, Joseph and Trev Lynn Broughton (1997), Introduction to *The Infernal Desires of Angela Carter: Fiction, Femininity, Feminism* (London: Longman), pp. 1–23.

Carter, Angela (1966–68), Journal MS88899/1/91, Angela Carter Papers Collection, The British Library, London.

—— (1968–69), Journal MS88899/1/92, Angela Carter Papers Collection, The British Library, London.

—— (1969–70), Journal MS88899/1/93, Angela Carter Papers Collection, The British Library, London.

—— (1972), *Heroes and Villains* (London: Picador).

—— (1977), Journal MS88899/1/96, Angela Carter Papers Collection, The British Library, London.

—— (1989–90), Journal MS88899/1/99, Angela Carter Papers Collection, The British Library, London.

—— (1998a), 'Notes from the Front Line', in *Shaking a Leg: Collected Journalism and Writings*, ed. Jenny Uglow (London: Penguin), pp. 36–43.

—— (1998b), 'That Arizona Home', in *Shaking a Leg: Collected Journalism and Writings*, ed. Jenny Uglow (London: Penguin), pp. 275–9.

—— (1998c), 'Jessica Kuper (ed.), The Anthropologist's Cookbook', *Shaking a Leg: Collected Journalism and Writings*, ed. Jenny Uglow (London: Penguin), pp. 86–8.

—— (1998d), 'Munch and Antibiotics', *Shaking a Leg: Collected Journalism and Writings*, ed. Jenny Uglow (London: Penguin), pp. 223–7.

—— (1998e), 'An Omelette and a Glass of Wine and Other Dishes', in *Shaking a Leg: Collected Journalism and Writings*, ed. Jenny Uglow (London: Penguin), pp. 96–100.

—— ([1974] 2006), 'Master', in *Burning your Boats* (London: Vintage), pp. 75–80.

—— (2010), *The Infernal Desire Machines of Doctor Hoffman* (London: Penguin).

—— (undated), Journal MS88899/1/110, Angela Carter Papers Collection, The British Library, London.

Lévi-Strauss, Claude (1962), *The Savage Mind* (Chicago: University of Chicago Press).

—— (1963), *Structural Anthropology*, trans. Claire Jacobson and Brooke Grundfest Schoepf (New York: Basic Books).

—— (1970), *The Raw and the Cooked: Introduction to a Science of Mythology Volume 1*, trans. John and Doreen Weightman (New York: Harper Torchbooks).

—— (2011), *Tristes Tropiques*, trans. John Weightman and Doreen Weightman (London: Penguin).

Sage, Lorna (1994) 'The Fate of the Surrealist Imagination in the Society of the Spectacle', in Lorna Sage (ed.), *Flesh and the Mirror: Essays on the Art of Angela Carter* (London: Virago), pp. 98–116.

—— (2007), *Angela Carter*, 2nd Edition (Tavistock: Northcote House Publishers).

Yeandle, Heidi (2015), 'Angela Carter, Thomas Hobbes and Jean-Jacques Rousseau: Surviving the Apocalypse in *Heroes and Villains*', in Thomas E. Bishop and Jeremy R. Strong (eds), *Imagining the End: Interdisciplinary Perspectives on the Apocalypse* (Oxford: Inter-Disciplinary Press), pp. 55–82.

Yoshioka, Chiharu (2001), 'Contextualizing Angela Carter: Fiction, Enlightenment, and the Revolutionary Tradition', PhD Thesis, University of East Anglia.

7

Angela Carter's 'rigorous system of disbelief': religion, misogyny, myth and the cult

Marie Mulvey-Roberts

IN RESPONSE TO LORNA Sage's question in a 1977 interview as to whether 'one needs still to be anti-God', Angela Carter was in no doubt, saying, 'Oh yes! It's like being a feminist, you have to keep the flag flying. Atheism is a very rigorous system of disbelief, and one should keep proclaiming it. One ought not to be furtive about it' (Sage 1977: 57). Carter debunked religion through two short stories demystifying the Fall, and another re-evaluating the representation of Mary Magdalene in European art. She also produced an iconoclastic film on the life of Christ through painting called *The Holy Family Album* (1991) and satirized religious practice from medieval Catholicism in *The Infernal Desire Machines of Doctor Hoffman* (1972) to that of a modern Messiah in *The Passion of New Eve* (1977), via a re-imagining of Charles Manson's infamous sex cult, responsible for the brutal murder of the film actress Sharon Tate, discussed in detail here for the first time. Carter's atheism informed her feminist, political and ideological outlook on the world, while her approach to religion was part of her 'demythologising business' (Carter, 1997c: 38). She used radical scepticism to attack religion which, in having been built on myths, she saw as 'extraordinary lies designed to make people unfree' (38), a witty inversion of Christ's dictum: 'And ye shall know the truth, and the truth shall make you free' (John 8:32, KJV).

As a teenager, Carter freed herself from the Anglican faith of her mother, which had involved attending a church service every Sunday. By the start of the 1960s, when she moved to Bristol, she was an avowed atheist.[1] Her brother Hugh responded rather differently to his upbringing by becoming an accomplished church organist and choir master.[2] The baroque extravagances of his sister's writing may have been a reaction against the Calvinism on the paternal side of her family. Her father, Hugh Stalker, came from the Calvinist north east of Scotland, the Aberdeenshire 'godly town' (1997b: 17) of Macduff and her great-great grandmother had 'the stern face of a Kirk-goer' (15). Her paternal grandfather, however, was 'the village atheist' (18), though not of sufficient conviction to refrain from hedging his bets over the after-life by leaving five pounds in his will to the minister. To his annoyance, his wife treated the Sabbath as a day of rest, and every week piled Sunday's washing into a bucket for the next day. His granddaughter continued his legacy in the belief that 'nothing is sacred' (108), though she did admit that there is 'something sacred about the cinema', as a place of shared revelation (Evans: 1992). Carter's atheism was bound up with 'an absolute and *committed materialism* – i.e., that *this* world is all that there is and in order to question the nature of reality one must move from a strongly grounded base in what constitutes material reality' (1997c, 38; emphasis in original). For this reason, she was mildly irritated by enquiries over the 'mythic quality' of her writing because of her conviction that 'all myths are products of the human mind' (38). As a component of mythology, religious belief fell under her iconoclastic axe. In an interview with Anna Katsavos, Carter explained that her understanding of myth included what people might take on trust, such as the stories in the New Testament (Katsavos, 1994: 12). These are underpinned by the Genesis story of creation and the doctrine of the Fall, to which she continually returned (see Jennings, 2012: 165). By the 1980s, she saw the Women's Movement as instrumental in dismantling phallocentric culture which was founded on Judaeo-Christianity, eloquently challenged by the speechlessness of the prelapsarian wolf girl in 'Wolf-Alice' (1979) and 'Peter and the Wolf' (1985).

'Wolf-Alice' and 'Peter and the Wolf'

The heroine of 'Wolf-Alice' is brought up in the forest by wolves until she is discovered in a wolf's den, next to the body of her bullet-riddled foster mother. After being taken to live with nuns in a convent, the Mother Superior tries teaching her to thank God for her rescue from the wolf pack but the feral girl's reaction is to defecate and urinate in a corner of the chapel. For this blasphemy, she is exiled to the 'unsanctified household' (Carter, 1981: 120) of the Duke, one of Carter's reincarnations of the anti-clerical and blasphemous Marquis de Sade. This scabby lycanthropic and vampiric Duke makes use of the Christian cross as a scratching post and laps holy water from a church font, as if it were an animal's drinking trough. Clearly, Wolf Alice feels more at home with another animal human cross-over. She is identified with the prelapsarian 'world of talking beasts and flowers' (1981: 121) when, according to the historian, Flavius Josephus, a first-century Roman-Jewish scholar, 'all living things spoke the same language' (Kugel, 2009: 99). This was at the time of the Garden of Eden before 'the mouth of all the beasts and cattle and birds and whatever walked or moved was stopped from speaking' (99) the same language,[3] owing to Adam and Eve's sin of disobedience in eating the forbidden fruit from the Tree of Knowledge of Good and Evil. This marked the transition from a collective, holistic consciousness of the oneness of nature to a dislocated human self-consciousness, manifested by the separation of self from other.[4]

In raising the question of whether the Fall can ever be reversed, Carter asks, 'how can the bitten apple flesh out its scar again?' (1981: 121). The image of a wounded apple serves as a metaphor for the female body, for whom 'Mutilation is her lot' (121). This refers to the Freudian fable of how a young boy 'falls' (Jennings, 2012: 167) into knowledge of sexual difference, on seeing for the first time a female without a penis and assumes that she has been castrated. For Carter, Freud was another mythologizer whose belief-system she relished dismantling. His representation of woman as an embodiment of lack reinforced the notion of her otherness as a marker of inferiority. Because of Eve's subversive role in defying God and tempting the first man, all women are bequeathed greater suffering, particularly in connection with sexuality and reproduction, though for both sexes, the Fall triggered shame in the naked human body. This painful self-consciousness, indicative of the sexual repression enshrined within Judeo-Christianity, does not affect the animal kingdom nor Carter's wolf girl, whose 'nakedness, without innocence or display, was that of our first parents, before the Fall' (1986: 86).

Liberation from this self-consciousness sets the scene for the climactic turning point in Carter's 'Peter and the Wolf'. The title hero tracks down his long-lost cousin, stolen as a baby from her parents' home by wolves and brings her to live with his grandmother. The chaos which ensues culminates in his grandmother dying from her festering hand, having been bitten by her feral granddaughter. Desperate for atonement, Peter turns to religion. He embarks upon extreme fasting during Lent, lashing himself on Good Friday, and resolves to become a priest. One day, after his cousin has been dramatically rescued by wolves and returned to the wild, he catches sight of her drinking from a river and witnesses her exposed genitals and the sight of her suckling wolf cubs. The shock releases his pent-up grief for his grandmother, which also has the effect of freeing him from the constraints of his priestly vocation and a future life of celibacy into 'the vertigo of freedom' (1986: 86). The world opens up to him, like a latter-day Garden of Eden, allowing him to experience undifferentiated nature. For the first time, he sees the mountain of his home as though it were part of himself. This epiphany comes about because Peter is able to accept his wolf cousin and her new family with open arms, despite her being 'hairy as Magdalen in the wilderness' and for whom 'repentance was not within her comprehension' (86).

The Wrightsman Magdalene

Mary Magdalene, the ultimate fallen woman, is invariably seen in a state of perpetual repentance. In the short story, 'Impressions: The Wrightsman Magdalene' (1993), Carter critiques her representation within European art by focusing on the seventeenth-century painting of *The Penitent Magdalene* by Georges de La Tour (see figure 3). Acknowledging that the penitential part of the Magdalene appears only from the waist upwards, Carter wryly notes that the problem had always been in the nether regions anyway, signalled by the colour of her skirt – scarlet for a scarlet woman. Magdalene, however, is characterized more by her hair than her attire and, as Carter reminds us, is the patron saint of hairdressers. In some paintings, the hairiness substitutes for clothing, grown to protect the modesty of the naked penitent (see Warner, 1995: 359). In the Old Testament, women with long flowing locks were usually associated with prostitutes. Carter is not entirely convinced by the penance of this penitent harlot, and interprets her act of washing Christ's feet and drying them with her hair as, 'the kind of *gaudy gesture* a repentant prostitute *would* make' (1993: 143; emphasis in original). Even though she is not identified in the gospels as a sexually transgressive woman, her name was given to the Magdalene laundries as places to cleanse wayward women, and where their hair was cut short. Carter visualizes Magdalene's sins of the flesh as forming a hair shirt in the present, wrought from desires of the past. Mortification for this 'Venus in sackcloth' (141) is evident from the way in which she 'belts her own hair round her waist with the rope with which, each night, she lashes herself, making a rough tunic of it' (142). Carter is repelled by the odour of sanctity reeking from Donatello's carving of Magdalene, which portrays her as exposed to the elements, 'dried up by the suns of the wilderness, battered by wind and rain, anorexic, toothless, a body entirely annihilated by the soul' (143) (see figure 3). Her bony hands are clasped together in prayer. Carter equates such penitence with sadomasochism, seeing self-punishment as its own reward (see 143). A further mythologizing of the composite Magdalen was that of desert hermit, through which Carter imagines her as having the freedom to abandon speech and grunt with the animals, signifying a release from the Lacanian law of the father. But this is no Garden of Eden. Through such representations, Magdalene became the victim of a medieval hagiography, which conflated her with the Coptic desert anchorite Mary of Egypt, the patron saint of penitents.

Magdalene has a dialectic relationship with that other Mary, referred to in Carter's opening sentence: 'For a woman to be a virgin and a mother, you need a miracle; when a woman is not a virgin, nor a mother, either, nobody talks about miracles' (Carter, 1993: 140). Carter suggests that if Magdalene been a virgin mother and not 'a sacred whore' (146), Georges de La Tour would have portrayed her with a baby instead of a skull on her lap. This *memento mori*, a Carteresque 'plea for mortality' (Sage, 1994: 59), fills the space of a baby, a *memento vivere*, or reminder of the infinite perpetuation of life itself, as opposed to the myth of an 'after-life'. In 'Peter and the Wolf', the hero glimpses these material intimations of immortality through the portal of his wolfish cousin's exposed labia. In this deft repost to Freudian penis envy, Peter has 'a view of a set of Chinese boxes of whorled flesh that seemed to open one upon another into herself [...] his first, devastating, vertiginous intimation of infinity' (Carter, 1986: 83). This wild-girl eventually gives birth to wolf cubs. Magdalene, however, is defined in the negative, as 'the not-mother' (Carter, 1993: 140). The sight of her contemplating a candle-flame reflected in the mirror triggered, for the author, the memory of giving birth to her son Alex. During the nineteen hours Carter spent in

3 Penitent Magdalen sculpture (1455) by Donatello, Museo dell'Opera del Duomo, Florence.

4 Original cover of *American Ghosts & Old World Wonders* published by Chatto & Windus in 1993.

labour, she too watched a candle flame, only one from within her own mind's eye.

The Holy Family Album and *The Infernal Desire Machines of Doctor Hoffman*

In her televised surrealist documentary on the life of Christ, *The Holy Family Album*, a baby is filmed emerging messily from the birth canal and delivered straight into the nativity's leading role. The sight of a mother bloodily giving birth violently clashes with sanitized and static representations of the birth from within Christian iconography. This disruptive image, with its sound track of a crying newborn, clashes with the solemn procession of paintings relating to the nativity, accompanied by sacred choral music. Carter's portrayal of the life of Jesus, through Western paintings, resembles a sequence of photographs in God's family album, which include a series of images of Madonna and child. The idea for the film might have been gestating as far back as 1977 when *The Passion of New Eve* was published, in which paintings of the Virgin and child are used to reprogramme Evelyn, who has undergone a forced surgical sex-change that transforms him into Eve:

> I recall particularly three video-tale sequences designed to assist me to adjust to my new shape. One consisted of reproductions of, I should think, every single Virgin and Child that had ever been painted in the entire history of Western European art, projected upon my curving wall in real-life colours and blown up to larger than life-size, accompanied by a sound track composed of the gurgling of babies and the murmuring of contented mothers; this was intended to glorify the prospect before me. (72)

Carter sees religious paintings of the Madonna and child as propaganda for inscribing roles for women as wives and mothers. In her film, God the father comes off badly as an absent father. She suggests that Jesus's preference for his single-parent mother prompted God to arrange for the crucifixion of his son, saying: 'He was a cruel father. Remember he planned all this' (184).[5]

After its broadcast in the run-up to Christmas in 1991, this bold exegesis led to calls from offended Christians to ban the film. Lorna Sage described *The Holy Family Album* as 'a piece of deliberate blasphemy against the Almighty' (1994: 59), though Carter told an *Observer* journalist that she had not intended the film to be blasphemous, 'because I don't believe that you can blaspheme against something which does not exist' (*Observer*, 1 December 1991). Elsewhere, she quips that compared to the French, the British regard blasphemy as silly (see 1997a: 68) yet, at the time the film was being made, it was still illegal in Britain, a fact pointed out by John Ellis, the producer, to Max Ernst's wife, Dorothea Tanning. He might have been only half-joking when he said that he hoped they would not be spending Christmas in jail (see Crofts, 2003: 170). As Charlotte Crofts suggests, Carter had difficulty reconciling a society which censored sex, and yet 'worships sadomasochistic images of the bleeding Christ' (184). In the script, she re-named the crucifixion, 'cruci*fiction*' (184; emphasis added) to draw attention to the fact that it *is* an image. Its repeated use in ritual and sacred art, as a means of religious indoctrination, serves to crucify Christ over and over again.

The cruelty enshrined in religious ideology, through suffering, martyrdom and sacrifice, is satirized in an episode in *The Infernal Desire Machines of Doctor Hoffman*, based on the sadomasochistic theology of a race of centaurs. These form the congregation of the Church of the Horse, a satire on medieval Christianity, and a reworking of the talking horses or Houyhnhnms, in Book Four of Swift's *Gulliver's Travels* (1726). On a low hill (Golgotha), there is a curious tree that is part horse skeleton, into which consecrated nails have been hammered. This is where two visitors to this equine dystopia, Desiderio and Albertina, are taken and narrowly escape being sacrificially killed by having iron shoes nailed to their feet with red-hot nails in readiness for their union with the celestial herd. This conflation of a scene from a blacksmith's forge with that of a torture chamber of the Inquisition, as well as Good Friday's main event, marks the centaurs' valediction to their human guests. Having no word for 'visitor' or its equivalents, the centaurs initially regard the newcomers as an irritating distraction from 'the majestic pageant of their ritual lives' (Carter, 1982a: 226), but eventually incorporate them into their liturgy. The rhythms of their days are regulated by ritual and they recite the entirety of their scriptures throughout the year, concluding in the death and resurrection of the Sacred Stallion, followed by forty days of mourning, corresponding to Lent and then a three-day feast, the equivalent of Easter. 'Daily life was meaningless to them for all they did was done in the shadow of the continuous passion of the Sacred Stallion and only this cosmic drama was real to them' (212). Inhabiting cyclical rather than linear time; the centaurs' liturgical calendar is a 'timeless medium' (214) or eternal present that would have been familiar to the medieval mind. Similarly, committed Christians experience the Passion, death and Resurrection of Christ as transhistorical and contemporaneous, so that 'the time of the theophany becomes actual' (Eliade, 1996: 393). This is explained in a section on 'Sacred Time and the Myth of Eternal Renewal' in *Patterns in Comparative Religion* ([1958] 1996) by Mircea Eliade, a book which Carter refers to in her papers at the British Library archive.[6] For the centaurs, the immediacy of myth and ritual time is reinforced through physical pain, whether brought about by tattooing, flagellation or the flaying alive of an unfaithful wife and castration of her lover, who is then forced to eat his own penis raw.

While religion is the driver for such barbarisms, classicism provided the vehicle which best expressed the centaurs' nobility. Carter draws attention to the Junoesque appearance of a roan mare and compares a group of centaurs to Greek masterpieces. Yet in *The Infernal Desire Machines of Dr Hoffman*, the centaurs' see themselves as degenerate copies of the horse god they worship, which parallels how Christians perceive themselves and their parents as imperfect versions of the Holy Family. The Middle Ages witnessed a growing revival of the classics, which emphasized the dignity of man. The Greek cult of the body was diametrically opposed to penitential corporeal medievalism with its scourging of the flesh. However, the religious fanaticism of Carter's centaurs allegorizes the way in which the classical world had been corrupted by the extremes of Christianity.

The centaurs' sacramental mind-set is fundamentally medieval: their sovereign myth is that everything has significance, even the most insignificant household tasks such as mucking out or collecting water. This divine and 'dramaturgical' (Carter, 1982a: 221) perception of life was characteristic of Christians in the Dark and Middle Ages, for whom all things sublunary were symbolic of spiritual counterparts or, in the words of Thomas Howard, 'everything meant everything, and that it all rushed up finally to heaven' (1989: 13). For the centaurs, this even extends to dung, an intertextual nod to Swift's scatological satire. Treated as a type of spiritual manure, Carter compares it obliquely to the bread and wine of Holy Communion:

> these hippolators believed their god revealed himself to them in the droppings excreted by the horse part of themselves [...] Shit signified his presence among them. Their Holy Hill was a dung heap. The twice daily movement of their bowels was at once a form of prayer and a divine communion. (211–12)

Despite the equation of the sacramental with the excremental, the centaurs do not stoop to coprophily, though that could hardly be said of the Marquis de Sade, who brings together the scatological and the sacred in *One Hundred and Twenty Days of Sodom*, written in 1785, in which whores defecate on communion wafers. The title of Carter's *Nothing Sacred* (1982) is likely to be homage to a line from Sade's poem *La Vérité* (1787), 'il n'est rien de sacré' (quoted by Roche, 2006: 159). Carter writes about *One Hundred and Twenty Days of Sodom* in *The Sadeian Woman* (1979), along with Sade's *Justine* (1791), whose virtuous heroine is forced to partake in monastic coprophagy. Sade's sadism and blasphemy function as an expression of Enlightenment anti-clericalism. His place in the history of ideas was established by Georges Bataille, whose *Story of the Eye* (*Histoire de l'oeil*, 1928) was admired by Carter as part of that 'fine European tradition of anti-clericalism' which puts sacrilege, blasphemy and pornography in the service of 'human freedom' against the restrictive laws of Judeo-Christianity, which she referred to as a 'nauseating madness' (1997a: 68–9). By eroticizing the ascetic traditions of flagellants, including the penitential scourging of the flesh, Sade was carrying out a political act in the name of *liberté*. In *The Infernal Desire Machines of Doctor Hoffman*, the centaurs adopt a creative way of inflicting pain on themselves for the sake of religion by tattooing their upper human parts in gloriously coloured designs. They resemble living illuminated medieval manuscripts, the image, rather than the word, made flesh, only their handiwork is closer to the intensely painful Japanese practice of *irezumi*. Carter was living in Japan at the time she was writing the novel and was aware of this method of tattooing for spiritual and decorative purposes, which covered much of the surface of the body with mythological beasts and characters from myths and folktales.[7] The skin of the centaurs is intricately embroidered with equine images to remind them of their more perfect selves, the supreme example of which is the Stallion, the epitome of sacred masculinity.

Within this theocracy, women rank as the lowest of the low, doing most of the humdrum, back-breaking work, usually out in the fields. Their inferior status goes back to the sins of a mythological Mother figure, the Bridal Mare who, after having been impregnated by her husband, the Sacred Stallion, is unfaithful with the Black Archer. Worse still, the adulterous couple kill and eat him, paralleling the Catholic mass. When the Bridal Mare brings forth the child of her illicit union, she gives birth to the Sacred Stallion. The absurdity of him being reborn as his own child, is a parody of the paradox of God being born as his own son through the mysteries of the Holy Trinity and Immaculate Conception. Because of her betrayal, the Bridal Mare is a 'penitent sinner' (222) who, like Eve and Mary Magdalene, is another archetype in the pantheon of feminine weakness. The misogynistic theology of the centaurs condones the ritual rape and degradation of women to assert male authority and virility. But their punishment does not end there. Female centaurs are tattooed more extensively and thus more painfully than the males: 'For they believed women were born only to suffer' (208).

The Passion of New Eve and Charles Manson

The elevation of the suffering woman to the point of deification manifests in the mythoclastic novel, *The Passion of New Eve*. Here the movie star Tristessa de St Ange, 'Our Lady of the Sorrows' (Carter, 1982b: 71), performs her rites of despair on the altar of the silver screen, exposing her scars in much the same way as 'a medieval saint points to the wounds of his martyrdom' (6). Sadness, saintliness and Sade are encoded within her very name, the second part of which derives from Sade's novel, *Philosophy in the Bedroom* (1795), in which the libertine Madame de Saint-Ange initiates the young girl Eugenie into sadism. Around Tristessa, the studio has created not just a mystique but a mythology, akin to the myth of the eternal woman and, as Carter observes: 'A critique of these symbols is a critique of our lives. Tristessa. Enigma, Illusion. Woman? Ah!' (6) This secular icon is worshipped by the hero Evelyn, the recipient of 'the flickering blessings of the divine Tristessa' (8). Yet, as he will discover, her sex is a mere projection, an illusion going beyond cinema, since the screen goddess is, in fact, a man masquerading as a woman. Tristessa literalizes Judith Butler's theory of gender as performance, which ironically Evelyn comes to embody after being surgically transformed into a woman, when she falls into the hands of Mother, the 'Grand Emasculator' (49). Doubling up as mad scientist and earth goddess, this Holy Mother is an 'incarnated deity' (49), who has surgically modified her own body by grafting two tiers of nipples onto her chest to become 'her own mythological artefact' (60). She debunks the Garden of Eden as the place where Adam was born by pointing out to Evelyn that the garden lies between her thighs. This turns upside down the Genesis creation myth that Eve was created from Adam's rib by reinscribing the biological imperative that man is born from woman. Mother, as the self-appointed 'Castratrix of the Phallocentric Universe' (67), has been conveniently trained as a transsexual surgeon, and conceives the radical plan of surgically modifying Evelyn so that he (or rather she) can give birth to a new 'Messiah of the antithesis' (67). Declaring war on biblical myth, Mother takes on the role of Angel Gabriel by breaking the news to Evelyn that he will be transformed into the New Eve and impregnated with his own sperm. Her prophecy that the child of this virgin mother will revolutionize the world, has a familiar ring. Powerless to resist, Evelyn is forcibly changed into Eve, but manages to avoid insemination by escaping into the desert.

Before long the now New Eve is captured again, only this time by another Messianic cult. Her wail, 'At whose mercy is poor Eve now?' (85), is akin to the lament of Sade's Justine, who also passes from one set of abusers to another. In common with Justine, Eve's fate is to be a sex slave, only hers has a distinctly twentieth-century twist. She is taken to Zero, the one-eyed and one-legged poet, who has a harem of seven women, just the right number for servicing his sexual needs for every day of the week with a different partner. Zero is based on the musician and poet Charles Manson, who recruited young women into his sex cult known as 'the Family' and demanded love-making seven times a day (see Sanders, 1973: 56). The unmistakable parallels between Zero and Manson, and concomitant level of detail, indicate that a likely source for Carter would have been Ed Sanders' *The Family: The Story of Charles Manson's Dune Buggy Attack Battalion* ([1972] 1973).[8] Evidence that Zero is based on Charles Manson appears in a notebook in the Angela Carter archive of the British Library (Add. MS 88899/1/103). Here she writes: 'Manson: the poet: Zero' (55). On a page headed 'Manson's theory of sexuality' (72), she writes that women have no souls and were slaves, 'fucking 7 times a day' and 'ritual foot-kissing'. Earlier she notes that Eve 'is ritually married to Manson' and that the women in 'Manson's gang' are treated worse than the mastiffs, later changed in the novel to pigs.[9]

Both Manson and Zero are sex gurus, who have the hubris of the madman, false prophet and confidence trickster (see Storr, 1996: xi–xvii). They exemplify the reiterative nature of religion and cults; their exploitation of women is also indicative of how patriarchy depends on repetition through which, as Judith Butler has argued, the performance of gender depends (Butler, 1990). Zero is not only a reincarnation of Manson but also repeats Manson's crimes using a Messianic smokescreen. The Manson family's murders hit the headlines while Carter was visiting the United States during late July to early September 1969. The news rudely awoke the hippy pipe-dream of peace and love wafting from the consciousness-raising days of 1968, which saw a proliferation of religious and cultish beliefs. Carter could certainly understand their appeal, saying how we can scare ourselves and get into 'culs-de-sac of infantile mysticism' at a time when 'false prophets, loonies and charlatans freely roamed the streets' (1997c: 37).

Manson convinced his devoted followers that he was the Messiah and introduced himself as Jesus Christ to a priest, even simulating the Crucifixion, using ropes instead of nails in an LSD infused ceremony, on the aptly named Hill of Martyrdom. Zero also succeeds in inspiring blind love in his women, 'postulants in the Church of Zero' (Carter, 1982b: 87), to whom they dedicate themselves mind, body and soul. Adoration towards charismatic, manipulative and narcissistic gurus is characteristic of potentially dangerous cults when reinforced by strict rules of obedience, punishment and threats. For example, Zero has a bull-whip and Manson warned of cutting off his women's breasts. Their respective anointed followers had been manipulated by the force of misogyny, mind-altering drugs and the indoctrination of a reality-distorting guru patter, so that for Zero's acolytes, 'The ranch-house was Solomon's Temple; the ghost town was the New Jerusalem; the helicopter his chariot of fire, his prick his bow of burning gold, etc etc etc' (100).

Eve's initiation into the cult is to be raped by Zero. Likewise, Manson used sex as a method for inducting girls into his unholy Family, boasting: 'I am the God of Fuck' (Sanders 1973: 31) and claimed to have revived the sexy side of Christ before its suppression by the Apostolic Fathers. Both gurus readily exploited the rhetoric of the sexual revolution and in 1968, Manson witnessed the Summer of Love at its epicentre in San Francisco. As Sheila Jeffreys points out in her critique of the sexual revolution, *Anti-Climax: A Feminist Perspective on the Sexual Revolution* (1990), instead of a woman being sexually available for just one man, she was now expected to be accessible for more. Zero and Manson, while retaining their status as sex gods, took advantage of this sexploitation by sending their women out to earn money through prostitution. In a sex cult, the phallus of the guru can be elevated to an object of divine worship, as in the case of Zero, whose votaries serve as vessels for his sacred member and holy seminal fluid. Their pretence that his semen was life-sustaining over-compensated for his inability to father 'a new breed of Americans' (1982b: 94). He blames his infertility on Tristessa, claiming that she had given him a spiritual vasectomy by way of the cinema screen, for, as Carter realized, a screen goddess can only ever be a sterile illusion. Eve's love guru is convinced that the only way in which he can replicate more Zeros, rather than continue to ejaculate blanks, is to sacrifice Tristessa. Evelyn plays tribute to his film idol with spermatozoa, while watching her on the cinema screen as she plays the role of a castrating femme fatale, at the same time as he is sexually exploiting an unnamed woman. Evelyn's misogyny will single him out as the chosen one for a future sex-change, thus enabling him to bring forth the Messiah. While Evelyn suffers castration, Zero is protected from it during oral sex by insisting that members of his harem have their incisors removed. This connects to a legend that after an over-zealous female disciple bit Manson's 'sacred' member in two, he miraculously healed himself. Manson would order his female disciples to 'strip and suck' (Sanders, 1973: 119) members of motor-bike gangs, whose initials SS stood for Satan's Slaves and the Straight Satans, as part of his Messianic plan. These acts of female sex slave subordination were intended to coerce the bikers into co-operating as a military wing, once the Family instigated the race war which would herald the start of Armageddon.

Manson predicted that blacks would rise, kill millions of whites and wipe out the government, thereby paving the way for him to dominate the world in the Second Coming, as both Christ and the Devil. In *The Passion of New Eve*, civil war has already broken out in the United States between various political, gendered and racial groups, resulting in Evelyn losing his new university post in New York after the building is taken over by a militant black group. For both Manson and Zero, these race riots marked the start of a holy war within a greater apocalyptic narrative.[10] The eschatology of Armageddon can provide cult leaders with a framework to strengthen their stranglehold on devotees by using a parallel time-line operating on a cosmic or millennial scale, which reinforces a collective sense of their existence outside the social order. Zero and Manson had both spent time in jail and incited their followers to become outlaws, in possession of illegal guns, drugs and stolen cars. Their stolen vehicles were converted into dune buggies to form a battalion, the equivalent of the sand-sleds used by the militant women in their isolated desert world. The cults of Zero and Manson formed a self-contained community, which was geographically isolated in remote ranches in the Southern Californian desert. Mason and his followers lived at the Spahn's Movie Ranch, which had been used as a film set for westerns. It was an appropriate setting for their make-believe world and keys into Zero's obsession with a movie star. Aided by a ban on books and psychedelic brainwashing, Manson created his own insane fantasy world; similarly, Zero 'no longer needed news of the world, since he manufactured it himself to his own designs' (Carter, 1982b: 101).

According to Manson's masterplan, the Family would descend to The Hole, a bottomless pit in Death Valley, from where they would attack cities with the hairy locusts of the Abyss from the Book of Revelations. From this, Carter may have gleaned her idea for Beulah, the subterranean metropolis occupied by Mother and her single-breasted warrior women in *The Passion of New Eve* and, incidentally, it was widely reported in the newspapers at the time that Sharon Tate's breast had been cut off by her attackers (Bugliosi, [1974] 2015: 28), which turned out to be untrue. Even though Manson made use of the language from the Book of Revelations in his prophecies, he actually named the coming cataclysm 'Helter Skelter', after a track from the Beatles' *White Album*. Unbeknown to the Fab Four, they had been transformed by Manson into the four horsemen of the Apocalypse. Another song from the album, 'Piggies', had particular resonance for Manson, as he interpreted it as an allusion to his prime hate target, the white elite whom he denounced as, 'Pig Christian wealthy Americans'. The word 'PIG' would be written in the blood of his victim, Sharon Tate, at the crime scene. Zero debased his women by decreeing that they share their beds with pigs, who must be treated as substitute babies. Treating pigs as sacred animals, Zero gives these little lords of creation more latitude than his wives, who are obliged to communicate in grunts. Almost as if to parody the Garden of Eden, as well as to reinforce the lowly status of women, Zero uses the language of the beasts when addressing his sex slaves. Similarly, Manson made a rule that the mothers speak gibberish to the children, banning the word 'why'. Such control over language is another means of turning cult members into cyphers of their guru. The word 'Nullity' (1982b: 102) appears in the novel as a synonym for 'Zero', a name which Carter probably borrowed from Sanders' *The Family*. Here may be found a reference to a youth in Manson's circle called Zero, recruited for his kleptomaniacal abilities (see Sanders, 1973:

164).[11] Giving neophytes different names is another common practice amongst gurus for the purpose of creating a new identity within the cult. For instance, two of Zero's women are known as 'Apple Pie' and 'Tiny', while Manson 'blessed' (39) Susan Atkins as 'Sadie Mae Glutz', whose new first name Carter probably adopted for another of Zero's women.[12] Appearance was also controlled by the master. For example, Zero insisted that the women have pudding-basin hair-cuts and during their trial the Manson women shaved their heads in imitation of their leader. Yet the mastery of the guru over his submissive women is never entirely one-sided, for as in the case of Zero, 'Their obedience ruled him' (Carter, 1982b: 99).

Manson enjoyed testing the obedience of 'Charlie's girls' by lining them up against a hay-stack and seeing how close to them he could hurl a machete. In *The Passion of New Eve*, Zero throws knives at a poster of his *bête noire*, Tristessa, inflicting multiple stab wounds on her 'elegiac body [...] hilts, the blades of which were embedded behind her in the wooden wall, quivered all over her' (1982b: 91). This has an unnerving similarity with the fate of another movie star, Sharon Tate, the wife of the film director Roman Polanski and the most well-known victim of the Manson family murders, who was stabbed sixteen times by members of the Manson gang. Her brutal murder, along with that of four others, was the catalyst for the apocalyptic Helter Skelter,[13] when intruders entered her secluded house, overlooking Benedict Canyon and West Hollywood. There is a fictional parallel in how Zero and his followers break into the remote Californian glass house of Tristessa, a shrine to fame and celebrity, to trigger their own version of Armageddon. Tristessa's house had a circular glass staircase and it seems likely that Carter used Sanders' description of a house, named after the large spiral staircase it contained, called The Spiral Staircase house. Located in the Topanga Canyon region of Los Angeles, this was where the Manson family stayed the previous summer (See Sanders, 1973: 42). The trashing of Tristessa's house relished by Zero and his girls parallels a comment made by Tex Watson, one of the Manson family murderers, that 'It was fun to tear down the Polanski residence' (Sanders, 1973: 232). In Tristessa's house of glass, Zero and his clan discover a waxwork museum memorializing those who lost their lives to fame: Valentino, James Dean, Marilyn Monroe, Jean Harlow and, most significantly, Sharon Tate 'in a tide of golden hair, she, poor girl, stabbed to death by mad people' (1982b: 117). When

Tristessa is discovered lying in a bier, she resembles another movie star simulated 'Immortal' (142), or even a corpse, but when her robe is seized by a dog, she is sufficiently alive to fling a bible at her attacker. Zero's attempt to destroy and humiliate Tristessa, a rival deity in the form of an emasculating screen goddess, is to hang her by the wrists from a steel beam. While this reenactment of her crucifixion film role (see 116) is another reminder that 'Suffering was her vocation' (8), it also makes a macabre connection with Sharon Tate, who was tied by a white nylon rope around her neck to a beam in her home before being murdered. In the chaos that Zero and the women wreak upon the glass house, wax effigies are dismembered and limbs and torsos jumbled up, including the body parts of Sharon Tate. Susan Atkins (Sadie) would later complain to cellmates that Tex had ordered her to leave before she could mutilate the bodies, a detail which may have some bearing on Carter's description of the waxwork body parts floating in the swimming pool (see Carter, 1982b: 142), which is also reminiscent of Billy Wilder's film about a faded Hollywood star, *Sunset Boulevard* (1950). Unlike her real-life counterpart who dies with her unborn child,[14] Tristessa survives the murderous love cult, only to be killed later by the leader of a militant Christian cult, a boy soldier who believes that he is Jesus Christ. After being exposed as a female impersonator, Zero forces him to marry Eve in a mock wedding. Her subsequent impregnation as 'the fruit of the tree of knowledge' (146) is another parody of the Fall.

Unsure whether she is at the beginning or the end of the world, Eve is driven by teleological curiosity. In an apocalyptic conclusion to the novel, time runs backward, in keeping with Mother's desire to reset the clock of father time. But Eve, now reborn and with the prospect of usurping Old Adam, sees through the myth of this Earth Mother to discover that she is just a crazy old woman, soon to die, and already redundant. As stated by Mother's daughter Leilah, also known as Lilith, the name of Adam's first wife: 'Historicity rendered myth unnecessary' (173). This must be Carter's wishful thinking, though she was too much of a realist to make it her last word. As the new Eve sails off to give birth, the reader is left wondering if she is the harbinger of a new myth and whether this is just the same old story being told all over again. In *The Sadeian Woman*, Carter derides the mythic representations of women, declaring that 'Mother goddesses are just as silly a notion as father gods' and identifies myth as a form of 'consolatory nonsense' (1979: 5) to dull the pain of reality. But it is the pain of religion, whether it be the penitential tortures of the centaurs or the suffering of Zero's women enslaved in a cult of nullification, that can be seen as extreme fictional manifestations of Carter's proselytizing atheism.

Notes

I would like to thank Martine Hennard Dutheil de la Rochère and Anna Watz for their helpful comments on this chapter.

1. I am indebted to Edmund Gordon for this information in an email, 1 September 2016.
2. Recordings of him playing sacred music are still available.
3. This was indicated in the Jewish *Book of Jubilees*, written during the second century BC.
4. For a parodic approach on the Fall, see also Carter, 1996, 58–67.
5. On p. 10 of the script, Carter writes in pencil in the margin: 'Its [sic] Eluard, Aragon & André Breton, I think – the anti-God squad. They'd like to take that baby away to a place of safety but the Father won't let them in', Add. MS 88899/1/60 ('The Holy Family Album'). I would like to thank Martine Hennard Dutheil de La Rochère for reminding me of this and for the reference.
6. Angela Carter Papers: British Library, Western Manuscripts, Add. MS 88899/1/96, created 1977. Martine Hennard Dutheil de La Rochère first alerted me to Carter's reference to this book in an email, 29 August 2016.
7. Corinna Sargood's lino cut frontispieces of Carter's two *Virago Book of Fairy Tales* (1990 and 1993) are of a similarly tattooed man and woman.
8. She may also have read a later book, *Helter Skelter: The True Story of the Manson Murders* (London: Arrow Books [1974], 1992), written by Vincent Bugliosi (with Curt Gentry), who was the prosecutor for the Tate trial.
9. I am grateful to Scott Dimovitz for drawing my attention to this part of the archive.
10. For a discussion on how gurus make use of the apocalypse, see Hall (with Schuyler and Trinh) (2000).
11. Christopher Zero is a Manson Family member mentioned in Ed Sanders, *Sharon Tate: A Life* (Boston, MA: Da Capo Press, 2016), p. 264.
12. Sadie Mae Glutz's baby was called Zezo Ze-ce-Zadfrak. Regarding naming, in a novel based on the Manson Family entitled *The Girls*, the

heroine is called Evelyn and when she first meets Manson, fictionalised as Russell, he shortens it to Eve (see Cline, 2016: 117).
13 Those looking for an explanation for the atrocity mistakenly linked it to human sacrifice, connecting it to Tate's first major film role, *Eye of the Devil* (1966).
14 Sharon Tate was heavily pregnant with the child of Roman Polanski, who had recently made a film about witchcraft, *Rosemary's Baby* (1968), about a woman who gives birth to the devil.

References

Butler, Judith (1990), *Gender Trouble: Feminism and the Subversion of Identity* (London: Routledge).
Bugliosi, Vincent with Curt Gentry ([1974] 2015), *Helter Skelter: The True Story of the Manson Murders* (London: Arrow Books).
Carter, Angela (1979), *The Sadeian Woman: An Exercise in Cultural History* (London: Virago Press).
—— 'Wolf-Alice' ([1979] 1981), *The Bloody Chamber* (Harmondsworth: Penguin), pp. 119–26.
—— ([1972] 1982a), *The Infernal Desire Machines of Doctor Hoffman* (London: Penguin).
—— ([1977] 1982b), *The Passion of New Eve* (London: Virago Press).
—— ([1985] 1986), 'Peter and the Wolf', *Black Venus* (London: Picador Press).
—— (1993), 'Impressions: The Wrightsman Magdalene', *American Ghosts & Old World Wonders* (London: Chatto & Windus).
—— ([1974] 1996), 'Penetrating to the Heart of the Forest', in *Burning Your Boats: Collected Short Stories* (London: Vintage), pp. 58–67.
—— ([1979] 1997a), 'Georges Bataille: Story of the Eye', in *Shaking a Leg: Collected Journalism and Writings*, ed. Jenny Uglow (London: Chatto & Windus), pp. 68–9.
—— ([1983] 1997b), 'My Father's House', in *Shaking a Leg: Collected Journalism and Writings*, ed. Jenny Uglow (London: Chatto & Windus), pp. 15–19.
—— ([1983] 1997c), 'Notes from the Front Line', in *Shaking a Leg: Collected Journalism and Writings*, ed. Jenny Uglow (London: Chatto & Windus), pp. 36–43.
Cline, Emma (2016), *The Girls: A Novel* (London: Chatto & Windus).
Crofts, Charlotte (2003), *'Anagrams of Desire': Angela Carter's Writing for Radio, Film and Television* (Manchester: Manchester University Press).
Dimovitz, Scott A. (2016), *Angela Carter: Surrealist, Psychologist, Moral Pornographer* (London and New York: Routledge).

Eliade, Mircea ([1958] 1996), *Patterns in Comparative Religion* (Lincoln and London: University of Nebraska Press).
Evans, Kim (dir.) (1992), *Angela Carter's Curious Room*, Omnibus, BBC1, 15 September.
Hall, John R. with Philip D. Schuyler and Sylvaine Trinh (2000), *Apocalypse Observed: Religious Movements and Violence in North America, Europe, and Japan* (London and New York: Routledge).
Howard, Thomas ([1969] 1989), *Chance or the Dance? A Critique of Modern Secularism* (San Francisco, CA: Ignatius Press).
Jennings, Hope (2012), 'Genesis and Gender: The Word, the Flesh and the Fortunate Fall in "Peter and the Wolf" and "Penetrating to the Heart of the Forest"', in Sonya Andermahr and Lawrence Phillips (eds), *Angela Carter: New Critical Readings*, (London: Bloomsbury), pp. 165–175.
Katsavos, Anna (1994), 'An Interview with Angela Carter', *Review of Contemporary Fiction*, 14:3, 11–17.
Kugel, James L. ([1998] 2009), *Traditions of the Bible: A Guide to the Bible as It Was at the Start of the Common Era* (Cambridge, MA: Harvard University Press).
Roche, Geoffrey (2006), 'Black Sun: Bataille on Sade', *Janus Head*, 9:1, 157–80.
Sage, Lorna (1977), 'The Savage Sideshow: A Profile of Angela Carter', *The New Review*, 4 (39/40), 51–7.
—— (1994), *Angela Carter* (Tavistock: Northcote House Publishers).
Sanders, Ed (1973), *The Family: The Story of Charles Manson's Dune Buggy Attack Battalion* (St Albans: Panther Books).
Storr, Anthony (1996), *Feet of Clay: Saints, Sinners, and Madmen: A Study of Gurus* (New York: The Free Press).
Warner, Marina (1995), *From the Beast to the Blonde: On Fairy Tales and their Tellers* (London: Vintage).
Watz, Anna (2017), *Angela Carter and Surrealism: 'A Feminist Libertarian Aesthetic'* (London: Routledge).

8

'Clothes are our weapons': dandyism, fashion and subcultural style in Angela Carter's fiction of the 1960s

Catherine Spooner

CARTER'S FICTION IS REPLETE with references to clothes and, in particular, to the heady possibilities afforded by dressing up: Melanie in *The Magic Toyshop* (1967), climbing a tree in her mother's wedding dress; Leilah in *The Passion of New Eve* (1977) with her fabulous harlot's wardrobe; Fevvers in *Nights at the Circus* (1984) dazzling the circus audience with her bottle-blonde hair and ambiguously fake wings. Critical attention to this aspect of Carter's writing has characteristically inhered around her fiction of the later 1970s onwards, and its explicit interest in the performativity of gender and feminine masquerade. Carter's attitudes to dress, however, were forged in the heady atmosphere of the 1960s and that decade's riotous celebration of subcultural style as a form of resistance. Carter's writing of the 1960s is explicitly informed by her interest in subcultural style, and the sartorial defiance enacted by the emergent counterculture. In the 1960s novels, *Shadow Dance* (1966), *The Magic Toyshop*, *Several Perceptions* (1968), *Heroes and Villains* (1969) and *Love* (1971), clothing operates overtly as a mode of opposition to a dominant culture that is constructed as conservative, middle-class and patriarchal.

Throughout her work, Carter repeatedly returns to the idea of feminine subjectivity as being constructed through a kind of dressing up box of visual props, which both constrain their wearers through a series of stereotyped images and liberate them through performativity and play. For the majority of critics, this liberatory impulse is increasingly emphasized in her writings of the later 1970s onwards. They characteristically read the emphasis on women's agency in these works as resolving a more problematic constraint by conventional gender scripts in the earlier fiction. Paulina Palmer, for instance, considers how, 'The representation of woman entrapped in male-scripted forms of masquerade in her early writings is replaced in her later works by images of women subversively "playing with mimesis"' (Palmer 1997: 32). Similarly, Christina Britzolakis suggests that in Carter's later novels she 'create[s] heroines who are no longer the puppets of male-controlled scripts but who use theatricality and masquerade to invent and advance themselves' (Britzolakis 1997: 51). Not only are these strategies rooted in the material practices of late 1960s style, but in Carter's earlier novels they are understood as such and used as a means of commenting on the rewards and limitations of the contemporary alternative scene. Moreover, in these works, the most interestingly attired characters are frequently men. Paying close attention to how the style revolution impacted on conventional forms of masculinity in the 1960s can help make sense of the less coherent gender politics of these texts, in which Carter explores countercultural rebellion through dandyism and androgyny.

Carter's focus on style enables her to critique the gendering of subculture itself as a predominantly masculine arena. She repeatedly returns to the male dandy as initiating a kind of crisis in patriarchal culture, as his power inheres, like that of women, in his 'to-be-looked-at-ness'. Through his experimentation with style, for Carter, the dandy rebels against the dominant order and asserts his mastery of the modern culture of images. However, as he 'watches himself being looked at', to adapt John Berger's phrase, he experiences a decentring of subjectivity that is often catastrophic (Berger, 1990: 47). The emphasis on dressing up in these novels instigates the dissolution of the 'authentic' subject prized in subcultural discourses and the inauguration of a more fluid, decentred model of subjectivity.

The boy in the djellibah

In 1960s Britain, popular culture was newly established as an object of intellectual analysis: not only through the dissemination of French semiotics in texts such as Roland Barthes' *Mythologies* (1957), which Carter read and admired; but also through the establishment of the Birmingham Centre for Contemporary Cultural Studies (BCCCS) by Richard Hoggart in 1964. Although critics more frequently note Carter's debt to Barthes, her approach to popular culture bears many similarities to the work done at the BCCCS by Stuart Hall,

Dick Hebdige, Angela McRobbie and others in the late 1960s and 1970s. Carter's fiction anticipates and animates many of the ideas that would be developed in some of the BCCCS's most influential works on subculture, such as Jefferson and Hall's *Resistance Through Rituals* (1975) and Dick Hebdige's *Subculture: The Meaning of Style* (1979).

British subculture in the 1960s was more visibly variegated than in the USA: if Mods and Rockers dominated the first half of the decade, then Teddy Boys still lingered on from the 1950s, and psychedelic bohemia merged into a full-blown hippy culture by the end of the 1960s. Meanwhile, Caribbean immigrants developed their own alternative communities based around ska and reggae. In her twenties, Carter participated in the alternative folk scene. In provincial cities such as Bristol, where Carter lived in the 1960s and where three of her novels from that time are set, subcultures mixed and merged promiscuously into a loosely defined alternative scene. Nevertheless, this melting pot of looks and lifestyles was united in its sense of opposition to a dominant culture defined as staid and middle-class.

Carter set out her attitude to fashion early on in a kind of manifesto published in *New Society* in 1967, called 'Notes for a Theory of Sixties Style'. The essay encapsulates in highly condensed form some of the major sartorial concerns of her fiction of the 1960s and throughout her career, and reveals her close engagement with the sartorial iconography of popular culture. The year 1967 was pivotal in pop culture, the year in which psychedelia went mainstream: the year of, among others, *Sergeant Pepper*, *The Piper at the Gates of Dawn*, *Their Satanic Majesties Request*, *The Velvet Underground and Nico* and *Are You Experienced?* The distinction between subcultural and mainstream style was increasingly eroded as a small group of metropolitan taste-makers gained increasing exposure in the mainstream press.[1] Nevertheless, the looks associated with 'Swinging London' were still regarded as confrontational by the majority, particularly outside the capital. Carter, according to biographer Edmund Gordon, sported a 'Jimi Hendrix cut' and a series of over-sized floppy hats at the time, and was described by a friend as going 'out of her way to be and look eccentric' (Gordon, 2016: 103).

Unsurprisingly, in this context, the overwhelming tendency of the *New Society* piece is towards viewing style as rebellion: 'Clothes are our weapons, our challenges, our visible insults', Carter states (1997:

105). Significantly, the collective pronoun suggests that Carter positions herself as part of this generational shift, a participant rather than merely an observer. The rebellion she identifies is articulated in a variety of ways, from androgyny and dandyism to bricolage, and, notably, these strategies are gendered. Indeed, many of the figures who interest Carter most in this essay are men, and this is reflected in the flamboyant male characters featured in her work of this period, from Honeybuzzard of *Shadow Dance* to Kay and Viv of *Several Perceptions*, Jewel of *Heroes and Villains* and Buzz of *Love*.

Androgyny is, significantly, the prerogative of men in Carter's essay, as, more predictably, is dandyism. These two aesthetic strategies are aligned in their shared rebellion but otherwise clearly distinguished in the article, although in her fiction this distinction is less clear. Carter validates hippy style for its subversion of conventional authority, embodied in 'the boy in the djellibah' (a long, loose-fitting robe also known as a kaftan) and in the Rolling Stones' 'style of calculated affront' with its 'anti-parent, anti-authority' appeal. Carter considers that in the 'sexually ambiguous' garments worn by these men, 'the class battle in Britain [...] is redefining itself as the battle of the generations' (1997: 107). These sartorial battle lines are readily detected in iconic images of the era, such as Ted West's photographs of the Rolling Stones smoking outside Chichester Magistrates Court during their 1967 appearance on drugs charges: Mick Jagger's and Keith Richards' long hair, paisley ties, striped trousers and flamboyant jewellery create a stark contrast with the police attendants in traditional uniforms behind them. Similarly, in *Love*, the heroine Annabel's parents, 'a man and a woman in casual, expensive clothes who smelled of soap and money' confront her brother-in-law Buzz, who wears 'nothing but a pair of filthy white sailor trousers holed, here and there, with acid' (Carter, 1988: 28).

Dandyism is similarly positioned as confrontational by Carter and is a striking feature of British subcultural fictions of the immediately preceding period. The unnamed narrator of Colin MacInnes's *Absolute Beginners* (1959) describes crossing a London square 'in my new Roman suit, which was a pioneering exploit in Belgravia, where they still wore jackets hanging down over what the tailor calls the seat' (MacInnes, 2001: 21). Carter's take on dandyism, however, marks a significant departure from MacInnes's protagonist's heroic modernity in that she explicitly reads it through Albert Camus's

The Rebel (1951). In this work Camus proposes that dandyism is 'an aesthetic [...] of negation' (Camus, 2013: 29). It is performative, defined through the responses of its audience who form the dandy's 'mirror'. In order to maintain this audience's attention, the dandy 'is always compelled to astonish' and therefore 'is, by occupation, always in opposition' (2013: 29). The provocation Camus specifies as the dandy's *modus operandus* Carter identifies in the Hell's Angels, 'perfect dandies of beastliness' (Carter, 1997: 107). The Hell's Angels' 'outlaw dress' is a carefully cultivated aesthetic and as such is a *performance* of nihilism (1997: 107). It is a kind of dandyism as anti-dandyism: one that overturns the stereotype of the dandy as immaculately groomed man of fashion yet also exposes the existential challenge to mortality at its heart.

From bricolage to schizophrenia

If anti-authoritarian androgyny and beastly dandyism are principally the province of men, then the feminist potential of subcultural style is embodied, for Carter, in what Dick Hebdige (following Claude Lévi-Strauss) would later call bricolage, the practice of intervening in the cultural construction of meaning through the recontextualization of semiotic objects (Hebdige, 1987). Subcultural bricolage is founded in 'the "radical" collage aesthetic of surrealism' and thus speaks directly to Carter's ongoing fascination with surrealist aesthetics (Hebdige, 1987: 120). For Hebdige, bricolage is quintessentially expressed through punk's appropriation of the swastika and the safety pin. Carter's description of a young woman attending a party in 'a Mexican cotton wedding dress [...] her grandmother's button boots [...] her mother's fox fur [...] and her old school beret' describes a similar process through which 'All these eclectic fragments, robbed of their symbolic content, fall together to form a new whole' (Carter, 1997, 106). Carter's young woman expresses the new interest in vintage style of the mid-to-late 1960s, one embodied in the iconic Chelsea boutiques *Granny Takes a Trip* and *I Was Lord Kitchener's Valet*, both of which opened in 1966 (although *Kitchener's* had previously existed as a Portobello Market stall). Carter's description also recalls a feature on Jane Ormsby-Gore in the January 1966 edition of British *Vogue*, in which the society heiress and style leader (and reputed inspiration for the Rolling Stones' 'Lady Jane') is described as:

scour[ing] the Portobello Road and antique shops and markets throughout the land, searching for handfuls of Venetian lace, rich embroideries, and beautifully made clothes of any age and kind. She has boots of Russian leather, endless shirts of cream and white lace, embroidered velvet coats falling almost to the ankle, striped silk stockings, huge plumes of ostrich and egret tumbling from floppy 1900s hats, and, above all, a jewel box stuffed with glittering treasures. (Gibbs, 1966)

The photographs of Ormsby-Gore feature her wearing an eclectic selection of vintage clothes, including a white linen and lace Victorian dress resembling a wedding dress and, notably, her great-grandmother's Edwardian motoring hat. In the *Vogue* article, Carter's *New Society* piece, and the naming of *Granny Takes a Trip*, the stylish young woman is explicitly presented as acknowledging, recontextualizing and liberating the clothes of a previous generation. Moreover, these vintage clothes are not representative of distant history, but of a time still within living memory and intimately connected to the wearer by family ties.

This passion for the past erupted, by 1967, into what Jenny Lister calls a fashion for 'fancy dress or "costume"' (Lister, 2016: 237). This stimulated a huge second-hand clothing industry that can be viewed as parallel to the antiques business run by Morris and Honeybuzzard in *Shadow Dance*; indeed, Morris and Honey are described as buying 'three fringed and beaded Edwardian evening dresses at the auction sale', which they prominently display in their shop window (Carter, 1994: 111). Jennifer Le Zotte describes how

> By 1967, Londoners were desperate to uncover forgotten caches of old clothes everywhere. Large department stores threw huge divestment auctions [...] digging into stores of unsold stock from bygone eras. Heirs brought heavy trunks out of cold storage, revealing dead marchionesses gowns and musty-feathered hats. Amateur playhouses marketed hoards of century-old clothing. Sotheby's auctioned a rediscovered stockpile of ballet costumes from the founder of the Ballets Russes in the first decade of the century. (Le Zotte, 2017: 147)

Second-hand clothing was in many ways as confrontational as the other style strategies Carter describes. Angela McRobbie notes how for the previous generation,

> markets for old clothes and jumble-sales in the 1960s remained a terrifying reminder of the stigma of poverty, the shame of ill-fitting

clothing, and the fear of disease through infestation [...] Hippy preferences for old fur coats, crêpe dresses and army great-coats, shocked the older generation for precisely this reason. (McRobbie, 1989: 34)

If, for Carter, the men of the 1960s challenge authority through androgyny or dandyism, then women do so through creative play, or 'fancy dress' (1997: 106). Subcultural bricolage, in its recontextualizing of iconic garments, emancipates girls 'from the stiff forms of iconic sexuality' (1997: 109).

The process of recontextualizing style can be seen in action in Barbie, the American girl who drifts through the second half of *Several Perceptions*. Barbie, whose name suggestively recalls the iconic American fashion doll, appears to have no other purpose in the novel except to exemplify the emancipatory potential of mid-60s style.[2] She variously appears in 'Dayglo green stockings, purple and orange smock and [...] a blanket or poncho of various brilliant wools', 'a loose dress of brilliant green velvet which glowed like wet moss', 'a loose smock of brilliant printed fabric [...] peacock feathers in her hair' and 'a backless silver lamé gown obviously borrowed from Mrs. Kyte's historic hoard' (Carter, 1995: 82, 88, 139, 130). In borrowing the gown from faded, reclusive theatrical star Mrs. Kyte and using it to dance in, Barbie unshackles it from its earlier meaning and converts it into a joyous and unfettered celebration of her own sexuality: 'Her marmalade mane, all stuck with artificial flowers, hung down her bare, sun-tanned tawny back and her lamé tail slithered like a fish; she was a wet mermaid. She was laughing and jingling with metal bracelets' (1995: 130). The rapid slippage within two sentences from historic starlet to (artificial) child of nature to mermaid to the exotic Oriental maiden suggested by the bracelets suggests that Barbie can, through clothes, inhabit and enjoy any number of iconic images of femininity without being defined by any of them. Moreover, as Angela McRobbie points out, 'There is in [the second-hand] milieu a [...] refined economy of taste at work. For every single piece rescued and restored, a thousand are consigned to oblivion' (McRobbie, 1989: 29). The process of finding, selecting and repurposing the dress thus reveals Barbie not as passive consumer of past fashions but as an active shaper of taste.

While Carter's tone in *Several Perceptions* is celebratory, there is a dark undercurrent: Barbie's liberation of Mrs. Kyte's dress is part of her war on time, as she tells Joseph, 'He's here, there and everywhere and he always wins out in the end', although she 'looked so healthy, normal and full of gaiety and colour' that her message appears to be lost on him (Carter, 1995: 140). In *Shadow Dance*, Carter more explicitly offers an alternative to the recycling of past images of femininity through the character of Emily, who to Honeybuzzard's disgust finds the Edwardian dresses he salvages 'would not fit' her 'strong, thick-waisted, post-world-war-two figure', unconstrained by corsetry (Carter, 1994: 111). Working-class Emily's Mod-influenced style is aspirational, a female version of MacInnes's heroic modernity, comprising angular haircut, denim miniskirt, striped sweater, 'bright white knee socks' over stockings, 'two-tone, lace-up, low-heeled shoes in red and green' and a scooter pennant on her duffel-bag (Carter, 1994: 55). Her lack of fit with a previous generation's images of femininity is directly contrasted with the doomed Ghislaine, who 'all the clichés fitted' (1994: 3). The 'healthy, normal' physicality of Barbie and Emily appears to allow an authentic expression of self that is not permitted to the physically and emotionally damaged Ghislaine, who loses control over her own image and allows herself to be manipulated by patriarchal culture.

There is an underlying darkness in the *New Society* piece too. Emancipation through fancy dress, Carter suggests, has a cost in the disintegration of the self: 'a relaxation from one's own personality and the discovery of maybe unexpected new selves' (Carter, 1997: 106). Here, Carter throws off the discourses of authenticity characteristically generated within subcultural writings (and within hippy culture) and anticipates instead the 'schizophrenic' subject of postmodernity proposed by Fredric Jameson (1991: 25–31). Jon Savage notes how in late 1966, 'Something very strange was happening to time in pop culture', citing pop music (The Beatles' 'Tomorrow Never Knows' and the 1920s vaudeville revival) and television (*Adam Adamant Lives*), as well as the vogue for second-hand clothes. He declares:

> The unitary drive of modernism had accelerated way beyond the point of sustainability. Under this pressure, time was beginning to fragment, from forward motion into a sequence of loops, into either the perpetual now or the historical periods sourced at will by an overloaded media. (Savage, 2015: 397)

The excavation of past styles provokes confusion between past, present and future that replaces the unity of the ego with a series of discontinuities, a process that may induce a sense of euphoria or of profound disorientation. A key response to this disorienting new state, according to Savage, was camp, 'all-pervasive in autumn 1966 [...] not just an expression of deviancy or cool or distance but a basic way of processing data, of dealing with an onrush of information from many different times and viewpoints, a method of navigating a schizophrenic consciousness' (2015: 400). Elizabeth Wilson similarly notes how late 1960s style combined camp, 'the pastiche and artificiality latent in the ransacking of old clothes for new styles', with the apparently contradictory 'cult of the authentic' (Wilson, 1985: 194). This camp tone is crucial to understanding Carter's depiction of gender roles through clothes in the 1960s and beyond. Carter's embrace of a postmodern world of sartorial play and performance embodied in subcultural style enables her to critique the ideologies of authenticity and naturalness that permeate hippy culture and subcultural discourse more generally.

Bricolage remains ambivalent, then: it decentres the subject but in doing so creates a subject that is suggestively pathological and in danger of disintegrating completely – the fate of several of Carter's 1960s characters, both male and female. In *Shadow Dance*, for example, the malevolent dandy Honeybuzzard states, 'I like – you know – to slip in and out of me [...] I would like to have a cupboard bulging with all different bodies and faces and choose a fresh one every morning' (Carter, 1994: 78). As Marc O'Day observes, Honeybuzzard's embrace of a performative model of self

> reveals the degree to which hippie notions of naturalness and authenticity were themselves artificial, mythical constructs no less than the mainstream commercial products against which hippies defined themselves. No one can be simply natural or authentic any more: these are just options among a variety of roles and acts; they have to be cultivated just like the others. (O'Day, 1994: 37)

Nevertheless, for Honeybuzzard, the price of this ideological critique is a descent into psychosis. He ends the novel singing to himself and cradling a plaster Christ, his hair trailing 'like mad Ophelia's' (Carter, 1994: 179). Annabel of *Love* meets a similar fate, 'as indifferent to the obscene flowers of the flesh as drowned Ophelia' (Carter, 1988, 102–3). Ophelia is, of course, a stage character, a stylized performance of madness – and one that was further crystallized through nineteenth-century art, most notably Millais's painting of 1851–52, which Carter particularly admired. Annabel deliberately rejects the natural and authentic, dying her hair and having a beauty makeover in preparation for her suicide, so that she becomes 'a marvellous crystallization retaining nothing of the remembered woman but her form' (Carter, 1988: 104). Needless to say, the price of this apotheosis into an artificial being is her death.

The politics of style

Carter's interest in forging a new kind of subject through style recalls a range of commentators from the late 1960s, but most strikingly, an early essay by foundational BCCCS member Stuart Hall. 'The Hippies: An American Moment', originally published in 1968 and anthologized in revised and extended form in the Penguin paperback *Student Power* in 1969 (the year Carter was writing her first draft of *Love*), presaged the BCCCS' later works' inclination to read subcultural style as expressive of social and political meaning. The essay is striking for the way in which its description and analysis of hippy culture coincides with that of Carter's fiction of this period, with many features mapping directly onto *Love*, from middle-class Annabel's 'disguise of poverty' to Buzz's obsession with his American father's Apache or Mohawk ancestry and the way that Lee and Annabel 'continue to "shadow" the student role they have so recently abandoned' (Hall 1969: 175, 174). For Hall, echoing Carter's earlier essay, 'The Hippies have not only helped to define *a style*, they have made the question of *style itself* a political issue' (1969: 194, emphasis in original). Hall argues that behind the 'apparently-patternless eclecticism' of hippy culture – a phrase that brings to mind Carter's young woman in her eclectic party ensemble – is 'a direct dialectical contra-posing of alternative values to the sacred values of the middle class' (1969: 195).

For Hall, the hippies are 'second or third wave partisans in a new kind of guerrilla warfare' that can be read as 'an attempt to *prefigure* a new kind of subjectivity' (1969: 196, emphasis in original). This 'revolution in the head', as a book on The Beatles memorably put it (MacDonald, 2008), is intended to overthrow the status quo by 'unravel[ing] it from within', changing engrained patterns of thought and thus its oppressive and repressive ideological structures (Hall, 1969: 196). Nevertheless, the hippies' '*tactical* withdrawal' from dominant middle-class values and lifestyle ultimately fails to realize its revolutionary potential because resistance to the state is experienced in individual terms rather than as a collective political movement (1969: 195, emphasis in original). Hall divides the 'generational underground' into the two poles of 'expressive' and 'activist', focused respectively on style and direct political action; the hippies' 'stress on the personal, the psychic, the subjective, the cultural, the private, the aesthetic or bohemian' locates them decisively at the former pole (1969: 198–9).

When Carter talks about clothes as 'our weapons' and the Rolling Stones' drugs case as 'generation warfare', she engages with a similar conception to that of Hall: of counterculture as a kind of guerrilla movement dismantling the culture from within. Here, too, the aim of this warfare is to establish new models of subjectivity: as Carter puts it, 'a new attitude to the self' (Carter, 1997, 106). This new attitude is explicitly liberating for women precisely because, for 1960's feminism, the personal is newly political. Privileging 'expressive' revolt through style segues readily into the feminist revaluing of the subjective, private and domestic/leisure spheres. Yet in her fiction, Carter remains powerfully ambivalent about this emancipatory project: yes, it liberates women from the 'stiff forms of iconic sexuality', yet it does not enable social revolution on a broader scale. The Afterword to *Love*, written in 1987, acknowledges this in envisaging an activist future for the surviving female characters, comprising Greenham Common, communal living, miners' strike support demos and careers in social work.

The tensions between the liberation of the individual subject and collective social change are implicit rather than explicit in most of Carter's late 1960s novels, but come to the fore in more deliberate fashion in the speculative fantasy of *Heroes and Villains*. Carter stressed that the 'pastiche Gothic' framework of the novel enabled her 'to examine some intellectual problems about politics that were beginning to exercise me' (1975: 132–3). In this novel, Carter's sartorial guerrilla strategies of androgyny, dandyism and bricolage are presented in concentrated form. Figured in terms of actual warfare, these expressive strategies are temporarily allowed an activist dimension. The book wears its countercultural credentials on its sleeve: as Carter explicitly acknowledged, it borrowed its title from a Beach Boys single of 1967, which was a top 10 hit in the UK just two or three months prior to her beginning writing in January 1968 (Carter, 1975: 133). The album on which the track featured, *Smiley Smile*, had cover art inspired by Henri Rousseau and was also, according to Edmund Gordon, a direct inspiration for Carter's novel (Gordon, 2016: 119). The song's theme of cultural exile from the city to a war-torn frontier and its depiction of a doomed cross-cultural love affair loosely resonates with the novel's imagery.

Heroes and Villains differs from Carter's other 1960s novels in that it eschews realist settings in provincial bohemia for a speculative, post-apocalyptic world. The continent on which the world is set is not specified and is deliberately fantastic (radiation poisoning has warped the plant life and wild beasts escaped from zoos thrive in the woods) but in its renewed wilderness state, it resembles early colonial America. In this world, the counterculture has become enlarged to become a separate, oppositional culture that directly threatens and resists the dominant culture. The 'Barbarians' resemble hippies in their communal style of living and their resistance to conventional forms of authority and order, which is embodied in the dominant culture of 'the Professors'.

The difference between the two rival communities is expressed through dress. The Professors wear 'browns and sepias, black, white and various shades of grey'; their clothes are 'muted and restrained' (Carter, 1981a: 39). In their drab respectability they resemble the stereotyped parent generation of the 1960s, but their 'clean and proper [...] shirts and dresses white as paper, suits as black as ink' also recall the attire of America's Puritan settlers, underlining the resemblance of the post-apocalyptic landscape to the 'new-found land' of 1600s America (1981a: 4). The Barbarians are the disinherited Native Americans in this reimagined continent, evoking what Hall calls the 'elevated status' the counterculture afforded Native American culture (Hall 1969: 178). The Barbarians repurpose materials and garments they plunder from the Professors' settlements in a form of bricolage that is simultaneously practical necessity and subversion. Here Carter recalls Lévi-Strauss's original use of the term bricolage as the opposite of scientific thinking (embodied in the novel by the Professors) and a feature of 'primitive' societies in which 'the rules of [the] game are always to make do with "whatever is at hand"' (Lévi-Strauss, 1972: 17). The heroine, Marianne, secretly watching a procession of Barbarians through the forest, observes:

The women wore trousers or long, cumbersome skirts made out of stolen blankets, or stolen cloth, or leather, or fur. They had blouses, some beautifully embroidered, and rough, sleeveless jackets usually of either fur or leather; some wore Soldiers' jackets though the black leather had been transformed by the application of beads, braiding and feathers. They were all decorated with astonishing, tawdry jewellery, some of it plainly salvaged from the ruins and of great age, some weirdly fashioned from animal bones and baked clay. Their hair was wound with ribbons and feathers; their faces were painted a little round the eyes or else tattooed with serpentine lines [...] Most were barefoot, although some wore stolen boots or sandals made of straw. (Carter, 1981a: 13)

The Barbarian women's mixture of vintage 'found' pieces, customized military garments, authentically crafted jewellery and garments, and an impulse to adornment, clearly recalls late 1960s hippy styles. For Marianne, this first signals a remote exoticism, and then her initiation into a world of magical thinking, where the community sets store on amulets and talismans. Having abandoned the Professors for the Barbarians, she is dressed in a 'shirt [...] of fine wool, originally woven and sewn in a Professor's village for intellectuals to wear but now it was covered all over with red and yellow daisies and little chips of mirrors, a gaudy and totally changed garment' (1981a: 39). Its customized purpose symbolizes her transition into the 'gaudy' Barbarian world, and the chips of mirrors are both a means of warding off the evil eye and suggest the disintegration of the stable and unitary self the Professors' world presupposes and punitively insists upon. Mrs Green, a woman who has also abandoned the Professors' world, compares the Barbarians' impulse to adornment with that of children: 'Bright colours, beads, things that shine. They're like kids, I tell you' (1981a: 39). Her words suggest a residual attitude to 'primitive' peoples retained from Professorial culture. Besides the Native Americans who opposed the Puritan settlers, the Barbarians resemble the Celtic barbarians who ultimately overthrew Rome: the child Jen wears 'a tunic of long-haired fur that made her look like a little Ancient Briton' (1981a: 43). These images are overlaid onto those of the counterculture to create an over-determined sense of threat.

The Barbarians are led by Doctor Donally, a renegade Professor who uses his superior knowledge of ritual and illusion to manipulate and entrance the tribe and who closely recalls the countercultural icon

Dr Timothy Leary, disgraced Harvard professor, LSD guru and media *provocateur*. Donally's scrawled slogans on the walls of the dilapidated mansion where the Barbarians make their home evoke Leary's mantra, 'Turn on, tune in, drop out'. His principal pawn is the beautiful and violent Jewel, a Byronic hero of sorts who recalls androgynous 1960s icons Jim Morrison and, most particularly, Mick Jagger (the heroine's name, Marianne, taking on additional resonance here due to Marianne Faithfull's high-profile relationship with Jagger 1966–70).[3] In Jewel and his brothers, Carter combines Jagger's anti-authoritarian sexuality with the beastly dandyism of the Hell's Angels (who she researched while writing the novel, Gordon relates, by reading Hunter S. Thompson's 1966 exposé) (Gordon, 2016: 120).

Through Jewel, Carter fully explores the limitations of dandyism as a mode of cultural resistance. Clothes are, literally, Jewel's weapons. He and his brothers go into combat wearing elaborate war paint and hairstyles to frighten their enemies; he wears an array of trinkets and amulets that ward off ill fortune including his adversaries' weapons. However, in becoming so fully subsumed to the power of the visual image, Jewel has become unmoored from an authentic self: 'He was like a work of art, created, not begotten, a fantastic dandy of the void whose true nature had been entirely subsumed to the alien and terrible beauty of a rhetorical gesture. His appearance was abstracted from his body, and he was wilfully reduced to sign language' (1981a: 71–2). Jewel has become an object to be looked at; as for Camus's dandy, his identity is dependent on the gaze of others. His translation to visual image has feminized him; Marianne tells him that with his 'jewels, paints, furs, knives and guns' he is 'like a phallic and diabolic version of female beauties of former periods' (1981a: 137). But for this 'dandy of the void', the relaxation from one's own personality does not bring the discovery of unexpected new selves, but merely the dissolution of self. As he dresses one final time to confront the Soldiers, Marianne catches a glimpse of his painted face reflected in the mirror and repeats hysterically, 'You aren't yourself this morning' (1981a: 146). There is no one else for him to be; death is inevitable.

In *Heroes and Villains*, Carter describes a world in which style *is* politics and where it as advisable, as Donally's aphorism proposes, to 'MISTRUST APPEARANCES, THEY NEVER CONCEAL ANYTHING' (1981a: 60, upper case in original). Accordingly, Jewel the beastly dandy is a hollow man: 'He was a coloured structure and, the coat opened, might reveal only the lining of its own back, no body inside' (1981a: 74). He fantasizes Donally flaying his tattooed skin and wearing him as a robe on ceremonial occasions, recalling at the same time his mentor's abortive attempt to create a 'Tiger Lady' by tattooing a little girl with tiger stripes (1981a: 86). The death of the dandy (and of the dandy's creator, Donally) apparently initiates a crisis in patriarchal culture, as there is no single person left in charge. But as Lévi-Strauss proposes, 'The significant images of myth, the materials of the bricoleur, are [...] defined by two criteria: they have *had a use* [...] and *they can be used again* either for the same purpose or a different one if they are diverted from their previous function' (Lévi-Strauss, 1972: 35, emphasis in original). Anyone can wear the tiger skin: the void left by Jewel's death may, it is implied, be filled by Marianne, who tells Donally's son, 'I'll be the tiger lady and rule them with a rod of iron' (1981a: 150).

Carter left Britain at the end of the 1960s and spent three years living in Japan, an experience she said radicalized her as a woman (Carter, 1992: 28). Critics have dated Carter's feminism from this period, treating the period in Japan as a kind of watershed in her work. Nevertheless, as I have shown, her fascination with performative models of gender was forged in the late 1960s, in the crucible of the counterculture and its politics of style. If men are often placed at the centre of these texts, their masculinity is interrogated, precisely through their relationship with clothes. Through the figure of the dandy, Carter exposes the dark side of the 1960s image factory and allows her male characters to suffer the consequences of becoming an object of the gaze. If the emancipatory potential of fancy dress is less visible for her female characters in her 1960s novels than it would be in her later work, she ruthlessly places the unitary masculine subject under attack. In this guerrilla warfare on the dominant culture, the price to be paid may be complete disintegration of the self. Despite the bleakness of this insight, however, there is room for hope: in the dissolution of the patriarchal subject, a new world order is intimated, one in which the tiger ladies of the future are ready to don their skins.

Notes

1 Angela McRobbie offers the reminder that 'this entrepreneurial dynamic has rarely been acknowledged in most subcultural analysis', pointing to

the preconceptions about 'selling out' within both subcultures themselves and sociological analysis that lead to consumerism being either ignored or recuperated as deriving from external market forces (1989: 36).
2 Carter's character's eclectic and glamorous ensembles perhaps make her an early version of one of Carter's 'living dolls'. The Barbie doll was first launched by Mattel in the United States in 1959. A new Mod style of Barbie with a swinging wardrobe was introduced in 1967, supporting the connection. However, in the UK in the 1960s, Barbie was dramatically outsold by her British rival Sindy, so Carter may have simply chosen the name as sounding particularly all-American.
3 Marianne Faithfull is, coincidentally, also the daughter of a Professor of Italian literature and closely related to Leopold von Sacher-Masoch, author of *Venus in Furs* (1870).

References

Berger, John ([1972] 1990), *Ways of Seeing* (Harmondsworth: Penguin).
Britzolakis, Christina (1997), 'Angela Carter's Fetishism', in Joseph Bristow and Trev Lynn Broughton (eds), *The Infernal Desires of Angela Carter: Fiction, Femininity, Feminism* (London and New York: Longman), pp. 43–58.
Camus, Albert ([1951] 2013), *The Rebel* (London: Penguin).
Carter, Angela (1975), 'Notes on the Gothic Mode', *The Iowa Review* 6.3, 132–4.
—— ([1969] 1981a), *Heroes and Villains* (Harmondsworth: Penguin).
—— ([1967] 1981b), *The Magic Toyshop* (London: Virago).
—— ([1971] 1988), *Love* (London: Picador).
—— (1992), *Nothing Sacred: Selected Writings* (London: Virago).
—— ([1966] 1994), *Shadow Dance* (London: Virago).
—— ([1968] 1995), *Several Perceptions* (London: Virago).
—— ([1967] 1997), 'Notes for a Theory of Sixties Style', in Angela Carter, *Shaking a Leg: Journalism and Writings*, ed. Jenny Uglow (London: Chatto and Windus).
Gibbs, Christopher (1966), 'Fashion Special: Jane Ormsby-Gore', British *Vogue*, January, http://ciaovogue.blogspot.co.uk/2010/07/january-1966-uk-vogue.html, accessed 29 July 2017.
Gordon, Edmund (2016), *The Invention of Angela Carter: A Biography* (London: Chatto & Windus).
Hall, Stuart (1969), 'The Hippies: An American Moment', in Julian Nagel (ed.), *Student Power* (London: Merlin Press).
—— and Tony Jefferson (1975), *Resistance through Rituals: Youth subcultures in post-war Britain* in *Working Papers in Cultural Studies* no 7/8 (Birmingham: The Centre for Contemporary Cultural Study).

Hebdige, Dick ([1979] 1987), *Subculture: The Meaning of Style* (London: Routledge).
Jameson, Fredric (1991), *Postmodernism, or, The Cultural Logic of Late Capitalism* (London: Verso).
Lévi-Strauss, Claude ([1962] 1972), *The Savage Mind* (London: Weidenfeld and Nicholson).
Le Zotte, Jennifer (2017), *From Goodwill to Grunge: A History of Secondhand Styles and Alternative Economies* (Chapel Hill, NC: University of North Carolina Press).
Lister, Jenny (2016), 'British Fashion 1966–70: A State of Anarchy', in Victoria Broackes and Geoffrey Marsh (eds), *You Say You Want a Revolution? Records and Rebels 1966–1970* (London: V&A Publishing), pp. 226–243.
MacDonald, Ian ([1994] 2008), *Revolution in the Head: The Beatles' Records and the Sixties* (London: Vintage).
MacInnes, Colin ([1959] 2001), *Absolute Beginners* (London: Allison and Busby).
McRobbie, Angela (1989), 'Second-Hand Dresses and the Role of the Ragmarket', in Angela McRobbie (ed.), *Zoot Suits and Secondhand Dresses* (Basingstoke: Macmillan), pp. 23–49.
O'Day, Marc (1994), '"Mutability is Having a Field Day": The Sixties Aura of Carter's Bristol Trilogy', in Lorna Sage (ed.), *Flesh and the Mirror: Essays on the Art of Angela Carter* (London: Virago), pp. 24–58.
Palmer, Paulina (1997), 'Gender as Performance in the Fiction of Angela Carter and Margaret Atwood', in Joseph Bristow and Trev Lynn Broughton (eds), *The Infernal Desires of Angela Carter: Fiction, Femininity, Feminism* (London and New York: Longman), pp. 24–42.
Savage, Jon (2015), *1966: The Year the Decade Exploded* (London: Faber and Faber).
Wilson, Elizabeth (1985), *Adorned in Dreams: Fashion and Modernity* (London: Virago).

9

Desire, disgust and dead women: Angela Carter's re-writing women's fatal scripts from Poe and Lovecraft

Gina Wisker

ANGELA CARTER'S WRITING IS crucial to the rebirth of Gothic horror in the late twentieth century, and an impetus to read, or re-read, myth, fairy tale and the work of Edgar Allan Poe and H.P. Lovecraft – each significant, acknowledged influences. Carter's work deconstructs the consistently replayed, cautionary narrative of myth and fairy tale in which (mainly young) women are first represented as objects of a prurient idolatry, then sacrificed to reinstate the purity and balance which their constructed presence apparently disturbs. Carter shows it is possible and essential to tell other stories. When she turns on her horror influences, she continues this exposé of the representation of women as objects of desire and disgust, springing as it does from ontological insecurity and deep-seated confusions concerning sex and power. Revising and rewriting constraining narratives, Carter's work draws us into the rich confusions of the language, the psychology, the physical entrapments and artifices and the constraining myths, which both Poe and Lovecraft play out through their representations of women, and which her work re-enacts to explode and re-write. As a late twentieth-century feminist, Carter critiques, parodies and exposes the underlying sexual terrors, the desire and disgust fuelling representations of women as variously dead or deadly. Reading early work, 'The Snow Child' (1979), 'The Man Who Loved a Double Bass' (1995) and 'The Loves of Lady Purple' (1974), the chapter moves to re-reading parts of her later work, including *Nights at the Circus* (1987). Imaginatively re-stirring the potion of myth, fairy tale and horror, Carter's women reject the roles of victims, puppets, pawns, of deadly sexual predators or hags, instead defining and seizing their own sexuality and agency, having the last laugh.

Horror, fairy tale, myth

Angela Carter creates her radical work partly in response to the material around her: 'I found most of my raw material in the lumber room of the Western European imagination' (1983: 19), and her own reactions against constructions and representations of women, through which she became aware of constraining versions and expectations: 'it was, therefore, primarily through my sexual and emotional life that I was radicalized – that I first became truly aware of the difference between how I was and how I was supposed to be, or expected to be' (1983: 72). Linden Peach comments that Angela Carter's stories 'deconstruct the processes that produce social structures and shared meanings, evident, for example [...] in the way in which the manifestation of the female body in her works disrupts the social construction of women as Woman' (Peach, 1998: 4).

Fairy tales are a rich source to plunder and reimagine in order to tell different stories about performance, vulnerability, control and defiance so, 'Carter, like many feminist critics, recognizes fairy tales as a reactionary form that inscribed a misogynistic ideology' (Peach, 1998: 74). The brothers Grimm, Perrault and sources in tales of the women whose work they retold, reappear, reworked throughout her novels, short stories, poetry, drama and critical pieces. Carter acknowledges then writes back against her influences, including those of horror: 'I'd always been fond of Poe and Hoffman [sic] – Gothic tales, cruel tales, tales of wonder, tales of terror, fabulous narratives that deal directly with the imagery of the unconscious – mirrors; the externalized self; forsaken castles; haunted forests; forbidden sexual objects' (Carter, Afterword to *Fireworks*, 1974: 132–3). Edgar Allan Poe and H.P. Lovecraft are the focus here, although Hoffmann's influence on Carter has been explored by Paulina Palmer (2017). Poe's own dark mixture of the romantic and the salacious offers a model for a deep-seated cultural fascination with sex and death in which women are desired, destroyed, and desired even more exquisitely when they are post mortem, for as he explains: 'the death, then, of a beautiful woman is, unquestionably, the most poetical topic in the world – and equally is it beyond doubt that the lips best suited for such topic are those of a bereaved lover' (Poe, 1966: 165). Myths of masculinity and men in power get short shrift in Carter's work. She refuses to replay victim rescue narratives such as that of Andromeda tied on the black rocks off Jaffa, awaiting the slavering sea beast, saved by Perseus, while in *The Magic Toyshop* (1967), that favourite tale of Renaissance artists and twentieth-century poets, the rape of Leda by Zeus metamorphosized into a swan gets the comic treatment. The lumpy homemade phallic swan in the makeshift cellar theatre reflects the fantasies of Uncle Philip, arch patriarch of toys who treats people as puppets. The scene ridicules without reducing the terror involved for Melanie, unwilling actor in a version of a disturbing powerful rape myth managed by unlicensed godliness. This is a familiar trajectory for Angela Carter's Gothic horror, which utilizes parody and critique without dissipating the damaging horror of the source.

My fascination with Carter's horror began with *The Magic Toyshop*, which undermines myth's licensing of rape fantasy and woman as manipulated object (Wisker, 1984). This developed into locating her engagement with the masters of horror, particularly Poe (Wisker, 1997, 2006), and latterly into probing resonances and responses to work by H.P. Lovecraft (1970 [1928]), who celebrated Poe and his influence (Wisker, 2015). Carter's Gothic and horror have been increasingly widely explored, often in response to 'The Company of Wolves' (Crofts, 1998), difficulties re-writing the fairy tales (Duncker, 1984) and in considering the female Gothic body (Mulvey-Roberts, 2016). It emerged as a popular theme in the recent Angela Carter conference organized by Marie Mulvey-Roberts and Charlotte Crofts in Bristol, where Carter studied and lived (2017).

Carter's earthiness and ridicule, which undermine without ever underestimating the perversity, violence and accompanying terror wielded by male mythic and economic power over women's bodies, run throughout her work. She exposes the control behind the cautionary tale and the destructive otherizing informing the treatment of women and sexual or romantic relations in myth, fairy tale and the work of Poe and Lovecraft. Julie Kristeva's (1988) and Helen Cixous' (1976) theories of the transfer of fear, as well as loathing and disgust onto the abject body of the constructed other is enlightening here. Kristeva talks of:

> Our disturbing otherness, for that indeed is what bursts in to confront the 'demons', or the threat that apprehension generated by the protective apparition of the other at the heart of what we persist in maintaining as a proper, solid 'us'. By recognising *our* uncanny strangeness we shall neither suffer from it nor enjoy it from the outside. The foreigner

is within me, hence we are all foreigners. If I am a foreigner, then there are no foreigners. (Kristeva, 1988: 192; emphasis in original)

Working beyond Lacan and Freud, Kristeva and Cixous show this transfer as based on otherizing elements of the self. It is a reflection which stares back at the one reflected, and onto which can be loaded everything that terrifies and disgusts, everything produced from an abjected self to enable the self to move on, having offloaded onto another what both attracts and terrifies. In this respect, Carter's use of reflection, parody and performance are her vehicles of demystification, of debunking pomposity, abjection and perverse power alike. Her use of medieval and eighteenth-century originated bawdy earthiness, grotesque and carnival, punctures perverse pomposity, showing how we might construct and represent what we desire and fear, but we can also fly free from the constricting worldviews of those in power who would restrict freedom and development, as Fevvers, the winged aerialiste in *Nights at the Circus* (1987) realizes when a teenager in Ma Nelson's friendly brothel that:

> Sealed in this artificial egg, this sarcophagus of beauty, I waited, I waited [...] although I could not have told you for what it was I waited. Except, I assure you, I did not await the kiss of a magic prince sir! With my two eyes I nightly saw how such a kiss would seal me up in my appearance forever. (39)

Romance is seen as potential entrapment. Carter revels in exposing and satirizing such constraining myths, internalized and suffered by mainly female victims. Rape of the vulnerable and women's spiteful jealousy are also exposed, for example in 'The Snow Child' (1979).

'The Snow Child' (1979) – a miniature

'Midwinter – invincible, immaculate' (193), so the story begins.

Carter replays and reveals the narrative trajectory of fairy tale and myth in her own fairy tale, 'The Snow Child' (1979a). Like a tiny toy snowstorm paperweight, this miniature releases and lays bare, rather than restrains or civilizes, a rape fantasy driven by male sexual power over a vulnerable, constructed female object. Aloft on their lovely horses, moving through the land they own, ride the Count and his indulged, beautiful wife. His lust drives him to conjure into being a snow child. Elemental tensions between his desire for the sexual victim of his dark fantasies and his wife's sexual jealousy wrench the rich clothes from the Countess and fling them onto the child. His fantasy dresses his vulnerable victim, makes her into what he desires, then, violating her, he kills her. In a trice, in just over a page, the rape of a child conjured from lust dissolves, traceless, into snow. The trajectory is familiar, commonplace, and in this tale it is pared to essentials: vulnerable child-woman, sex object constructed from the fantasy of a powerful man, violated and destroyed. But this is an Angela Carter story. Even here the erased event, the repressed tale, ends in a little comeback. Bowing, his stature and marital courtliness reinstated, the Count picks up from the snow a rose, all that remains of the girl, and hands it to his lovely wife, who drops it. 'It bites!' she said (1979a: 194). Carter's ending splices horror and fairy tale. As this powerful comeback shows, the girls and women in Angela Carter's work do not learn to fear, obey and remain static, the puppets are not confined to their elaborate boxes. She exposes and rewrites the reification and rape fantasies played out in fairy tale and classic myth, then further reveals and undercuts the mysogyny in the great male horror writers, Edgar Allan Poe and H.P. Lovecraft.

Poe and Lovecraft – women and sex – desire, disgust and death

Edgar Allan Poe and H.P. Lovecraft, masters of horror, are major influences on Carter, who writes out of and back against their versions of sexual terrors, which render the constructed, terrifying female as beautiful, deadly revenant (Poe), or vile hag, shameful, miscegenating grandmother coupling with sea creatures and bringing on humankind the wrath of the Elder gods, the end of the world (Lovecraft). Both of these extremes are products of imaginations roiling in sexual repression, finding an outlet in reifying and variously destroying women. Carter imagined the origins and upbringing of Poe (born in Boston) and Lovecraft, whose Providence, Rhode Island, she visited, exploring his context and his grave. She consulted their papers and letters, reimagining the sources of extreme responses to sex and women, which infuse their work.

When she homes in on the influential work of Poe and Lovecraft, Angela Carter draws us into the rich confusions of the language, the psychology, the physical entrapments and artifices, the constraining myths, which both authors play out through their representations of women, and which she re-enacts to expose, explode and re-write. Carter unpicks and challenges the fascination Poe and Lovecraft have with the myths of women as monstrous, vulnerable, enthralling (Lovecraft and Bishop, 'Medusa's Coil', 1939), as deadly hags (Lovecraft, 1970: 'The Dreams in the Witch House (1932) and 'The Dunwich Horror' (1928)), as capable of luring travellers and students to hell, coupling with the devil or inhuman creatures (Lovecraft, 1970: 'The Shadow over Innsmouth' (1936)) or as sirens, performative puppets, reified artistic objects and revenants (Poe, 1966: 'Berenice' (1835); 'The Oval Portrait' (1842); 'Ligeia' (1838); 'Eleonora' (1842)).

Both Poe and Lovecraft were initially brought up as only children, mainly by their mothers. Following his mother's death, Poe was adopted by the Allans (and temporarily moved to England) and Lovecraft was brought up by his (spinster) aunts. Poe's parents were in the theatre, as strolling players, and when his father died, his mother continued to perform on the stage, nightly dying as Ophelia, and being reborn post performance. In her short story 'The Cabinet of Edgar Allan Poe' (1985), Carter imagines the young Edgar hiding in a costume basket, fixated on linking beauty and sexuality with performance, death and the return of the beloved, a trope played out in 'Eleonora' (1842) and 'Ligeia' (1838).

Poe's horror is often melodramatic, emphasizing the playing of roles, making it a fit choice for Hammer movies in the 1960s. Later, Lovecraft identifies his own debt to Poe, with a chapter on Poe's horror tales in *Supernatural Horror in Literature* (1927), where he calls Poe the 'deity and fountain-head of all modern diabolic fiction' ([1927] 1973: 53). Lovecraft argues that Poe moves beyond earlier authors of horror because he refuses to conform to happy endings, avoids didacticism, and establishes psychological horror. Carter also finds and replays in her own writings the physical and psychological horror in the work of earlier authors, including Webster and Tourneur, the Jacobean revenge dramatists and, of course, Shakespeare (see her 'John Ford's *'Tis Pity She's a Whore*' 1994).

Carter takes issue with the representation of evil, as well as of sex and sexuality, in both Poe and Lovecraft, saying of Poe that:

> The Gothic tradition in which Poe writes grandly ignores the value systems of our institutions; it deals entirely with the profane. Its great

themes are incest and cannibalism. Character and events are exaggerated beyond reality, to become symbols, ideas, passions. Its style will tend to be ornate, unnatural – and thus operates against the perennial human desire to believe the world as fact. ('Afterword' to *Fireworks*, 1974: 122)

While of Lovecraft she notes that:

> Lovecraft tacitly assumes that the 'unnameable' is the temporary embodiment of a free-form, cosmic evil like a blasting dew. This is a convention of the genre in which he works. Some of the consolatory quality of the tale of supernatural terror lies in this; that it removes evil from the realm of human practice and gives it the status of a visitation from another realm of being. It is an affliction. It is a possession. (Carter, 1998)

Her attack focuses first on their refusal to see evil as essentially human, a product of the human mind and behaviour. But she uses her skills of critical parody to perfection on their representations of sex as unnatural and demonic, leading to lasting disruption and disease of mind and body, of individual and generations, of women as the source of such tempting evil, and of their representation as manipulated performers. Carter undermines the destructive delusions of Poe, Lovecraft, myth and fairy tale without underestimating the damage and terror, offering instead a balance between polarities, earthy realism, alongside high Gothic moments of horror and fantasy, and an energetic agency.

Carter and Poe –dead women, returned lovers

The version of Edgar Allen Poe and H.P. Lovecraft which Carter uncovers and dramatizes exposes their representations of women, sexuality and sex as variously fascinating, lurking, terrifying and disgusting. She shows these two as masters of horror whose works fundamentally influence the genre, and as locked into both the idealization of women and the sexual hang-ups of their age.

In 1977 in a television interview with Les Bedford, Carter defines Poe's influences on her work: 'I have a kind of familial attachment to Poe. I've used him a lot decoratively, but never structurally. I don't know if that makes sense. […] I've used a lot of the imagery from Poe. I say I've used it, I've used it as a starting point for imagery of my own' (Bedford, 1977). For Poe, women are performative, objects of desire, and sex and death are inextricably linked, a response conditioned in his childhood and adulthood, losing both his mother, and his young wife/cousin. Poe himself appears as a character in 'The Cabinet of Edgar Allan Poe', one of Carter's short stories in *Black Venus* (1985a) and is a reminder of E.T.A. Hoffmann's 'The Sandman' (1816) and Robert Wiene's *The Cabinet of Dr Caligari* (1920). In this tale, young Edgar hides in the costume basket: 'Now and then, as a great treat, if he kept quiet as a mouse, because he begged and pleaded so, he was allowed to stay in the wings and watch; the round-eyed baby saw that Ophelia could, if necessary, die twice nightly. All her burials were premature' (58) After marrying his thirteen-year-old cousin Virginia Clemm, variously described as angelic and beautiful, 'a lady angelically beautiful in person, and not less beautiful in spirit' (Wagenknecht, 1963: 183), Poe witnessed his young wife wasting away with tuberculosis. Women, beauty and allure are linked with death in Poe, and Carter responds directly to the elision, to the underlying values and representations of women in his work.

'The Oval Portrait' (1842) has a male artist painting a female model, who slowly fades and dies as the portrait becomes more lifelike, as if it is draining her. Carter replays this deadly danger of the male gaze as a warning to young women in 'The Bloody Chamber' (1979), where, in Bluebeard's castle, an impoverished young wife on her wedding night finds herself reflected in a myriad of mirrors in which 'A dozen husbands impaled a dozen brides while the mewing gulls swung on invisible trapezes in the empty air outside' (17). Poe's poem 'Annabel Lee' (1849), which deals with another young woman doomed to an early death, has echoes in the figures of the emotionally unstable woman, the Ophelia-obsessed Annabel, whose life ends in suicide, and her husband, Lee, in Carter's novel *Love* (1971).

Poe's equation of sex and death can be seen in how women are portrayed in his fiction: as performing, manipulated objects, their allure lasting beyond seeming death. In his stories, often a woman's power comes back to haunt the one who outlasted or killed her, in the form of a ghostly embodiment of a second wife, or a returned spectral self ('Eleanora', 1842; 'Ligeia', 1838).

Carter and Lovecraft – disgusting spawning, formless evil

While Poe's fascination is with idealized, beautiful, dead women, Lovecraft has no such fascination, only fear and disgust. His response to and representation of women is based on distaste at sex and procreation, which expresses itself in miscegenation. Lovecraft's horror focuses on the culpability of women duped and overwhelmed by alien others, who produce spawn debasing any line of inheritance and purity. Lovecraft's women are guilty of coupling with the devil, apes, fishy folk, Elder gods, and bringing unsuspecting ruin on individuals and humankind. His world of horror, his weird, sees individual acts as part of the grander plot from the Elder gods beyond the dark skies, in the ocean depths, the above, beyond, behind and beneath. The leaky door of this betrayal of humankind to eventual destruction is the weakness of women. Lovecraft's women are not beautiful and seductive, even Marceline in 'Medusa's Coil' (1939) is overblown, and finally recognized as a huge black snake inhabiting a human body. Mostly his women are hags, mothers to monsters, whose deformity renders them disgustingly much less than human, and terrifying, dangerous. If Lovecraft enacts women's sexual actions as disgusting, so he also depicts sex as disgusting. Exploring Lovecraft's early reading of the Puritans and acknowledgement in his papers and letters that he found sexuality debasing and degenerate, Bruce Lord argues that Lovecraft 'places sex in direct opposition to intellect and the pursuit of intellectual ends' (2004: online) S.T. Joshi notes that at age eight, when reading about sex, Lovecraft decided it was not of interest and instead equated restraint and intellect with human development. Lovecraft argued that sex was 'a mechanism which I rather despised or at least thought non-glamorous because of its purely animal nature & separation from such things as intellect & beauty – & all the drama was taken out of it' (Joshi, 2001: 30). And that restraint and Puritan behaviour were vastly preferable. Carter challenges the sexual terrors which lurk or spew out in Lovecraft's work. Her linking of his weird horror, and a kind of hysterical sexual repression emerges in her wonderful image:

> Is it any wonder, when evil finally manifests itself, that it does so as an obscene and huge ejaculation? 'Out of the fungus-ridden earth steamed up a vaporous corpse-light, yellow and diseased, which bubbled and lapped to a gigantic height in vague outlines, half human and half monstrous' ('The Shuttered House'). The doctor who posthumously refrigerated himself leaves behind him, when the machinery breaks down, pools of 'something unutterable', a ghastly pus. 'A burst of multitudinous and leprous life – a loathsome, night-spawned flood of organic corruption [...] seething, stewing, surging, bubbling like

serpent's slime' ('The Lurking Fear'). On examination, this stream proves composed of uncountable thousands of dwarfed, monkey things, oddly reminiscent of the teeming homunculi early researchers observed when they put semen under the micro-scope. This pus-like matter turns out to be the last of an old Dutch colonial family. Evolution has wound them backwards; they have reverted to their own seminal fluid in three generations. (Carter, 1998: 443–7)

Evil in Carter is real; it imprisons, tortures, kills bodies and minds, and one emanation of it is the perverse dehumanization and objectification of women as puppets, performers, sexual objects for consumption and destruction in the service of lust, self aggrandizement and bizarre beliefs. In her use of bawdy and satirical comedy in the midst of prurience and violence acting as idolatory, Angela Carter exposes and undermines Poe's idolatry and preference for ideas, man-manipulated idealized women, and Lovecraft's embrace of the weird and utter abjection of women as culpable of betraying humankind.

Both authors write about the kind of voyeuristic ownership enabled when constructing an artistic image of a beautiful woman. Poe's 'The Oval Portrait' (1842) and Lovecraft and Zealia Bishop's 'Medusa's Coil' (1939) reveal the need to control the representation of woman and, in the latter tale, women's deviant sexual allure and power, as Marceline is possessed by a disgusting black snake, and the focus on her otherness (she is from New Orleans, and a Creole) leaks Lovecraft's racism through his sexism. Both tales replay without irony the power and sexual ownership which is instead exposed and critiqued in Robert Browning's powerfully unsettling poem 'My Last Duchess' (1842), where a tyrannous, obsessive nobleman owns the right to display a portrait of his dead wife, whose smiles were jealously owned by him, and whose breath was stopped along with her smiles. Browning's Duke has power over the lasting image, the woman's sexual identity, life and death. Neither Poe nor Lovecraft ironize this kind of compulsive love and control through reification. But, like Browning, Carter does.

Carter reacts against the deification, artistic reification, and then sacrifice, of woman as sexual object constructed from male heated fantasy in a wide range of her work, including 'The Snow Child' (1979), 'Unicorn' (1966), the short story 'The Loves of Lady Purple' (1974), Uncle Philip's sadistic control of Melanie as sexualized child puppet in *The Magic Toyshop* (1967), and both Christian Rosencreutz and the Grand Duke's perverse representation of Fevvers as goddess or owned art object, each constructed from their heated brains, each to be manipulated and either petrified or destroyed in *Nights at the Circus* (1987).

Poe's treatment of the horror of incarceration and bodily destruction ('The Cask of Amontillado' (1846); 'The Pit and the Pendulum', (1842)) reminds us of the incarceration of women as forms of living dead dolls for the sexual pleasure of punters visiting Madame Schreck's brothel in *Nights at the Circus* (1987), and the short story 'The Scarlet House' (1977). Houses are engulfing, locations of entrapment, torture and domestic incarceration. Poe's representation of the house, heredity and family as a deadly, incestuous trap in 'The Fall of the House of Usher' (1839) is echoed in that of the house of the puppeteer Uncle Philip in *The Magic Toyshop* (1967), where incest is actually a way of fighting back, undermining his power. Carter also re-writes 'The Fall of the House of Usher'(1839), by turning the story backwards on itself in 'Through a Text Backwards: The Resurrection of the House of Usher'(1988), in which Carter's reversal of the death of the cursed incestuous twins, and the destruction of the lowering family house, built over a dark tarn, re-enacts the revivification of the dead beloved, that favourite Poe trope emphasizing both the inevitability of their demise, and yet ending on a note of uneasy threatened calm.

'The Man Who Loved a Double Bass' (1962)

Poe's reification and idolatry, as well as Lovecraft's disgust at miscegenation, also lurk behind the early 'The Man Who Loved a Double Bass' (1962). Carter's story is of an ill-fated love for a double bass, a curvy wooden musical object caressed, played and slept with by a travelling musician in the Fens. Just by imaginatively turning the loved one into a wooden double bass, which can never refuse his advances, she emphasizes the reification of woman as sex object. The musician adores and sleeps with his double bass, a fetishistic set of behaviours tolerated by the rest of the group. Jameson, the transient double bass player, offloads his sexual needs for a static, faceless, limbless, female companion onto the double bass herself, Lola, his permanent companion. She comes to life from wood under the caresses of his fingers on her strings, and is bought appropriate drinks by the rest of the band: 'Her shape was that of a full-breasted, full-hipped woman, recalling certain primitive effigies of the Mother Goddess so gloriously, essentially feminine was she, stripped of irrelevancies of head and limbs' (1962: 3). The influences of Carter's teenage years, which saw fights between Mods and Rockers down South – Clacton, Brighton and Eastbourne – play out through her work here with the warring rival posers in the pub where the band play. First, the jealous destruction of the wooden double bass, smashed into shavings after turmoil in the Fenland pub, and then the musician's bereft, desperate, guilt-ridden suicide play up and simultaneously expose and ridicule the sexual perversion of such idolatry. Lola is described as 'firewood', 'splinters', her case a 'coffin' emptied of the pieces of her 'corpse' (1962: 9).

'The Loves of Lady Purple' (1974) and
Nights at the Circus (1987)

Carter's 'The Loves of Lady Purple' (1974) and her mature, marvellous, later novel, *Nights at the Circus* (1987) take the idolatry, reification, possession and preference for dead women into the context of people as puppets, puppets as people, and brothels as galleries of the living dead. This may be seen as a response to Poe's fixation with the untimely death of constructed beauties such as the narrator's cousin 'Berenice' (1835), whose grave clothes appear to suggest she survives her interment, whose teeth are collected post mortem in a box, and 'Ligeia' (1848), where the possession is by an undead woman whose eternal longevity is both sexualized and controlled.

In 'The Loves of Lady Purple' (1974), Carter interjects this deadly, prurient idolatry with a vampire doll fed up with being manipulated and playing out the dark terrors and fantasies of punters, turning into a living woman with a will of her own, master of her own sexuality. Much more dangerous than Lola, the wooden double bass, Lady Purple is part of a mass fantasy, as the punters collude with the man who manipulates and created her and her cruel tale. 'The Loves of Lady Purple' is an exposé of sadistic sexual fantasy, since the puppet is a construct of an eternal whore, men's fetish and fantasy, an object of desire and disgust manipulated nightly to perform whoring roles. Born from the fevered brain of the Asiatic Professor, playing on the fevered brains of the punters, she is dressed up for their fantasies, forced to perform them, and then punished for this performance, hung up and put away. This enacts Kristeva's argument concerning otherizing, and abjection (1988). Sexual perversities and the dehumanizing of women unite, grown from a total lack of self-awareness of their origins in the men's minds. Her eyes, rubies, her mother of pearl teeth in a permanent smile, Lady Purple cannot speak, but the Professor, his voice of fur and honey (44), speaks through her. She is 'contagious as evil', forced to enact terrible sexual and violent deeds while performing the story of 'her' life, written by the Professor, composed of a series of performances of desire, in her 'miraculous inhumanity' (48), representing the 'petrification of a universal whore' (47), visiting men 'like the plague' (47). With the utilization of baroque instruments for sexual torture, she is the 'quintessence of eroticism' (43). As a marionette, all her movements are 'calculations in an angular geometry of sexuality' (44), brought to life by the Professor's skilful manipulation. She is larger than life, infecting those who desired her, and is, finally, herself punished in the show, because this then exorcizes the evil, having laid it on her, and all involved can both enjoy the perverse show, and feel exonerated at her demise. But the puppet, behaving like a woman, performing deeds which feed from and punish the fervid imagination, responds to the Professor's kiss like some anti-romantic Sleeping Beauty. Her artificial hair turns back to grow into her scalp, and she comes to life. Lady Purple, wooden, overdressed, manipulated puppet, vampire woman, turns on her Svengali, draining him of his blood to fuel her own system. Seizing her own sexual and economic agency she heads off into the night to set herself up in the town's brothel.

Carter explores the polarities of constraint, imprisonment and freedom. Freedom to imagine and to construct versions of the self are expressed in *Nights at the Circus* (1987) through Fevvers, the winged woman who flies away from being turned into a victim of romance, prostitution, ritual sacrifice, or reification, and instead constructs *herself* as a performance, a feathered intacta, who genuinely flies, a puzzle for others, which she finds satisfying as well as lucrative. About to be a sacrifice to a series of esoteric gods whose names resemble those of ancient religions or Lovecraft's *Necronomicon* (a fictional grimoire or textbook of magic), Fevvers escapes the Gothic mansion and heated incantations of Christian Rosencreutz, whose powerful voice in the House of Lords denies women the vote and equal human status to men, under the guise of idolizing them, and whose name reminds of a variety of nonsense controls imposed by a variety of religious systems.

Artifice and reification are familiar in Gothic horror, where people become objects, and objects come alive in a terrifying and strange reversal. Objects of performance can be objects of desire and disgust. Sacrificing these constructs onto offloaded desires and fears offers a moment of purification, of escape from self, a moment of promise of some kind of eternity, escape from the death of the performed self. Constructing an idol of lust and evil, or one to be trapped or sacrificed, offers an opportunity for control for the constructor and controller. In *Nights at the Circus* (1987), the Grand Duke, master of another Gothic castle filled with the icons and trappings of powerful masculinity, seeks to own a version of woman as a performing doll. He has an ice swan dripping into jewels downstairs, while upstairs, seducing/being seduced by Fevvers, his plan is to shrink and trap a real bird woman in a Fabergé egg. A golden bird on a golden swing, reduced in size to the doll-like miniature fitted inside the egg, any revelation or seeming live appearance controlled by his management of the hinges and the mechanism, the bird woman, Fevvers, would in his plan be disempowered, reduced, dehumanized, trapped and rendered docile in a permanent performance or silence. The Grand Duke has designs to turn a woman into an object of control, to place a shrunken Fevvers as a golden bird in a golden cage. Fevvers turns his perverse dream against itself, while simultaneously recognizing that her own greed has landed her there in the first place 'The cage was empty. No bird stood on that perch, yet. Fevvers did not shrink, but was at once aware of the hideous possibility that she might do so' (192).

Controlling the Duke's sexual activity, she escapes as the ice sculpture table decoration of herself as a swan melts into free flowing water. This is not just a reflection, it is also a sexual release; for at the same time as Fevvers stimulates the Duke, she also takes control. His temporary ecstasy brings on the ice sculpture of the swan, her alter ego the sculpted swan, beautiful but destined to melt – as she disempowers him, seeking that moment of orgasm to escape both control of her as a sexual being and control of her as an object of a construct of his fantasy. So when she earlier exposes Christian Rosencreutz, she escapes the power that wealth enables. Each man has a heavy reeking masculinity. Rosencreutz tries to cast her as a reflection of his desires and fears, the Grand Duke as an object for manipulation. Whether an idol, a deity steeped in the mystic claptrap wielded by religious and political power – incantation, spells, entire cosmologies of constant and controlling doctrines and rules of belief – or constraint in a gilded cage, in a bejewelled egg, dancing when only wound up, each fate for Fevvers derives from their constructing her as a desired and feared other, and their wishes to manipulate and destroy, sacrifice or control her. Carter exposes this otherizing, this disgusted idolatry with sex and woman seen as perversion and contamination. Neither Rosencreutz nor the Duke fully offload sexual and cosmic guilt onto vile, hideous, deceitful woman, as does Lovecraft, nor do they manage to first celebrate and then contain, reify, destroy yet deify post mortem their object of desire, as does Poe, who finds the most extreme beauty, the most extreme sexual satisfaction in a dead woman.

Fevvers' agency is powered by her down to earth, bawdy self, her control of her own performance, her materialistic cold self-awareness and energy in the face of beliefs in the controlling power of universes of wealth, idolatry and perversity, which these men have constructed and managed. Fevvers flies or shrinks and escapes, free, her own fantastic construct. A winged woman seems genuinely to fly, rather slowly like a real bird, rather than a dressed up performer, and also to guffaw and be vulgar, vulnerable and in control. Taking ownership of her own performance, Fevvers refuses to be anyone else's reflection, manipulated doll or sacrificial victim. She undercuts, exposes, refuses the roles, denies the systems and talks back to the discourses of power which attempt to reduce, manage and destroy her – and lands large, solid, real and free with the last laugh. Carter's carnival and bawdy, the essentially earthy, counteracts the heated constructs of minds wound up in self-loathing, manipulation, desire, sexual and xenophobic othering and reifying.

Like a bawdy cockney, Carter's work is a performance of an extreme. Her representations of the down to earth amidst the magical and/or perverse constraining constructs which society offers women and men, and which they imbibe, take in, ingest, reproduce, then assert, that which they are fettered by to reveal the mind-forged manacles of behavioural and psychological control.

> I believe that all myths are products of the human mind and reflect only aspects of material human practice. I'm in the demythologising business … How that social fiction of my 'femininity' was created by means outside my control, and palmed off on me as the real thing […] This investigation of the social fictions that regulate our lives – is what I've concerned myself with consciously since that time. (Carter, 1983: 70–1)

Carter's famous demythologizing quotation is not just about escape from myth and fairy tale but, as with Roland Barthes' own views (1957) on myth, springs from culturally internalized constructions. In *Nights at the Circus* (1987), in the midst of the high Gothic and artifice, the controlling plans of both Christian Rosencreutz and the Grand Duke would seal Fevvers up as a religious sacrifice to eternal youth, or an object of entertainment, a golden bird on a golden bough, an ornament of perverse imagination, a winged flying cockney Venus. The demythologizing can be focused both on her realization of the earthy usefulness of money, which she is to be paid for her collusion, on the debunking of the powerful men's underpinning theorizing, and on Fevvers' realization of the necessity of self-preservation and escape.

Carter shows that we internalize performance as real, we construct ourselves as reflections which then entrance us, so in 'Alice in Prague *or* the Curious Room' (1993), the Alice figure comes out from and goes back through the mirror, to reveal how the magical world is both freeing and a trap. Also entrapping is film, and its dream factory, Hollywood. In 'The Merchant of Shadows' (1989) the producer has lasted, pretending to be his own aged partner of the opposite sex, and in *The Passion of New Eve* (1977), Tristessa, the ideal woman, born a man, represents performance of woman as icon.

Celebration of sexual energy as liberation is at the heart of many of the stories, as it is with Melanie revelling in her own body at the end of *The Magic Toyshop* (1967), and in Carter's dealings with de Sade, most notably in *The Sadeian Woman* (1979). What she critiques is dehumanization through objectification as puppet, icon or sexual slave, finding the most disturbing example (beyond the double bass and the whorish marionette) with the tableaux vivants in Madame Schreck's brothel cellar in *Nights at the Circus* (1987). Here there are static embodiments of perverse versions of woman as sexual object, succumbing by design or accident to the plans of others to work out desire, disgust and death.

Fuelled by a vital element of socialism, Carter's women always recognize the power of economics, as they do of sexual energy, which she refuses to condemn. On the one hand, she is a product of the liberated 1960s and 1970s herself, and in the vanguard of writing about women and sexual power, who are turning the tables. On the other hand, she is using the Gothic to reveal and manage the contradictory or paradoxical.

In the famous comment in 'Notes from the Front Line' Carter acknowledges, 'I am all for putting new wine in old bottles, especially if the pressure of the new wine makes the old bottles explode' (1983: 69). Her revisiting of fairy tale, myth and horror challenge their misogyny and reification.

The hang ups and perversities she saw in fairy tale, myth, Poe and Lovecraft are her target and her source material. Carter's women are not willing victims, static sex objects devoid of identity, power and voice, neither are they prudes or sexless. These positive versions are enacted when women fly free like Fevvers and choose their own mates, and later when her women deliberately dress up to re-enact their performative bawdy youth, as do the twins in *Wise Children* (1991). Agency is the clue. Carter's women construct themselves and their sexual selves, and at the core of this is her wonderful bawdy debunking of the terrified prurience of both Lovecraft and Poe, the one representing the figure of the beloved as most beautiful when dead, the other representing his greatest terrors as wayward grandmothers who prefer beasts and pass on their sick heritage, and seeing sex as a terrifying spume of evil. As a late twentieth-century feminist, Carter critiques, parodies and exposes the underlying sexual terrors, the desire and disgust fuelling representations of women as variously dead or deadly in fairy tale, myth and in the work of the two great masters of Gothic horror, Poe and Lovecraft. Carter shows it is possible and essential to tell other stories, revising and rewriting these received, constraining myths, particularly ones in which women reject the role of puppets and pawns (*The Magic Toyshop*, 1967; *Nights at the Circus*, 1987; 'The Loves of Lady Purple', 1974), seizing their sexuality and agency, having the last laugh.

References

Barker, Pat (2006), 'Angela Carter: Clever, Sexy, Funny, Scary', *Independent* (22 January), www.independent.co.uk/arts-entertainment/books/features/angela-carter-clever-sexy-funny-scary-524246.html, accessed 26 November 2018.

Barthes, Roland (1957), *Mythologies* (Paris: Editions du Seuil).

Botting, Fred (2002), 'Aftergothic: Consumption Machines and Black Holes', in Jerrold E. Hogle (ed.), *The Cambridge Companion to Gothic Fiction* (Cambridge: Cambridge University Press).

Browning, Robert ([1842] 1994), 'My Last Duchess', *Dramatic Lyrics* (New York: Dover Publications).

Carter, Angela (1966), 'Unicorn', *Vision Magazine* (May), 1.

—— (1971), *Love* (London: Virago).

—— (1972), *The Infernal Desire Machines of Dr Hoffman* (London: Rupert Hart-Davis).

—— (1977), *The Passion of New Eve* (New York: Harcourt Brace Jovanovich).

—— ([1997] 1995), 'The Scarlet House', in *Burning your boats: The Collected Short Stories* (London: Chatto & Windus).

—— (1979a), 'The Snow Child', in *The Bloody Chamber and Other Stories* (London: Gollancz), pp. 91–2.

—— (1979b), 'The Bloody Chamber', in *The Bloody Chamber and Other Stories* (London: Gollancz), pp. 7–40.

—— (1979c), 'The Company of Wolves', in *The Bloody Chamber and Other Stories* (London: Gollancz), pp. 110–18.

—— (1979d), *The Sadeian Woman: An Exercise in Cultural History* (London: Virago Press).

—— ([1967] 1981), *The Magic Toyshop* (London: Virago Press Limited).

—— (1983), 'Notes from the Front Line', in M. Wandor (ed.), *On Gender and Writing* (London: Pandora), pp. 69–77.

—— (1985a), *Black Venus and Other Stories* (London: Chatto & Windus).

—— (1985), 'The Fall River Axe Murders', in *Black Venus and Other Stories* (London: Chatto & Windus), pp. 101–21.

—— (1987), *Nights at the Circus* (London: Chatto & Windus).

—— ([1974] 1987a), 'Afterword', in *Fireworks: Nine Profane Pieces* (London: Virago), pp. 132–3.

—— ([1974] 1987b), 'The Executioner's Beautiful Daughter', in *Fireworks: Nine Profane Pieces* (London: Virago), pp. 13–22.

—— ([1974] 1987c), 'Flesh and the Mirror', in *Fireworks: Nine Profane Pieces* (London: Virago), pp. 61–70.

—— ([1974] 1987d), 'Master', in *Fireworks: Nine Profane Pieces* (London: Virago), pp. 71–80.

—— ([1974] 1987e), 'The Loves of Lady Purple', in *Fireworks: Nine Profane Pieces* (London: Virago), pp. 23–38.

—— (1988), 'Through a Text Backwards: The Resurrection of the House of Usher', *Metaphores* (14–15 January).

—— (1991), *Wise Children* (London: Chatto & Windus).

—— (1993), 'Alice in Prague *or* the Curious Room', in *American Ghosts & Old World Wonders* (London: Chatto & Windus), pp. 121–40.

—— ([1989] 1993), 'The Merchant of Shadows', in *American Ghosts & Old World Wonders* (London: Chatto & Windus), pp. 66–85.

—— (1994), 'John Ford's *'Tis Pity She's a Whore*', in *American Ghosts & Old World Wonders* (London: Vintage), pp. 20–45.

—— ([1962] 1995), 'The Man Who Loved a Double Bass', in *Burning Your Boats: The Collected Short Stories* (London: Chatto & Windus), pp. 3–10.

—— ([1985] 1996), 'The Cabinet of Edgar Allan Poe', in *Black Venus and Other Stories* (London: Vintage]), pp. 32–42.

—— ([1968] 1998), 'The Hidden Child (Stories and Tellers)', in *Shaking a Leg: Collected Journalism and Writings*, ed. Jenny Uglow (London: Vintage), pp. 443–7.

Cixous, Helen ([1975], 1976), 'The Laugh of the Medusa', in E. Abel and E.K. Abel (eds), *The Signs Reader: Women, Gender, and Scholarship* (Chicago: University of Chicago Press), pp. 279–97.

Crofts, Charlotte (1998), 'Curiously Downbeat Hybrid or Radical Retelling? Neil Jordan's and Angela Carter's *The Company of Wolves*', in Deborah Cartmell, I. Q. Hunter, Heidi Kaye and Imelda Whelehan (eds), *Sisterhoods Across the Literature / Media Divide* (London and Sterling, Virginia: Pluto Press), pp. 48–63.

Duncker, Patricia (1984), 'Re-imagining the Fairytales: Angela Carter's Bloody Chambers', *Literature and History*, 10:1 (Spring), 3–14.

Gordon, Edmund (2016), *The Invention of Angela Carter: A Biography* (London: Chatto & Windus).

Hill, Rosemary (2012), 'Hairy Fairies'. Review of *A Card from Angela Carter* by Susannah Clapp, *London Review of Books*, 34: 9 (10 May), pp. 15–16. www.lrb.co.uk/v34/n09/rosemary-hill/hairy-fairies, accessed 26 November 2018.

—— (2015a), 'Rediscovering Angela Carter's Poetry: Images that Stick and Splinter in the Mind', *Guardian* (Friday 30 October), https://www.theguardian.com/books/2015/oct/30/rediscovering-angela-carter-poetry accessed 26 November 2018.

—— (2015b), *Unicorn: The Poetry of Angela Carter* (London: Profile Books).

Hoffman, E.T.A. (1816), 'The Sandman', *The Night Pieces* (Berlin).

Joshi, S.T. (2001), *H.P. Lovecraft: A Life* (West Warwick, RI: Necronomicon Press).

Kristeva, Julia (1988), *Strangers to Ourselves* (New York: Columbia University Press).

Lord, Bruce (2004), 'The Genetics of Horror: Sex and Racism in H.P. Lovecraft's Fiction', www.thephora.net/forum/archive/index.php/t-41 907.html accessed 26 November 2018.

Lovecraft, H. P. (1965), *Selected Letters Vol. I*, ed. A. Derleth and D. Wandrei (Sauk City, WI: Arkham House).

—— (1970), 'The Dunwich Horror' [1928], 'The Dreams in the Witch

House' [1932] and 'The Shadow over Innsmouth' [1936], in *'The Lurking Fear' and Other Stories* (London: Panther).
—— ([1927] 1973), *Supernatural Horror in Literature* (Mineola, NY: Dover Publications).
—— and Z. Bishop (1939), 'Medusa's Coil', *Weird Tales*, 33:1, 26–53.
Mulvey-Roberts, Marie (2016), *Dangerous Bodies: Historicising the Gothic Corporeal* (Manchester: Manchester University Press).
—— and Charlotte Crofts co-organizers of 'Fireworks: The Visual Imagination of Angela Carter', conference, Royal West of England Academy and the Arnolfini City Campus, University of the West of England, Bristol, 9–10 January 2017.
Munford, Rebecca (2013), 'Poe, Baudelaire and the Decomposing Muse', in *Decadent Daughters and Monstrous Mothers: Angela Carter and the European Gothic* (Manchester: Manchester University Press), pp. 71–10.
Palmer, Paulina (2017), 'Uncanny Representations of the Marionette and Clockwork Figurine in the Fiction of Angela Carter and their Connections with E.T.A. Hoffmann's Stories', conference, Bristol, 9–10 January.
Peach, Linden (1998), *Angela Carter* (Basingstoke: Macmillan).
Perrault, Charles (1697), *Tales and Stories of the Past with Morals* (France, n.p.).
Poe, Edgar Allan (1966), 'Annabel Lee' [1849], 'Berenice' [1835], 'Eleanora' [1842], 'Ligeia' [1848], 'The Cask of Amontillado' [1846], 'The Fall of the House of Usher' [1839], 'The Oval Portrait' [1842], 'The Pit and the Pendulum' [1842] in *Complete Stories and Poems of Edgar Allan Poe* (New York: Doubleday Dell Publishing Group, Inc.).
Wagenknecht, Edward (1963), *Edgar Allan Poe: The Man Behind the Legend* (Oxford: Oxford University Press).
Wisker, Gina (1984), 'Woman Writer, Woman Reader, Male Institution: The Experience of a Contemporary Women's Writing Seminar', *Literature Teaching Politics*, 3, 18–31.
—— (1997), 'The Revenge of the Living Doll: Angela Carter's Horror Writing', in J. Bristow and T.L. Broughton (eds), *The Infernal Desires of Angela Carter: Fiction, Femininity, Feminism* (Harlow: Longman), pp. 116–31.
—— (2006), 'Behind Locked Doors: Angela Carter, Horror and the Influence of Edgar Allan Poe', in R. Munford (ed.), *Revisiting Angela Carter: Texts, Contexts, Intertexts* (Basingstoke: Palgrave Macmillan), pp. 178–98.
—— (2013), 'Spawn of the Pit: Lavinia, Marceline, Medusa and All Things Foul: H.P. Lovecraft's Liminal Women', in D. Simmons (ed.), *New Critical Essays on H P Lovecraft* (Basingstoke: Palgrave Macmillan), pp. 31–54.
—— (2015), 'Speaking the Unspeakable: Women, Sex and the Dismorphmythic. Lovecraft, Angela Carter, Caitlin R. Kiernan and Beyond', in S. Moreland (ed.), *The Lovecraftian Poe: Essays on Influence,*

Reception, Interpretation and Transformation (Bethlehem, PA: LeHigh University Press).

Filmography
Cabinet of Dr Caligari, The (1920), dir. Robert Wiene.

Television
Bedford, L. (1977), 'Angela Carter: An Interview', Sheffield University Television, February.

10

The 'art of faking': performance and puppet theatre in Angela Carter's Japan

Helen Snaith

ON 26 MARCH 1969 Angela Carter received the news that she had been awarded the five hundred pound Somerset Maugham Travel Award for her novel, *Several Perceptions*, published in the previous year. Carter used the money to travel to America with her then-husband, Paul Carter, before embarking upon her sojourn to Japan alone. Reflecting on Carter's time abroad Sarah Gamble remarks that, 'Japan provided [her] with new insights which energized her writing for years afterwards' (1997: 16); Lorna Sage saw Carter's time abroad as a 'rite of passage', in which she stepped into the 'looking-glass world of a culture that reflected her back to herself as an alien' (1994: 24–6). Both Susan Fisher (2001) and Charlotte Crofts (2003; 2006) offer a substantial analysis into Carter's time abroad and what it means to be 'other'. For Fisher, Japan offered a way for Carter to be the 'other' 'in a far more definitive way than her life in England' (2001: 171). Deliberately avoiding the dangers of 'straightforwardly situating Japan as an intellectual playground for the development of Carter's aesthetic', Crofts focuses on a postcolonial reading of Carter's journalism, radio plays and short fiction, arguing that an exploration of the racial dynamics in her work is pertinent to understanding the 'strengths and the limitations of Carter's political strategies in relation to her engagement with Japan' (2006: 87).

Recent publications on Carter have also offered new insights into her time in Japan. Sozo Araki's *Seduced by Japan: A Memoir of the Days Spent with Angela Carter, with 'Her Side of the Story' by Natsumi Ikoma* (2018; translated, annotated and introduced by Natsumi Ikoma) provides a new insight into Carter's personal and professional life during her time abroad. Araki, who was Carter's lover while she was living in

Japan, 'teases and reveals much about Japanese customs, ways of life, and Japanese views on foreigners, especially Caucasians' (Ikoma in Araki, 2018: ix). According to Araki, Carter felt that Western people were 'prepossessed with the Judeo-Christian concepts on sin and punishment. This made them culturally exceptional in the world [...] She regarded Japanese culture as frankly mysterious' (Araki, 2018: 44).

In addition to Araki's memoirs, Edmund Gordon's biography *The Invention of Angela Carter* (2016) draws heavily on the Angela Carter Papers available at the British Library: Gordon's access to the archival material challenges the popular view of Carter as the 'benevolent white witch' of English Literature (Rushdie, 1992). Most notably, it is Gordon's focus on Carter's time in Japan that has received considerable attention in literary reviews, indicating that we have much to learn from this relatively unknown period in Carter's life. Described by Max Liu as the place where Carter 'found the settings for some of her best stories' (2016), representations of Japan are littered throughout Carter's short stories, essays, and the one novel she wrote during her time abroad: the illusionary city 'full of mirages' (3), which appears in the first chapter of *The Infernal Desire Machines of Doctor Hoffman* (1972) is clearly a 'dream-version of Tokyo' (Gordon, 2016: 175). Likewise, the 'self-contained society' (76) of the river people in chapter three has clear similarities with the Japanese – the women, for example, paint their faces white with eyebrows 'some three inches above the natural position' (79), an aesthetic Fisher links to the beauty tricks of the Heian period court ladies (2001: 170). The body modification practiced by the centaurs in chapter seven is a reference to the Japanese art of *irezumi*: 'what I had taken for clothing was the most intricate tattoo work I have ever seen. These tattoos were designed as a whole and covered the back and both arms' (203). Carter's essays for the *New Society* between 1970 and 1972 also demonstrate a fascination with Japanese culture, and her contributions include topics ranging from manga comic books, tattooing, and all-male bars. Furthermore, Carter continued to write essays about Japan well beyond 1972, and her later contributions to the *New Society* include a review of Nagisa Oshima's film *Ai No Corrida* (1978), plus literary commentaries on Murasaki Shikibu's *The Tale of Genji* (1976) and Jun'ichirō Tanizaki's *Naomi* (1986).[1]

Drawing on her journals and the short stories she produced during her time in Japan, this chapter explores representations of authenticity in Carter's work through two channels. Firstly, it assesses the extent to which Carter's own authentic self can be interpreted from her archival records and her semi-autobiographical short stories that appear in her collection *Fireworks* (1974), written during her time in Japan. Displaying a 'self-conscious exoticism' (Fisher, 2001: 169) Carter performs the role of 'other' in Japan: a role that has been scripted for her, and one that she is complicit in sustaining. However, Carter capitalizes on this position 'recognis[ing her] own artificiality' through the physical estrangement from our home-selves (Sage, 1994: 27). Secondly, artificiality will be explored through an analysis of Carter's experiments with Japanese puppet theatre *bunraku*. Purposefully avoiding 'the danger of over-realism' instead delivering 'stylization in art and not literal fidelity' (Keene, 1990: 124), it is the 'art of faking' (Buruma, 2001: 69) that is so pertinent to *bunraku* theatre, an idea that resonates with Carter's own ideas of in/authenticity.

Carter as 'other' in Japan

Reflecting on Carter's decision to travel to Japan, Paul Barker remarks that 'It is hard now to appreciate how strange a decision this was. Japan was then simply a place that made cheap toys, imitation Western branded goods, and had done many horrible things in the war. No one knew anything about it' (1995). Carter gave a range of reasons as to why she chose to travel to Japan, claiming that she wanted to live 'in a non-Judeo Christian culture', and that it met her 'stringent criteria for a bolthole' (Clapp, 2012: 31) In an interview with Lisa Appignanesi (1987) Carter cites her love of Japanese cinema as one of the reasons for her visit. She comments, 'I was very fond of Japanese films, and when I won this prize, somebody said to me, "Now you can go to Japan". So I had to'. In her journals, Carter describes her arriving for the first time as akin to descending into an 'electric city where nothing was what it seemed at first and I was absolutely confused (Add MS 88899/1/81).

Carter's description of her arrival into the illuminated world of Japan encapsulates her experiences in a country she describes as 'the domain of the marvellous' (Add MS 88899/1/81). Her arrival into Japan transcends the boundaries between reality and fiction, as she moves beyond the looking glass to a world where, not only is everything unfamiliar and unknown to *her*, but in which she is unknown and unfamiliar *herself*. Descending into the unknown, into the 'city [of] delusion', 'nothing but a hall of mirrors' (Add MS 88899/1/81), Carter's language is suggestive of the themes that permeated her fiction produced during her time in Japan. Her comments act as a premeditated gesture towards the backdrop of *The Infernal Desire Machines of Doctor Hoffman*: just as Carter describes Tokyo being full of 'apparitions', so too does Desiderio live in a constant 'flux of mirages', mirroring Carter's language that 'Nothing in the city was what it seemed – nothing at all!' (Carter, 2010: 3). The city, she came to feel, was 'a living image of impermanence', its weirdly mutable landscape provoking 'an uneasy suspicion that nothing is real' (Add. MS 88899/1/80).

For the first time in her life, Carter was perceived as an outsider because of the colour of her skin: as a Western Caucasian woman, she stood out. In an essay she wrote for the *New Society* in 1970, 'Tokyo Pastoral', she recalls being surrounded by young Japanese children who were intrigued (and wary of) the 'first coloured family' on the street, hearing the 'rustle of innumerable small voices murmuring the word: *Gaijin, gaijin, gaijin* (foreigner), in pure, repressed surprise. We spy strangers. *Asoka*' (1997: 234). Inverting the Westernized use of the term 'coloured', Carter deliberately positions herself as an outsider, and as 'other' to the Japanese. In her journals she describes feeling in 'a state of permanent estrangement' (Add. MS 88899/80/1): yet, Carter utilizes her position as 'other' in order not only to observe Japanese cultural and social norms, but as a means of observing her own Western culture, for 'there is no point in studying another culture if this does not tell us anything about our own' (Buruma: 2001: xi). Carter comments in her journals that:

> The foreigner cannot escape a perpetual sense of foreignness; at ways defined as 'foreign' he lives on the twilit margins of a society that allows its denizens no half-measures. I am trying to create this sense of foreignness in every possible way in my narrative. (Add. MS 88899/1/80)

Carter's deliberate integration of 'otherness' resonates throughout *Fireworks*. For instance, in 'A Souvenir of Japan', Carter's narrator refers to herself as 'inexpressibly exotic' and a 'fabulous beast' (2009b, 8), deliberately inverting the Occidental narrative of the Orient towards the West. Likewise, in the essay 'Poor Butterfly'

(1972), Carter further explores this reversed voyeuristic practice by examining the treatment of Caucasian bar hostesses working in Tokyo. Employed in one of these bars during her time in Japan, Carter describes white women as 'exotic extras', with 'foreign girls' being able to demand more pay from the male Japanese clients. The hostesses become automatons, constructed under a 'blueprint for an ideal hostess' – a point exacerbated through Carter's claims that the hostesses 'do not really need to speak and no doubt soon will cease to do so' (1997a: 250). However, as Crofts points out, Carter's performance as an exotic extra 'has the affect of radicalizing her as a woman in relation to her own culture by amplifying the gender dynamics implicit in Western culture to such an extent as to make them recognisable as cultural constructions' (2006: 93). The position of foreigner for Carter appears to be a difficult one to reconcile: on the one hand the exoticism held an element of fascination – in 'A Souvenir of Japan' the narrator describes herself as 'an outlandish jewel' (2009b: 8). Yet, she also described herself as a 'female impersonator', and it is the same exotic qualities that categorize her as an interchangeable commodity, acting as no more than a 'masturbatory device for gentlemen' (1997a: 254). Although appalled by the 'intense polarity of the sexes' she simultaneously marvelled to see gender being so 'ludicrously exaggerated' (Add. MS 89102).[2] Carter's Japanese experience, Crofts claims, 'defamiliarised Western societal relationships by putting them in an alien context and exaggerating them' (2006: 93). It is perhaps no surprise, then, that Carter attributes Japan as the place where she 'learnt what it was to be a woman and became radicalised' (1982: 28).

There are some considerable difficulties in separating 'Carter as author' and 'Carter as narrator' during the novels and short stories she produced during her time in Japan. The crossover of language between her journals at the British Library is glaringly apparent, and *Fireworks* appears to openly experiment with the conflict between the fictional and the autobiographical. Michele Ryan-Sautour extensively explores the semi-autobiographical content of Carter's Japanese short fiction, linking Carter's 'growing emphasis on surface and image' and her attempts to 'metatextually foregroun[d] the performativity of the autobiographical confession'. If it is impossible to write outside of fiction, suggests Ryan-Sautour, then autobiography can *only* be perceived as an ongoing performance (2007: 66–7).

The short story 'Flesh and the Mirror' (2009c) serves as a prime example of the blurred boundaries between biography and fiction and Carter's 'authentic self'. During Carter's time in Japan, she returned to England twice: the first time was after she had spent her grant money; the second was to promote the publication of her novel *Love* in 1971. Her return to Japan both times was influenced by the relationship with her Japanese lover, and her desire to continue the relationship they had begun during her first trip. In 'Flesh and the Mirror' a nameless woman returns to Japan expecting to find her lover waiting for her: finding no one to meet her, she trawls the streets looking for him. Instead, she meets a stranger and they go to a love hotel together for one night of passion: the next morning the narrator departs, full of regret and remorse. Comparing this fictional narrative with Carter's journals and her correspondence to friends at the time, it is evident that 'Flesh and the Mirror' is based on actual events. When Carter returned to Japan in July 1971, after being in England for three months, Sozo was not there to meet her. Failing to find him, Carter found herself going to a love hotel with a stranger. She recalls the events in a letter to her friend Carole, telling her that it was 'an absolutely delirious night [...] a grand tour of Japanese eroticism' (Add. MS 89102).

Carter's reaction to her night with the man she calls 'Summer Child' differs in her letter to Carole from the final/fictional version that appears in 'Flesh and the Mirror'. The sequence of events that leads up to the one night stand are undoubtedly familiar in the short story, as the narrator laments 'however hard I looked for the one I loved, she could not find him anywhere and the city delivered her into the hands of a perfect stranger' (80). However, the narrator does not perceive the one night stand as triumphantly as Carter does: instead she is overcome with guilt for betraying her true lover. Upon catching sight of herself and the stranger entwined in an embrace in the mirror above the bed she reflects that,

> I saw the flesh and the mirror but I could not come to terms with the sight. My immediate response to it was, to feel I'd acted out of character. The fancy-dress disguise I'd put on to suit the city had betrayed me to a room and a bed and a modification of myself that had no business at all in my life, not in the life I had watched myself performing. (82)

Comparing the two versions, Gordon argues that despite their differences, they have 'equivalent biographical value', as they recall nearly identical events. Certainly, Carter is as likely to exaggerate the version of events in her letter to Carole as she does in the 'Flesh and the Mirror'. The best conclusion that we can draw, argues Gordon, 'is that their differing moods were both present in her encounter with the Summer Child' (2016: 187). As with her journals, Carter deliberately refuses to deliver a 'real' account of the tale, instead preferring to adopt a performance that is evasive of reality. Ryan-Sautour suggests that Carter's identity 'flickers throughout the text in a "now you see me, now you don't" dynamic' (2007: 58); the pronoun '"I" is not what it seems, or perhaps is only what it seems' and in Carter's 'literary landscape [...] "I" self-consciously "stages" a struggle with language, world, and self' (58, 69). In a critical assessment of Carter's journals from the period, alongside her novel and short stories, the fragmentary nature between the 'real' and the unreal is heightened in her fiction of the early 1970s. Just as in *Doctor Hoffman*, where Desiderio finds himself in a sea of mirages, unable to distinguish from what is real and what is not, so the readers find themselves in a similar position when interpreting Carter's time in Japan.

The 'art of faking': performance in Japan

Carter's struggles with authenticity during her time abroad can be understood on two levels. Firstly, due to the semi-autobiographical nature of her short story collection, it is difficult to interpret the truly fictional (and thus any truly authentic) experiences in her tales. Her role as 'other' is both deliberate and staged, although she capitalizes upon this position within her narrative. Secondly, authenticity and interpreting the 'real' is explored through Japan itself: that is, its culture, city and its traditions. *The Infernal Desire Machines of Doctor Hoffman*, for example, 'reveals the processes by which she transmuted her day-to-day experiences into strange, hallucinatory art' (Gordon, 2016: 175). Desiderio's home city, which comes under attack from the Doctor's hallucinations, is undeniably an imagined version of Japan, where boundaries between the real and the unreal are uncertain. Carter's imagery employed in *Doctor Hoffman* mirrors that of 'Flesh and the Mirror', where the narrator reflects how 'this city presents the foreigner with a mode of life that seems to him to have the enigmatic transparency, the indecipherable clarity, of dream' (79). Otherness for Carter thus becomes performative, as it is a role that she is unable to negotiate: 'And it is a dream he could, himself, never have dreamed. The stranger, the foreigner, thinks he is in control; but he has been precipitated into someone else's dream' (79).

In an interview with Ronald Bell, Carter reflects that 'the Japanese [...] have always wished to make themselves works of art' (1973: 35). Her observation correlates with a similar position put forward by Ian Buruma, in his rather aptly named social commentary *A Japanese Mirror: Heroes and Villains in Japanese Culture* (2001).[3] Much like Carter, Buruma claims that the Japanese 'are not interested so much in "real selves" and no attempts are made to hide the fake': instead, 'artificiality is often appreciated for its own sake' (2001: 69). Buruma uses the image of the looking glass to highlight the reflective nature that the traveller experiences during their time abroad. Perched 'on the extreme edge of Asia' Japan is 'the ideal place from which to observe the rest of world [...] Japan, at times, really does feel like the other side of Alice's looking glass' (2001: xi). Likewise, Carter writes in her journals that 'although I lived there, it always seemed far away from me. It was as if there were a glass between me and the world; but I could see myself perfectly well on the other side of the glass', and that 'I was [...] all the time, elsewhere, monitoring myself, standing a little apart from my body' (Add. MS 88899/1/81).

There are, however, some fundamental differences in the ways that Buruma and Carter perceive the Japanese, and their own respective roles as foreigners in Japan. In her interview with Bell, Carter comments that 'It's the fact that everything's the same and everything's different to what I'm accustomed to' (1973: 24), acknowledging the similarities between cultures. She goes on to say that 'There is a great deal of common ground between us – and then they freeze into Japanese attitudes, and then they are lost to me' (1973: 23). She does not find this difference unsettling, however; instead she finds it 'exhilarating', especially 'in situations where I'm not particularly close to the Japanese' (1973: 24). In comparison, the Japan that Buruma encounters is a 'long way from the austere, controlled, exquisitely restrained, melancholy beauty most people in the West have come to associate with Japan' (Buruma, 2001: 34), an approach that Carter mocks Buruma for taking. It 'is hard to tell from his tone [...] just how great his personal disappointment originally was when he discovered what he terms the "raunchy" side of Japanese culture' (1997: 266).

In a case of 'art-imitating-life' (or, in this case 'art-imitating-art'), Japanese theatrical traditions echo the sentiments of a cultural appreciation of artificiality. In particular, Japanese *bunraku* puppet theatre demonstrates the pertinent nature of 'faking it' through a variety of deliberate staging strategies and through promoting a relationship that is complicit with its audience engaging in its theatrical nuances: 'Performers do not try to seem informal or real, for it is the form, the art of faking, if you like, that is the whole point of the exercise' (Buruma: 2001: 69). Similarly, in *Nō and Bunraku* Donald Keene argues that the 'stylization in art and not literal fidelity is what the audience craves' and that the puppeteers must maintain a harmonious balance between 'realism and non-realism' (1990: 124).

A term coined in the nineteenth century, *bunraku* refers to 'the puppet theatre in Osaka descended from the one founded by Uemura Bunrakken (or, Bunraku-ken) some 150 years ago' (Keene, 1990: 120). Delivered on a much larger scale than its Western counterpart, the main spectacle of *bunraku* is its puppets, which stand around four feet tall. Unlike the marionettes of the West, they are free from the shackles of strings and each puppet is controlled instead by three highly skilled puppeteers, who are visible on stage. The main puppeteer (*omu-zukai*) is permitted to wear brightly coloured clothing, distinguishing him from his peers: the other two puppet masters are concealed in black. The performance is accompanied by a chanter, who stands to the side of the stage and provides the vocals for all of the 'characters'. A samisen player provides a musical accompaniment. Keene emphasizes that the three puppeteers must 'breathe' together to sustain the dramatic illusion of animation; if they are unable to work harmoniously with one another, the actions of the doll appear clumsy, awkward and unrealistic (1990: 127). Similarly, the harmonious alignment of the 'three writings' (Barthes, 1982: 48) of *bunraku* – the manipulator, the chanter and the samisen player – are crucial to sustaining an eloquent performance.

In Roland Barthes's *Empire of Signs* ([1970] 1982), he describes the puppeteers as 'agents of spectacle', who are perceived not as performers *per se*, but as an intricate part of the performance in which they are *exempt from meaning*. Barthes's remarks become all the more significant when one considers the fact he visited Japan in 1967, preceding Carter's own trip abroad by a matter of years. His role as a semiotician, coupled with a desire to 'discover a culture that despised depth', has a striking affinity with Carter's own interests in the Japanese aesthetic, as it was her time abroad where 'she found out the truthfulness *and finality* of appearances' (Sage, 1994: 26; emphasis in original).

Unlike Western puppet theatre, which seeks to conceal the mechanics of its art, *bunraku* ensures that these manifestations of artifice are clearly on display for the audience to see: it shows 'the gesture, lets the action be seen, exhibits simultaneously the art and the labour' (Barthes, 1982: 54). The very point of *bunraku* is that it *refuses to conceal* and so places the trinity of puppeteers on stage in full view of its audience: 'there is no reason to hide them. People want to see them so they can appreciate their skills' (Buruma, 2001: 69). *Bunraku* thus becomes 'immune to the temptation known in certain theatres of the West of trying to persuade it is watching reality and not a play' (Keene, 1990: 125).

Performance and authenticity in 'The Loves of Lady Purple'

The image of the marionette is by no means a new feature within Carter's works of fiction, and the symbolic metaphor of the marionette is extensively explored in her 1967 novel *The Magic Toyshop*. Following the death of her parents, Melanie is forced to live with her Uncle Philip, proprietor of a London toyshop. Peering into her uncle's basement puppet theatre for the first time Melanie finds 'puppets of all sizes [...] blind-eyed puppets, some armless, some legless, some naked, some clothed, all with a strange liveliness as they dangled unfinished from their hooks' (2006a: 67). Similarly, in 'The Loves of Lady Purple', Carter experiments with the image of the puppet: in her short introduction to *Expletives Deleted*, Carter indeed emphasizes the centrality of the tale of a marionette who, led by an Asiatic Professor, enacts a nightly performance, 'The Notorious Amours of Lady Purple'. In the play, a young Lady Purple seduces her foster father before murdering her foster parents: she then becomes a prostitute, the 'sole perpetrator of desire', and 'the object on which men prostituted themselves' (2009d: 36–7). At the end of her performance we see Lady Purple (acting as a woman) turn into a wooden puppet, a replica of herself. The performance comes to a close. One night, the Asiatic Professor notices a ripped seam in Lady Purple's shroud; a dropped stich, a seam undone. In an ominous foreboding of an unravelling world in which the real blends with the unreal, the Professor then leans in to kiss Lady Purple: she awakens, sucking the life from the puppet master. Renewed with life, Lady Purple frees herself from her strings and, in a move that mirrors her nightly performance, heads for the nearest brothel.

The Lady Purple marionette clearly draws on imagery from *bunraku* theatre (Sage, 1994; Fisher, 2001; Crofts 2006).[4] Led by an Asiatic Professor, a 'master of marionettes' (29) who is accompanied by his deaf nephew and a dumb orphan girl, Carter draws together her very own puppeteer trinity. Exercising an 'exquisite precision' in his act, with 'godlike [...] manipulations', the puppet master reveals the artifice of the mechanisms of his art, and in a direct homage to *bunraku*, his act is made 'all the more disturbing *because we know it to be false*' (27–8; emphasis added). Further references to Japanese puppet theatre are made throughout the tale: Lady Purple's performance is enacted to the accompaniment of the 'delirious *obbligato* of the [...] samisen' (34), and the star of the show is imitative of the Japanese geisha with a face as 'as white as chalk', and a wig 'of black hair arranged in a chignon' (31). The vibrant purple colour that she is adorned with, claims Fisher, is a direct influence from Japanese literature, and draws reference from Murasaki Shikibu, author of *The Tale of Genji*: *murasaki* meaning 'violet or purple' (2001: 168). Furthermore, Lady Purple's role as a prostitute in 'The Notorious Amours of Lady Purple, the Shameless Oriental Venus' is also closely interlinked with the Japanese language. *Kugutsu*, the first name given to puppets in Japan, is also the Japanese term for female prostitutes (Plowright, 2002: 100).

It is unclear from Carter's tale, argues Fisher, whether or not Lady Purple is a 'real woman changed into a puppet, or a puppet who comes alive', and she suggests that Lady Purple's performance is both 'within and beyond her control' (2001: 167). Lady Purple is instructed by the puppeteer to act out a gendered performance in the nightly plays; and yet, it is possible that the play itself is in imitation of Lady Purple's own life as a real woman. Thus, Lady Purple's role as a 'universal whore' (Carter, 2009d: 34) is maintained throughout her life as both a marionette and as a living, breathing woman, whose single purpose is to satisfy the needs of men. She is 'an incarnation of what the male-dominated society, symbolized by the puppeteer, cannot accept (in this case, excessive female sexuality) and therefore casts off in the figure of the monstrous woman' (Tavassoli and Ghasemi, 2011: 56).

Although Lady Purple is successful in breaking free of the strings that attach her to the role of marionette, she is trapped within a 'tautological paradox' in which she cannot perceive of anything beyond that of her nightly performances, and is open to only the 'scantiest notion of possibilities' (Carter, 2009d: 45). And, although she embodies the figure of the *femme fatale* when she awakens as she heads towards the nearest brothel at the end of the story, it is unclear whether or not 'she was renewed or newly born, returning to life or becoming alive, awakening from dream or coalescing into the form of a fantasy generated in her wooden skull by the mere repetition so many times of the same invariable action' (Carter, 2009d: 45). Behaving in accordance to 'pre-determined codes' (Tavassoli and Ghasemi, 2011: 56), the 'Butlerification'[5] of Lady Purple is complicit with the performative practices aligned with her gender. The repetitive motions that she has been forced to act out every night thus are performative of her social and gender norms, and her inability to shift away from this performativity acknowledges her compliance with these practices. This repetition is at once a 're-enactment and re-experiencing of a set of meanings already socially established' (Butler, 1990: 140). As Butler sets out in *Gender Trouble*: 'Such acts, gestures, enactments, generally construed, are *performative* in the sense that the essence or identity that they otherwise purport to express are *fabrications* manufactured and sustained through corporeal signs and other discursive means' (Butler, 1990: 185; emphasis in original). In a seemingly contradictory narrative, in which the puppet cuts loose from the physical constraints of her strings, Lady Purple is still unable to break free of her script, whether that be the script from her previous time as human, or that which she has been taught by the puppet master. She must simultaneously enact her role of a real woman, a 'mistress of the whip', performing a tale that not only mimics the hundreds of performances that have gone before, but complies with a gendered act that sees her fall into the demise of her sex: initially a real woman, at the end of her performance she becomes 'herself her own replica, the dead yet moving image of the shameless Oriental Venus' (39). In the final scene of 'The Notorious Amours of Lady Purple' the Professor's marionette is transformed from a woman into a wooden puppet – i.e. the thing that she really is – resulting in a double-layered performance that complicates the notions of performativity and authenticity. The progression of the narrative is a deliberate strategy devised by Carter, as she reflects 'How do we know what is authentic behaviour and what is inauthentic behaviour? […] Can the marionette in that story behave in a way she's not programmed to behave?' (Katsavos, 1994: 11). Despite her attempts, Lady Purple knows only how to follow the story that she has been taught to follow.

'The Executioner's Beautiful Daughter': performance and spectacle

In the analysis of Carter's Japanese tales – with particular emphasis on *bunraku* – it is important not to focus solely on the image of the marionette, as it is the supporting actors such as the chanter and the samisen player that contribute to the overall performance. Indeed, it is Carter's more subtle references to the art of *bunraku* that serve as the most fascinating to assess on a critical level, and it is the analysis of her more neglected tales that offers new readings of her work.

'The Executioner's Beautiful Daughter' was one of Carter's first short stories written in Japan while she was living 'in a room too small to write a novel in' (2006b: 459). Much like the other tales that make up the *Fireworks* collection, the tale 'dispense[s] almost entirely with such conventional trappings as character and plot […] and compel[s] attention via the play of language and ideas' (Gordon, 2016: 159). The opening paragraph presents a tableau frozen in time with 'whispering shifting sawdust freshly scattered over impacted surfaces of years of sawdusts clotted […] with blood shed so long ago'; 'the air is choked all day with diffuse moisture tremulously, endlessly on the point of becoming rain' (15–16). A tale that is 'absolutely static, […] it's all about words' (Gordon, 2016: 159). Carter constructs a narrative that experiments with performance and Japanese theatrical tropes.

There are elements of the tale that are unmistakably influenced by *bunraku*. In a story that sees an executioner behead his own son for committing incest with his only daughter, Carter integrates a counter-cultural narrative that incorporates popular Japanese themes such as love and death alongside familiar Carterian tropes developed throughout the 1960s, such as incest and an exuberant use of theatrical imagery. The dramatic backdrop of the highlands, in which plays a 'baleful almost-music […] repercussing in an ecstatic agony of echoes against the sounding boards of the mountain' (15), constructs a stage onto which the performance of the executioner will be carried out. The distant music is reminiscent of the samisen players who provide the sound for *bunraku* performances: the 'twanging, plucking and abusing with horsehair bows' (15) is antithetical to the harmonious background it should provide, and acts as an ominous foreboding to the events that lie ahead. The early pages of the story are littered with deliberate staging techniques and references to theatrical nuances – the executioner performs a 'hieratic ritual' and commands a 'dramatic silence' from his audience; the altar on which he beheads his victim is described as 'the canvas on which he exercises his art' (16–17). In a curious gesture which reveres in an artistic execution culminating in a *literal* execution, Carter's narrative suggests that 'art becomes far more important than life', an attribute she closely associates with the Japanese 'Because they make life an art and once you do that you forget how to live' (Bell, 1973: 26).

The execution, watched by the 'gnarled features' of the grinning audience, is sustained by its spectatorship, and maintains an authentic spectacle that is interpreted as a performance. The spectators are described with an 'intent immobility, wholly absorbed as they are in the performance of the hieratic ritual' (16), and the string band, accompanied by the 'screeching wail' of a 'choir of stunted virgins' is reminiscent of *bunraku* whose 'progress resulting from a steadily increased awareness of dramatic possibilities, may be measured in terms of the additional demands made on its audience' (Keene, 1990: 124). The audience take part in a 'violent "act of viewing"', in which 'complicity, intimacy and distance [...] work in tandem' (Robson, 2017: 103). The boundaries between the spectator, victim and the perpetrator in Carter's short story 'dissolve in a frenzy of identifications' (Adler, 2015: 237), in which the spectators experience a form of perverse pleasure at the violent performance carried out by the executioner.

Carter's deliberate use of theatrical tropes and the perception of performance makes it possible for the spectators to accept scenes in 'The Executioner's Beautiful Daughter' which would otherwise be abhorred. Recalling watching a performance of 'The Village School', Keene draws upon a scene in which a father examines the severed head of his son: 'the scene [...] would either fill the audience with terror or stir uneasy laughter if it were not acted with ritual formality'. The ritual act of the executioner ensures that he complies with a pre-mediated performance, and makes 'it possible for us to witness this scene without acute discomfort' (1990: 125). The audience become complicit in the performance of execution because they are no longer able to distinguish between authenticity and art: 'No hideous parody of the delights of the flesh would be alien to them ... *did they but know how things were, in fact, performed*' (22; emphasis in original). Like the executioner, they are scripted to a performance: other desires are unknown and thus unknowable with them.

There is also something to be said about the incestuous relationship between the executioner's children (his daughter, curiously, is absent from the main spectacle). A theme that Carter also explores in 'Penetrating to the Heart of the Forest' (1974), incest is typically a Western (Christian) taboo, and has not been abhorred in Japan until recently. However, conducting incest is not illegal in Japan: the incest law prohibiting it was abolished in 1881 and incestuous couples are allowed to have children. The Civil Code of Japan restricts family marriages, but the act of incest itself is not a crime. In both short stories Carter adopts a Western position, although this is considerably more drawn out in 'Penetrating to the Heart of the Forest', which imitates a narrative framework that is clearly a reference to Adam and Eve's fall, opening with an 'edenic landscape' (Jennings, 2012: 171) and a 'malign' tree at its centre. The two stories experiment with a hybrid narrative that intertwines an Occidental approach within an Oriental image.

Performance, art and artificiality are all familiar tropes within Carter's work. However, as is evidenced within this chapter, Japan permitted Carter to explore and experiment with the boundaries of fact and fiction; between the authentic and the inauthentic. Gordon's work provides an illuminating insight into Carter's time in Japan, paving the way for specific nuances (such as the influences of *bunraku* theatre) to be explored in greater detail. As the narrator reflects at the end of 'Flesh and the Mirror', 'The most difficult performance in the world is acting naturally, isn't it? Everything else is artful' (89). Destined to perform to a series of socially prescribed roles, artificiality becomes art itself, in a performance that all participants are complicit in sustaining.

Notes

1 Carter's review was published in the *New Society* in 1978, two years after the release of Oshima's film in 1976. Tanizaki's *Naomi* (1924) was translated into English by Anthony Chambers in 1985. Murasaki's *The Tale of Genji* was first published in c. 1021 – Edward Seidensticker was the first to publish a complete version of the novel in English in 1976.
2 Letter to Carole Roffe, 3 August 1971.
3 The title of Buruma's text is inimical to Carter's novel *Heroes and Villains*, which tells the tale of a post-apocalyptic dystopian world.
4 Although the imagery Carter draws upon in 'The Loves of Lady Purple' can be likened to *bunraku*, Lady Purple's nightly performance is *not bunraku*. The Professor is the only puppeteer who appears on stage with the marionette, breaking the unity of *bunraku*'s puppeteer trinity. Moreover, the performance takes place outside of Japan, 'in a country in Middle Europe' (28).
5 'Butlerification' is a term used by Joanna Trevenna in her 2002 essay 'Gender as Performance: Questioning the "Butlerification" of Angela Carter's fiction'. Trevenna suggests that Carter's presentation of gender acquisition is more aligned with theories put forward by Simone de Beauvoir in *The Second Sex* (1949) rather than those of Butler's *Gender Trouble*.

References

Add. MS: Additional Manuscripts
Add. MS 888899/1/80 Japan 1, Angela Carter Papers Collection, The British Library, London.
Add. MS 88899/1/81 Japan 2, Angela Carter Papers Collection, The British Library, London.
Add. MS 89102 Correspondence of Angela Carter and Carole Howells.
Adler, A. (2015) 'The Pleasures of Punishment: Complicity, Spectatorship and Abu Graib', in Charles J. Ogletree Jnr. and Austin Sarat (eds), *Punishment in Popular Culture* (New York and London: Routledge).
Appignanesi, L. (1987), *Angela Carter in Conversation* (London: ICA Video).
Araki, Sozo (2018), *Seduced by Japan: A Memoir of the Days Spent with Angela Carter, with 'Her Side of the Story' by Natsumi Ikoma*, ed. and trans. Natsumi Ikoma (Tokyo: Eihosha).
Barker, Paul (1995) 'The Return of the Magic Storyteller', *The Independent*, 8 January.
Barthes, Roland ([1970] 1982), *Empire of Signs*, trans. Richard Howard (New York: Hill and Wang).

Bell, Ronald (1973), *The Japan Experience* (New York: John Weatherhill, Inc.).
Bristow, Joseph and Trev Lynn Broughton (1997), *The Infernal Desires of Angela Carter: Fiction, Femininity, Feminism* (London and New York: Longman).
Buruma, Ian ([1984] 2001), *A Japanese Mirror: Heroes and Villains in Japanese Culture* (London: Jonathan Cape Ltd.).
Butler, Judith (1990), *Gender Trouble* (New York: Routledge).
Carter, Angela (1982), *Nothing Sacred: Selected Writings* (London: Virago).
—— (1983), 'Notes from the Front Line', in Michele Wandor (ed.), *On Gender and Writing* (London: Pandora), pp. 69–77.
—— ([1991] 1992), *Wise Children* (London: Vintage).
—— ([1966] 1995), *Shadow Dance* (London: Virago).
—— (1997a), *Shaking a Leg: Collected Writings*, ed. Jenny Uglow (Harmondsworth: Penguin).
—— ([1972] 1997b), 'Poor Butterfly', in *Shaking a Leg: Collected Writings*, ed. Jenny Uglow (Harmondsworth: Penguin), pp. 249–54.
—— ([1984] 1997c), 'Ian Buruma: A Japanese Mirror', *Shaking a Leg: Collected Writings*, ed. Jenny Uglow (Harmondsworth: Penguin), pp. 265–67.
—— ([1986] 1997d), 'Jun'ichirō Tanizaki: *Naomi*', in *Shaking a Leg: Collected Writings*, ed. Jenny Uglow (Harmondsworth: Penguin), pp. 267–70.
—— ([1978] 1997e), 'Japanese Erotica', in *Shaking a Leg: Collected Writings*, ed. Jenny Uglow (Harmondsworth: Penguin), pp. 354–7.
—— ([1967] 2006a), *The Magic Toyshop* (London: Virago).
—— ([1995] 2006b) 'Afterword to *Fireworks*', in *Burning Your Boats: Collected Stories* (London: Vintage), pp. 459–60.
—— ([1974] 2009a), *Fireworks: Nine Profane Pieces* (London: Virago).
—— ([1974] 2009b), 'A Souvenir of Japan', in *Fireworks: Nine Profane Pieces* (London: Virago), pp. 1–14.
—— ([1974] 2009c), 'Flesh and the Mirror', in *Fireworks: Nine Profane Pieces* (London: Virago), pp. 77–9.
—— ([1974] 2009d), 'The Loves of Lady Purple', in *Fireworks: Nine Profane Pieces* (London: Virago), pp. 27–46.
—— ([1972] 2010), *The Infernal Desire Machines of Doctor Hoffman* (Harmondsworth: Penguin).
Clapp, Susannah (2012), *A Card from Angela Carter* (London: Bloomsbury).
Crofts, Charlotte (2003), *'Anagrams of Desire': Angela Carter's Writing for Radio, Film and Television* (Manchester: Manchester University Press).
—— (2006), 'The Other of the Other: Angela Carter's "New Fangled" Orientalism', in Rebecca Munford (ed.), *Revisiting Angela Carter: Texts, Contexts, Intertexts*. (Basingstoke: Palgrave Macmillan), pp. 87–109.
Fisher, Susan (2001), 'The Mirror of the East: Angela Carter and Japan', in Susan Fisher (ed.), *Nostalgic Journeys: Literary Pilgrimages between Japan and*

the West (Vancouver: Institute of Asian Research, University of British Columbia), pp. 165–77.

Gamble, Sarah (1997), *Angela Carter: Writing from the Front Line* (Edinburgh: Edinburgh University Press).

—— (2006), *Angela Carter: A Literary Life* (Basingstoke: Palgrave Macmillan).

Gordon, Edmund (2016), *The Invention of Angela Carter: A Biography* (London: Chatto & Windus).

Jennings, Hope (2012), 'Genesis and Gender: The Word, the Flesh and the Fortunate Fall in "Peter and the Wolf" and "Penetrating to the Heart of the Forest"', in Sonya Andermahr and Lawrence Phillips (eds), *Angela Carter: New Critical Readings* (London and New York: Contiuum).

Katsavos, Anna (1994) 'An interview with Angela Carter', *Review of Contemporary Fiction*, 14:3, 11–12.

Keene, Donald (1990), *Nō and Bunraku: Two Forms of Japanese Theatre* (New York: Columbia University Press).

Liu, Max (2016), '*The Invention of Angela Carter: A Biography* by Edmund Gordon', book review: 'It will fascinate Carter's admirers', *The Independent*, 12 October.

Munford, Rebecca (ed.) (2006), *Revisiting Angela Carter: Texts, Contexts, Intertexts* (Basingstoke: Palgrave Macmillan).

—— (2013), *Decadent Daughters and Monstrous Mothers: Angela Carter and European Gothic* (Manchester: Manchester University Press).

Murasaki, Shikibu (1976), *The Tale of Genji*, trans. Edward Seidensticker (New York: Alfred A. Knopf).

Palmer, Paulina (1987), 'From "Coded Mannequin" to "Bird Woman": Angela Carter's Magic Flight', in Sue Roe (ed.), *Women Reading Women's Writing* (London: The Harvester Press), pp. 179–205.

Peach, Linden (1998), *Angela Carter* (Basingstoke: Palgrave Macmillan).

Plowright, Poh Sim (2002), *Mediums, Puppets, and the Human Actor in the Theatres of the East* (New York and Ontario: The Edwin Mellen Press).

Robson, M. (2017), 'Complicity, Intimacy and Distance: Re-examining the Active Viewer in Michael Haneke's Amour', *Studies in European Cinema*, 14:2, 103–17.

Rushdie, Salman (1992), 'Angela Carter, 1940–92: A Very Good Wizard, a Very Dear Friend', *New York Times*, 8 March.

Ryan-Sautour, Michelle (2007), 'Autobiographical Estrangement in Angela Carter's "A Souvenir of Japan", "The Smile of Winter" and "Flesh and the Mirror", *Études britanniques contemoraines revue de la Société d'Études Anglaises Contemporaines*, 32, 57–78.

Sage, Lorna (1994) *Angela Carter* (Plymouth: Northcote House).

Tanizaki, Junichiro ([1924] 2001) *Naomi*, trans. Anthony H. Chambers (New York: Vintage).

Tavassoli, Sara and Phavin Ghasemi (2011), 'A Rebellion Against Patriarchy: A Study of Gothic in Carter's Short Stories', *Journal of Research in Peace, Gender and Development*, 1:2, 53–60.

Trevenna, Joanne (2002), 'Gender as Performance: Questioning the "Butlerification" of Angela Carter's fiction', *Journal of Gender Studies*, 11: 3, 267–76.

Wisker, Gina (1997) 'Revenge of the Living Doll: Angela Carter's Horror Writing', in Joseph Bristow and Trev Lynn Broughton (eds), *The Infernal Desires of Angela Carter: Fiction, Femininity, Feminism* (London and New York: Longman), pp. 116–31.

—— (2006) 'Behind Locked Doors: Angela Carter, Horror and the Influence of Edgar Allan Poe', in Rebecca Munford (ed.), *Revisiting Angela Carter: Texts, Contexts, Intertexts* (Basingstoke: Palgrave Macmillan), pp. 178–98.

11

'I resented it, it fascinated me':
Carter's ambivalent cinematic fiction and the problem of proximity

Caleb Sivyer

Ambivalence, proximity, cinema

ANGELA CARTER WAS DEEPLY ambivalent about the cinema, loving its luminous images and larger than life stars, while being highly critical of both its representation of women and its masculine structure of looking. On one side, her passion for the cinema shines through her writings and interviews. Recalling her visits as a young girl to the Granada cinema in Tooting, Carter says that she 'fell in love with cinema', and not just its towering images, but also the 'dream cathedral of voluptuous thirties wish-fulfilment architecture' with its 'mix of the real and false' (2013f: 488–9). She claimed that her favourite film was Marcel Carné's *Les Enfants du Paradis* (1945), which produced in her a deep desire to 'jump through the screen [...] and live there, in a state of luminous anguish' (Jackson, 1986).[1] In the *Omnibus* documentary made during the last year of her life, she even claimed that there was 'something sacred about the cinema' because people could come together to share 'the same experience', the 'same revelation' (Evans: 1992). For a woman who 'lived to an unusual extent [...] in her own fantasies' and who claimed 'I'm a born fabulist', it should be no surprise that cinema's fabulous spectacles appealed to Carter enormously (Gordon, 2016: xvi).

On the other side, Carter was unsparing in her criticisms of cinema, especially with respect to Hollywood. Her exposure to alternative and radical forms of filmmaking, such as the French New Wave, helped her to see mainstream cinema's fantastic illusions in a more critical light. Jean-Luc Godard's films, for example, were 'an education in cinema and how to see it' (2013a: 465). As Carter became politicized in the 1960s, she learned to appreciate the ideological dimension to cinema. Later in life, she reflected that 'Hollywood had colonised the imagination of the entire world and was turning us all into Americans'. Consequently, she argued that 'A critique of the Hollywood movie is a critique of the imagination of the twentieth century in the West' (2013d: 466). One issue in particular that concerned her was Hollywood's 'cultural production of femininity' as an illusory yet tangible commodity, and its perpetuation of the dominant patriarchal structure of looking, whereby spectators are positioned as masculine and women are turned into passive, objectified and sexualized images (Haffenden, 1985: 85).[2] As she wrote in *The Sadeian Woman*, figures like Marilyn Monroe are 'imaginary prostitute[s]' who sell, 'not the reality of flesh, but its image', and are 'raped by a thousand eyes twice nightly' (2011: 76). Hollywood's visual worlds might be wonderfully seductive but they also perpetuated patriarchal ideology.[3] She therefore subjected Hollywood to her so-called 'demythologisation' project, exposing its cultural myths as what she called 'extraordinary lies'. She saw Hollywood as helping to maintain 'the social fiction of [...] femininity', a result of specific material and contingent practices, but which was 'palmed off [...] as the real thing', all in the service of heterosexual male desire (2013b: 47).

Despite these criticisms, Carter's passion for the cinema, including Hollywood, never wavered. She therefore maintained an ambivalent attitude towards cinema, one which appears clearest in her reaction to Hollywood's global dominance: 'I resented it, it fascinated me' (2013f: 5). Other critics have noted this before: Catherine Neale refers to Carter's 'simultaneous deconstruction and celebration of Hollywood' (1996: 102), while Charlotte Crofts argues that Laura Mulvey's concept of 'passionate detachment' could be used to describe Carter's own 'engagement with the cinema' (2003: 103).[4] However, in making sense of the role of cinema in Carter's fiction, most critics tend to stress the negative side, focusing on how her texts demythologize filmic illusions or are inspired by anti-illusionistic cinema. Sarah Gamble argues, for example, that Carter's early novels are inspired by Godard's anti-naturalistic and anti-Hollywood cinema, which constantly reminds spectators that they are watching a film and thus breaks their identification with the fiction. In addition to illuminating the influence of the French New Wave upon Carter's writing, this line of interpretation attempts to make sense of her controversial representation of violence against women. Gamble argues that the 'mannered presentation' common to both Godard and Carter 'results in a portrayal of female subjectivity that is entirely devoid of naturalism, so that the audience is kept in a state of constant awareness that what they are seeing or reading is an invention' (2006: 46). The representation of violence against women is justified, therefore, on the grounds that it is exhibited 'for the purpose of inspection and critique' (2006: 59). From this perspective, then, it is Carter's interest in anti-illusionistic cinema that is seen as informing her fiction.

While this is a legitimate line of interpretation, it downplays Carter's love of cinema as illusion and the influence of Hollywood film on her fiction. It even runs the risk of representing her as hostile towards Hollywood, perhaps even towards cinema itself.[5] Part of this danger stems from emphasizing the influence of Godard's filmic techniques upon Carter's writing practice. As Todd McGowan argues, the approach of radical filmmakers like Godard is 'actually a fundamentally anti-cinematic one' because it sees fascination, illusion and identification – fundamental aspects of the cinematic apparatus – as a problem to be transcended (2007: 8). The radical spectator for Godard is someone not taken in by the cinematic illusion, but who holds the images at a distance and recognizes them as constructed. Therefore, if Godard is taken as the model for the influence of cinema on Carter's fiction, it might give the impression that she was primarily preoccupied with breaking traditional cinematic techniques and criticizing the cinematic apparatus. However, as some of Carter's remarks above make clear, and as this chapter shows in its analysis of her fiction, she was also clearly fascinated by the way that traditional cinema utilizes spectator identification to create seductive illusions. Indeed, I would argue that part of what makes Carter's work distinctive is her wholehearted engagement with illusion, fantasy and visual pleasure on their own terms rather than simply dismissing them as something to be seen through.[6] Carter takes this approach because she recognizes that in order to understand cinema's illusions, it is necessary to grapple with the desires invested in them by spectators. Knowing that an image is not real is not enough to transform spectators into radical subjects since it leaves untouched their desires.[7]

This chapter, therefore, looks at how Carter takes cinematic illusions seriously, and shows that it is by pushing such illusions to their logical extreme that her texts arrive at a more robust critique – a critique not just of cinema but of desire.[8] It focuses on two of her most cinematic novels, *The Infernal Desire Machines of Doctor Hoffman* ([1972] 2010) and *The Passion of New Eve* ([1977] 2008),[9] texts whose protagonists are obsessed with images because of the way they provide erotic pleasure without threatening their sense of mastery. They therefore embody what Adam Phillips refers to as 'the self-protective modern individual', whose dilemma is that he 'doesn't (and does) want to get too close to the things and people that excite him' (2010: 59).[10] Cinema seemingly solves this dilemma because it offers spectators pleasure held at a safe distance. As McGowan usefully explains, Hollywood cinema creates what he calls 'proximity from a distance': the spectator is given an imaginary sense of proximity to the images on screen, while simultaneously being kept at a safe distance from them. This then 'allows the spectator to avoid any encounter in the cinema that might challenge or alter the spectator's subjectivity' (2007: 2). I argue that, unlike Godard's technique of increasing spectator distance, Carter increases the sense of proximity between her protagonists as spectators and the images they gaze at, thereby forcing them to confront their desires.[11] This, though, has dramatically different consequences in each text.

Doctor Hoffman's infernal cinematic machines

Although *The Infernal Desire Machines of Doctor Hoffman* is not explicitly concerned with cinema, its narrative of a scientist attempting to control the collective imagination through technologically created images can be read as an allegory of twentieth-century visual culture. Indeed, Elaine Jordan suggests that Doctor Hoffman can be read as an authoritarian movie director, what Carter calls the 'Merchant of Shadows', for he is 'the producer of cultural representations which control desire and perception' (2007: 215).[12] Hoffman takes Hollywood's colonization of the imagination to its logical extreme by bombarding the world with autonomous images, whose forms are drawn, he claims, from the collective unconscious of its citizens. As a result, people become completely enchanted by Hoffman's mirages as the line between the real and the artificial is blurred.[13] Indeed, at one point in the narrative, we learn that the desire machines were in fact invented as an extension of the cinematograph: building on film's ability to capture 'time irrefutably past', the desire machines give 'autonomy' to the image, freeing it from its imprisonment on the screen (2010: 116–17).[14] In effect, Hoffman has transformed the world into a series of vast, interactive cinematic spectacles. Opposing this, however, is the Minister of Determination, a staunch advocate of Enlightenment reason, who desperately attempts to destroy the Doctor's mirages. He sets up a totalitarian state designed to differentiate, at all costs, the real from the unreal, and disparagingly likens Hoffman's mirages to the 'early days of cinema' because 'all the citizens are jumping through the screen to lay their hands on the naked lady in the bathtub!' (2010: 35). The Minister tasks Desiderio, the novel's protagonist, with locating and destroying Hoffman's desire machines, and his journey through this mirage-filled world is represented like a series of cinematic scenarios as he moves 'from one tableau to another, "still" after "still", quickened into movement by a kind of optical illusion – as in [...] a film' (Sage, 1992: 169). However, Desiderio has the blasé and detached attitude of an experienced film spectator: 'I felt as if I was watching a film in which the Minister was the hero and the unseen Doctor certainly the villain; but it was an endless film and I found it boring for none of the characters engaged my sympathy' (2010: 21).

However, one character does pique Desiderio's interest, thereby increasing his identification with Hoffman's film: the Doctor's own enigmatic and alluring daughter Albertina, who arrests Desiderio's gaze with the 'spell of the [movie] personality' (Benjamin, 1999: 224). Like the ever-changing images in a kaleidoscope, Albertina takes on a number of guises, first appearing to Desiderio as a 'persistent hallucination' on the 'borders of [...] sleep' (2010: 22). She is, in Maggie Tonkin's words, 'fantastically mutable', for she takes various forms, including a black swan, a woman with translucent skin, a bandaged young boy, and an androgynous figure dressed in the most extravagant manner (2012: 82). Albertina is also clearly eroticized for a male gaze: in a pornographic peep-show her face appears 'intermittently' and tantalizingly on a wax figure engaged in sexual congress, and later she shows up as a scantily clad proprietor of a brothel. At one point in the narrative, it becomes abundantly clear that Albertina is herself an image, for Desiderio observes her 'flicker a little; then waver continuously', before vanishing completely (2010: 161). Eventually, he learns that she is indeed one of Hoffman's mirages, a masculine-scripted image of femininity 'maintained [...] by the power of [Desiderio's] desire' (2010: 243). This both excites and frustrates Desiderio in equal measure, for Albertina's status as an image means that she is held at a safe distance yet always out of reach. At one point, he pictures her as a magic trick which disguises 'a living being beneath' because 'such tricks imply the presence of a conjurer', and his ultimate ambition is 'to rip away the ruffled shirt and find out whether the breasts of an authentic woman swelled beneath it' (2010: 40). Hoffman has therefore created an image that is both too excitingly near and too frustratingly far from the spectator's gaze.

Desiderio's ambivalent desire for Albertina drives his narrative forward, yet when he finally reaches the object of his desire he experiences only horror. Up close, Albertina unsettles Desiderio's position of observation by reflecting back his own gaze: 'In the looking glasses of her eyes, I saw reflected my entire being whirl apart and reassemble itself innumerable times' (2010: 241). Like Hollywood film, Albertina is ultimately a mirror, reflecting back the spectator's own desires. Furthermore, when standing before Hoffman's desire machines, Desiderio learns that the Doctor plans to enslave him in an endless act of sexual congress with Albertina in order to fuel his vast cinematic apparatus. As an allegory of Hollywood cinema, *The Infernal Desire Machines of Doctor Hoffman* therefore suggests that by confronting the fantasy, the spectator comes to recognize that his desire not only maintains the spectacle but is dependent on it and that this also involves a relinquishing of autonomy. During this 'grotesque denouement', Albertina stands naked before Desiderio's gaze, the distance between spectator and image completely eroded. However, rather than consummate his long-frustrated desire, Desiderio murders both her and Hoffman, and destroys the desire machines (2010: 258). His violence is motivated by his anxiety at getting too close to the image (Albertina) because this proximity forces him to confront the logic of his desire. However, his attempt to free himself from this fails, for he continues to be haunted by both her image and his desire for the rest of his life: as he confesses at the end, 'I close my eyes. Unbidden, she comes' (2010: 265). It is as if Desiderio had murdered Albertina and destroyed the desire machines as an attempt to destroy his dependence on her and on images, even to destroy his very desire. Through this narrative, Carter dramatizes Hollywood's fantasized solution to the problem of (male heterosexual) desire and exposes its ideological position by pushing its structure to the logical extreme. Hoffman's mirages are effectively more Hollywood than Hollywood because they increase the sense of proximity between spectator and image. In doing so, though, it forces the spectator, Desiderio, to confront the logic of his desire, and because this is traumatic, it ends in violence.

The passion of the cinema

While *The Infernal Desire Machines of Doctor Hoffman* provides a good insight into Carter's passion for illusionistic cinema, a much more comprehensive engagement appears in *The Passion of New Eve*, a text that is arguably her most explicit ode to, and critique of, Hollywood. The narrative centres on Evelyn, a young man obsessed with Hollywood's sexualized images of woman, who is forcibly transformed into a woman to become the titular New Eve. With this central plot device, wherein the male spectator in effect turns into the very thing he gazes at voyeuristically, Carter is able to have her protagonist experience life from both sides of the camera/gaze. This dramatizes once again how an increase in the proximity between spectator and image undermines Hollywood's system of proximity from a distance. Additionally, and in a similar way to her representation of Albertina, Carter has Evelyn's object of desire, the Hollywood star Tristessa de St Ange, turn out to be a male transvestite, once again highlighting the notion that Hollywood's images of femininity are a product of, and for, male heterosexual desire. This functions as a more literal increase in proximity, for it is when Eve comes face to face with Tristessa that she discovers the man behind the image.

The novel begins by highlighting both Hollywood's proximity from a distance and Evelyn as a typical heterosexual male spectator as he stares voyeuristically at Tristessa on the silver screen without the threat of her returning his gaze. He recalls how she was 'billed [...] as "The most beautiful woman in the world"', and that he had come to see her once again in order to pay her 'a little tribute of spermatozoa' (2008: 5). Several comments in this opening scene also make clear Evelyn's preference for the image of a woman over her flesh-and-blood counterpart. At one point he confesses that he 'only really loved [Tristessa] because she was not of this world' and that he became 'disillusioned [...] when [he] discovered [...] [her] humanity' (2008: 8). Furthermore, while admitting to being aroused by Tristessa's exquisite suffering on the screen, upon discovering that the girl he brought to the cinema is crying at the thought of losing him, Evelyn can feel only furious embarrassment (2008: 8–9).[15] Evelyn's fascination with cinematic images of femininity clearly stems from the fact that, in McGowan's words, because such images are held at a safe distance, the spectator can 'avoid any encounter in the cinema that might challenge or alter [his] subjectivity' (2007: 2). This also has an explicitly gendered aspect too, for as E. Ann Kaplan argues, 'the sexualization and objectification of women', seen most prominently in Hollywood narrative cinema, 'is designed to annihilate the threat that woman [...] poses' – the threat, that is, of sexual difference. The camera 'fetishizes the female form [...] so as to mitigate woman's threat' (1993: 31). Tristessa's image appeals to Evelyn, therefore, not just because it is held at a safe distance, but because femininity as sexual difference is masked. Hollywood's images of femininity are thus doubly held at bay from their presumed male spectator.

The opening scene features other ways of looking at Tristessa's image, which not only suggest a different sense of proximity between spectator and image, but call attention to the blind spots of Evelyn's gaze. Firstly, there is Eve's retrospective narrative gaze as she looks back on herself as a man and on the images of Tristessa. From Eve's radically different perspective, she is able to see what Evelyn cannot: that Tristessa's performance is not of some natural and eternal femininity but a masquerade or impersonation of womanliness. Eve notes that Tristessa 'executed her symbolic autobiography in arabesques of kitsch and hyperbole', and that 'no drag-artiste felt his repertoire complete without a personation of her magic and passionate sorrow' (2008: 5–6). This relay of looks – Eve looking back at Evelyn, who in turn is gazing at Tristessa – also introduces a sense of distance between spectator(s) and image, giving this scene of observation a self-conscious quality. Secondly, Eve also recalls observing another kind of spectator in the audience, whose point of view she only now appreciates with her added knowledge. There are a number of 'sentimental queers' in the audience, for whom Tristessa's image signifies not erotic pleasure but a source of sympathetic identification. These men 'had come to pay homage' to Tristessa because she 'perfectly expressed a particular pain they felt as deeply as, more deeply than, any woman' (2008: 5). By identifying with, rather than objectifying Tristessa, these queer spectators break down the construction of distance between spectator and image that is intrinsic to Hollywood cinema, and are therefore open to the possibility of being transformed by this experience.

Evelyn's attachment to Hollywood's illusionistic images is so strong that it even influences his perceptions and behaviour outside the movie theatre. During his time in New York, it is as if he lives out a series of cinematic scenarios. As he puts it at one point, he sits 'agog in [his] ring-side seat' before the spectacle of New York, seemingly resistant to the possibility of being transformed by any encounters (2008: 15). As Gamble notes, Evelyn is a 'detached spectator, unable to believe that he is not still in a movie theatre' (1997: 121). As she goes on to observe, *The Passion of New Eve* thus anticipates Jean Baudrillard's argument that the heart of the cinema in America is to be found, as he puts it, 'all over the city, that marvellous, continuous performance of films and scenarios' (2010: 58). Baudrillard refers to this breakdown of the distinction between the original and the copy (and between the real and the simulated) as the 'hyperreal'; given the way that this occurs in *New Eve* through the cinema, I want to suggest that Evelyn lives in a 'hyper-reel' New York, in which he experiences the real as reel.[16] To adapt Baudelaire's image of modern man, Evelyn, the postmodern man, becomes a 'cinema equipped with consciousness'.[17]

Evelyn's cinematic consciousness also affects his perception of women, so that he sees them as characters in his personal film. Before arriving in New York, Evelyn imagines the city inhabited by 'a special kind of crisp-edged girl with apple-crunching incisors and long, gleaming legs like lascivious scissors' (2008: 10). Woman is here visualized as a *femme fatale*: simultaneously erotic and threatening. It is no surprise, then, that when he starts a sexual relationship with a black prostitute named Leilah, he visualizes her in this iconography, similarly fantasizing about her 'legs [...] coiled or clasped around [his] neck' (2008: 19). Evelyn also gazes at her with what Crofts calls the 'fetishising lens' of the movie camera (2003: 93), dissecting Leilah's body into discreet parts: 'pointed breasts', 'tense and resilient legs', 'black mesh stockings', and 'fetishistic heels six inches high' (2008: 19–20). In an interview a decade later, Carter provides a possible source of influence for this in her description of a scene from *Double Indemnity* (1944): 'I think of Barbara Stanwyck's descent down the stairs [...] First, you see the stiletto-heeled shoe then the ankle with the chain around it, then the legs and the full, rich shine of her stockings. You know she is going to be a femme fatale long before you even see her face' (Jackson, 1986).[18] As in *Double Indemnity*, Evelyn's fetishizing gaze blinds him to the notion that Leilah may be manipulating him by purposely performing this spectacle of male-scripted femininity. Their relationship indeed 'follows the arc of the *noir* script from the hero's sexual obsession with the *femme* through his need to punish her' (Tonkin, 2012: 191). Not only does Evelyn violently beat Leilah on occasions as punishment for disturbing or disobeying him, but he eventually abandons her after he gets her pregnant and she undergoes a botched abortion. However, this 'noir script' comes to a dramatic holt when Evelyn is captured by a group of militant feminists led by Mother and forcibly transformed into a woman as part of her plan to overthrow patriarchal society.

Increasing proximity

In being transformed into a woman, Evelyn is effectively forced to change roles in his cinematic life, from the private 'noir' detective to the woman as sex object. It is also as if Evelyn had been transported to the other side of the camera, no longer occupying the position of the masculine observer but now in the position of woman subjected to the male gaze. However, while she will experience being the object of masculine vision, her own internal perspective is more complicated, for being given the body of a woman is not the same thing as being given her point of view. Indeed, immediately after surgery, Eve feels split between her psychic reality as a man and her new bodily appearance as a woman. Gazing at herself for the first time in a mirror, Eve explains, 'I saw a young woman who, though she was I, I could in no way acknowledge as myself, for this one was only a lyrical abstraction of femininity to me, a tinted arrangement of curved lines' (2008: 74).[19] Recognizing this split, it might be more appropriate to refer to 'Eve/lyn' rather than 'Eve' or 'Evelyn' in order to mark the ambiguity of gender and sex represented here.[20] What is also worth noting is that in referring to femininity as 'a lyrical abstraction', Eve has begun to appreciate that gender may be more of a social construction than she had previously imagined. Crucially, though, it is only in adopting the place of the fantasy, that is, in becoming a woman, that Eve is able to see this. Furthermore, Eve now occupies, paradoxically, both the position of the male observer and the woman as sex object: 'They had turned me into the *Playboy* center fold. I was the object of all the unfocused desires that had ever existed in my own head. I had become my own masturbatory fantasy. And – how can I put it – the cock in my head, still, twitched at the sight of myself' (2008: 75). Eve's observation turns out to be prescient, for she discovers that her appearance was the result of 'a consensus agreement' on what constituted the 'ideal woman', and was 'drawn up from a protracted study of the media' (2008: 78). In a sense, then, Evelyn is turned into the kind of image he used to gaze at voyeuristically, thereby increasing his sense of proximity to such images. The distance between spectator and image that Hollywood creates has been eliminated so that he is no longer just a detached and masterful observer, but also an observable object.[21]

Mother attempts to create a unified woman in Eve, however, by following up the plastic surgery with what she calls 'psycho-surgery', a technique that consists of subjecting Eve to hours of 'video-tape sequences' of images connected with femininity and the female sex (2008: 71–2). The aim is clearly to force Eve to identify with these images, thereby removing the distance separating spectator from image, in the hope that she becomes, essentially, a woman.[22] However, because the psycho-surgery includes masculine-scripted images of femininity, including Tristessa, there is the danger that Eve will only internalize the structure of the male gaze so that she will learn to present herself as an object for masculine vision.[23] Hence, eliminating the distance between Evelyn as spectator and Tristessa as image actually reproduces the patriarchal version of woman. As narrator, Eve recognizes that Tristessa demonstrates 'every kitsch excess of the mode of femininity', rather than some supposedly natural female sex, making her a rather ironic model of woman (2008: 71). Consequently, Eve wonders if this was secretly part of Mother's plan all along. Whatever the case may be here, this section of the text certainly upsets the system of proximity from a distance, with Evelyn turned into one of Hollywood's images of woman, in effect embracing his fantasy more fully.

Hollywood's proximity from a distance is further upset in two other important scenes, whereby the veil of objectification and sexualization that conceals the threat of sexual difference is removed. The first example is a scene that was actually cut from the published text and so appears only in Carter's manuscripts for *New Eve* held at The British Library. It takes place during Evelyn's imprisonment but before his transformation into Eve. Mother leads him into a dome-shaped building to watch 'a picture show' that is described as 'mercifully brief but unmercifully affecting' (1973: 32). After a number of phallic images are projected onto the ceiling of the dome, such as Apollo rockets, the lips of a woman's vulva appear, thereby threatening Evelyn's position of safety as an observer:

> the image of her oozing hole, in full, natural colour, was instantly projected upon the centre of the dome so that we were all at once walled about with her most intimate flesh, & of which the archetechtronics [sic] were so perfect that her hairy corona occupied the place where the skirting board would have been. (1973: 33)

Evelyn's feeling that he was 'walled about with her most intimate flesh' suggests a threat of engulfment, an allusion to the *vagina dentata*. This monstrous image of femininity upsets his masculine idea of woman as passive and thus suggests a different model of cinematic spectatorship, one that anticipates the work of Barbara Creed. With reference to Mulvey's foundational work, Creed argues that many models of feminist film theory fail 'to theorise the presence of woman as active monster', as master of the sadistic gaze, and the consequent masochistic gaze of the male spectator (1993: 153). In this excised and exorcized section of the novel, the projected image of a woman's genitals gazes back threateningly at the male spectator. It is a revelation of the disavowed sexual difference that Hollywood's fetishized images of femininity conceal, breaking down the proximity from a distance so that the images appear threateningly close. By forcing a closer proximity between spectator and image, Mother in effect forces Evelyn to see what he was blind to previously: sexual difference and his position as voyeur.

A similar scenario is present in the published text, during Eve's imprisonment by the sadistic poet Zero. This functions as a repetition and revision of the opening scene of *The Passion of New Eve*'s opening scene, with Zero also watching a Hollywood movie starring Tristessa. However, as with the scene analysed above, the fetishizing veil and proximity from a distance both break down so that the threat of sexual difference becomes horrifyingly apparent and threateningly close. In an allusion to the Medusa's petrifying gaze, Zero claims that Tristessa 'magicked away his reproductive capacity via the medium of the cinema screen' (2008: 104). As he explains, it was during a cinematic adaptation of *Madame Bovary* that Tristessa's eyes 'had fixed directly upon his and held them', eyes that '[grew] to giant size' as a result of Zero having taken mescaline. He then felt that 'her eyes consumed him in a ghastly epiphany. He'd felt a sudden, sharp, searing pain in his balls' and with 'visionary certainty, he'd known the cause of his sterility' (2008: 104). Unlike the previous scene, there is a suggestion that, under certain circumstances, Hollywood cinema itself can terrify the straight male spectator. It is as if the woman on-screen had temporarily evaded the Hollywood apparatus and reached out subversively and menacingly to the male spectator. The unilateral viewing situation breaks down so that the spectator perceives the character on screen as gazing back at him. Like Louise Brooks in *Pandora's Box* (1929), Tristessa returns the male gaze 'and with interest', in Carter's words (2013e: 473). Through this extreme increase of proximity between spectator and image, Eve comes to see Hollywood's production of femininity and the masculine observer anew.

Facing filmic fantasies

Eve's re-vision of Tristessa and of her own way of seeing reaches an apotheosis when she comes face to face with the Hollywood star.[24] 'Stars encourage us to face our fantasies', Graham McGann observes, and meeting Tristessa certainly forces Eve to face a number of hers (1991: 326). The most obvious of these comes from the revelation that Tristessa is in fact a male transvestite, which forces Eve to reassess and see anew Hollywood's production of femininity, not as the image of a natural and eternal femininity, but an elaborate male fantasy. Carter claims that the inspiration for this was the advertising slogan for *Gilda* (1946) – 'There was never a woman like Gilda' – observing that 'only a man could think of femininity in terms of that slogan' (Haffenden, 1985: 85).[25] Similarly, Tristessa embodies the idea that 'woman is indeed beautiful only in so far as she incarnates most completely the secret aspirations of man' (2008: 129).[26] However, I want to examine two fantasies in particular that relate more directly to the issue of proximity.

The first of these concerns the disavowal of the woman's body in Hollywood's images of femininity. Long since retired, Tristessa now hides, paradoxically, in a transparent glass palace in the desert. One room functions as a mausoleum for Hollywood's fallen stars, filled with waxwork figures of Jean Harlow, James Dean and Marilyn Monroe amongst others. Upon seeing Tristessa's prone body laid out upon a bier, Eve mistakenly believes her to be dead. More significantly, Eve struggles to see her as more than an image: observing that Tristessa was 'so like her own reflection on the screen it took my breath away', adding that 'that spectacular wraith might have been only the invention of all our imaginations and yet, all the time, she had been real' (2008: 118). Despite this acknowledgement, though, Eve continues to see only the cinematic Tristessa:

> It was as if all Tristessa's movies were being projected all at once on that pale, reclining figure so that I saw her walking, speaking, dying, over and over again in all the attitudes that remained in this world, frozen in the amber of innumerable spools of celluloid from which her being could be extracted and endlessly recycled in a technological eternity, a perpetual resurrection of the spirit. (2008: 119)

Beyond Eve's own desiring gaze, this passage suggests that Hollywood's scopic regime effaces the female body in its production of an infinitely reproducible commodity that masquerades as a unique feminine essence.[27] That Tristessa's body appears masked by her cinematic images also chimes once again with the work of Baudrillard and his concept of the simulacrum. Leonard Wilcox explains that, for Baudrillard, 'images, signs, and codes engulf objective reality; signs become more real than reality and stand in for the world they erase' (1991: 346–7).[28] Once again, the reel subsumes the real. More than masking the female body, Hollywood is also pictured as vampiric for, as Eve suggests, it is 'as if the camera had stolen, not the soul, but [Tristessa's] body and left behind a presence like an absence' (2008: 123), a being with 'no ontological status, only an iconographic one' (2008: 129).[29]

Coming into close proximity with Tristessa not only helps Eve to appreciate the former's role as a screen but also as a mirror for the spectator's desires. Moving towards Tristessa was, Eve says, like moving 'towards [her] own face in a magnetic mirror' (2008: 110). The idea of woman as a mirror was an important part of Hollywood's development. Carter notes that Greta Garbo was instructed by director Rouben Mamoulian during the shooting of *Queen Christina* (1933) to 'keep her face a perfect blank, so that the audience could read into her features whatever they felt should be the appropriate response' (2013g: 497). One consequence of this is that such images of femininity do not challenge the male spectator, and thus work in tandem with Hollywood's system of proximity from a distance. However, as with Desiderio and Albertina, Eve's getting close to Tristessa's actual body breaks this safe proximity to produce not pleasure but horror: approaching Tristessa, Eve says that she 'did not feel a sense of homecoming, only the forlorn premonition of loss'. 'It was', she continues, 'like finding [herself] on the brink of an abyss', producing a 'giddiness that seized [her] and shook [her]'. Most importantly, Eve confesses that only much later would she come to understand that this was an abyss that opened onto herself (2008: 110). As Dani Cavallaro argues, the 'reflection cannot grant a sense of conclusive fulfillment [sic]' but instead reminds spectators of 'the inevitability of separation, disconnection and bereavement. Beholding its illusory plenitude, we seek confirmation of our own solidity but only find evidence for a splitting between subject and object which in turn replicates our internal – and incurable – self-divisions' (2011: 87). As with *The Infernal Desire Machines of Doctor Hoffman*, then, *New Eve* also suggests that the gap between spectator and image is crucial for sustaining but also hiding the fact that it is the former's desire that maintains the latter.

Wrapping up the celluloid

Despite Eve's experience of horror at this point, the final part of her narrative reveals a more hopeful resolution to the problem of proximity than was the case in *The Infernal Desire Machines of Doctor Hoffman*. Unlike Desiderio, Eve's confrontation with Hollywood's illusions and her own position as spectator results in a successful coming to terms with her desire; from here, she is then able to leave behind her obsession with Hollywood and the economy of the gaze in search of new beginnings. The first part of this resolution involves a final confrontation with Tristessa, a cinematic experience that not only produces pleasure but also transforms Eve's subjectivity. During a sexual encounter in the desert that brings their cinematic love affair to a crescendo as spectator and Hollywood star merge, Eve describes how they 'peopl[ed] this immemorial loneliness with all we had been, or might be, or had dreamed of being, or had thought we were' (2008: 148). Unlike Desiderio's and indeed Eve's own earlier experience of horror at coming face-to-face with her fantasy, this encounter appears expansive and generative. In contrast with Hollywood's system of proximity, which protects the spectator from any transformative encounter, Eve and Tristessa both appear to multiply selves. Indeed, this encounter even transforms Eve in a corporeal sense, for she later discovers that she has become pregnant with Tristessa's child. Once again, Eve sees 'fragments of old movies playing like summer lightning on the lucid planes of [Tristessa's] face' (2008: 149), but this becomes a shared visual experience as 'every modulation of the selves we now projected upon each other's flesh' (2008: 148). Eve's view of sex and gender is also now more expansive and open to ambiguity: 'what the nature of masculine and the nature of feminine might be [...] I do not know' (2008: 149–50). Now that the distance separating spectator from image has been completely erased and Eve confronts Tristessa directly, she is able to grasp her own desires, appreciate better the ambiguity of identity, and embrace change.

In the final part of Eve's narrative, she then effectively exorcizes her cinematic consciousness and scopophilia in search of new beginnings. In another revision of the opening scene, Eve leaves behind her obsession with Hollywood's visual economy inside the enclosed and darkened space of a cave by the sea. By contrast with the cinema theatre, the cave is uncomfortably small, so that Eve's dominant experience is tactile rather than visual: she squeezes through a number of tunnels, 'fold[ing]' her body 'into the interstice of rock' (2008: 179–80). Whereas the economy of the gaze allows the spectator to hold the image at a safe distance, this tactile experience forces a direct encounter between bodies. As well as the more obvious symbolism of the cave as womb, Eve also turns to a literary rather than a cinematic metaphor to describe this experience, imagining herself 'pressed as between pages of a gigantic book' (2008: 180). There is also a symbolic rejection of Hollywood's narcissistic and voyeuristic visual economy represented by two objects that Eve finds in the cave: a broken mirror, 'cracked right across many times so it reflected nothing' and a signed publicity photo of Tristessa, which Eve tears into 'pieces' (2008: 181–2).

The high point of this rejection of Hollywood occurs during a surreal experience in which both Eve's sense of self and time itself seem to come undone, which she explains not in terms of cinema's flat images but the corporeality of its celluloid. In the cave, Eve experiences time 'running back on itself' so that the words 'duration' and 'progression' appear 'meaningless', and an abyss opens up once again, producing 'a sensation of falling' (2008: 182–3). The body is then foregrounded as Eve squeezes through a womb-like fissure, its walls like 'meat and slimy velvet', shuddering and sighing, and rippling with a 'visceral yet perfectly rhythmic agitation' as if 'ingest[ing]' her body (2008: 184). At this point, when proximity from a distance has been replaced by direct bodily contact, Eve has a final cinematic vision: as if watching a film of the Earth's evolutionary history in reverse, Eve sees '[r]ivers neatly roll[ing] up on themselves like spools of film' which then 'turn in on to their own sources' (2008: 185). With this metaphor of the celluloid curling up into itself like a film in reverse, it is as if Hollywood's illusions are finally being packed away, Tristessa's luminous image receding into darkness.[30] With this affirmative experience of an abyss, Eve is able to accept the emptiness behind the cinematic image. After embracing Hollywood's fantasies up close, Eve is able to come to terms with her desire and end her enthrallment to the cinematic scopic economy in favour of a new sense of corporeality: after being expelled from the cave in an act of rebirth, this new Eve sails off into the ocean before her, pregnant with Tristessa's child. Although Tristessa continues to haunt Eve's dreams, as Albertina does Desiderio's, Tristessa's house, 'the glass mausoleum that had been [Eve's] world [...] is [now] smashed' and she is able to 'start from [her] conclusions' (2008: 191).

What I hope to have shown in my readings above is that while it may be true that Carter's early works emulate the anti-illusionistic filmic techniques of filmmakers like Godard, later texts like *The Infernal Desire Machines of Doctor Hoffman* and *The Passion of New Eve* employ cinematic-inspired techniques that instead increase the sense of proximity between spectator and spectacle – heightening the illusion as it were – as a more productive way of confronting not just the illusory images of (predominantly Hollywood) cinema but the very desires of the spectators themselves, desires that imbue the images with power. What could be called Carter's late cinematic texts, then, use the illusionistic tools of Hollywood cinema in order to deconstruct its fantasies from within, by effectively giving the (heterosexual) male spectator too much of what he wants in order to force a confrontation with his desire. In this way, the two texts analysed above show us that a more fruitful critique of the illusions of traditional cinema can only emerge from a confrontation with our desires for such imagistic illusions.

Notes

1 Carter refers to *Les Enfants du Paradis* as her favourite film in 'My Maugham Award' (2013h: 251).
2 As critics have noted, Carter's fiction shares much with feminist film theory as it was developing in the 1970s, in particular the pioneering work of Laura Mulvey (1975).
3 Carter did, however, find alternative models of femininity even within mainstream film. She was fascinated by actors like Mae West, Marlene Dietrich and, especially, Louise Brooks, for the way they portrayed femininity as both powerful and as a social construction or masquerade. In the case of Brooks, Carter was impressed with her confrontation with the male gaze in her performance in *Pandora's Box* (1929): 'Like Manet's Olympia, she is directly challenging the person who is looking at her; she is piercing right through the camera with her questing gaze to give your look back, with interest' (2013e: 473).
4 Mulvey's phrase is from 'Visual Pleasure and Narrative Cinema' (1975).
5 No doubt part of the reason critics are hesitant to take Carter's love of cinematic illusionism seriously or at face-value is to avoid the criticism that her work indulges in dangerous fantasies and illusions. By emphasizing the self-conscious quality of her writing practice, critics are able to fend off this critique by arguing that Carter's works hold such dangerous fantasies at a distance – as social constructions rather than natural realities.
6 To put it in terms of Marx's concept of commodity fetishism, Carter's fiction does not represent a straightforward critique of the structure of fetishism by dismissing it as illusory in favour of the so-called real relations of existence. Rather, she engages with the structure of desire which fetishism depends upon in order to understand why subjects continue to believe in the illusory promises of the commodity despite cynically knowing that it is a fantasy.
7 See for example the work of Slavoj Žižek, who frequently argues that the cynicism of contemporary consumers does little to challenge the ideology of capitalism, for despite knowing that the claims made by advertisers are illusory, consumers continue to purchase the commodities. As McGowan puts it with reference to anti-illusionistic cinema, 'Subjects adopt a position of cynical distance in which the transparency of the game becomes part of the game itself' (2007: 10). It is for this reason, I argue, that Carter takes cinematic fantasies seriously rather than simply demythologizing them as social fictions or lies.
8 This is not to suggest that Carter's demythologization of cinematic illusions is unimportant, and indeed I will note some instances of this in my

analysis of her work. However, because critics have already pointed out how her texts deconstruct or demythologize cinematic fantasies, I will concentrate instead on how her texts also embrace such filmic fantasies as a different, even complementary, approach.

9 Hereafter, these will be referred to as *Desire Machines* and *New Eve* respectively.
10 It is worth noting that Carter was also fascinated with psychoanalysis, a phenomenon that arose almost in tandem with the invention of the cinema. Furthermore, the relationship between psychoanalysis and cinema has been a particularly fertile one throughout the last century.
11 This then might suggest David Lynch as a better comparison with Carter's fiction than Godard, at least as McGowan understands Lynch's filmic techniques. See *The Impossible David Lynch* (2007).
12 Carter's phrase is from a later short story entitled 'The Merchant of Shadows' (1993).
13 The desire machines in a sense literalize Walter Benjamin's notion of film as introducing an 'unconscious optics' to its audience (1999: 230). Carter herself made a similar connection when she described the Granada cinema at Tooting as 'like the unconscious itself [...] public and private at the same time' (2013f: 489).
14 In this respect, the desire machines look forward to the invention of personal computers and, especially, smart devices, which allow spectators to view seemingly any image and in any time or place.
15 Indeed, on at least three occasions in the opening pages, Evelyn confesses that he cannot remember the girl's name. On one occasion, he refers to her as 'some girl or other' (2008: 5).
16 For more on the hyperreal and the simulacrum, see Jean Baudrillard (1994).
17 Charles Baudelaire refers to modern man as a 'kaleidoscope equipped with consciousness' (1964: 9).
18 Tonkin has also explored the representation of Leilah as *femme fatale*, noting that Carter draws on both the 'Decadent iconography instigated by Baudelaire' and on 'later cinematic versions' (2012: 140).
19 The lack of recognition from the mirror-image casts this scene as a reversal, and perhaps parody, of Jacques Lacan's 'mirror-stage' hypothesis (2006).
20 For the sake of stylistic ease, however, I will continue to use 'Eve' and 'Evelyn', depending on the context.
21 This then challenges his omnipotence as a spectator since he now recognizes the gaze of the Other. For a classic account of visuality in terms of a struggle between the self and the Other, see the section of Jean-Paul Sartre's *Being and Nothingness* entitled 'The Look' (1969).

22 It should be clear that there is a contradiction here in Mother's project: while she appears to be an essentialist when it comes to sex and gender, she goes to elaborate lengths to produce a woman through technical means. The latter actually foregrounds the notion of gender as a technology, as something produced by various discursive acts and bodily inscriptions. For more on gender as a technology, see Teresa de Lauretis (1987).
23 In this way, *New Eve* shares much with John Berger's *Ways of Seeing*, published in the same decade.
24 The importance of the term re-vision here is helpfully illustrated by Adrienne Rich when she writes that 'Re-vision – the act of looking back, of seeing with fresh eyes', is for women not just 'a search for identity' but a 'refusal of the self-destructiveness of male-dominated society' (1993: 167).
25 As Rita Hayworth herself famously quipped, 'Men go to bed with Gilda, but wake up with me' (Herbert, 2002: 7).
26 Some critics have also argued that this scenario is suggestive of the concept of 'womanliness as a masquerade', a concept pioneered by the psychoanalyst Joan Riviere. As Kate Webb argues, the film stars who inspired Tristessa 'were so manifestly queens of artifice, creatures of dream and design' that 'they flaunted an idea only previously rumoured in books: that femininity itself was a drag act' (2010). Stephen Heath explains the concept of masquerade in terms of cinema: 'The masquerade is obviously at once a whole cinema, the given image of femininity'. Heath turns to Marlene Dietrich as an example of the cinematic masquerade: 'Dietrich wears all the accoutrements of femininity *as* accoutrements, does the poses as poses, gives the act as an act [...] Dietrich gives the masquerade in excess and so *proffers* the masquerade, take it or leave it, holding and flaunting the male gaze; not a defence against but a derision of masculinity' (1986: 57).
27 This passage has strong affinities with Benjamin's essay 'The Work of Art in the Age of Mechanical Reproduction', in which he writes of how mechanical reproduction erodes the authenticity of the original work of art. He also argues that the cult of the movie star is Hollywood's strategy for obscuring this erosion (1999).
28 Again, this has a particularly gendered dimension as, through mainstream cinematic practices, woman is associated with the flatness of the image. Mary Ann Doane, for example, writes: 'The woman's beauty, her very desirability, becomes a function of certain practices of imaging – framing, lighting, camera movement, angle. *She is* thus, as Laura Mulvey has pointed out, *more closely associated with the surface of the image than its illusory depths*, its constructed 3-dimenional space which the man is destined to inhabit and hence control' (1982: 76, emphasis added).

29 This functions as a cinematic version of Edgar Allan Poe's 'The Oval Portrait', in which a painter captures his wife on the canvas so that once the painting is complete she dies (2003).
30 There is a similarity here with Carter's brilliantly inspired essay on Poe's 'The Fall of the House of Usher', in which she retells the story by reversing the narrative order, comparing it to playing a movie backwards: 'I decided that I would invert "The Fall of the House of Usher" – play it backwards, in the same way as one can play a movie backwards, and see what face is shown to me, then, and what story that face told about the Ushers and their author' (2013i: 590).

References

Baudelaire, Charles (1964), 'The Painter of Modern Life', in *The Painter of Modern Life and Other Essays*, ed. and trans. Jonathan Mayne (London: Phaidon), pp. 1–40.

Baudrillard, Jean ([1981] 1994), *Simulacra and Simulation*, trans. Sheila Faria Glaser (Ann Arbor: University of Michigan Press).

—— ([1986] 2010), *America*, trans. Chris Turner (London: Verso).

Benjamin, Walter (1999), 'The Work of Art in the Age of Mechanical Reproduction', in *Illuminations*, trans. Harry Zorn (London: Pimlico), pp. 211–44.

Berger, John (1972), *Ways of Seeing* (London: Penguin).

Carter, Angela (1973), *Angela Carter Papers: 'The Passion of New Eve'* (London: The British Library), Add. MS 88899/1/5.

—— ([1983] 2013a), 'Jean-Luc Godard', in *Shaking a Leg: Collected Journalism and Writings* ed. Jenny Uglow (London: Vintage, 2013), pp. 464–6.

—— ([1983] 2013b), 'Notes from the Front Line', in *Shaking a Leg: Collected Journalism and Writings* ed. Jenny Uglow (London: Vintage), pp. 45–53.

—— ([1978] 2013c), 'Femmes Fatales', in *Shaking a Leg: Collected Journalism and Writings* ed. Jenny Uglow (London: Vintage), pp. 427–32.

—— ([1987] 2013d), 'Robert Coover: *A Night at the Movies*', in *Shaking a Leg: Collected Journalism and Writings* ed. Jenny Uglow (London: Vintage), pp. 466–9.

—— ([1990] 2013e), 'Barry Paris: *Louise Brooks*', in *Shaking a Leg: Collected Journalism and Writings* ed. Jenny Uglow (London: Vintage), pp. 472–9.

—— ([1992] 2013f), 'The Granada, Tooting', in *Shaking a Leg: Collected Journalism and Writings* ed. Jenny Uglow (London: Vintage), pp. 488–9.

—— ([1979] 2013g), 'Acting it Up on the Small Screen', in *Shaking a Leg: Collected Journalism and Writings* ed. Jenny Uglow (London: Vintage), pp. 495–9.

―――― ([1970] 2013h), 'My Maugham Award', in *Shaking a Leg: Collected Journalism and Writings* ed. Jenny Uglow (London: Vintage), pp. 250–2.

―――― ([1988] 2013i), 'Through a Text Backwards: The Resurrection of the House of Usher', in *Shaking a Leg: Collected Journalism and Writings* ed. Jenny Uglow (London: Vintage), pp. 589–99.

―――― (1993), *American Ghosts & Old World Wonders* (London: Chatto & Windus).

―――― ([1992] 2006), 'Author's Introduction', in *Expletives Deleted: Selected Writings* (London: Vintage).

―――― ([1977] 2008), *The Passion of New Eve* (London: Virago).

―――― ([1972] 2010), *The Infernal Desire Machines of Doctor Hoffman* (London: Penguin).

―――― ([1979] 2011), *The Sadeian Woman: An Exercise in Cultural History* (London: Virago).

Cavallaro, Dani (2011), *The World of Angela Carter: A Critical Investigation* (Jefferson: McFarland & Company).

Creed, Barbara (1993), *The Monstrous Feminine: Film, Feminism, Psychoanalysis* (London: Routledge).

Crofts, Charlotte (2003), *'Anagrams of Desire': Angela Carter's Writing for Radio, Film and Television* (Manchester: Manchester University Press).

Doane, Mary Ann (1982), 'Film and the Masquerade: Theorising the Female Spectator', *Screen*, 23:3–4, 74–88.

Evans, Kim (dir.) (1992), *Angela Carter's Curious Room*, Omnibus, BBC1, 15 September.

Gamble, Sarah (1997), *Angela Carter: Writing from the Front Line* (Edinburgh: Edinburgh University Press).

―――― (2006), 'Something Sacred: Angela Carter, Jean-Luc Godard and the Sixties', in Rebecca Munford (ed.), *Re-visiting Angela Carter: Texts, Contexts, Intertexts* (Basingstoke: Palgrave), pp. 42–63.

Gordon, Edmund (2016), *The Invention of Angela Carter: A Biography* (London: Chatto & Windus).

Haffenden, John (1985), *Novelists in Interview* (London: Methuen).

Heath, Stephen (1986), 'Joan Riviere and the Masquerade', in Victor Burgin, James Donald and Cora Kaplan (eds), *Formations of Fantasy* (London: Methuen), pp. 452–61.

Herbert, T. Walter (2002), *Sexual Violence and American Manhood* (Cambridge, MA: Harvard University Press).

Jackson, Rosemary (1986), 'Angela Carter', *Bomb*, 17, http://bombmagazine.org/article/821/angela-carter.

Jordan, Elaine ([1994] 2007), 'The Dangerous Edge', in Lorna Sage (ed.), *Flesh and the Mirror: Essays on the Art of Angela Carter* (London: Virago), pp. 201–6.

Kaplan, E. Ann (1993), *Women and Film: Both Sides of the Camera* (London: Routledge).
Lacan, Jacques (2006), 'The Mirror Stage as Formative of the I Function as Revealed in Psychoanalytic Experience', in *Écrits*, trans. Bruce Fink (London: Norton), pp. 75–81.
de Lauretis, Teresa (1987), *Technologies of Gender: Essays on Theory, Film, and Fiction* (Bloomington: Indiana University Press).
McGann, Graham (1991), 'Biographical Boundaries: Sociology and Marilyn Monroe', in Featherstone, Hepworth and Turner (eds), *The Body: Social Process and Cultural Theory* (London: Sage), pp. 325–38.
McGowan, Todd (2007), *The Impossible David Lynch* (New York: Columbia University Press).
Mulvey, Laura (1975), 'Visual Pleasure and Narrative Cinema', *Screen*, 16:3, Autumn, 6–18.
Neale, Catherine (1996), 'Pleasure and Interpretation: Film Adaptations of Angela Carter's Fiction', in Deborah Cartmell, I.Q. Hunter, Heidi Kaye and Imelda Whelehan (eds), *Pulping Fictions: Consuming Culture Across the Literature/Media Divide* (London and Chicago: Pluto Press), pp. 99–109.
Phillips, Adam (2010), *On Balance* (London: Hamish Hamilton).
Poe, Edgar Allan (2003), 'The Oval Portrait', in *The Fall of the House of Usher and Other Writings* (London: Penguin), pp. 201–4.
Rich, Adrienne ([1971] 1993), 'When We Dead Awaken: Writing as Re-vision', in Barbara Charlesworth Gelpi and Albert Gelpi (eds), *Adrienne Rich's Poetry and Prose* (New York: Norton), pp. 166–77.
Sage, Lorna (1992), *Women in the House of Fiction* (Basingstoke: Macmillan).
Sartre, Jean-Paul (1969), *Being and Nothingness*, trans. Hazel E. Barnes (London: Routledge).
Tonkin, Maggie (2012), *Angela Carter and Decadence: Critical Fictions/Fictional Critiques* (Basingstoke: Palgrave Macmillan).
Webb, Kate (2010), 'Angela Carter at the Movies', *Daily Telegraph*, 3 May, Available at: https://katewebb.wordpress.com/2010/05/03/angela-carter-at-the-movies-daily-telegraph/, accessed 12 November 2018.
Wilcox, Leonard (1991), 'Baudrillard, DeLillo's *White Noise*, and the End of Heroic Narrative', *Contemporary Literature*, 32:3, 346–65.

12

The rough and the holy: Angela Carter's marionette theatre

Maggie Tonkin

'"LIVE" THEATRE – THOUGH it might be better to call it "undead" theatre – used to embarrass me so much I could hardly bear it, that dreadful spectacle of painted loons in the middle distance making fools of themselves' (Carter, 2013: 495): these scathing remarks, made in 'Acting it Up on the Small Screen', an essay published in *New Society* in 1979, reveal much about Angela Carter's view of classic British theatre. Her characterization of classic British theatre as 'undead' echoes Peter Brook, who, in his seminal work of dramatic theory published a decade previously, *The Empty Space* (1968), draws distinctions between deadly, rough, holy and immediate theatre. Brook argues that these are not watertight categories but moments that co-exist, even within the same work. The deadly theatre – the theatre of cliché, predictability, formula – he compares to the 'deadly bore': one who operates 'at the bottom instead of the top of his possibilities' (2008: 45). According to Brook, although deadly theatre can be found everywhere, from grand opera to Brecht, it gravitates to productions of Shakespeare:

> Of course, nowhere does the deadly theatre install itself so securely, so comfortably and so slyly as in the works of Shakespeare. The Deadly Theatre takes easily to Shakespeare. We see his plays done by good actors in what seems like the proper way – they look lively and colourful, there is music and everyone is all dressed up, just as they are supposed to be in the best classic theatres. Yet secretly we find it excruciatingly boring. (2008: 12)

Carter similarly objects to the accoutrements of period drama, excoriating British actors who, she claims, 'adore period costume and facial hair; that's what they went to RADA for' (2013: 497). She goes on to argue that the 'peculiarly external quality of the British school of acting, as if it were done in the third person, suits the personation of posturing fakes very well' (2013: 498). Such 'posturing fakes' have now inherited television where they 'spread themselves across all three channels mopping and mowing and rolling their eyes and scattering cut-glass vowels everywhere' (Carter, 2013: 495). Her early infatuation with the stage – she is on record as saying that 'Like so many girls, I passionately wanted to be an actress when I was in my early teens' (Carter, 1983: 74) – gave way to a rejection so total that, 'Blushing for them', she gave up going to the theatre 'some time in the late 1950s' (2013: 498, 495).

Her repudiation of the classic British theatre notwithstanding, the theatre figures largely in Carter's oeuvre. As a corollary, the tropes of theatricality and performativity are pervasive motifs within the critical reception of her work, with a particular focus on the performativity of gender. Susan Fisher, for instance, argues that, 'Throughout her works, from the basement puppet theatre of *The Magic Toyshop* (1967) to the Shakespearean farce of *Wise Children* (1991), Carter uses metaphors of performance to explore the notion that all social behaviour, including gender, requires us to adopt roles' (1999: 165). Indeed, so pervasive is this metaphorical reading of theatricality in Carter's work that, according to Joseph Bristow and Trev Lynn Broughton, 'the most insistent feature of current Carter studies [...] is her interest in that bundle of tropes – theatricality, spectacle and play-acting – now commonly associated with theory and (cultural) politics of gender as performance' (1997: 14).

In contradistinction to the tradition of reading performance and performativity metaphorically, this chapter explores the representations of performance in Carter's work *literally*, that is to say, as modes of theatrical performance. In so doing, it seeks not to challenge but rather to augment the dominant tradition of reading performance metaphorically by considering how specific modes of theatricality function to denaturalize the real in Carter's work. Apart from the Shakespearean turn in her last novel, *Wise Children*, Carter's representations of theatricality are of demotic forms: travelling players, freak shows, the music hall, marionettes and the circus. I am particularly interested in analysing Carter's preference for demotic theatrical practices over proscenium arch drama in the light of debates about the British theatre that were current during her writing career, which spanned the late 1950s until the early 1990s. These decades saw great changes in the British theatre, with the establishment of state funding for the arts, the ascendancy of a new generation of playwrights, such as those associated with the English Stage Company at the Royal Court Theatre, and the emergence of alternate theatrical modes influenced by European dramatists and theorists as well as Asian cultural traditions. This chapter will take the depictions of the marionette theatre in *The Magic Toyshop* (1967) and 'The Loves of Lady Purple' (1974) as exemplary of Carter's interest in demotic theatrical forms, and will situate them historically against the debates about theatricality current at their time of writing. Peter Brook's notions of deadly, rough and holy theatre will be pivotal to the analysis.

Post-war British theatre and naturalism

The dominant narrative of the post-war British theatre runs something like this. In the early war years, there was a blanket closure of theatres, but by 1945 the London theatre scene was thriving, with 'reviews, light comedies, revivals of classics by noted actors including John Gielgud, Laurence Olivier and Ralph Richardson, and the occasional highly successful new work, such as Noel Coward's *Blithe Spirit*' (Shellard, 1999: 2) appealing to a wide audience base. Commercial theatre in the West End, dominated by the entrepreneur-manager Binkie Beaumont, was characterized by long runs of lavishly staged works, while the Old Vic, led by Laurence Olivier and Ralph Richardson, was the mainstay of serious drama, mounting acclaimed productions of Shakespeare and 'the classics', with the company acting as national cultural ambassadors during 1945 tours to Paris, occupied Germany and even the then recently liberated Belsen concentration camp.

Nevertheless, as Dominic Shellard points out, the peace brought significant challenges, most notably the paucity of new work by serious British playwrights and the dominance of London over the regions (1999: 2). The government response to this was to involve itself in the funding and direction of the theatre to an unprecedented degree. Having noted the important role played by the arts in keeping up morale during the war, in 1946 the Labour Government established a national body, the Arts Council of Great Britain, to administer state subsidies to the arts. Although this funding was heavily concentrated in the capital, regional theatre companies were also set up and funded, including the Bristol Old Vic and repertory companies in Guildford, Ipswich, Canterbury and Derby (Shellard, 1999: 6). The Stratford-based Shakespeare Memorial Theatre, renamed the Royal Shakespeare Company (RSC) in 1961, had something of a renaissance too, launching the directorial career of Peter Brook in 1946 and forging an unlikely alliance with Binkie Beaumont, which enabled his 'talent' to alternate working in the West End with seasons at Stratford.

Despite the injection of funding into regional companies, the vast majority of government money was funnelled into the professional London theatre. The Arts Council was primarily interested in buttressing the metropolitan theatres as the pinnacle of British drama, and in promoting that theatre as an instrument of national identity. The idea of a national theatre company, one that could 'set a standard for the production of drama in a national setting worthy of Shakespeare and the British tradition' (Stafford Cripps, cited in Rebelatto, 1999: 61) had been mooted since the war, and in 1963 the Old Vic Company was subsumed into the newly formed National Theatre of Great Britain. At the second reading of the National Theatre Bill, which legislated the establishment of this new company, Conservative MP Oliver Lyttleton, who was later appointed inaugural chairman of the board of the National Theatre, declared with nationalistic fervour, 'A national theatre in Great Britain would help to keep undefiled the purity of the English language ... by setting a standard springing from the glorious English of Shakespeare' (cited in Rebellato, 1999: 61).

Perhaps partly as a consequence of this desire for a theatre of 'undefiled purity', post-war British theatre operated under considerable constraints. Censorship was operative until 1968, with 42 plays banned in the period 1945–68 on various grounds, including indecency, defamation, improper representation of the monarchy, incitement to crime or a breach of the peace, and offending religious sentiment. Homosexual acts were not decriminalized until 1968, and until 1958 there was an absolute ban on the representation of homosexuality on the stage.

Against this conservative background, the 1956 première of John Osborne's *Look Back in Anger* at the Royal Court Theatre was something of a bombshell. Featuring a love triangle between a young married couple and another woman set in a working-class flat, the play explored the frustrations of working-class lives, marital infidelity and class and generational antagonisms. It has been claimed that audiences gasped at the sight of an ironing board onstage, and were appalled by the lead actor's non-standard BBC pronunciation. Both of these claims underline the middle- and upper-class bias of most British drama of the period. Many historians cite Osborne's play as a watershed moment in post-war British theatre, crediting it with ushering in a new era of contemporary play-making; as Dan Rebellato puts it, albeit parodically, 'At the Royal Court, *Look Back in Anger*, John Osborne's fiery blast against the establishment burst onto the stage, radicalizing British theatre overnight' (1999: 1).

Osborne's play did indeed usher in a new era of realism in the British theatre, yet arguably *Look Back in Anger* changed little stylistically, merely exchanging an out-dated, metropolitan, middle-class-based form of naturalism for a contemporary, regional, working-class one. By and large, British drama in the late 1950s and 1960s – the period to which Carter refers – retained its naturalist bent, remaining relatively impervious to the anti-illusionist and absurdist drama being developed in Europe. During this period, European drama companies had appeared on British stages, including Brecht's Berliner Ensemble. Becket's *Waiting for Godot* and *Endgame*, along with plays by Genet, Sartre, Cocteau and other lesser-known European playwrights, had been performed in Britain, sometimes having extended and highly successful runs. The expressionistic and absurdist staging of these works, and the quite different acting techniques they demanded, with far greater importance placed on the body, and less on the 'Beautiful Voice' – the mainstay of British acting that Carter derides with her reference to 'cut glass vowels' – had certainly had an impact on British actors and directors (Hayman, 1979: 130). But although there was a subsequent degree of theatrical experimentation in Britain – most notably the Sunday night seasons at the Royal Court Theatre, Peter Brook's Theatre of Cruelty season with the RSC in 1964, and Joan Littlewoood's *Oh What a Lovely War* – the dominant mode well into the 1970s remained that of naturalism (Hayman, 1979: *passim*).

And it is this naturalism that stuck so forcefully in Carter's caw. She makes this point forcefully in 'Acting it Up', declaring that it was '"naturalistic" acting that drove me out of the theatre [...] all those years ago' (Carter, 2013: 498). Carter's aversion to theatrical naturalism is one of the motivating forces behind the turn to demotic theatrical forms in her fiction. Her objection to classic British acting and actors is not simply that they are hams, but that they are hams in thrall to an ideology. According to Carter, the cardinal sin of the classic actor is an unthinking adherence to the ideology of naturalism, which, in its slavish reproduction of surface detail, produces a 'fictive reality' (Carter, 2013: 498). Naturalism 'necessitates the creation of an illusion as an end in itself', which differentiates it from realism: 'naturalism as a mode which deals with the recreation of reality as a credible illusion is quite a different thing from the mode of realism itself, which is a representation of what things actually *are* like and must, therefore, bear an intimate relation to truth or else, well, it isn't any good' (Carter, 2013: 498).

Carter's attack on naturalism in the theatre is very much in keeping with her critique of realism in fiction. In the 'Afterword' to *Fireworks*, her first collection of short stories, many of which were written during 1969–72, the period she lived in Japan, she explained her admiration for the tales of Hoffmann and Poe. Carter states that 'the tale differs from the short story in that it makes few pretences at the imitation of life [...] The tale does not log everyday experience, as the short story does; it interprets everyday experience through a system of imagery derived from subterranean areas behind everyday experience, and therefore the tale cannot betray its readers into a false knowledge of everyday experience (Carter, 1974: 121–2). Her embrace of the non-naturalistic modes of the tale, allegory, the fantastic and magic realism can be seen as part of a generalized repudiation of fictional realism as creating 'false knowledge of everyday experience'. Her embrace of demotic forms of theatre – puppetry, music hall and musical comedy, freak shows, the circus and so forth – is analogous to her repudiation of fictional realism. These demotic theatrical forms are non-naturalistic and thus do not make 'pretences at the imitation of life'.

They are also, of course, all instances of what Brook terms 'rough theatre', in which the 'most vital theatrical experiences occur outside the legitimate places constructed for the purpose' (Brook, 2008: 74). The rough or non-legitimate theatre is the theatre of crudity, dirt and disorder. According to Brook, 'it is most of all dirt that gives the roughness its edge; filth and vulgarity are natural, obscenity is joyous; with these the spectacle takes on its socially liberating role, for by nature the popular theatre is anti-authoritarian, anti-traditional, anti-pomp, anti-pretence' (2008: 76). Brook notes that in the twentieth century every attempt to revitalize the theatre has seen a return to these rough sources: Meyerhold turned to the music hall and the circus, Brecht to cabaret, Littlewood to the funfair. He make the additional point that the word 'popular' does not convey the full sense of the rough theatre, which encompasses 'bearbaiting, ferocious satire and grotesque caricature', all qualities that were present in 'the greatest of rough theatres, the Elizabethan one' (Brook, 2008: 77). In the rough theatre then, violence, cruelty and social critique are inextricable from popular entertainment.

Of the 'rough' theatrical modes depicted in Carter's work, puppetry is the most non-naturalistic. One of the most ancient forms of theatre, puppetry is thought to have originated at least 3,000 years ago as an aspect of religious ceremony, perhaps deriving from the use of ceremonial masks (Baird, 1965: 28–43). It is mentioned in works by Herodotus and Xenophon from the fifth century BC, as well as in the ancient Indian epic, the *Mahabarata*. Yet, in many cultures, the sacred or religious aspect of puppetry has been lost over time, and it has come to be regarded more as a popular entertainment. This is less the case in Asian cultures, in which puppetry has retained its religious associations to some degree, and also serves as a mode for the transmission of national epics and fables. It is, however, particularly noticeable in Europe, where the French *Grand Guignol*, the English Punch and Judy, the Russian *Petrushka* and the Italian puppet versions of the *Commedia dell'arte* have all come to be viewed as rough theatre, which is frequently aimed at children. However, in the early twentieth century the European theatrical avant-garde was drawn to puppetry as a counter-practice to the dominant paradigm of naturalism, and it is this avant-garde counter-practice, as well as demotic puppetry traditions, on which, this chapter will argue, Carter draws.

Carter's marionette theatres

There are two depictions of puppetry in Carter's oeuvre: Uncle Philip's basement marionette theatre in her second novel, *The Magic Toyshop* (1963), and the Asiatic Professor and his marionette, Lady Purple, in 'The Loves of Lady Purple', from her first collection of short stories, *Fireworks* (1974). It should be noted that Carter makes it explicit that these are marionettes – defined as 'jointed figure[s] operated from above by rods, wires or strings' (McCormick, 2004: ix) – rather than generic puppets. According to scholars, the term 'marionette' derives from the French 'little Marie', purportedly because the Virgin Mary figured largely in early religious puppet plays (Baird, 1965: 67), but in Carter's hands the marionette invariably has a blasphemous and transgressive function. This is most evident in the tale, 'The Loves of Lady Purple'.

'Lady Purple' has a double structure: a frame narrative that relates the devotion of the Asiatic Professor, a virtuoso puppet master, to his marionette, the Lady Purple, and an embedded play script, 'The Notorious Amours of Lady Purple, the Shameless Oriental Venus' that is enacted nightly in his puppet theatre. The play script relates the history of Lady Purple, an orphan who seduces, robs and murders her foster father before running off to the 'pleasure quarters' to become a mistress of perversity, a veritable Sadean Juliette who destroys all her lovers. Eventually, after contracting a fatal – presumably syphilitic – illness, she is rejected by the townsfolk and reduced to 'scavenging on the seashore', there practising 'extraordinary necrophilies on the bloated corpses' the sea brings in (Carter, 2006: 47). At this point her 'dry rapacity had become entirely mechanical'; she loses her humanity and 'became a marionette herself, herself her own replica, the dead yet moving image of the shameless Oriental Venus' (Carter, 2006: 47).

In contrast to the cautionary narrative contained in the play script, in the frame narrative the marionette Lady Purple comes to life, kills the puppet master and sets his booth on fire, then heads off to the nearest brothel to ply her trade. The unmarked narrative voice comments on the paradox of the marionette liberating herself from her master only to freely pursue her own exploitation in the brothel thus:

> she did not possess enough equipment to comprehend the complex circularity of the logic which inspired her for she had only been a marionette. But, even if she could not perceive it, she could not escape the tautological paradox in which she was trapped; had the marionette all the time parodied the living or was she, now living, to parody her own performance as a marionette? (Carter, 2006: 51)

With its depiction of the fraught power relations between female puppet and her male master, 'Lady Purple' readily lends itself to an exploration of the performativity of gender. Writing in general terms about Carter's deployment of the motif of the puppet, Paulina Palmer contends that her early texts represent 'woman as a puppet, performing scripts assigned her by a male-supremicist culture (1997: 31). For Gina Wisker, the female puppet in 'The Loves of Lady Purple' is an expression of the patriarchal fear of the *femme fatale* and an enactment of the voyeuristic fantasy of watching the 'sexually provocative' woman perform her perversities and be punished for them (2006: 185). While I concur with theses analyses, I am interested in the theoretical underpinnings of Carter's choice of the marionette to enact her 'tautological paradox'. What is it about the marionette that makes it an ideal metaphor for patriarchal power relations, and to what traditions of puppetry does Carter's iteration of the marionette speak?

In a recent interview with Natsumi Ikoma, Carter's Japanese lover Sozo Araki revealed that Carter took a keen interest in Kabuki theatre and Joruri puppet theatre – the latter a synonym for Bunraku – while she lived with him in Tokyo, during which time she wrote the tale (Ikoma, 2017: 86). In both these theatrical forms, Ikoma explains, 'an extremely elegant and stylized femininity is put on show by a male actor in the former or by a puppet in the latter, further consolidating the fact that "femininity" is a performance' (2017: 86). Several undated entries in Carter's journals from the period make the connection to Bunraku explicit, such as 'Lady Purple (the Oriental Venus)/A Bunraku puppet that comes to life' (*Angela Carter Papers: Japan* 1, n.d. MS 88899/1/80 no pag), which is repeated more than once. Other entries, again undated, suggest that Carter was also thinking about 'Lady Purple' in relation to the specifically Western forms of the Gothic, automata and the peep-show, such as:

Automata – the Gothic Venus
Jeweled puppets with chalk-white faces, wigs of human hair & headdresses made mirror, of looking-glass, jeweled mirrored puppets
Lady Purple, the oriental Venus
A being at once magnificent and preposterous
She lies in the Peep-show (*Angela Carter Papers: Japan* 1, n.d. MS 88899/1/80.no pag)

To date, most critics have situated 'The Loves of Lady Purple' solely in relation to the traditions of Japanese puppetry. Thus Susan Fisher claims that 'the style of puppetry practised by the Asiastic Professor is clearly "*bunraku*"' (Fisher, 1999: 168), a claim that Charlotte Crofts seconds in her reading (Crofts, 2006: 101). However, as I shall show, this claim is only partially accurate, and, in its investment in reading the text in relation to Carter's stay in Japan, it ignores the specifics of the Professor's art. This chapter argues that the Professor practises a composite form that combines aspects of *bunraku* with Western puppetry traditions, and that the tale demands to be read in relation to both Japanese and Western puppet traditions. Specifically, it argues that the Western literary tradition of the animate puppet, the turn to puppetry by the early twentieth-century European theatrical avant-garde, and Brook's notions of the rough and the holy theatre, are key theoretical frames for reading Carter's tale.

Let us first consider the claim that 'Lady Purple' is a depiction of *bunraku*. According to puppetry scholar Donald Keene, *bunraku* developed as a highly stylized form of puppetry in the early eighteenth century, later taking its name from Bunrakken, a master puppeteer who founded the Bunraku Theatre in Osaka in 1872 (1965: 19–33). As this suggests, *bunraku* is performed in dedicated, permanent theatres, in contrast to Western puppetry, which has mostly been practised by itinerant players. *Bunraku* is a highly literary form, with a large repertoire of plays written specifically for it. Another distinguishing feature of *bunraku* is the visibility of its three essential human participants: the chanter, who sits to one side of the stage reciting the play text; the samisen player, who provides the musical accompaniment; and the puppet operators. The operation of the puppets is also highly distinctive. Each main character puppet has three operators: the principal and the two assistants. In scenes with multiple puppets, over twenty operators may be onstage simultaneously (Tilakasiri, 1982: 69), and the stage has special trenches running crossways in which the operators stand to facilitate the movement of the puppets. The puppets themselves are a unique composite of rod, glove and lever puppet; with some having inner strings by which the facial features can be manipulated by the hand of the operator (Keene, 1965: 50).

To consider 'Lady Purple' solely in reference to this tradition is clearly problematic. The tale does indeed make references to Japan, such as with the statement that the Professor has 'the wistful charm of a Japanese flower' (Carter, 2006: 42), and the description of Lady Purple as an exaggerated geisha-like figure (2006: 43). There is also a specific allusion to *bunraku* in the reference to the accompanying samisen playing of the 'dumb girl' (2006: 44). It could, moreover, be argued that the embedded play script itself reflects the densely literary nature of the traditional form. However, the mode of operating Lady Purple does not fit the definition of *bunraku*. Crucially, the narrative voice stresses that this puppet is a marionette. The Asiatic Professor is 'a master of marionettes' (2006: 41), who places 'his marionette in a specially constructed box' (2006: 43). Lady Purple's mode of operation is that of a marionette, with the Professor 'crouched above the stage directing his heroine's movements' (2006: 44). In lieu of the tripartite operators of the *bunraku* puppets, along with the chanters and samisen players, in 'Lady Purple' the Professor alone operates the marionette, as well as chanting her narrative 'in his impenetrable native tongue' (2006: 44).

Furthermore, there are several indicators that locate 'Lady Purple' within the traditions of the European marionette theatre, rather than *bunraku*. The naming of the puppet master as the Asiatic 'Professor' is one such example. As John McCormick writes in *The Victorian Marionette Theatre*, 'proprietors of marionette shows in the nineteenth century commonly added the title "professor" to confer respectability to their calling' (2004: 17). The itinerant nature of Lady Purple's entourage also links it to the European tradition, in which performances were given in a variety of venues from theatres, music halls, village halls, to – most commonly – fairgrounds. Indeed, Carter's characterization of the fairground itself as a 'diaspora of the amazing' (Carter, 2006: 43) speaks to descriptions of nineteenth-century fairs, in which 'rope-dancing and acrobatics, performing monkeys and bears, conjuring tricks and peepshows' co-existed with the 'phantasmagorias, dissolving views, ghost shows, panoramas, and other such visual items' that often featured in the marionette shows themselves. (McCormick, 2004: 9). The Asiatic Professor's infatuation with his marionette also echoes a number of anecdotes in the oral traditions of European puppetry. McCormick relates that when the celebrated Holden's company visited Istanbul in 1882, 'an Armenian photographer fell in love with their Cinderella and stole her', and notes that some puppeteers 'have half believed that their puppets possessed a life of their own' (2004: 65).

Such infatuations, of course, also speak to the long literary tradition of granting animate status to the inanimate puppet or doll, which date from Ovid's Pygmalion and Galatea through to Collodi's Pinocchio and Hoffmann's Olympia. 'Lady Purple's' specific allusions to Ovid's Pygmalion and Galatea have already been mapped out by

Sallye Sheppeard (2001: 36), but I would argue that the tale references an even broader tradition. Lady Purple's callous murder of her doting puppet master reflects the latent cruelty and amorality with which animate puppets are frequently imbued in the literary tradition of the animate puppet. As Tzachi Zamir points out, the 'misuse of its capacities' is implicit in every literary representation of puppets; the puppet's acquisition of agency is at the cost of the puppeteer's evacuation of volition, which is 'proportionately sucked out' (2010: 390), with the puppeteer frequently 'tricked, attacked, or even killed by his own creation' (2010: 392).

However, 'Lady Purple' sits not only within the European literary tradition of the animate puppet, but is also informed by the 'poetics of performance' of puppetry, which links Plato's cave to the European avant-garde of the early twentieth century. Whereas Olga Taxidou cites Plato's preference for puppets – the *neuropasta* of the Eleusinian mysteries – over human actors as the origin of this discourse, for many scholars the German Romantic writer Heinrich von Kleist's 'On the Marionette Theatre' is its ur-text. In this 1810 essay, Kleist stages a conversation about the relative merits of human dancers and puppets between two friends, one of whom is a celebrated dancer. The latter is enamoured of dancing marionettes, which he believes are superior to their human equivalents. This superiority, he claims, stems from the absence of affectation and relative weightlessness of the puppets, but more importantly, from their absence of consciousness. According to the dancer, there is an inverse correlation between grace and thought: 'grace returns after knowledge has gone through the world of the infinite, in that it appears to best advantage in that human bodily structure that has no consciousness at all – or has infinite consciousness – that is, in the mechanical puppet, or in the God' (Kleist, 1972: 26).

Kleist's valuation of the puppet over the human performer informs the experimentation of the early twentieth-century theatrical avant-garde, which was preoccupied with what Taxidou refers to as the 'man or marionette debate'. According to Taxidou, this debate was an attempt to answer the questions, 'Is the human form the appropriate material for art, can it ever free itself from verisimilitude and psychological expressivism, can abstraction be ever fully rendered through the use of the human form?'(2005: 225). Writers and practitioners as diverse as Alfred Jarry, with his famous *Ubu Roi,* the Bauhaus artist Oscar Schlemmer, British theatre director and theorist Edward

Gordon Craig, and Soviet constructivist director Vsevolod Meyerhold were significant players in this debate, which greatly influenced Brecht's notion of the alienation effect.

Meyerhold credits Craig with being the first to fling down 'a challenge to the naturalistic theatre' (Senelick, 1981: 114); indeed, Craig published the first English translation of Kleist's essay in his journal, *The Marionette*, in 1918. His own essay, 'The Actor and The Übermarionette' echoes Kleist's thesis. 'Art', Craig claims, 'arrives only by design [...] in order to make any work of art it is clear we may only work in those materials with which we can calculate. Man is not one of these materials' (cited in Taxidou, 2005: 228). Marionettes, on the other hand, offer endless possibilities for design. Their lack of interiority makes them ideal models for abstract, stylized modes of performance, which elicit an audience response characterized by distance and estrangement, just as their associations with childhood and religion evoke naivety and wonder in spectators (Taxidou, 2005: 228–9). While Meyerhold and Craig responded differently to the possibilities puppets offer – Meyerhold developing a system of biomechanics to train his actors to resemble puppets, and Craig replacing his actors with puppets – for both directors, the marionette offered a way to escape the stranglehold of naturalism.

Carter's representations of marionettes need to be situated not only within the history of this theatrical 'man or marionette' debate, but also within the related history of literary representations of the animate puppet. In both of these histories the puppet is privileged as an uncanny object that fundamentally broaches the subject–object divide and unsettles notions of autonomy and free will. As uncanny objects, Carter's marionettes enact Freud's dictum that the uncanny is the name for 'everything that ought to have remained secret and hidden' that comes to light (Freud [1919] 1953–74: 224). In 'Lady Purple' the marionette's decision to return to the brothel makes visible the structural forces and social conditioning that determine so called 'choice'; the female puppet can only choose that which she knows to be available to her. Free will is thus shown to be an illusion, because choice is always socially constrained. As Zamir argues, 'The puppet's resistance to its operator intimates a more complex set of relations with autonomy than a mere lack of freedom implied in the clichéd association of marionettes with determinism. The allure of puppets surely partakes of the fascination with tragedies and fate such as

Oedipus or *Macbeth*, which highlight the illusion of self-determination' (2010: 392).

The marionette's absence of interiority is fundamental to the reader's realization of the illusory nature of free will, hence the puppet acts as a literary version of Brecht's alienation device. According to Brook, Brecht took Craig's insight that useless information on the stage diverts the audience's attention away from true apprehension of a play's theme, so he 'cut out superfluous emotion, and the development of characters and feelings that related only to the character' (2008: 84). Too much characterization is opposed to the play's needs (2008: 85). Carter's choice of a marionette to illustrate her theme is predicated on its complete absence of emotional life or interiority – those bedrocks of the fictional illusion of character – the corollary of which is a lack of audience identification. Like Brecht, Carter is here using the absence of characterization in order to provoke alienation so as to 'shock us into bringing the best of our reason into play' (Brook, 2008: 81), rather than appealing to the affective response of the reader.

The audience's affective engagement with Melanie, the protagonist of *The Magic Toyshop*, whose forced interactions with marionettes are key to her developing consciousness, are considerably more complex. Since Melanie, as the focalizer of the text, undergoes significant trauma with the loss of her parents and her relocation to the oppressive Gothic household of her Uncle Philip Flower, the reader is likely to invest emotionally in her narrative. In this case, Carter uses marionettes as a means, not of provoking an alienation effect in the reader, but within Melanie herself. Melanie's forced participation in Uncle Philip's puppet rendition of 'Leda and the Swan', in which she endures mock-rape by an enormous swan marionette that descends upon her from above, crystallizes her realization of her own powerlessness under patriarchy. Initially she had mocked the swan puppet as 'dumpy and homely and eccentric' (Carter, 1981: 165), but when it forces her onto her back on the stage as if to rape her, 'All her laughter was snuffed out. She was hallucinated; she felt herself not herself, wrenched from her own personality, watching this whole fantasy from another place' (1981: 166). Melanie experiences this moment as one of psychic annihilation and profound self-alienation, in which her sense of her own subjectivity and agency is shattered. Thereafter she experiences herself as a thing: 'She was a wind up putting away doll, clicking through its programmed movements. Uncle Philip might have made her over, already. She was without volition of her own' (1981: 118). Melanie's alienation stems from the realization that she is akin to one of Uncle Philip's puppets, which realization had been presaged by Finn's observation, 'He's pulled our strings as if we were his puppets' (1981: 152).

Carter deploys marionettes as agents of estrangement in both the texts under discussion, and her fictional depictions of the marionette theatre as a space in which either the reader or the protagonist come to a realization of the nature of reality resonate with Brook's notion of the holy theatre. According to Brook, the holy theatre 'could be called The Theatre of the Invisible-Made-Visible' (2008: 47), as it is a privileged space in which the symbolic structures underpinning the everyday can be brought to light. But whereas Brook argues that the rough theatre, in which he includes the puppet theatre, and the holy theatre have a 'true antagonism to one another' (2008: 80), Carter depicts them as deeply imbricated, or even one and the same. In her fictional deployments of the marionette theatre, the Rough – the non-naturalist theatre, in other words – is precisely that which allows the 'system of imagery derived from subterranean areas behind everyday experience' to shock the reader or the character into knowledge (Carter, 1974: 121–2). As alienation devices, Carter's marionettes embody her rejection of naturalism on the page as well as the stage.

Towards the end of her life Carter's attitude to the British theatre had clearly softened, as evidenced by her acceptance of a commission to write an adaptation of Franz Wedekind's *Lulu* for the National Theatre in 1987, and her 'narrow-eyed' fury when it was never produced (Clapp, 1995: ix). Of course, Wedekind's play is not in the naturalist tradition, and by the 1980s the British theatre – even that bastion of 'undefiled purity' itself, the National Theatre – had been transformed into something far more polyglot and experimental than the institution that had embarrassed her so in the 1950s. But, her late involvement with mainstream British theatre notwithstanding, the deployment of demotic theatrical forms throughout Carter's oeuvre is underpinned by her unremitting rejection of naturalism. As this exposition of her invocation of the literary tradition of the animate puppet, and the theatrical 'man or marionette' debate in 'The Loves of Lady Purple' and *The Magic Toyshop* illustrate, the theatrical elements of Carter's fiction – so often read through the critical frame of gender performativity – are also engagements with the ideologies and aesthetics of performance *qua* performance.

References

Baird, Bill (1965), *The Art of the Puppet* (New York: Ridge Press/Macmillan).
Bristow, Joseph and Trev Lynn Broughton (eds) (1997), 'Introduction', in *The Infernal Desires of Angela Carter: Fiction, Femininity, Feminism* (London and New York: Longman), pp. 1–23.
Brook, Peter ([1968] 2008), *The Empty Space* (London: Penguin Modern Classics).
Carter, Angela, British Library, London, Add. MS 88899/1/80 *Angela Carter Papers: Japan 1*. N.d.
—— (1967), *The Magic Toyshop* (London: Virago).
—— (1974), 'Afterword', in *Fireworks: Nine Profane Pieces* (London: Quartet), pp. 121–2.
—— (1983), 'Notes from the Front Line', in M. Wandor (ed.), *On Gender and Writing* (London and Boston: Pandora Press), pp. 69–77.
—— (2006), 'The Loves of Lady Purple', in (*Fireworks* 1974) reprinted in *Burning Your Boats: Collected Stories* (London: Vintage), pp. 41–51.
—— ([1979] 2013), 'Acting it Up on the Small Screen', in J. Uglow (ed.), *Shaking a Leg: Collected Journalism and Writing* (London: Vintage), pp. 495–9.
Clapp, Susannah (1995), 'Introduction', in Mark Bell (ed.), Angela Carter, *The Curious Room: Plays, Film Scripts and an Opera* (London: Chatto & Windus), pp. vii–x.
Crofts, Charlotte (2006), '"The Other of the Other": Angela Carter's "New-Fangled" Orientalism', in R. Munford (ed.), *Re-visiting Angela Carter: Texts, Contexts, Intertexts* (Houndmills, Basingstoke: Palgrave Macmillan), pp. 87–109.
Fisher, Susan (1999), 'The Mirror of the East: Angela Carter and Japan', in S. Fisher (ed.), *Nostalgic Journeys: Literary Pilgrimages between Japan and the West*. Proceedings of a Conference held in Vancouver, British Columbia, September 1999 in honour of Kinya Tsuruta (CJR Japan research Series), pp. 165–77.
Freud, Sigmund ([1919] 1953–74), 'The Uncanny' (1919), James Strachey (ed.), in collaboration with Anna Freud, assisted by Alix Strachey and Alan Tyson, *The Standard Edition of the Complete Psychological Works of Sigmund Freud*. Vol. 17 (1917–19) (London: The Hogarth Press and the Institute of Psychoanalysis), pp. 217–56.
Hayman, Ronald (1979), *British Theatre Since 1955* (Oxford: Oxford University Press).

Ikoma, Natsumi (2017), 'Encounter with the Mirror of the Other', *Angelaki: Journal of the Theoretical Humanities*, 22:1 (March), 77–92.

Keene, Donald (1965), *Bunraku: The Art of the Japanese Puppet Theatre* (Tokyo: Kodansha International).

von Kleist, H. (1972) 'On the Marionette Theatre', trans. T.G. Neumiller *The Drama Review: TDR*, 16:3, 22–6.

McCormick, J. (2004), *The Victorian Marionette Theatre* (Iowa City: University of Iowa Press).

Palmer, Paulina (1997), 'Gender as Performance in the Fiction of Angela Carter and Margaret Atwoood', in Joseph Bristow and Trev Lynn Broughton (eds), *The Infernal Desires of Angela Carter: Fiction, femininity, Feminism* (London and New York: Longman), pp. 184–97.

Rebellato, Dan (1999), *1956 and All That: The Making of Modern British Drama* (London: Routledge).

Senelick, Laurence (1981), 'Moscow and Monodrama', *Theatre Research International*, 6 (Spring), 109–124.

Shellard, Dominic (1999), *British Theatre Since the War* (New Haven and London: Yale UP).

Sheppeard, S. (2001), 'Angela Carter's Oriental Venus: Myth and Metaphysics in 'The Loves of Lady Purple', *The Publications of the Mississippi Philological Association*, 35–42.

Taxidou, Olga (2005), 'Actor or Puppet: the Body in the Theatres of the Avant-Garde', in Dietrich Scheunenmann (ed.), *Avant-Garde/Neo-Avant-Garde* (Amsterdam: Rodopi), pp. 225–239.

Tilakasiri, J. (1982), *The Puppet Theatre of Asia* (Ceylon: Department of Cultural Affairs).

Wisker, Gina (2006), 'Behind Locked Doors: Angela Carter, Horror and the Influence of Edgar Allan Poe', in R. Munford (ed.), *Re-visiting Angela Carter: Texts, Contexts, Intertexts* (Houndmills: Palgrave Macmillan), pp. 178–98.

Zamir, Tzachi (2010), 'Puppets', *Critical Inquiry*, 36:3 (Spring), 386–409.

Index

Adam Adamant Lives 173
Adam and Eve 147, 156, 218
Adler, A. 217
Alexander, Sarane
   Surrealist Art 110
      'The Necrophile' 110
Alloway, Lawrence 87
Alma Tavern Theatre 6
Andermahr, Sonya and Lawrence Phillips
   Angela Carter: New Critical Readings 14
Andromeda 184–5
Angel Gabriel, The 157
Angela Carter Papers Collection, The
      British Library Archive 123, 128, 154, 157, 163, 205, 208, 233, 254
Angela Carter Society, The 7, 15
anthropology 9, 13, 127–9, 142
Anzieu, Didier
   The Skin-Ego 64, 75
Apostolic Fathers, The 158
Appignanesi, Lisa 120, 206
Aragon, Louis 103, 105, 108, 163
Araki, Sozo 6, 100, 101, 119, 122, 209, 254
   Seduced by Japan: A Memoir of the Days Spent with Angela Carter, with 'Her Side of the Story' by Natsumi Ikoma 204–5
Arcimboldo, Guiseppe 26, 27, 49
Arden, John 84
Armstrong, Paul B. 76
Arp, Jean 17
Artaud, Antonin 103, 106, 120
Arts Council of Great Britain, The 248–9
Atkins, Susan 161–2
Aylesford Review, The 81, 83, 85, 86, 93, 94, 96, 100

Bacchilega, Christina 44–5
Bachelard, Gaston
   The Poetics of Space 1, 46, 53
Baggini, Julian 45
Baird, Bill 252–3
Balász, Béla 77
Ballard, J.G. 114
Ballets Russes, Les 171
Balmer, Derek 84
Barker, Paul 206
Barthes, Roland 44, 46, 198
   Empire of Signs 212–13
   Mythologies 167
Bartók, Béla
   Duke Bluebeard's Castle 77
Bashō, Matsuo
   The Narrow Road to the Deep North 119
Bassnet, Susan 98
Bataille, Georges
   Story of the Eye 155
Bath 3, 6
Baudelaire, Charles 9, 99, 100–1, 111–12, 114–19, 121–2, 231, 241
   'Les Bijoux' 112
   'Correspondances' 120

Baudelaire, Charles (cont.)
   Les Fleurs du mal 99, 108, 112, 115, 118
   Fusées 105, 121
   Hygiène 121
   Journaux intimes 121
   Mon Coeur mis à nu 105, 121–2
   Oeuvres posthumes 121
   Petits poèmes en prose, aka *Le Spleen de Paris* 117–18
   'Le Revenant' 119
   'Sed non satiata' 113, 115
   'Spleen' 117
   Spleen et ideal 115
Baudrillard, Jean 231, 236, 241
Beach Boys, The
   'Heroes and Villains' 176–7
   Smiley Smile 177
Beake, Fred 96
Beatles, The
   'Helter Skelter' 160
   'Piggies' 160
   Sgt. Pepper's Lonely Hearts Club Band 168
   'Tomorrow Never Knows' 173
   The White Album 160
Beaumarchais, Pierre-Augustin 66
Beaumont, Binkie 248–9
Beauvoir, Simone de
   The Second Sex 219
Beckett, Samuel
   Endgame 250
   Waiting for Godot 250
Bedford, Les 189
Bell, Mark 32
Bell, Roland 211, 217
Bellmer, Hans 103, 108
Belsey, James
   The Sixties in Bristol (ed.) 84
Benjamin, Walter 227, 241
   'The Work of Art in the Age of Mechanical Reproduction' 242
Benoît, Jean
   Execution of the Testament of the Marquis de Sade 110, 121
Benson, Stephen 44–5
Berger, John
   Ways of Seeing 113, 167, 242
Berliner Ensemble, The 250
Bertrand, Sergeant François 110

Bettelheim, Bruno
   The Uses of Enchantment: The Meaning and Importance of Fairy Tales 75
Better Books (bookshop) 84
Birmingham Centre for Contemporary Studies, The 167–8, 175
Blake, William 59, 61, 72
   A Vision of the Last Judgement 73
Bloodaxe Books (publisher) 84
Bolter, Jay and Grusin, Richard 29–30
The Book of Beasts 87
The Book of Jubilees 163
Borden, Lizzie 11
Borges, Jorge Luis 98
Botelho, Inês 50
Boyars, Marion 108
Breakthru New International Poetry Magazine 84
Brecht, Bertolt 88, 246, 250, 252, 258, 259
Breton, André 89, 100–3, 105, 108, 118–20, 163
   L'Amour fou 100–3, 120
   Arcane 17, 103
   hasard objectif 100
   Manifesto of Surrealism 119
   'Le Marquis de Sade a regagné' 105
   Nadja 100, 103
   'L'Union libre' 105
   Les vases communicants 100, 103
bricolage 1, 11, 28, 51, 95, 169–70, 172, 174, 176–7
   see also patchwork
Bridges, Margaret 28
Bristol 3–4, 6–7, 9, 14–15, 81, 83–4, 86, 92, 94–5, 99, 145, 168, 185, 249
   Clifton 3–4, 6
Bristol Arts Centre, The 84
Bristol Old Vic, The 249
Bristol University 99
Bristow, Joseph and Trev Lynn Broughton
   The Infernal Desires of Angela Carter: Fiction, Femininity, Feminism (eds) 14, 128, 247
British Broadcasting Corporation (BBC)
   Angela Carter's Curious Room 2, 14
British Poetry Revival 82–4
British theatre 246–50, 260

Index

Britzolakis, Christina 167
Brontë sisters 52
Brook, Peter 249
  The Empty Space 246, 248, 251–2, 255, 259, 260
  Theatre of Cruelty 250
Brooks, Louise
  in *Pandora's Box* (dir. Georg Wilhelm Pabst) 235, 240
Browne, Sir Thomas
  Vulgar Errors 87
Browning, Robert
  'My Last Duchess' 192
Bucher, Ulrike and Finka, Maro 8, 45
Bugliosi, Vincent and Gentry, Curt
  Helter Skelter: The True Story of the Manson Murders 160, 163
Bunrakken, Uemura 212, 255
Bunraku Theatre, Osaka 255
Buñuel, Luis
  L'Âge d'or (A Idade do Ouro) 119
Buruma, Ian 11, 206
  A Japanese Mirror: Heroes and Villains in Japanese Culture 211, 213, 219
Butler, Judith 156–7
  Gender Trouble 215, 219

cabinet of curiosities 1–2, 8, 13, 26, 47–8
  see also Kunstkamer
Calder and Boyars 108, 120
Callil, Carmen 110
Camus, Albert
  The Rebel 169–70, 179
cannibalism 5, 189
Carné, Marcel
  Les Enfants du Paradis 223, 240
Carrington, Leonora 106, 111
  'La Debutante' 111
Carroll, Lewis 48
  Alice's Adventures in Wonderland 5, 25
  Through the Looking Glass and What Alice Found There 25
Carter, Angela
  'Acting it Up on the Small Screen' 246, 250–1
  'The Alchemy of the Word' 100–1, 118
  American Ghosts and Old World Wonders 21, 26, 32

  'Alice in Prague *or* The Curious Room' 1, 5, 21, 25–6, 48, 120, 198
  'Gun for the Devil' 21, 32–4
  'Impressions: The Wrightsman Magdelene' 10, 20, 60, 148–51
  'In Pantoland' 21
  'John Ford's *Tis Pity She's a Whore*' 31–2, 188
  'Lizzie's Tiger' 92
  'The Merchant of Shadows' 22, 198, 226, 241
  Angela Carter's Book of Wayward Girls and Wicked Women 111
  'The Art of Horrorzines' 35
  'Black Panther' 92
  Black Venus 21, 122, 190
  'Black Venus' 112
  'The Cabinet of Edgar Allan Poe' 21, 188, 190
  'The Fall River Axe Murders' 21
  'The Kiss' 23
  'Overture and Incidental Music for *A Midsummer Night's Dream*' 23–5
  'Peter and the Wolf' 146–9
  Black Venus's Tale 112–14
  The Bloody Chamber and Other Stories 2–3, 6, 8–10, 21, 58–77, 92, 99, 111, 120–1, 140, 142–3
  'The Bloody Chamber' 8, 47, 60–4, 67, 70–1, 75–6, 110–12, 120, 190
  'The Company of Wolves' 2, 5, 21, 65–6, 71–2, 185
  'The Courtship of Mr Lyon' 67, 70
  'The Erl-King' 66, 69, 70, 76
  'The Lady of the House of Love' 6, 21, 23, 30, 35, 67, 70–1
  'Puss-in-Boots' 5, 66, 68
  'The Snow Child' 66, 69–70, 183, 186–7, 192
  'The Tiger's Bride' 65–6, 143
  'The Werewolf' 68–9
  'Wolf-Alice' 64–5, 72, 76, 110, 146–8
  Bristol Trilogy 3
  Burning your Boats: Collected Short Stories 35
  'The Classical Hollywood Cinema' 20

Carter, Angela (*cont.*)
  'Come Unto These Yellow Sands' 23
  Come Unto These Yellow Sands: Four Radio Plays 2
  The Curious Room: Collected Dramatic Works, ed. Mark Bell 14, 17, 36
  'The Dark Tower' 93, 96
  Expletives Deleted 19, 213
  'Fictions Written in a Certain City' 117
  Fireworks: Nine Profane Pieces 2, 7, 12, 100–1, 129, 139, 206, 208, 216, 252
    'Afterword' 184, 188–9, 251
    'The Executioner's Beautiful Daughter' 12, 216–18
    'Flesh and the Mirror' 21, 100, 209–10, 218
    'The Loves of Lady Purple' 11–12, 183, 192, 194–5, 199, 213–16, 219, 248, 252–7, 260–1
    'Master' 129–30, 139–42
    'Penetrating to the Heart of the Forest' 21, 218
    'A Souvenir of Japan' 100, 207–8
  Heroes and Villains 3, 10, 127, 129–34, 142, 166, 169, 176–80, 219
  The Holy Family Album 4, 10, 145, 151–3, 163
  'The Horse of Love' 85, 91
  The Infernal Desire Machines of Doctor Hoffman 7, 10, 12, 98, 102, 107–8, 110–11, 119, 127–30, 133–9, 142, 145, 153–6, 205, 207, 210, 225–9, 237, 239, 241
  'Japanese Snapshots' 96
  'Life-Affirming Poem About Small, Pregnant White Cat' 85, 92, 93
  Love 3, 14, 118, 166, 169, 174–6, 190
  Lulu 13
  The Magic Toyshop 3, 5, 11, 13–14, 43, 94, 166, 185, 192–3, 198–9, 247–8, 252, 259–61
  'The Man Who Loved a Double Bass' 183, 193–4
  'The Mother Lode' 46
  'Munch and Antibiotics' 142
  'My Cat in her First Spring' 85, 92–3
  'My Father's House' 46
  'My Maugham Award' 240
  Nights at the Circus 3, 11, 13, 15, 51, 92, 112, 166, 183, 186, 192–9
  'Notes for a Theory of Sixties Style' 168, 173
  'Notes from the Front Line' 82, 90–1, 103–4, 128, 199
  'An Omelette and a Glass of Wine and Other Dishes' 142
  'On the Down' 94
  The Passion of New Eve 3, 7–8, 10, 12, 20, 42, 59, 103, 108, 111, 145, 152, 156–63, 166, 198, 225–6, 229–39, 241
  'Poem for a Wedding Photograph' 85, 92
  'Poor Butterfly' 207–8
  'The Quiltmaker' 26
  The Sadeian Woman: An Exercise in Cultural History 3, 7, 59, 96, 103, 107, 109, 111, 121, 155, 162–3, 198, 224
  'The Scarlet House' 7, 40, 49–55, 193
  Several Perceptions 3, 94, 166, 169, 172–3, 204
  Shadow Dance 3, 5–6, 43, 81, 85–6, 94–5, 112, 166, 169, 171, 173–4
  Shaking a Leg: Collected Journalism and Writings 35
  'The Snow Pavilion' 47
  'That Arizona Home' 128
  'The Thirteenth Key of Basil Valentine' 86–7
  'Through a Text Backwards: The Resurrection of the House of Usher' 193, 243
  'Through the Looking Glass' 81
  'Tokyo Pastoral' 207
  'Two Wives and a Widow' 86–7, 90–1, 96, 117
  'Unicorn' 81, 85–9, 91, 192
  Unicorn: The Poetry of Angela Carter 8, 80, 96, 117
  'Vampirella' 21, 30, 35
  'Venus Testudo Graeca' 89, 91
  Virago Book of Fairy Tales, The 163
  'William the Dreamer's Vision of Nature' 86–7, 117

Index

Wise Children 13, 20, 112, 129, 199, 247
Carter, Paul 6, 7, 92, 204
Cavallaro, Dani 43–6, 237
Caws, Mary Ann
   The Poetry of Dada and Surrealism 120
Chagall, Marc 5, 17
Chambers, Anthony 219
Char, René 120
Chardin, Teilhard de 130
Chatto & Windus 80
Christ, Jesus 145, 152
Cixous, Helen 185, 186
Clapp, Susannah 17–18, 206, 260
   A Card from Angela Carter 15, 17, 41, 55
Clemm, Virginia 190
Cline, Emma
   The Girls: A Novel 164
Cocteau, Jean 250
Coexist Gallery, The 15
Commedia dell'arte 252
Conan Doyle, Sir Arthur 24
Coover, Robert 34
Cottingley Fairies, The 24
Coward, Noel
   Blithe Spirit 248
Craig, Edward Gordon 257–9
   'The Actor and the Über-marionette' 258
   The Marionette 258
Creed, Barbara 234
Crevel, René 103, 105
   Le clavecin de Diderot 104–5
Cripps, Stafford 249
Crofts, Charlotte 15, 152–3, 185, 204, 208, 214, 224, 231, 254
   'Anagrams of Desire': Angela Carter's writing for Radio, Film and Television 4, 18, 31, 33–4, 36
Crofts, Charlotte and Marie Mulvey-Roberts (eds)
   Pyrotechnics: The Incandescent Imagination of Angela Carter 14
Crowe, Rankin 81
Cunliffe, Dave
   Poetmeat (magazine) 83
Curry, Neil 81
Czerny, Carl 60

Da Vinci, Leonardo
   Paragone 59
Dadd, Richard 23–4
Dali, Salvador 101, 108, 121
Dean, James 161, 235
Debussy, Claude 60, 63
   La Terrasse des audiences au clair de lune 20
decadence 19, 47, 58, 61–2
Dee, Dr John 27
Deleuze, Gilles and Félix Guattari
   Mille Plateaux 70–1, 77
Descartes, René 101
Desnos, Robert 108
   La Liberté ou l'amour 108
Desnos, Youki 101
Dietrich, Marlene 240, 242
Dimovitz, Scott 2, 44, 120–1, 163
Doane, Mary Ann 242
dolls 48, 103, 181, 193, 196–7, 256, 259–60
   Barbie 181
   Sindy 181
Donatello
   Penitent Magdalen 149–50
Donne, John
   'Catch a Falling Star' 48–9
Donovan, Josephine 75
Dorson, Richard M.
   Folk Legends of Japan 119
Double Indemnity (dir. Billy Wilder) 231
Dowson, Jane and Alice Entwistle
   A History of Twentieth-Century Women's Poetry 82
Duke Bluebeard's Castle (dir. Michael Powell) 77
Dunbar, William
   'The Tretis of the Twa Marrit Wemen and a Wedo' 86–7, 90
Duncan, Andrew 83–4, 88
Duncker, Patricia 73, 185
'Duodecim claves' or 'Twelve Keys' 87
Durkheim, Émile 130
Duval, Jeanne 105, 112, 114–16, 119, 121–2
Dworkin, Andrea 109

Easton, Alison
 Angela Carter: Contemporary Critical Essays (ed.) 14
Electronic Literature Association, The 34
Eliade, Mircea
 Patterns in Comparative Religion 153–4
Ellis, John 152
Elouard, Paul 101, 103, 105, 120, 163
English Stage Company, The 248
Ensor, James
 The Foolish Virgins 60
Ernst, Max 103, 108, 152
Evans, Kim 14, 36, 146
Exposition inteRnatiOnale du Surréalisme, (E.R.O.S.), 1959–60 104, 120

Faber & Faber 122
Fabergé 196
fairy tales 3, 5–6, 9, 21–2, 24–5, 35, 47, 58, 63–4, 70–5, 99, 114, 116, 119, 163, 182–7, 189, 198–9
 Bluebeard 3, 8, 47, 50, 60, 62, 64, 66, 70, 77, 112, 119, 121, 190
 Cinderella 119
 Jack and the Beanstalk 71
 Little Red Riding Hood 64, 70
 Puss in Boots 5, 66, 68
 Sleeping Beauty 195
 Tom Thumb 72
 see also folk tales
Faithfull, Marianne 179, 181
Falmer, Tessa
 The Forest Assassins 5
fantasy 21, 44, 52, 69, 77, 85, 91, 93, 160, 176, 185–7, 189, 192, 194, 196, 215, 225, 228, 232–3, 235, 237, 240, 254, 259
Feiler, Paul 84
Feinstein, Elaine 114
femininity 12, 41–2, 48, 62, 82, 172–3, 197, 224, 227, 229–36, 240, 242, 254
feminism 2, 8–9, 11, 14, 40–3, 45–6, 58–60, 74, 80–2, 102–4, 109–11, 114–20, 145, 158, 170, 176, 180, 182, 184, 199, 232, 234, 240

Filimon, Eliza Claudia 42
Fini, Leonor 121
Finlay, Ian Hamilton 84–5
Fish, Stanley 45
Fisher, Susan 204–6, 214, 247, 254
Five Quiet Shouters: An Anthology of Assertive Verse 83, 85, 92–6
Fleming, Ian 87
folk music 2, 6, 9, 168
folk tales 2, 6, 58, 66–7, 73, 119, 140, 155
 see also fairy tales
Foucault, Michel 42
Fragonard, Alexandre-Évariste 60, 75
Frankova, Milada 49
Frayling, Christopher
 Inside the Bloody Chamber 6
Freud, Sigmund 147, 186, 258

Gala Dali 101
Gamble, Sarah 41–2, 45, 53, 204, 224–5
 Angela Carter: A Literary Life 15
Garbo, Greta 236
Gauguin, Paul
 Out of the Night We Come, into the Night We Go 20, 60
Gauthier, Xavière 9, 101, 107
 'Anagrammes, jeux de mots, contrepétries' 106
 'L'Echec surréaliste' 106
 'L'espoir surréaliste' 105
 'Perversions' 106
 Surréalisme et sexualité 100, 102–8, 110–1, 118, 120–1
Geering, Ken 84
Genet, Jean 250
Genette, Gérard 121
getangelacarter.com 6, 14, 15
Gibbs, Christopher 170–1
Gielgud, John 248
Gilda (dir. Charles Vidor) 235, 242
Ginsburg, Alan 82
Godard, Jean-Luc 223–6, 239, 241
Goethe, Johann Wolfgang von
 'Erlkönig' 66
 Faust 72
 Wilhelm Meister 66

Goldsworthy, Kerryn 74
Gordon, Edmund 6, 15, 80, 95, 99, 110, 117–19, 163, 168, 177, 179, 210, 216, 223
  The Invention of Angela Carter 205
Goulding, Simon 43
Gounod, Charles 60
  'Walpurgisnacht' 72
Granada cinema, Tooting, The 223, 241
Grand Guignol, Le Théâtre du 252
Granny Takes a Trip (shop) 170–1
Grimm brothers 58, 184

Haffenden, John 2, 39, 105
Hall, John R. 163
Hall, Stuart 167–8
  'The Hippies: An American Moment' 175–6
Hammer movies 188
Haraway, Donna 46
Harlow, Jean 161, 235
Harpers and Queen 90
Hassall, Christopher 77
Hayman, Ronald 250
Hayworth, Rita 242
Heath, Stephen 242
Hebdige, Dick 167–8, 170
  Subculture: The Meaning of Style 168
Hegel, Georg Wilhelm 101
Hell's Angels 170, 179
Hendrix, Jimi
  Are You Experienced? 168
Hennard Dutheil de la Rochère, Martine 47, 73–4, 116, 118–19, 121, 163
  'From "The Bloody Chamber" to the *Cabinet de Curiosités*' 30
  '"La magie des voix dans la nuit": transcréation des contes de Perrault chez Angela Carter' 35
Herodotus 252
Hicks, Anne 84
Hicks, Jerry 84
Hill, Rosemary 95
Hobbes, Thomas 142
Hoffmann, E.T.A. 184, 251
  'The Sandman' 190
Hoggart, Richard 167

Holden's company 256
Hollywood 223–6, 228, 230, 233–9, 242
Holman Hunt, William 5
  The Shadow of Death 4
Holzer, Layla
  The Snow, The Crow and the Blood 15
Howard, Thomas 154
Hughes, Ted 85, 114
Hulton, Pontus
  'The Arcimboldo Effect' 26
Huw Weldon Best Arts Programme, BAFTA 14

I Was Lord Kitchener's Valet (shop) 170
Ikoma, Natsumi 6, 254
  'Her Side of the Story' 204–5
incest 5, 32, 64, 75, 188–9, 193, 216, 218
intermediality 7, 18–26, 28–31, 33–6, 58, 66, 72
  see also multi-disciplinary
International Federation of Independent Revolutionary Art 120
Iser, Wolfgang 45, 76

Jackson, Rosemary 223, 231
Jagger, Mick 169, 179
Jameson, Fredric 173
Jarry, Alfred
  Ubu Roi 257
Jefferson, Tony and Hall, Stuart
  Resistance through Rituals 168
Jeffreys, Shiela
  Anti-Climax: A Feminist Perspective on the Sexual Revolution 158
Jennings, Hope 147, 218
John Llewellyn Rys Prize 14
Joosen, Vanessa 45
Jordan, Elaine 226
Jordan, Neil
  The Company of Wolves 75
Josephus, Flavius 147
Joshi, S.T. 191

Kahlo, Frida 4, 107, 111
Kaplan, E. Ann 230
Kappeler, Susanne 109
Katsavos, Anna 146, 216

Keene, Donald 206
  Nō and Bunraku: Two Forms of Japanese Theatre 212–13, 217–18, 255
Kirkus Reviews 98
Kleist, Heinrich von
  'On the Marionette Theatre' 257–8
Krieger, Murray 69
Kristeva, Julia 41, 185–6, 194–5
Kugel, James L. 147
Kunstkamer, or *Wunderkammer* 26, 27, 48
  see also cabinet of curiosities
Kuper, Jessica
  The Anthropologist's Cookbook 142

Lacan, Jacques 186, 241
Lamba, Jacqueline 120
Lang, Andrew 67
Langland, William
  Piers Plowman 87, 117
Lappas, Catherine 75
Lauretis, Teresa de 242
Lautréamont, Comte de 49
Le Zotte, Jennifer 171
Leach, Edmund
  Claude Lévi-Strauss 10
Leary, Dr Timothy 178–9
Leavis, F.R. 99
Leda 185
Lefebvre, Henri 42
Leone, Sergio 33
Lessing, G.E.
  Laocoon 59, 60–1
Levi, Eliphas
  'Great Pentacle from the Vision of Saint John' 74
  The Key of the Mysteries 74
Lévi-Strauss, Claude 9–10, 127–42, 170, 177, 180
  From Honey to Ashes 129
  Mythologiques 128, 136–7
  The Origin of Table Manners 129
  The Raw and the Cooked: Introduction to a Science of Mythology 10, 128, 136–8, 140–2
  The Savage Mind 10, 128–9, 132
  Structural Anthropology 127, 129
The Listener 96
Lister, Jenny 171

Littlewood, Joan 252
  Oh What a Lovely War 250
Liu, Max 205
Lochhead, Liz 114
The London Magazine 86
Longley, Michael 85
Lord, Bruce 191
Louvel, Liliane 62, 74
  Le Tiers pictural: pour une critique intermédiale 33–4, 36
Louvel, Liliane and Verley, Claudine 77
Lovecraft, H.P. 11, 183–93, 197, 199
  'The Dreams in the Witch House' 188
  'The Dunwich Horror' 188
  'The Lurking Fear' 191–2
  Necronomicon 195
  'The Shadow over Innsmouth' 188
  'The Shuttered House' 191
  Supernatural Horror in Literature 188
Lovecraft, H.P. and Bishop, Zealia
  'Medusa's Coil' 188, 191–2
Lynch, David 241
Lyttleton, Oliver 249

Macbeth, George 83
McCarthy, Cavan 81, 83, 86, 94, 100
McCarthy, Cormac
  Cities of the Plain 31
  No Country for Old Men 31
McCormik, John 252
  The Victorian Marionette Theatre 256
Macdonald, Ian W. 32
  Revolution in the Head: The Beatles' Records and the Sixties 175
McGann, Graham 235
McGowan, Todd 225–6, 240
  The Impossible David Lynch 241
MacInnes, Colin
  Absolute Beginners 169
McRobbie, Angela 167–8, 171–2, 180–1
Madame Bovary (Gustave Flaubert) 234
Magdalene laundries 148–9
Magdalene, Mary 145, 148–51, 156
Magritte, René 120
  La Dame 104–5, 116, 120
  Le Viol 120
Mahabarata 252
Maitland, Sara 114

Index

Mallarmé Stéphane 117
The Man in Black (*Appointment with Fear*) 18
Mandelstam, Ossip 114
Manet, Edouard
   La Dame à l'évantail ou La Maîtresse de Baudelaire 113
   Le Déjeuner sur l'herbe 113
   Olympia 240
Manson, Charles 10, 145, 157–62
Mansour, Joyce 103–4, 106, 111
March-Russell, Paul 22
marionettes 12, 198, 212–16, 219, 246–8, 252–60
   see also puppets
Marx, Karl 240
Mary of Egypt 149
Masefield, John
   Box of Delights 18
Massumi, Brian 77
Mattel 181
Medusa, the 234
Mendelssohn, Felix
   Op. 21 (Overture to *Midsummer Night's Dream*) 24
   Op. 61 (Incidental Music to *Midsummer Night's Dream*) 24
Meschonnic, Henri 9, 67, 76, 99, 117
Meyerhold, Vsevolod 252, 258
Millais, John Everett
   Ophelia 175
Milton, John 86
misogyny 47, 82, 158–9, 199
Mitchell, W.J.T. 8, 59–62, 76
   What do Pictures Want? 74
Mods and Rockers 194
Molan, Christine 6, 15
Monroe, Marilyn 161, 224, 235
Moreau, Gustave
   Sacrificial Victim 20, 60, 77
   Salome 77
Morris, Tina
   Poetmeat (magazine) 83
Morrison, Jim 179
Mozart, Wolfgang Amadeus
   The Marriage of Figaro 66
multi-disciplinary 2, 5, 13–14
   see also intermediality

Mulvey, Laura 224, 234, 240, 242
   'Visual Pleasure and Narrative Cinema' 240
Mulvey-Roberts, Marie 14–15, 185
Munford, Rebecca 112
   Decadent Daughters and Monstrous Mothers: Angela Carter and European Gothic 19
   Re-visiting Angela Carter: Texts, Contexts, Intertexts (ed.) 14, 19
Murai, Mayako 119
Murnau, F.W.
   Nosferatu 23

Nadar 114, 122
Nairn, Tom 114
Nanicelli, Ted
   A Philosophy of the Screenplay 31–2
National Theatre Bill, The 249
National Theatre of Great Britain, The 249, 260
Neale, Catherine 224
New Music in the South West 15
New Society 168, 171, 173, 205, 207, 219, 246
'New Tales' 114
Next Editions 112–13, 122
Northam, Christopher 15
Northern House (publisher) 84
Nouvelle Vague, La (New Wave, The) 118, 223–4

Observer, The 152
O'Day, Marc 174
O'Keefe, Georgia 3
Old Vic, The 248–9
Olivier, Laurence 248
Olympia (E.T.A. Hoffmann's) 256
Omnibus documentary 223
Ong, W.
   Orality and Literacy 75
Oppenheim, Meret 111
   Le Festin 104, 120
Ormsby-Gore, Jane 170–1
Osborne, John
   Look Back in Anger 249–50
Oshima, Nagisa
   Ai No Corrida 205, 219

Pacheco, Ana Maria
   The Banquet 5
Palmer, Paulina 166–7, 184, 253–4
patchwork 26, 51
   see also bricolage
Peach, Linden 43, 184
Pearce, Alexander Robert 149
performativity 12, 29, 60, 73, 166, 170, 174, 180, 188–9, 199, 208, 210, 215, 247, 253
Perrault, Charles 9, 58, 67, 73, 184
   Contes du temps passé 99
   The Fairy Tales of Charles Perrault 99
Perseus 185
Petrushka 252
Phillips, Adam 226
Picard, Michel 69, 76
Pickard, Bill 84
Pink Floyd
   The Piper at the Gates of Dawn 168
Pinocchio (Collodi's) 256
Pinsky, Robert 89
Piranesi 2
Plato 101, 257
Playboy 232
Plowright, Poh Sim 214
Poe, Edgar Allen 11, 41, 116–17, 121, 183–5, 187–90, 193, 197, 199, 251
   'Annabel Lee' 99, 190
   'Berenice' 188, 194
   'The Cask of Amontillado' 193
   'Eleanora' 188, 190
   'The Fall of the House of Usher' 193, 243
   'Ligeia' 188, 190, 194
   'The Oval Portrait' 188, 190, 192, 243
   'The Pit and the Pendulum' 193
   'The Raven' 117
Poet and Printer Press 83
Poetry and Audience (magazine) 83
Polanski, Roman 161
   Rosemary's Baby 164
Pontalis, Jean-Bertrand 107–8, 110
Portobello Road 170, 171
postmodernism 44, 46, 48, 173–4, 231
Pound, Ezra 85

Pousin, Nicolas 60
Praz, Mario 120
Prévert, Jacques 103, 105
Punch and Judy 252
puppets 5, 11–12, 39, 55, 167, 183, 185, 187–8, 192–5, 198–9, 206, 212–15, 219, 247, 251–60
   see also marionettes
Pussy (musical) 5–6
Puvis de Chavannes, Pierre 60
Pygmalion and Galatea (Ovid's) 256–7

Queen Christina (dir. Mamoulian, Rouben) 236

Rainer, Arnulf
   The Wine Crucifix 4
Ray, Man 108
Ray, Man and Paul Eluard
   Les Mains libres 121
Raymond, Marcel
   De Baudelaire au surréalisme 99, 100, 117–18, 120
Rebellato, Dan 249–50
Redgrove, Peter 85
Redon, Odilon 60
Reid, Brenda 32
Resnais, Alain 118
Reverdy, Pierre 89, 100, 118
Rich, Adrienne 242
Richards, Keith 169
Richardson, Michael 25
Richardson, Ralph 248
Rimbaud, Arthur 117
Riviere, Joan 242
Robinson, Fiona 14
Robson, M. 217
Roche, Geoffrey 155
Roffe, Carol 118, 209–10, 219
Rolling Stones, The 169, 176
   'Lady Jane' 170
   Their Satanic Majesties Request 168
Rops, Félicien 60
Rossini, Gioachino
   The Barber of Seville 66
Rothenstein, Julian 112
Rousseau, Henri 177
Rousseau, Jean-Jacques 142

Royal Academy of Dramatic Art (RADA) 247
Royal Albert Hall Poetry Incarnation, The 82
Royal Court Theatre, The 248–9, 250
Royal Shakespeare Company, The (RSC) 249–50
Royal Society of British Artists, The 87
Royal West of England Academy, The 4
Rudolph II, Archduke 1, 26, 48
Rushdie, Salman 21, 39, 205
Ryan, Marie-Laure 19, 29
Ryan, Marie-Laure and Jan-Noël Thon
    Storyworlds Across Media: Toward a Media-Conscious Narratology 19–20
Ryan-Sautour, Michelle 31, 208, 210
    'The Intermedial Trajectories of Angela Carter's Wolf Tales' 35
    'Intermediality and the Cinematographic Image in Angela Carter's "John Ford's *Tis Pity She's a Whore*"' 36

Sabatier, Apollonie 105
Sacher-Masoch, Leopold von
    Venus in Furs 181
Sade, Donatien Alphonse François, Marquis de 105–16, 108–19, 111, 119–20, 147, 155, 198, 253
    Justine 155, 157
    One Hundred and Twenty Days of Sodom 154–5
    La philosophie dans le boudoir 106, 121, 156
    'La Vérité' 155
Sage, Lorna 6, 52, 83–4, 128, 145, 152, 204, 206, 213–14, 227
    Flesh and the Mirror: The Art of Angela Carter (ed.) 13
Sage, Sharon 15
Saint Cecilia 61, 74
Sanders, Ed
    The Family: The Story of Charles Manson's Dune Buggy Attack Batalion 157–61
    Sharon Tate: A Life 163
Sargood, Corinna 6, 163

Sartre, Jean-Paul 250
    Being and Nothingness 241
    'The Look' 241
Satan's Slaves 159
Savage, Jon 173–4
Schlemmer, Oscar 257
Schober, Regina 29
Schubert, Franz 67
    The Erlkönig 66
Schumann, Robert 70
    Märchenbilder or *Fairy Tale Pictures* 73
Seagal, Naomi 75
Seidensticker, Edward 219
Senelick, Laurence 258
Sewell, Father Brocard 81, 83, 85–6, 92, 94, 100
sex, sexuality 10–11, 13, 24–5, 39, 41–3, 47, 51, 64, 88–90, 93, 95, 100–6, 108, 112, 114, 118–22, 145, 147–8, 152–3, 156–60, 169, 172, 176, 179, 183–99, 208, 214–15, 224, 227, 228–38, 242, 249, 254
Shakespeare Memorial Theatre, The 249
Shakespeare, William 86, 188, 246–9
    Macbeth 258–9
    A Midsummer Night's Dream 24–5
    Sonnet 130 115–16
    The Tempest 23–4
Shellard, Dominic 248–9
Sheppard, Robert
    The Poetry of Saying 83
Sheppeard, Sallye 257
Shikibu, Murasaki
    The Tale of Genji 119, 205, 214, 219
Shônagon, Sei
    The Pillow Book 119
Sivyer, Caleb 15
Smith, A.C.H. 15, 84
Smith, Ali
    foreword to *British Women Short Story Writers: The New Woman to Now* 22, 35
Smith, Joan 18
socialism 2, 80, 198
Somerset Maugham Award 14, 204
Sophocles
    Oedipus 258–9

Sotheby's 171
Soupault, Philippe 120
Spencer, Stanley
   Wedding at Cana Bride and Bridegroom 4
Stalker, Hugh Jnr. 145
Stalker, Hugh Snr. 146
Stanwyck, Barbara 231
Stoppard, Tom 84
Storr, Anthony 157
Straight Satans, The 159
Strange Worlds: The Vision of Angela Carter (exhibition) 2, 4–5
Strauss II, Johann
   The Bat (Die Fledermaus) 66
   'Kennst du das Land wo die Zitronen blühen?' 66
Student Power 175
Suleiman, Susan Rubin 108, 121
'Summer Child' 209, 210
surrealism 2, 4, 7, 9, 25–8, 45, 48–9, 89–90, 98–111, 115, 118–21, 151, 170
   Surrealist Manifesto 48
Sutton, Philip 113
Švankmajer, Jan
   Alice 25–8, 33, 48
   Faust 33
Svengali 195
Swift, Jonathan
   Gulliver's Travels 107, 153–4
Swinging London 168
Swiss Papers in English Language and Literature (SPELL) 28
Syvret, Miss (Carter's French teacher) 117

Tanizaki, Jun'ichirō
   Naomi 205, 219
Tanning, Dorothea 104, 152
Tate, Sharon 10, 145, 160–2, 164
   Eye of the Devil (dir. Thompson, J. Lee) 164
Tavassoli, Sara and Phavin Ghasemi 214–15
Taxidou, Olga 257–8
Tchaikovsky, Pyotr Ilych
   The Snow Maiden 66

Tebb, Barry 85, 93–4
Tenniel, Sir John 25–6
Thévoz, Michel 73
Thomas, Karima 48
Thompson, Hunter S. 179
Tiffin, Jessica 44–5
Tilakasiri, J. 255
Tlaloc 81, 83, 85–6, 100
Tomlinson, Charles 84
Tonkin, Maggie 99, 112, 117, 121, 227, 232, 241
Tour, Georges de la
   The Penitent Magdalene, aka *The Magdalene and Two Flames* 20, 148
Tourneur, Cyril 188
Trevenna, Joanna
   'Gender as Performance: Questioning the "Butlerification" of Angela Carter's fiction' 219
Triolet, Elsa 101
Triquarterly 93, 96
Trotsky, Leon 120
Trouille, Camille Clovis 108
   Luxure (Dolmancé au château de la Coste) 109
   Voyeuse 109
Tzara, Tristan 120
   Manifeste Dada 119

Universities' Poetry 83, 85, 93

Valentino, Rudolph 161
Vallorani, Nicoletta 43–4
Velvet Underground, The
   The Velvet Underground and Nico 168
Verdi, Guiseppe 60
Vernant, Jean-Pierre 62, 74
Vieux-Colombier, Le Théâtre 120
The Village School (by Izumo Takeda) 217
Virago 109, 110
Virgin Mary 253
Vision (Carter's poetry magazine) 81, 84–6
Vitrac, Roger 120
Vivaldi, Antonio 70
Vogue 170–1

Wagenknecht, Edward 190
Wagner, Geoffrey 115
Wagner, Richard 60
  'Liebestod' 66, 71
  Tristan und Isolde 66
Waley, Arthur (trans.)
  The Tale of Genji 119
Walz, Marie Emilie 117
Warner, Marina 74
Waterhouse, John William
  Saint Cecilia 74
Watson, Tex 161, 162
Watteau, Jean-Antoine 60
Watz, Anna 99–100, 102, 107, 111, 118–21, 163
Webb, Caroline 68, 76
Webb, Kate 242
Weber, Max 130
Webster, John 188
Wedekind, Franz
  Lulu 260
West Country 3, 6
West End, The 248–9
West of England College of Art 15, 84
West, Mae 119, 240
West, Ted 169
Western Daily Press 15
Wheatley, David 32

White, T.H. 87
Wiene, Robert
  The Cabinet of Dr Caligari 190
Wilcox, Leonard 236
Wilder, Billy
  Sunset Boulevard 162
Wilson, Elizabeth 174
Wisker, Gina 41, 185, 254
Wittgenstein, Ludwig 119

Xenophon 252

Yeandle, Heidi
  Imagining the End: Interdisciplinary Perspectives on the Apocalypse 142
Yeats, W.B.
  'The Indian to His Love' 122
Yoshioka, Chiharu 128
'The Young Contemporaries Exhibition' 87

Zamir, Tzachi 257–9
Zero, Christopher 163
Zeus 185
Zezo-Ze-Ce-Zadfrak 164
Zipes, Jack 65
Žižek, Slavoj 240

EU authorised representative for GPSR:
Easy Access System Europe, Mustamäe tee 50,
10621 Tallinn, Estonia
gpsr.requests@easproject.com